A CROWN OF ASH AND FLAME

A. ROUCHER

Roucher

The Crown of Ash and Flame

To my wife, Sheila —my toughest proofreader and kindest critic. Thank you for catching my mistakes (and reminding me that commas do, in fact, matter).

I owe a special thanks to Nathan Crocco and Jim Rush, whose thoughtful edits and honest feedback strengthened this manuscript at every stage. Their patience and precision were invaluable.

Table of Contents

Roucher

Prologue
The Kingdom That Was

Long ago, the Kingdom of Valebrook stood unshaken beneath the stars. Its banners flew high above green valleys and golden fields, and the rivers sang of peace. Magic was known, but carefully guarded, woven through song, stone, fire and thought. It was entrusted to only the wisest of the mage born. At its heart ruled King Reynard the Just, a warrior with fire in his blood and mercy at his hand. At his side, Queen Elenora, a blade of the north, who was iron willed and fiercely beloved. Together, they forged a realm not of dominance but of balance. From them, came two sons. The first, Rayner, born beneath the Harvest Moon, strong of will and steady of hand. The second, Cole, born in a storm, with laughter in his voice and magic burning behind his eyes. They grew in light, beneath the watchful eyes of knights and mages, of mothers who led and fathers who bled. In the end, light, no matter how bright, always casts a shadow.

Malrik, a once-trusted advisor, was seduced by an ancient and forbidden path. He called it blood magic, for it was born from the lifeforce of others, old as the bones of the earth. Where most feared it, Malrik embraced it. He called it strength. He called it destiny. He said the crown should bow to him, and when it didn't, he tore the kingdom apart to take it. He poisoned the guard. He shattered the Veil between life and death. He unleashed horrors older than language. One cold, gray morning, the towers of Valebrook burned.

King Reynard died on the palace steps, his sword shining even in death. Queen Elenora vanished into fire. Sir Worric, The Captain of the Guard, led the children to safety, and the world changed. Rayner became a fugitive prince, who would be hunted by Malrik his entire life. Cole, a hidden ember, taken to Azor for safe keeping. The kingdom fell silent, but stories lived in whispers during slumber. Now, as winter breaks over the ruined peaks... Now, as shadows grow in forgotten places... Now, as prophecy stirs and ancient powers awaken... Four friends return to the land that made them. To find what was lost. To right what was broken.

CHAPTER 1

Eldara did not begin as a continent of hills and hearth-fires, but as a vibration in the Weave, the great, invisible lattice of elemental threads that underlies all creation. Lorekeepers call that earliest instant the First Pulse: a moment when raw possibility quivered, bled light, and collapsed into form. From that quiver came stone and sky, wind and tide, and lastly memory, the latent awareness that causes rivers to remember their banks and mountains their shape.

Unlike planes forged by single deities, Eldara appears to have been self-assembling: its rivers braid in spirals that mirror the Weave's flow, its ley-lines radiate like spokes from a central hub, and even its animals dream in geometric patterns. Ancient flame-sigils discovered beneath Brevenhall speak of "worlds born as echo", hints that the realm is one harmonic reverberation of a far older cosmos. Whether some guiding mind "strummed" the Weave first, or whether the Weave itself is conscious, remains the oldest debate in Eldaran scholarship.

When the land cooled, Eldara was a quilt of contradictions: volcanoes steamed beside frost-choked gulfs, and forests of silver-leaf grew atop glassy desert flats. Nomadic sapiens, the Dawn Tribes, wandered this raw theatre. Their obsidian tools and bone flutes, occasionally unearthed in the Fissure Fields near Dunmar, are etched with spiral sigils identical to those seen in the Codex of Binding, suggesting that even these proto-peoples knew the Weave as song.

In the far northeast, where Greymire's mist now rolls over bog-reeds, primordial wetlands birthed the first herb-witches. They spoke of lights beneath the fen surface, "trapped starlings", that taught them to coax medicine from rot. To the south-west, hunter bands settled along rivers later called Stonebrook and Ashbrook, carving early hearth circles that remain beneath modern cottages. Their scarcity of stratified burial mounds indicates a culture focused on motion over monarchy.

Roughly three millennia ago came Eldara's first organized order: the Firekeepers. They arose in what is now Brevenhall, after a rain of meteoric cinders seeded the valley with slag-glass and unpredictable vents. Legends claim one ember-storm birthed sentient flame-spirits; the Firekeepers bargained with these entities, offering them veneration in exchange for thermal balance. Through ritual, they learned to bind volcanic aggression, steering magma away from settlements, quick-forging unbreakable steels, and inventing fire-milling. With fire mastered, mortals looked outward. City-states flared along fertile rivers and mineral-rich ridges: Valebrook, "Crown of the Lowlands," began as a fortified trading depot straddling two rivers. Its first monarch, Queen Myrena of the Stag, unified grain clans by offering them Weave-lit irrigation runnels, embryonic aqueducts whose keystones still glow faintly at midsummer. Windmere and Thistlewatch emerged as coastal and highland watch-posts, guarding sea and sky routes.

In the north-west, Embernest leveraged volcanic ash to fertilize wine-terraces, bridging mercantile ties with Valebrook that endure to this day. By the midpoint of this era, royal banners outgleamed tribal totems. Yet the Weave was not silent: mages, descendants of the Firekeepers and fen-witches, took courtly posts, forming a loose council later codified as the Weavebound Circle. Their charter insisted that "No throne stand without mage, no mage act without mercy." It was in this period that Azor first appears in chronicles, advising King Reynard's father on harmonic ley-tax policy (a gentle harvesting of ambient magical pressure to fund public works).

Eventually, under King Reynard the Bold, scattered duchies pledged oaths to Valebrook, forming what scholars dub the Old Kingdom. Its guiding document, the Balance Charter, married knightly chivalry to elemental stewardship: nobles swore to guard not only subjects, but also "the pulse of river and root." Ashbrook, Stonebrook, and Eldwyre thrived as agrarian satellites; Hollow-mere, once a haunted mire, became a safeguarded alchemical preserve.

Within this golden stretch the Weave seemed placid. Knights undertook individual Trials of Character, Fortitude, and Fear (Sir Worric's cave ordeal among them), reinforcing the Charter's ethos that power must be tested inwardly before exercised outwardly, but balance is fragile. A court mage named Malrik grew obsessed with the Weave's deepest strata, particularly its resonance with lifeblood. Where others saw harmony, he saw leverage: blood, pulsing iron-rich, vibrated on a lower frequency that could overwrite local Weave threads. His early experiments promised medicines against plague; his later rituals devoured those plagues, along with the living hosts. Exiled, Malrik fled beyond Harrowcrest Mountains, raising his Black Bastion atop cliff and rift. Blood magic warped the land around it, birthing the Dark Expanse: a scarred corridor where time seems to echo out of sequence, river water runs scarlet at dusk, and spells falter like broken lutes. Vornholt, just north of this corridor, embraced his creed, carving orchards that bleed and brewing fear-tonics for his legions. The Balance Charter shattered with them: the realm's ley-lines buckled, storms lost their seasons, crops hissed with static. Knights fell; mages quailed. Eldara stood on the cusp of unsung ruin.

Present Day

The edge of the forest was silent, with the occasional clanging sounds of metal hitting wood echoing out. It was not yet mid-morning, but Rayner was already sweating. His day started like most days, swordsmanship in the morning followed by bow hunting in the afternoon. Sir Worric watched on as Rayner continued to hit the wooden Pell with his sword.

"Mind your footing" Sir Worric barked.

Rayner paused for a second to catch his breath. His arms were heavy and his hands ached.

"Again" shouted Sir Worric.

Rayner continued practicing, as sweat poured down his face. His only thought was that he could not wait until it was time for bow practice. He was not very good with a bow, but at least he could rest from swinging the heavy sword. As Rayner and Sir Worric finished their training for the day. Rayner could barely lift his arms up. He did not understand why he had to constantly train every day.

"Why must I train day in and day out?" asked Rayner.

Sir Worric stared at Rayner and replied "One day I may not be here to save you. You need to be able to take care of yourself in a fight".

Rayner scoffed and rolled his eyes. "Fight, what fight? And save me from what?" questioned Rayner.

The sun had long since dipped below the trees, casting long shadows across the glade as Rayner stumbled through the cottage door. His tunic clung to him with sweat, and his arms ached like they were made of stone. Dirt streaked his hands. His forearms were bruised, and a thin scrape crossed the bridge of his nose, courtesy of a botched parry that Sir Worric had corrected with the flat of his blade. He kicked off his boots at the door, wincing at the stiffness in his back. The scent of roasted root vegetables, garlic, and slow-cooked meat hit him like a warm embrace. His stomach growled. Loudly.

"Thought you might crawl back in," came Sir Worric's voice from beside the hearth.

The old knight stood by the iron pot, stirring with one hand while holding a battered mug of mead in the other. He wore no armor now, just a loose linen shirt, rolled at the sleeves, and the familiar, unimpressed look he often reserved for Rayner's foot-work.

"You're cooking?" Rayner asked, collapsing into the wooden chair at the table, letting his head drop back with a groan.

Sir Worric grunted. "If you can call it that."

A moment later, he brought over a chipped plate and set it before Rayner. Steam curled into the air. The plate held roasted carrots and parsnips, a portion of honey-glazed turnips, and two generous slices of venison stew pie, the crust golden and flaky, the meat inside swimming in a thick gravy with rosemary and mush-rooms. Rayner didn't speak. He just dug in. The first bite melted in his mouth, rich and savory, the crust soaking up the gravy like sponge. His eyes half-closed as the warmth spread through his chest and eased the ache in his bones. He tore into a slice of bread, slathered with butter and garlic, and used it to mop up the juices. Sir Worric poured him a mug of cider and finally sat opposite him with his own plate, watching in amused silence as Rayner devoured half the pie in three bites.

"I take it training was hard," he said.

Rayner chewed, nodded. "Brutal."

Sir Worric sipped his cider. "Good."

The fire popped in the hearth, casting orange light across the stone walls and the stacked swords on the mantle. Outside, the forest hummed with the chirping of night creatures. Inside, it was warm, quiet, grounded. After a long pause, Rayner sat back and rubbed his jaw.

"You think I'm ready?" he asked.

Sir Worric leaned forward, elbows on the table. "No one ever is, but you're farther than most."

Rayner looked down at his plate, at the crumbs and streaks of gravy. The hunger was gone, but something fuller had replaced it. He wasn't just being trained. He was being forged, and tonight, at this table, in the glow of the fire and the weight of a mentor's silence, he felt it. He was becoming more than a boy with a sword. He was becoming a knight.

The fire crackled low in the hearth, casting flickering light against the stone walls of the cottage. Outside, the trees of Ashbrook whispered in the wind, their branches brushing softly against one another like old men trading secrets. Inside, the scent of smoke, sweat, and supper hung in the air. Rayner sat cross-legged on the rug by the hearth, a damp cloth pressed against his shoulder, a bruise forming near the collarbone. Sir Worric sat in his favorite chair nearby, boots off, mug in hand, staring into the flames like they held the answers to things too old to name. For a long time, neither spoke., but then, after a deep breath,

Sir Worric said, "You know, I wasn't ready either."

Rayner looked up. "For what?"

"For my first real fight." He leaned forward, placing his mug on the floorboards.

"Not drills. Not patrols. A real battle. Swords drawn. Friends dying."

Rayner sat straighter, the cloth slipping from his shoulder. Sir Worric rarely spoke of his past, not in detail, anyway.

"It was in the north, near the border of Wyrvale," Sir Worric continued, eyes fixed on the flame.

Wyrvale was tucked between the mist-shrouded cliffs of the Greycrown Highlands lies the village of Wyrvale, a quiet place where the mountains speak in wind and the stones remember footsteps long vanished. Few travel to Wyrvale by accident, and fewer still leave without carrying its whispers.

The village itself clings to a sloping hillside, where moss-covered cottages huddle together as though seeking warmth from the cold breath of the cliffs. The homes are built from stacked riverstone and aged timber, their rooftops thatched with woven grass and insulated by old bark. Smoke curls from squat chimneys, fragrant with pine and peat. At the center of the village stands the Stone Moon, a towering crescent-shaped monolith, older than memory and carved with glyphs none can read. The villagers believe it marks the spot where the moon once touched the earth. Children leave offerings of flowers, feathers, and painted stones at its base, and it is said to hum softly during the solstice.

Wyrvale's people are hardy, quiet folk, herders, stonemasons, and gatherers of rare mountain herbs. Their dialect is thick with old words, and they keep the traditions of the ancestors alive with seasonal festivals, silent mourning rituals, and midnight songs sung to the stars. Every autumn, the Nightfire Festival lights the vale with hundreds of floating lanterns, each carrying a prayer to those beyond the veil.

The village is surrounded by forested slopes and narrow goat trails, leading to hidden caves, ice-fed streams, and long-forgotten watchtowers buried by landslides. Many believe that the mountains around Wyrvale hide ancient runes, relics of the Weave's first rise, and others whisper that blood magic once tainted the earth here, leaving the soil strange and the shadows longer than they should be.

Despite its isolation, Wyrvale is known among herbalists and alchemists for its rare blossoms, especially veilroot, a glowing plant said to enhance magical focus. Azor himself is rumored to have visited the village in his youth, trading spellwork for a satchel of the flowering herb.

There is no true inn in Wyrvale, but a longhouse called Stonehome serves weary travelers with stew, strong mead, and a place beside the hearth. Its keeper, an old woman named Tessa Hollowborn, claims to be the last living descendant of the village's founders, and she has eyes that seem to see through men, rather than at them.

Wyrvale is not a place of grandeur or gold. It does not seek the world, nor beg the world to seek it. But those who find their way to its fog-veiled paths often say the same thing: they leave changed. For in Wyrvale, the wind tells stories older than kings, the stones sing softly beneath your feet, and for a moment... the world feels like it remembers you.

"The village had been overrun by raiders, mercenaries mostly. Hired steel without a cause. We'd heard stories of what they did to the last town. Burned it down with the people still inside. Women. Children."

He reached for the mug again and took a slow sip.

"I was nineteen. Young. Arrogant. Full of the same fire I see in you. Thought I'd swing a sword once or twice, shout a clever line, and come out a hero." He chuckled bitterly.

"Turns out, real fights aren't like stories. They're noise. Chaos. Pain and mud and screaming."

Rayner swallowed. "What happened?"

Sir Worric leaned back in the chair, arms crossed. The fire lit up the lines on his face, made his eyes glint with something far older than battle.

"We marched in before dawn. Thirty of us. Thought we'd catch them sleeping, but they were waiting. Ambush. Arrows from the tree line, blades in the brush. Men I'd trained with for two years dropped in seconds." He paused. When he spoke again, his voice was quieter.

"I froze. Right there in the mud, sword drawn. Couldn't move. Couldn't breathe. Everything I'd learned... gone."

Rayner didn't interrupt. He couldn't. The idea of Sir Worric, his pillar of strength, paralyzed in fear was hard to picture.

"I remember one of the older knights shouting at me: 'Move, boy!' But I couldn't. Until..."

Sir Worric looked down at his hand. It trembled, just slightly.

"Until a man charged me. Big. Axe in hand. Screaming. I thought I was dead."

"What did you do?" Rayner asked, barely above a whisper.

"I ducked." Sir Worric gave a short laugh. "He swung, and I dropped. Pure reflex. His axe buried itself in a tree behind me. Before I could think, I drove my sword through his side."

Rayner stared.

"That was it. No style. No flourish. Just survival. My first kill. I still remember the look in his eyes."

The fire popped, and for a moment the silence stretched.

"I wanted to vomit," Sir Worric said. "Afterward. My hands shook. My knees buckled, but I kept fighting. Not because I was brave, but because the others needed me."

Rayner shifted closer. "How did you keep going?"

Sir Worric looked at him now, really looked at him.

"Because I realized something that day. Being ready... that's a lie we tell ourselves. No one's ever ready. Not truly. We're just tested. Again, and again, and every time, we either stand... or fall."

Rayner absorbed the words like a sponge, the heat of the fire and the weight of the moment pressing down around him.

"I thought you were fearless," he admitted.

"I'm not," Sir Worric said plainly. "I've never been. I'm just someone who's learned to step forward anyway."

He leaned forward and poked at the fire with the iron rod, sending sparks into the chimney.

"You want to be a knight, Rayner?" he asked.

Rayner nodded. "Yes."

"Then know this: it's not about perfection. It's not about glory. It's about what you do when everything falls apart. When you're bruised, bleeding, and afraid. You don't fight for a name. You fight for the ones beside you. For the people behind you. That's what makes a knight."

Rayner stared into the flames. "I want to be that," he said quietly. "Even if I'm not ready."

Sir Worric's eyes softened. He leaned back in his chair. "You will be. Because you'll keep showing up. You'll keep getting back up. And because... I'll keep knocking you down until you stop making those sloppy parries."

Rayner snorted, just barely. "You're getting slower, old man."

Sir Worric chuckled. "Careful, boy. I may be old, but I hit like a horse."

They sat in silence again, the fire casting long shadows across the walls. Outside, the wind shifted. The stars began to rise. Inside, the weight of doubt had lightened. Not vanished, but tempered. Forged like a blade in heat. Rayner wrapped his arms around his knees and leaned his head back, closing his eyes, and in the warmth of the hearth and the presence of the man who'd raised him like a son, he began to believe: maybe he didn't have to be ready—he just had to be willing.

"Finish your chores and get some rest. Tomorrow is another day of practice," Sir Worric said with a small smirk on his face.

Rayner finished his chores and laid down in his bed. Rayner grew up in a small village to the west called Ashbrook. This village was one of sixteen villages in the realm of Eldara. The realm of Eldara consists of mountains, forests, rivers and countrysides. There are three mountain ranges in the realm of Eldara. The Eroded Mountains in the west. The Relentless Slopes lay to the east. Finally, the Ever-reaching Mountain range lay to the south. This particular mountain range surrounded the Dark Expanse, where evil dwells. There are three forests, which are home to many magical creatures not all which are known. The Whispering Woodland was to the west, the Wandering Forest to the east, and the Royal Forest just north of the kingdom. Many of the coastal villages relied on fishing, while the villages in the countryside relied on farming. In the southwest section of Eldara lay the Kingdom of Valebrook. This was once the home of the King and Queen of Eldara. A great battle took place many years ago and the kingdom was left in ruin.

The next morning, Rayner was awakened by Sir Worric.

"Rayner" Sir Worric shouted. "Today is your final day of training. Tomorrow we will begin the trials."

"Trials? What trials?" Rayner muttered.

Sir Worric chuckled and said, "Do not concern yourself with that now, focus on the day."

The scent of woodsmoke and spiced oats filled the cottage long before Rayner opened his eyes. Morning light crept in through the shutters, thin, gold slivers warming the old timber walls and the patchwork rug by the hearth. Somewhere outside, birds chirped above the rising mist that rolled through the Ashbrook woods, but within the stone and cedar walls of Sir Worric's cottage, all was calm and still. Rayner sat up from the cot tucked beneath the low-beamed ceiling. He stretched the stiffness from his arms, the ache of yesterday's training still lingering in his shoulders. His boots rested beside the fire, dry and warm. Across the room, the old knight was already at the hearth, stirring something thick in a cast-iron pot hung over the flames.

"Up at last," Sir Worric said without turning. "I thought you'd sleep through until supper."

Rayner grunted and shuffled over to the small round table. It was carved from a single slab of Ashwood, scarred with years of notches, knife marks, and the occasional burn from a misjudged ladle. Two mismatched chairs stood across from one another, one creaking more than the other. The inside of the cottage was simple, lived-in and stubborn, like its owner. Shelves of old tomes and whetstones lined the walls. A sword hung above the hearth, not for decoration, but close at hand. The wooden floor was swept clean, and bundles of herbs dangled from the ceiling rafters, drying in the smoke. The scent of thyme, sage, and old leather lingered every-where. Sir Worric ladled steaming porridge into two clay bowls, added a dash of cinnamon, and then, without ceremony, dropped a few slices of crisped ham and a soft-boiled egg on top. A hunk of dark rye bread and a pat of goat butter completed the meal.

"Eat," he said, setting it down in front of Rayner. "You'll need it if you're going to stop swinging like a drunk scarecrow."

Rayner smirked and picked up his spoon. The porridge was creamy and rich, flecked with barley and sweetened just enough with honey. The ham was thick and peppered, cooked in the pan until the edges curled. The egg split with the first bite, yolk running like sunlight into the oats. He soaked the bread into it all, savoring the quiet. Sir Worric ate standing, as he often did, watching the fire while chewing thoughtfully. For a few minutes, they didn't speak. Outside, the day waited, trials, sword drills, lessons in honor and restraint, but here, in the stillness of the hearth light, Rayner felt something deeper than instruction. He felt home, and though Sir Worric would never say it aloud, this morning ritual, the breakfast, the fire, the quiet, meant more than any battlefield could. Grabbing his sword and into the light of the morning.

"Sword Training, begin" said Sir Worric.

Rayner began his typical sword techniques, which consisted of parries, thrusts, cuts, and footwork. This was done all while Sir Worric watched. Something about Sir Worric was different today, the usual stern look was replaced with a slight smirk. Rayner wondered and began to worry about what the trials might include.

That evening it was late, having just finished their meal, they sat by the fire. The moon hung low over Ashbrook, casting pale light through the open shutters of the cottage. A breeze rustled the leaves outside, gentle and steady. Inside, the fire had died to glowing embers, and Rayner sat across from Sir Worric, still in his training tunic, arms crossed over his chest, brow furrowed in the way he always wore when chewing on something deeper than tactics. Sir Worric sat back in his chair, hands steepled, watching his young charge carefully.

"You want to know why we have the Trials," he said at last, voice low and steady. Not a question. A statement.

Rayner nodded. "You said mine was coming tomorrow, but you never told me what it is. Or why it's different for every squire."

Sir Worric tapped the arm of his chair once. Twice. Then leaned forward. "Because a blade that isn't tested will break," he said. "That's the truth of it."

The Trials have a long history and tradition in Eldara. Trails are given to a squire to earn the title of Knight. This is not for the faint of heart. The Trials consist of 3 phases, with obstacles that the squire must overcome. He poured himself a small measure of dark mead, untouched since supper.

"Let me tell you something, boy. Becoming a knight, it's not about the armor. It's not the sword, nor the vow. Those are symbols. Tools. The Trials... they find the man underneath."

Rayner didn't interrupt. Sir Worric's stories didn't come often, but when they did, they were worth more than any sword lesson.

"There are three trials every knight must pass," Sir Worric continued. "Not written in stone. Not always named, but they come for all of us." He held up a finger.

"First: The Trial of Character." Every knight is taught to protect, to serve, to hold to a code, but codes are easy when life is easy. The Trial of Character doesn't test your memory of the code; it tests your commitment to it when the world wants you to break it." Sir Worric's eyes clouded for a moment, lost in old shadows. "My trial came during the Siege of Garan Hold. I was young, newly knighted, barely twenty winters. A traitor within the hold offered me a chance to end the siege from inside, poison the well, kill the guards while they slept. It would've saved lives on our side. Ended the war before it began."

Rayner leaned forward. "What did you do?"

"I turned him in," Sir Worric said quietly. "Because a knight doesn't win wars like a coward. We fight clean. We win the right way, or not at all. We lost good men that day... but we kept our honor, and when the enemy finally yielded, it was with respect, not hatred. He looked at Rayner. The Trial of Character will ask you: What will you give up to stay true? If the answer is 'nothing,' then you're not ready." He held up a second finger.

"Second: The Trial of Fortitude. Not strength. Fortitude. Grit. The fire in your gut when your muscles give out and your bones scream. It's what separates warriors from legends."

He gestured to Rayner's bruised arm.

"Training is just the beginning. One day, you'll be made to march through a blizzard with no food. To stand when your brothers fall. To endure more than flesh was meant to carry." Rayner nodded slowly. He understood pain, but this sounded deeper.

"My squire," Sir Worric said softly, "before you... was a lad named Merren. Tough. Bright. He failed the Trial of Fortitude. Not because he was weak, but because he quit. The trial had him carry an injured man across a flooded plain. He made it four and gave up. Left the man behind."

Rayner's eyes widened. "What happened?"

"He wasn't knighted," Sir Worric said flatly. "He became a carpenter in Grayhill. Good man, but not a knight."

He let the words settle. Rayner sat in silence, absorbing the truth. Some trials weren't won with swords, but with will. Then Sir Worric raised a third finger.

"Third: The Trial of Fear. The worst of them. Fear isn't just the blade at your throat or the fire on your heels. It's the quiet voice inside your head that says: You'll fail. You'll die. You're not enough." He stared into the embers. "My trial came in the crypts of Hollowmere. We were tasked to retrieve a relic stolen by bandits hiding in those catacombs. Everyone knew the place was cursed. The air itself whispered madness. When the tunnel caved in behind me, and I was alone in pitch black, with only a torch and a sword, I had to walk blind into that dread. Every shadow felt like death."

Rayner whispered, "What was in there?"

"Nothing," Sir Worric said.

"That was the point. The fear was in my mind, but it felt real. My torch died halfway through. I had to follow the sound of dripping water, step by step, not knowing if I'd fall to my death or into the arms of a ghost."

He turned back to Rayner.

"The Trial of Fear is different for everyone. Sometimes it's a dream. Sometimes a vision. Sometimes a real enemy, but always, it strikes your deepest doubt."

Rayner sat still, firelight dancing in his eyes.

"So," Sir Worric said at last, "that's why we don't all take the same trial. Because no two men are shaped the same, and no two knights should be forged from the same mold."

He stood slowly, crossing to the shelf where his old helm sat. He picked it up, held it for a moment.

"I knew I was ready when I stopped hoping the trial would be easy. When I knew it would break me, and I still stepped forward."

He placed the helm back down and turned to Rayner.

"Yours will be tomorrow. I don't know what form it'll take, but I've seen you fight through pain. I've seen you stand up when others fall, and I know your heart, boy. Not perfect, but steady."

Rayner finally asked, "What happens if I fail?"

Sir Worric's eyes narrowed. "Then you stand up and try again. That's what makes you worthy."

Before the fall of the Old Kingdom, before Rayner was born, before Malrik ever whispered to the darkness beneath the palace, there was a man called Sir Worric of Ashbrook. Not yet a knight.

Not yet a captain. Just a soldier. With a sword, a scar, and something in his eyes that didn't break. This is his story. Sir Worric first fought in the War of the Broken Pines, when the kingdom's eastern provinces rebelled against the crown. Sir Worric was not yet a knight when the War of Broken Pines broke across the southern border like a wild storm. He was seventeen then, barely more than a boy, clad in ill-fitting chainmail and gripping a spear too long for his reach. His hands blistered beneath the leather, and his heart hammered louder than the war drums. The war began with smoke. The pines along the southern edge of Eldara had long marked the border with the fractured lands of Corvaine. When the Corvain warbands crossed the river with axes in hand and fire on their breath, they brought the woods down like thunder, clearing paths to march through. Forest villages burned. Ash hung in the air. And the young were called to fight.

Worric had never seen death before that summer. Not like this. The fighting in the pines was brutal, chaotic and close, between twisted trunks and smoldering roots. Men vanished in the mist; struck down by blades they never saw. The trees themselves wept sap like blood. He remembered his first kill. A Corvain raider, face painted black, rushing with a hooked blade. Worric had driven his spear forward on instinct. It struck true. The man fell without a sound. And Worric stood there, shaking, staring at the blood on his hands. But he didn't break.

He followed his captain deeper into the woods, where the fighting worsened. The pines burned day and night. Trees crashed around them like gods falling from the sky. At one point, the Eldaran line was nearly broken, hemmed in by fire and surrounded. Worric's captain was struck down, and for a moment the line wavered. It was then that Worric, bloodied, breathless, and barely standing, picked up his fallen captain's banner. He raised it above the smoke. He yelled until his throat tore, rallying the scattered men around him. And they answered. He held the line at the Stone Root Glade for six hours until reinforcements arrived, just long enough to turn the tide. Eldaran steel pushed the Corvain raiders back through the charred woods, across the river, and into legend.

Worric was not knighted that day. Nor the next. But word of the boy who held the banner spread to Valebrook. And in time, King Reynard would ask his name personally. Years later, when soldiers spoke of the War of Broken Pines, they didn't speak of kings or lords or highborn commanders. They spoke of a seventeen-year-old boy with soot on his cheeks, fire behind his eyes, and the will to stand when all else fell, and that boy became Sir Worric, the Iron Shield of Eldara.

Sir Worric expected to return to obscurity after the war. The King had seen him and heard of the boy who held the Northern Crossroad for three nights against rebel horsemen. So, when King Reynard began rebuilding the kingdom's peacekeeping forces, he sent for him. Their first meeting was brief. The King stood in his audience chamber, young but already composed. He had eyes that saw through lies, and a voice that didn't need to rise to carry weight.

"You're not a court man," he told Sir Worric. "That's good. I have enough of those." Sir Worric knelt.

"I serve the crown, my King."

King Reynard gave him one task: train a new generation of royal guards not the pampered ones who flinched at blood, but soldiers who would bleed for the people, not just the palace. Sir Worric accepted this daunting task.

Within five years, he was Sir Worric, Captain of the Royal Guard. He built the Royal Guard from nothing. Handpicked recruits were trained them not only in the sword and shield, but in judgment, restraint, and duty. The old guard called him too rigid. The nobles feared his honesty, but King Reynard trusted him completely.

"Sir Worric is my shield," the King once said. "And my sword when diplomacy ends."

He led the guard during the quelling of the Whisper Riots, protected the Queen during the Glassborn Assassination Attempt, and even saved Azor the Mage from a band of blade cultists in the western isles. He rarely smiled. He didn't drink. He spoke plainly and with purpose. However, watched everything, and he never failed.

Sir Worric first met Malrik during a council session. The man was charming, too charming. He was clever with words, quick to defer, but always smiling like he knew more than he should. Sir Worric didn't trust him. He told the King as much, but Malrik hadn't yet turned. Not openly. He was still just a lord with strange ideas and deep pockets.

"I will not accuse without cause," King Reynard said gently. "But I'll remember your warning."

Sir Worric watched and waited. He saw the signs. The disappearances. The whispers from the eastern marshes. A sickness of the soul spreading among nobles. When Malrik's betrayal finally came, it wasn't with fire, it was with a silence that stretched across the city like a cloak. Guards disappeared. The siege of Valebrook came fast and ended faster. Sir Worric fought like a dying storm. He was there when King Reynard made his final stand.

After, he took Rayner to the west and raising him as a son. Over time, Sir Worric saw something in the boy. He decided to train him and teach him the old code. He taught him how to fight, not just with steel, but with conviction, and for the first time in years, Sir Worric began to feel like the sword he carried wasn't just a memory. Rayner gave him purpose, a second chance, and a reason to believe that the kingdom, though shattered, was not dead.

CHAPTER 2

The First Trial

The sun hung low over the horizon as Rayner reached the banks of the Western River. His boots, caked with the dust of long-traveled roads, stopped just shy of the gleaming water, but the river, wider than he had imagined and glittering with strange silver hues, cut across his path like a living barrier. He scanned the riverbank. There were no bridges, no boats. Only reeds that whispered in the wind, and water that rippled with unnatural calm. Rayner stepped forward cautiously, but as his foot grazed the edge of the water, a voice as smooth as silk drifted through the air.

"Halt, wanderer."

Rayner jerked back, hand falling to the hilt of his sword. The water stirred. From its depths, three figures rose like mist given form: women, graceful and ageless, their skin shimmering like pearl, their hair trailing behind them like riverweed spun from moonlight.

They were river nymphs, spirits of the Western River, and they were watching him with eyes both curious and cold. Long before the kingdoms of men rose in Eldara, before Valebrook's walls and even before the Great Weave was first named by mortal tongue, the rivers flowed, wild and sacred. From those waters came the River Nymphs. Not born of flesh nor flame, but of current and echo, the River Nymphs are elemental spirits who dwell in the waterways that thread through the lands of Eldara. The oldest mages say they were not summoned, nor created, but rather awakened when the first snow melted on the Stoneheart Peaks and flowed into the Whispering River.

They are not gods, but are more than mortal. River Nymphs often appear as tall, luminous women, their skin the hue of polished pearl or riverstone, their hair flowing like water itself, sometimes braided with reeds, moss, or starlight. Their eyes shine with the colors of the rivers they protect: pale blue, green, silver, or gold. They are often serene, but their moods shift as swiftly as a stormed current. A Nymph can soothe a wounded traveler with a single touch or drown a warband in sudden fury. Each river in Eldara has its own Nymph, though some may share tributaries or wander during high tide or flood. Nymphs are tied deeply to memory. Waters carry more than life; they carry echoes of what has been. Mages of the old age would seek counsel from the River Nymphs by offering tokens, driftwood carved with runes, cups of honey-wine, or a song sung over still water. The Nymphs speak rarely, but when they do, their knowledge stretches far and deep. However, the Nymphs are bound by balance. They may bless, but they may also curse. Hunters who poison streams, soldiers who spill innocent blood near sacred springs, or kings who dam sacred waters often suffer sudden drownings, lost armies, or waterlogged fields.

The tallest stepped forward.

"Few mortals come to our waters uninvited," she said. "Fewer still survive the crossing."

Rayner swallowed hard. "I didn't come to challenge you. I seek to cross."

The second nymph, more youthful in form, tilted her head. "All seek something. What makes you worthy?"

"I'm not sure I am," Rayner said honestly.

The third, silent until now, gave a small smile. "Honest, this one. I like him."

The first nymph raised a slender hand. "We are the daughters of Western, guardian of the river. None may pass without trial. Will you face us, Rayner?"

Rayner's breath caught. "How do you know my name?"

They smiled as one. "We are the river. We remember all who speak their dreams to water."

With a nod, Rayner stepped forward. "Then I accept your trial."

The first nymph beckoned him closer. Her eyes glinted like wet stone.

"I am Naida, eldest of the river sisters. My trial is of strength, not of limb, but of soul."

Before Rayner could respond, the river surged upward and enveloped him like a cloak. In an instant, he was underwater, but he could still breathe. He floated in darkness until a vision flared before him. He saw himself as an infant, clutching his mother's hand. Then he saw her fall, vanish into flame and fire. The memory was real, but sharper now, as if the pain had never dulled.

"You cannot outrun the past," Naida's voice echoed in the water. "Show me your truth."

Rayner clenched his fists. He walked through the illusion, through the fires and the screams. The battlefield faded. Light returned. Naida stepped back, expression unreadable.

"You face your wounds. You may continue."

The second nymph floated forward, her laughter like wind chimes.

"I am Lira, keeper of the heart. My trial is of temptation."

She snapped her fingers, and Rayner blinked into a dreamlike vision. He was home. Fields of grain waved in the wind. A woman with dark hair smiled at him from the porch of a cottage. Children laughed. Peace. It felt real. So real it hurt.

"This can be yours," Lira whispered. "No more struggle. No more quest. Lay down your sword. Rest."

Rayner felt his knees weaken. He longed for this. Every part of him wanted to step into the vision and never leave, but something tugged at the edge of his mind, a voice, a promise made under stars and firelight. He turned away from the cottage.

"This isn't mine to claim yet. Not without sacrifice."

The vision dissolved. Lira's smile faded into something sadder, more sincere.

"Many would have stayed," she said softly. "You chose the harder path. You may go on."

The third nymph remained silent for a long moment. She was different, older, perhaps, or simply deeper. The river darkened as she rose from it, the currents swirling beneath her feet.

"I am Elyra, keeper of truth," she said. "My trial is not of strength or desire. It is of self."

Rayner braced himself. Elyra reached out, touching his forehead with one cool finger. The world went silent. Then came voices. Dozens. Hundreds. Rayner heard every word he had ever spoken in anger. Every doubt. Every betrayal of his own ideals. Every moment he had faltered, failed, lied, or given in to fear. The voices screamed, whispered, begged.

"You carry more than hope," Elyra said. "You carry darkness. Can you look upon it and not break?"

Rayner stood trembling. "I see it," he said through gritted teeth.

"And I still choose to fight."

Silence fell. The voices faded. Elyra nodded.

"Then you are not just a boy with a sword. You are a man with a purpose."

The river calmed. The mist lifted. The three nymphs stood side by side once more.

"You have passed our trials," Naida said.

"You have looked within and not flinched," added Lira.

"You may cross," Elyra finished.

A path of water lilies formed across the river, wide enough for one. He walked across the silver path, the river silent behind him, and vanished into the trees beyond. The nymphs watched until he was gone. Then, like reflections dissolving on disturbed water, they slipped beneath the surface once more. Sir Worric watched the entire trial from a distance and followed him over the lilies.

The Second Trial

The mountains rose like broken teeth from the earth's jaw jagged, uneven, and bleeding shadow into the sky. To call them "mountains" was generous. These were ruins of titanic spires, once taller than cloud line, now reduced to cruel ridges and valleys of shattered stone. Locals called them The Eroded. The air changed before Rayner ever set foot on the lower slopes. It turned dry, metallic, laced with the scent of sulfur and old fire. The grass thinned, and the soil turned to powder and grit, until every footstep crunched like bone underfoot. In the far distance, clouds spiraled unnaturally around the peaks, not from weather, but from ancient enchantments buried in the stone. The winds here didn't howl, they whispered. Sometimes in voices he almost recognized.

The first day of ascent was brutal. The slopes weren't steep, but they shifted, stones grinding beneath his boots, trails crumbling at their edges, each step uncertain. The rocks themselves were strange: gray-veined with deep crimson, like blood had been poured into their cracks and left to harden. Some of the stone bled when struck. Not liquid, but a fine dust that clung to his hands and smelled like something half-alive. Dry trees rose here and there; their branches twisted toward the sky like hands caught mid-curse. Their bark was white and smooth like bone, and their leaves, what few remained, sang when the wind passed through them, like flutes made of sorrow. Creatures did not live here. Not openly. Only the occasional glint of gold eyes behind a ridge, or the remnants of something that once resembled a bird but now looked more like a skeleton with wings. At one point, Rayner came across a statue half-buried in the shale. A knight, face broken, sword raised. He almost walked past it, until he realized the sword in the stone was real, not part of the sculpture, but pierced into the knight's spine from behind. He didn't touch it.

By midday on the second day, Rayner reached the Cracked Stair a natural rock formation that formed an uneven, perilous stair spiraling around the base of the second peak. Carved long ago by hands now forgotten, the steps were too narrow for safety, too wide to ignore. Some crumbled as he placed his weight on them. Others whispered spells of failure as he passed, and his own crushing fear of what lay ahead. On one shattered step, he slipped. Not far, just enough to feel the mountain notice him. That night, he slept in a shallow cave beneath the cliff. The fire he built sputtered against the cold, and the shadows danced like memories.

On the third day, Rayner descended into a hidden vale nestled between two ridgelines. The valley floor was soft with dust and the crushed remains of shattered skeletons, goats, men, monsters alike. Whatever lived here fed on hope, or at least the remnants of those who'd lost it. Stone pillars jutted from the ground at random, carved with runic lines that pulsed faintly under moonlight. He didn't read them. He just walked. Slowly. Carefully. The wind here didn't push, it pulled. Toward the cliffs ahead. Toward the trial. He camped by a spring that bubbled up from a glowing crack in the earth. The water tasted of copper. He woke with a burn across his palm, shaped like the symbol carved into the stones: a circle split down the center. Balance must break to be remade.

The Shard Ridge was the cruelest part yet. A stretch of wind-blasted ridgeline where razor-thin stones jutted from the earth like glass blades. Crossing it meant bleeding. No path, no shelter, only a tightrope trail wide enough for boots, too narrow for fear. Each gust of wind carried flecks of glass and dust. Rayner wrapped cloth around his face, his arms, and pressed forward as the shards cut at his clothes and skin, each step testing his resolve. He passed land-marks of those who failed. Small piles of armor, bones arranged in prayer, sometimes shields. He touched each one. Honored each one. One night, he encountered a figure carved from wind and ash, standing in the pass like a ghost.

By the fifth day, Rayner reached the last climb, a vertical scramble up the Teeth of the Sky. The clouds here moved back-ward. The stars above were warped. The world below vanished in mist. He climbed without ropes, using cracks in the stone and will alone, each movement aching, his body worn and bloodied. He passed the Remnants, statues shaped like men, but too tall, too thin, their eyes missing, their arms outstretched toward the peak. Whether they were once people or not, he couldn't say. He didn't stop to ask. Halfway up, he found a ledge, a narrow place carved by time. There, in a pile of wind-shaped stones, rested a sword: rusted, broken, bound in roots. He left his own blade beside it. A gesture.

The wind howled like a living thing, pulling at Rayner's cloak and stinging his cheeks with fine, frozen needles. Rayner squinted against the snow as he took another step upward, his climbing boots biting into the icy slope. Above him, the jagged summit of Eroded Mountain loomed, shrouded in mist and menace.

Snow began falling in lazy spirals that quickly thickened into a storm. The path narrowed into icy ridges. He'd traversed these with aching caution, pressing his hands into frozen earth, heart hammering as one foot slipped before catching again. Rayner's lungs burned with every breath. Around him, the world was a palette of white and gray. He kept moving. He had to. By late afternoon, the storm slackened, revealing a craggy plateau just below the summit. Rayner's fingers were numb, his lips cracked, and his thighs screamed with exertion, but a fire had lit inside him now. He was close.

He crossed the plateau with careful steps, aware of the cornices that could crumble underfoot. As he approached the final pitch Eroded Mountain Pass a gust of wind tore across the ridge. Rayner dropped to a crouch, bracing himself until it passed. Then he looked up and froze. Heart pounding, Rayner knelt and brushed away snow with trembling hands.

"I made it," he whispered.

A sudden gust of wind kicked up snow, but then it died again, leaving a stillness so profound it felt sacred. Rayner closed his eyes. There was only one climb left.

The Eroded Mountain Pass was the hardest part, but Rayner moved with steady determination. His hands found holds. His feet pressed against tiny ledges. He no longer thought of the pain, or the cold. Halfway up, the sun pierced the clouds, casting a beam of light across the slope. The snow glittered like powdered stars. For the first time in days, Rayner smiled.

Two hours later, with the last of his strength, he crested the Eroded Mountain Pass. He stood, panting, dizzy, and triumphant. The sky above was cobalt blue, and the land below stretched endlessly, valleys, rivers, distant peaks softened by mist. As the sun dipped low and the sky turned shades of violet and gold, Rayner sat at the summit, breathing in the silence, heart full. Tomorrow, he would descend, but tonight, he would rest at the roof of the world.

When he reached the top, he found no temple, no test, no fire-lit altar. Only a plateau of wind and silence. There, in the center, was a mirror of obsidian, untouched by time. Rayner stood before it. And the mirror showed him not his face, but every failure he feared. The world burning. He closed his eyes, and whispered: "I don't climb for power. The mountain accepted the answer. The wind stilled. And in the silence, Rayner felt a pulse beneath his feet, like a heartbeat. The ancient power of the weave, not to grant, but to test. He did not leave stronger. He left clearer. The descent was no easier. But the mountain did not fight him anymore. It watched. He passed the statue with the sword again. This time, it was gone. He crossed the shard fields with blood on his boots and a calm in his chest. The glass no longer cut. Rayner had passed the Eroded Mountains. He had walked the path of fear and left it behind. He had finished the second trial. He met with Sir Worric, who had taken a different route through the mountain pass.

The Third Trial

As Rayner and Sir Worric entered the Whispering woodland, they could hear strange sounds coming from a clearing up ahead. As they approached, they could see an old man with a younger man around Rayner's age. Rayner waited in the wood line as Sir Worric made his way towards the old man. Suddenly, Sir Worric greeted the old man with a warm embrace.

"Azor, it has been an age since we last saw each other" said Sir Worric.

Azor replied, "Good to see you my old friend".

Rayner crept from the Woodline towards them. He noticed the young man's apprentice looked peculiarly familiar, but he could not quite point it out. Azor introduced himself and his young apprentice.

"My name is Azor and this is my apprentice Cole" he said.

Sir Worric added "Azor was the mage to King many years ago".

Sir Worric pulled Azor aside to speak in private. Rayner and Cole just stood there staring back at one another.

Cole smirked and said "That is a very pretty sword you have there".

"Yes, and quite sharp" Rayner snickered back.

"Where are you from?" Rayner questioned.

"We reside in a small cabin deeper into the forest. We come out here to the edge of the forest for my training." Cole stated.

Rayner smiled "So you are in training as well".

Far from Rayner and Cole, Sir Worric whispered to Azor "Is that..." before he could finish his words, Azor nodded. "What are we going to do?"

"Nothing yet", said Azor.

They returned to the young men. They began to walk deeper into the Woodline. The trees began before the path ended. One moment, Rayner walked beside Azor and Cole through the edge of the highland trail. The next, the world narrowed into shadow and sound. The Whispering Woods rose before them like a green wall, thick-trunked trees with silver-veined bark, their branches interlacing like fingers sealing away the sky. Azor stopped, lifting his hand.

"This is as far as we go," the old mage said, his voice low. "Beyond here, the woods test what no sword can defend. This is not a trial of strength, Rayner. It is a trial of self."

Cole gave a half-smile. "Try not to punch the trees."

Rayner managed a smirk but said nothing. He touched the pommel of his sword, the one Sir Worric had given him. The metal felt colder now. He stepped forward. Azor raised his staff and whispered a phrase in the Old Tongue. The woods shimmered, just once, as if pulling breath. Then Rayner crossed the threshold, and the forest closed behind him.

Light here moved differently. It passed through the canopy in slivers and spirals, dancing over moss-draped roots and stones cracked with runes. The air smelled of cedar, loam, and rain that hadn't yet fallen. No animals stirred. No birds sang. But the trees... the trees whispered. Not loud, and not constant. Just enough that when Rayner moved, he swore he heard his name, or a question, soft and curious.

"Rayner... why do you carry the sword?" "Why do you follow a dead man's path?"

He tightened his jaw and pressed on.

A trail barely marked the forest floor, winding between trees twisted into impossible shapes, one like a serpent, another like a man reaching toward the heavens. As he walked, the canopy closed tighter. Daylight vanished. Then the woods spoke again. But this time, not in whispers.

Rayner stepped into a clearing and found himself on a battlefield. Wind howled. Smoke clung to shattered earth. Around him lay armored corpses, their tabards bearing his sigil: a rising sword over flame. His hands were slick with blood. His sword, longer, darker, was buried in the chest of a man kneeling before him. Quinn. Rayner stumbled back, horror rising in his throat. But Quinn didn't fall. He looked up.

"You chose this path. You chose command. You led us here."

The bodies stirred. Cole lay broken beneath rubble. Tristan's crossbow shattered beside his corpse. A horn blew. From the hill, Malrik descended, not old, not hunched, but in full vigor, smiling like a king of old.

"You have become me," he said.

Rayner dropped the sword. And the illusion shattered. The forest returned, but the pain did not vanish. Rayner walked deeper. Weaker. Each step cost more. The forest grew dense with hanging moss, the ground spongy and cold. Here, the trees whispered again, but not about war. About childhood.

"Do you remember when you first picked up a sword?"

Then he was there again, twelve years old, wooden blade in hand, facing Sir Worric in the yard behind his cottage in Ashbrook.

"Feet apart," Sir Worric barked. "Grip with both hands. Again."

Rayner blinked, he knew it wasn't real, but it felt real. The sun on his skin. The sweat. The ache. The hope.

"You think it's about glory," Sir Worric said, walking circles around him. "But it's not. It's about service. About sacrifice. Do you still want it, boy?"

The memory froze, and then Sir Worric turned, eyes sharp, piercing, as if pulled from the grave.

"You've lost your way, Rayner."

Rayner fell to his knees. His chest burned, not from physical wounds, but from the weight of all he carried.

"I don't know if I'm enough," he whispered. "I never was."

Yet, through the trees, a new voice came. One not of memory. It was Cole.

"You're not supposed to be enough alone, you stubborn idiot."

Rayner looked up. No one was there. But he rose anyway. At the heart of the woods stood the Mirror Tree. It was massive, its bark like burnished silver, its branches filled with hanging leaves that shimmered like glass. In its trunk, a mirror, smoother than ice, reflected not the forest, but Rayner alone. He stepped toward it. And the reflection changed. He saw himself as a boy. Then as a knight. Then a king. Then a tyrant. Then broken. Then gone. He placed his hand on the mirror and it spoke in his voice.

"Who are you without the sword? "Who are you when no one follows?" Rayner's hand curled into a fist.

"I am not perfect."

He drew the sword. Not in defiance. But in honesty.

"I am Rayner. I bleed. I break. But I do not give up. I serve. I protect. I choose."

The mirror shattered, not violently, but like petals falling. The shards drifted into the air and turned into leaves, blowing away on a wind that hadn't existed until now. The tree sighed, and the path lit ahead. Rayner emerged from the woods changed. Azor stood where he'd been, watching quietly. Cole leaned on his staff, trying not to look worried. Rayner didn't speak. He simply looked at them. Azor nodded.

"The sword can be taught," he said. "But the truth must be faced alone."

Cole clapped Rayner on the back. "Took you long enough."

Rayner finally smiled. The Whispering Woods fell silent behind them. The knight had passed his final trial, not with victory, but with truth, and that made all the difference.

Roucher

CHAPTER 3

Prior to the arrival of Rayner and Sir Worric, Azor and Cole were training.

"Again," Azor said, voice like low thunder.

Cole stood in the center of a stick-drawn circle, his brow slick with sweat, hands raised. Blue sparks danced between his fingers, sputtering like wet kindling. He grimaced, focused, and tried to shape the energy into form. Nothing. The sparks fizzled out.

"I am trying," Cole said through clenched teeth. "It's just this spell doesn't make sense."

Azor, seated on a log in the forest, arched an eyebrow.

"Magic is not meant to make sense. Not in the way a hammer or a blade does. It is will imposed upon the unseen. You think too much, boy. Feel more."

Cole dropped his hands with a sigh. "That's easy for you to say. You've been a High Mage for sixty years."

"Seventy-two," Azor corrected. "And I still fail. You think fire was the first spell I mastered? No. It was light. Then levitation. Then silencing spells so I could meditate without hearing the bloody hawks nesting in the trees."

Cole snorted. "And now?"

"Now I teach loud, impatient apprentices who think power comes with a flick of the wrist."

Azor stood, approaching the boy with measured steps. His eyes, pale and gleaming, held the weight of centuries.

"The spell I gave you is simple: summon fire from within. Not from air. Not from wood. From you. It's not about force. It's about balance."

Cole looked down at his hands. "Balance."

"Yes. Let me show you."

Azor raised his right hand and closed his eyes. A heartbeat passed. Then a flame bloomed in his palm not wild or raging, but calm, flickering gently like a candle on a still night.

"This is not a weapon," he said softly. "It is a conversation between soul and element. Do not command it. Invite it." He closed his hand, and the fire disappeared. "Now. You."

Cole inhaled. Slowly. He closed his eyes, feeling the lingering heat of the stick circle beneath his boots. He thought of warmth, of hearths and torches, of summer light peaking between the trees. He reached inward. A spark. Then a flicker, and then a flame. It hovered above his palm like a newborn bird, trembling with uncertainty. Cole's eyes flew open.

"I did it!"

The fire sputtered and vanished. Azor chuckled.

"Joy breaks focus. Still, not bad." Cole beamed despite himself.

"Will I be able to hold it longer soon?"

"In time. Magic grows like a tree slowly, and with struggle." Azor stepped back and gestured toward the tiny shelter. "Come."

"Why only one apprentice?" Cole asked. "You could have dozens.

Azor's smile faded. "Because magic is not a trade to be mass-produced. It's dangerous. Demanding, and personal. I take one because I must give all."

"Why did you choose me?" Cole asked quietly. "There must have been others. Smarter. More... noble-born."

Azor turned to him. "Hope."

Cole swallowed. "I won't let you down."

"You will," Azor said without malice. "Many times. That is how we learn."

Weeks passed, and Cole's magic grew. He could summon light to guide his steps through the forest, levitate quills to take notes, even warm a kettle with just a touch. The fire spell became a familiar companion not yet a weapon, but a tool.

The first years were slow, filled with silence and strange lessons. Cole learned to read not from books, but from tree bark, runes, wind-blown leaves.

Azor would say, "If you can read the wind, you can understand a man's thoughts. The elements do not lie."

Magic did not begin with sparks or explosions. It began with stillness. Azor never scolded. Never struck. He was maddeningly patient, more like a stone than a man. But when he spoke, the world seemed to hush to listen.

He began teaching Cole the basics of magic, not spells, but awareness.

"Magic," Azor explained, "is not a thing you do. It is a thing you feel. The world sings, and we answer."

He asked questions constantly, his mind as sharp as his heart was wild. One night, Cole awoke screaming. He had seen a dark figure, or what was left of him. A figure with black veins and empty eyes, reaching through shadow toward a burning Valebrook. Azor took this seriously.

"The boy is a conduit," he said to himself. "Malrik has tasted power far beyond our world. If Cole is to stand against him, he must learn not only control, but resolve."

From that day, their training deepened. Azor taught Cole ancient runes, the structure of magical languages, and the cost of imbalance in the Weave. For each spell, Cole learned a moral weight.

"He must never become what we fought to stop," Azor warned. "Magic is never just light or shadow. It is intention."

Cole learned the language of the flame first, Aurev, surna, kel. He lit candles with breath alone. By his ninth year, he could hold fire in his palm without fear. But Azor made him snuff it just as often.

"You must know when not to burn," he would say. "That's the difference between a pyromancer and a mage."

By the time Cole turned twelve, their home had shifted. Azor believed the world was a better teacher than walls. They traveled to Hollowmere, where the fog never lifted, and the people spoke in riddles. Cole learned to bend mist and walk through veils. He studied at the ruins of Faranhold, where he touched stones that remembered the time before kings. He slept beneath stars that no longer had names.

Azor grew distant during these years, not in heart, but in presence. He would often disappear at dawn, returning only after sundown. Cole learned to train alone. To fail and fail again. His hands burned. His feet froze. He was once nearly lost in a wraithwood storm, but he survived. By fifteen, he could duel with illusions. He could summon wind to guide an arrow or ice to seal a wound. But he had not smiled in months. Azor finally took him to the Silver Lake, a place of calm where the stars reflected so clearly, they seemed like a second sky. There, they sat beneath the moon, and Azor spoke words he had not spoken before.

"I was once like you. Wild with power. Blinded by it. I hurt more than I helped. I loved only knowledge." He looked at Cole then, his ancient eyes tired. "But you... You love people."

It was the first time Cole wept in Azor's presence. Not for pain. Not for anger. But for the love buried so deep it startled him when he saw it reflected back. At sixteen, Azor finally tested him.

The first trial was to walk into the Ebon Glen alone, where whispers wound around the ears and madness clung to the mist.

Cole was to retrieve a moonthorn flower, a rare bloom that only grew when it sensed courage. He walked for two days, fasting. He faced memories not his own. Saw visions of fire consuming his brother Rayner. Saw Sir Worric bleeding out on a hill. He screamed until his voice cracked. But he found the moonthorn. And it bloomed in his hands.

The second trial was of control. Azor summoned a being of raw flame, a fire revenant, and placed it in a sealed circle. Cole had to bind it using only words and will. The revenant clawed at the air, mocking him. It took hours. Sweat poured from Cole's brow. But he stood his ground, rooted not in rage, but in compassion. When the circle sealed, Azor merely nodded.

"You are not just strong," he said. "You are worthy."

Between his seventeenth and nineteenth year, Cole no longer needed constant teaching. Azor gave him books and scrolls, and Cole studied late into the night. He learned healing magic. Light magic. Illusions, wards, and the deeper language of the stars. But as Cole grew in power, he also grew restless.

When Cole was nearly twenty, Azor grew quiet again. Something shifted. He spent more time watching the skies. His staff never left his side.

"What is it?" Cole asked.

"The balance is tipping. The old magic stirs again."

Cole stiffened. The name sent a shiver up his spine. Azor looked toward the trees, as if seeing through them.

"It is time we return."

Cole's chest tightened. Fear and excitement tangled in his ribs. Azor both crafted and gifted the staff to Cole.

"A staff is not a toy, Cole. It's not even a weapon, though it can be. It is a burden. A mirror. And it will break you, if you are not ready."

Over the next few years, Azor taught him the foundations of the Weave: not just spells, but discipline, restraint, silence, and meaning. Cole grew stronger, smarter, but also more headstrong, more eager to prove himself. One autumn, when the leaves turned gold and bled crimson, Azor took him deep into the Whispering Woods, alone. There, Cole faced his trial: a night in a clearing where the Weave shimmered faintly in the air, where the trees listened. Spirits tested him, illusions of fear, temptation, anger. Cole resisted, barely. But it was enough. At dawn, Azor returned. He had been watching the whole time, hidden in the edge of the forest. Azor placed a bundle in Cole's hands. Wrapped in a leather cloth, warm from enchantment, was the staff. Carved from the heart of a Weavesap Tree, found only in the oldest parts of the forest. It glows faintly when magic is near. The wood shifts in tone with Cole's emotions. A single vein of sky-iron runs through its center, forged by Azor's own magic. The metal helps channel and stabilize spells. Set into the upper curve is a crystal of binding, a gift from a River Nymph. It reflects moonlight, even when the moon is gone.

"This is not just a staff. It is your anchor. Your voice when words fail. Do not wield it in anger. And do not lose it. It knows you now."

CHAPTER 4

The sun hovered low in the sky, bleeding amber over the treetops as Sir Worric and Rayner emerged from the whispering forest. Pine needles clung to their cloaks, and the scent of sap and damp moss clung to the air around them. After leaving the forest, where they had met Azor and Cole, they began their travel back to Ashbrook. Along the journey home, Sir Worric and Rayner were approached by a Village Elder, who told them about the Mountain men, who are tearing up villages and burning homes. The Elder asked Sir Worric and Rayner for help. Before even the rivers flowed or the first human kings walked the green fields of Eldara, the mountains stood, tall, jagged, and cold. From their stone hearts came the Ulgorim, known in later ages as Mountain Men, Stone Giants, or more respectfully in old dwarven, Tharnk'Dur, "those shaped of the earth." The oldest tales tell of Durmog the Peak-Father, a primordial titan who shaped the highlands with his bare hands. From his footprints rose the Eroded Mountains, and from shards of his bone and blood came his sons and daughters, the first giants.

The Ulgorim say only this: "We were born of stone and silence. We owe nothing to the stars above." Standing between 10 and 14 feet tall, the Ulgorim are carved as if from the mountain itself. Their skin ranges from granite-grey to pale slate-blue, and their bodies are heavily muscled, often layered in stone-like calluses that serve as natural armor. Their hair, when they grow it, resembles dry moss or tangled shale. Though most consider them brutes, this is far from the truth. The Ulgorim are a stoic and contemplative people, slow to act but decisive when stirred. They speak little, but when they do, it is often in poetry or metaphor. Their long lifespans, some living for five or six centuries, give them a perspective few mortals understand. They often wear hides from mountain beasts, hammered bronze, or furs of white wolves. Many carry war-clubs, axes forged from volcanic stone, or hammers passed down for generations, each weapon bearing its own name and history.

They had spent three days tracking signs of mountain men giants that dwelled in the crags to the north, known for raiding settlements when the snowmelt flushed the rivers fat with trout, but until now, they had only found broken trees and scattered prints.

Rayner walked slightly ahead, hand on the hilt of his sword, ever alert. At twenty summers, he moved with the eager stride of youth, his dark hair tied back, eyes sharp and curious. Beside him, Sir Worric moved more deliberately. Though his age pressed on his bones, his bearing remained proud, his armor worn but maintained, his steel gauntlets polished. The veteran knight had trained Rayner since the boy's nineth year, shaping him from a boy into a swordsman worthy of a banner. They reached the clearing near the river a wide bend with a flat embankment, choked with rushes and reeds. Birds scattered from the trees, and frogs leapt into the water.

Rayner halted. "Sir... Do you see that?"

Sir Worric followed his gaze. Across the river, just beyond the fallen logs, four massive shapes loomed like statues. They were not men at least, not as men ought to be. Their frames were massive, each towering at least ten feet tall, wrapped in furs, muscle and sinew rippling beneath leathery skin. One wielded a tree trunk as a club. Another had bones strung around his neck like trophies. Their eyes glowed faintly in the waning light pale and cruel.

"Giants," Sir Worric whispered. "And not the wild, solitary kind. These are clan-bound."

The nearest of the mountain men roared, deep and guttural, and leapt into the river. Water crashed around him like a burst dam.

The others followed, boots churning mud and fish alike as they charged across. Rayner unsheathed his blade with a hiss.

"Four of them. Do we run?"

"No time," Sir Worric growled, planting his feet and drawing his longsword. "Hold the line. Keep them from flanking us."

They met the first giant in the shallows. Rayner darted left, blade flashing toward the beast's leg. The giant swung its club, splintering a willow tree where Rayner had stood a second before. He struck again, slashing across the calf. Blood sprayed. The giant bellowed in rage. Sir Worric moved with brutal precision. His blade carved through the wrist of a giant mid-swing, severing it cleanly. The brute shrieked and dropped its weapon, crashing to its knees. Sir Worric drove his sword into its chest, twisting deep into the heart. The monster fell, twitching. The other three giants howled. One hurled a rock the size of a cartwheel. Sir Worric raised his shield, too late. The stone struck him square in the ribs, flinging him backward into a mossy boulder. He collapsed, groaning.

"Worric!" Rayner shouted, cutting deep into another giant's thigh before retreating toward his fallen mentor.

The odds turned. The remaining giants surged forward, sensing weakness. Rayner positioned himself in front of Sir Worric's body, sword raised, heart thundering in his chest. He remembered everything the knight had taught him: Watch the shoulders, not the hands. Let your feet guide your blade. Strike once, but true. The closest giant lunged. Rayner ducked low, rolled beneath the swing, and sliced across the Achilles tendon. The beast staggered, crashing into the shallows. Rayner leapt onto its back and drove his sword into the spine. It roared once, then went still. Another rushed him.

Rayner barely turned in time to parry a wild backhand, the blow knocking him sideways into the mud. He slid and scrambled to his feet, blood and sweat in his eyes. The giant raised its fist and then froze. Sir Worric, groaning and bloodied, had risen to one knee. He hurled his dagger with all the strength he could muster. The blade sank into the giant's eye. It screamed, clutching its face and stumbling blindly toward the trees. Only one remained. This one was the largest, chest like a barrel, face painted with blue streaks. It didn't roar. It smiled.

It spoke in a rumbling voice: "Boy fights well, but dies now."

It stepped over its fallen kin, raising a hammer carved from stone and bone. Rayner had no breath left. No strength, but he held the sword tight and stood his ground.

The giant charged. Rayner didn't move. He couldn't. His legs trembled. His arms burned. Just as the hammer came down, Sir Worric rose with a roar of his own and flung his broken shield. It struck the giant in the jaw. The impact slowed the hammer's descent just enough for Rayner to dive forward and thrust his sword straight through the beast's stomach. It collapsed on top of him. Darkness. Rayner awoke to the sound of water lapping against stone. A heavy weight pressed against his chest, but it wasn't the giant it was Sir Worric, dragging him by the collar out from under the massive corpse.

"Rayner," he rasped. "Breathe."

Rayner gasped. Cold air filled his lungs. He sat up, coughing mud and blood.

"You're alive," he managed. Sir Worric grinned grimly.

"Aye. For now." Rayner looked down.

Sir Worric's side was soaked with blood. The hit from the boulder had cracked ribs maybe worse. He couldn't walk. Without a word, Rayner sheathed his sword, slid his arms under the knights, and began to lift.

"You fool," Sir Worric hissed. "You'll throw your back"

"Quiet," Rayner muttered. "I'm not leaving you here."

He carried the knight across the river, each step slow and agonizing. The bodies of the giants floated behind them or lay sprawled in the shallows, staining the water red. Rayner didn't look back. The journey home took hours.

Through the twilight, then into full night, Rayner trudged across hills and glades, each step a battle. Sir Worric drifted in and out of consciousness, sometimes mumbling half-formed orders, sometimes warning Rayner about nonexistent threats. They passed the ancient stone road, then the hollow oak that marked the edge of the old wood. Moonlight guided them. Owls hooted above. Once, Rayner stumbled and both collapsed to the ground. He lay there, panting, tears stinging his eyes, but then he heard it the faint howl of a distant wolf. Close enough to be real.

"No rest," he muttered. "Not yet."

He lifted Sir Worric again at last, just before dawn, they made it home.

Sir Worric said to Rayner "Find Azor"

Sir Worric died on the riverbank. Rayner had carried him half a mile before he collapsed, knees buckling in the mud, his mentor's blood soaking through his cloak. The wound had been too deep. The mountain men had taken too much. Sir Worric's last words had been few, but clear: "Find Azor." Rayner buried him beneath an ash tree, where sunlight filtered through the canopy in broken shafts of gold. He laid Sir Worric's sword across the grave, then knelt beside it for what felt like hours. The forest offered no comfort only wind and the rustle of leaves, as if the world had already moved on. Rayner could not believe what had just happened the man he looked up to and admired was gone. Looking back, he wished he could have conveyed his gratitude for the training Sir

Worric had given him. He eyes swelled with tears, as he brushed them from his cheek, and picked himself up.

By nightfall, Rayner stood again. His hands were clenched. His jaw tight. He had one goal: find the mage Azor, and with him, Cole. Only they could guide him through the next chapter of the journey.

Rayner took the path that Sir Worric had previously taken to get to the Whispering Woodlands. This was a passage to the south of the mountain range where it meets a shallow peaceful river, easy to cross. He made his way through the shallow end of the Eroded Mountains.

"I am glad I do not have to climb that again." He thought to himself.

Finally, after 6 days of travel he arrived back at the Whispering Woodlands.

"Now, I just need to find Azor and Cole."

The forest was old older than maps, older than kingdoms. Trees with twisted trunks leaned across the trail like sentries. The path was overgrown, used only by deer, wolves, and ghosts. Rayner walked it alone, his sword sheathed at his back, a waterskin on his belt, and a broken heart in his chest. The first night, he made camp beneath a fallen pine, starting a small fire only after wrapping the flames in dirt and stone to avoid drawing attention. He dreamt of Sir Worric. In the dream, the knight stood atop a hill, his armor shining like the sun, but his face was shadowed, distant. Rayner called out, but Sir Worric said nothing. When Rayner woke, there were tears on his cheeks and frost on his cloak. He pushed onward.

At midday, he found the remnants of a campfire, still warm beneath the ash. Scorch marks spidered across the stones in strange patterns. Mage fire. Rayner knelt, tracing the edges. Cole's handiwork, likely. The fire had burned hotter than normal, as if fed by spellwork rather than wood, but no footprints. Whoever had made it had moved carefully. Still, it was something. Rayner followed broken twigs and a trail of faint heat through the underbrush, deeper into the forest's heart. The trees grew stranger here, white-barked, their leaves deep red even in summer. The air carried whispers. He came upon a clearing by dusk. At its center, a stone obelisk rose from the earth, carved with runes that shimmered faintly in moonlight. Azor's mark. Rayner stepped closer, and then the wind changed.

Something moved at the edge of the clearing. It stepped into view, a creature the size of a bear, cloaked in moss and bark, eyes glowing blue. Not beast, not man. A construct. A guardian. It raised a massive arm of vine-wrapped stone and pointed at Rayner.

"Turn away," it rumbled. "This place is not yours."

Rayner drew his sword. "I seek Azor of the Hollow Flame," he said.

The guardian's eyes narrowed. "Many seek him. Few are found worthy."

Rayner stepped forward. "Then test me."

The forest fell silent. Then the guardian charged. Rayner met the creature's weight with precision, dodging left, striking low. His sword sang as it cut through vines, sparking against enchanted stone. The guardian swung a massive limb, grazing Rayner's ribs and sending him rolling through the leaves. Pain exploded in his side, but he rose. Again, and again. Until finally, he drove his blade between two runes carved into the guardian's chest. The construct froze. The runes blinked out. The creature crumbled into vines and dust.

From the tree line, a voice called out. "Enough."

Azor emerged like a shadow unraveling. Tall, cloaked, his face marked with black ink tattoos and a long braid of white hair down his back. His staff crackled faintly with silver fire.

"You've bled enough to earn words," Azor said, voice deep as thunder. "Come. You are expected."

Azor led Rayner through veils of mist that parted at his gesture, revealing a glade filled with rune-etched stones and floating lanterns. Trees grew in perfect arcs overhead. Streams flowed in curves that defied gravity. It was a pocket of magic held together by sheer will, and there, beside a fire, sat Cole. He rose when Rayner entered, a grin breaking his face.

"Rayner" he called.

Azor spoke behind them. "The two of you are bound by fate, and now, fate demands you move quickly."

CHAPTER 5
Many Years Ago

"Be seated, both of you." "I will tell you a story."

Days before that fateful night, King Reynard called for a private council, just the king, myself, Sir Worric, Queen Elenora, and Lord Malrik. I remember how the firelight flickered that day. The tension in the King's jaw. The distant roll of thunder, though the skies were clear.

"Something walks beneath our feet," King Reynard said. "The crypt stones sweat. The wards strain. Azor, speak plainly."

"I did. I spoke of blood rites. Of necromantic sigils found carved into the trees in the high woods. Of villages burned, not by raiders, but by controlled fire, aimed with surgical cruelty. I spoke of a wound in the Veil, that invisible barrier separating life from death, that was growing wider every week. Someone is drawing from the old power," I said.

King Reynard turned to Malrik.

"You've long studied ancient texts. Have you seen anything like this?"

Malrik smiled, so slightly, so politely. "No, my king," he said. "But I will look deeper, if you wish."

"I saw it then. In his eyes. In the way he didn't blink. The lie."

"That night, I followed Malrik. Invisible, silent, cloaked in a spell that only three mages in the known world could cast. I watched him descend beneath the palace, through tunnels once sealed by the Hollow Flame. I followed him into the Chamber of Binding, a place even I feared, where the first kings buried their failed creations. There, I saw Malrik stand before a circle of bone. I saw him bleed into the stones. I heard the whisper of something

57

waking. A name spoken in a language that turned my stomach: Anek'Thur, the god of chained souls. I fled, and I knew what had to be done. The next morning, I appeared in full ceremonial robes, storming into the King's private garden where King Reynard was reading beside his son. "Malrik must be arrested," I said without formality.

Sir Worric rose instantly. "Why?"

I explained, but the queen frowned. "We have no proof."

I slammed a scroll down, marked with Malrik's blood signature, stolen from the circle.

"I watched him call to the dark. I felt the Veil stretch."

King Reynard looked tired. Older than his years. He had built a kingdom out of the ashes of civil war. Now it trembled again.

"I believe you," he said. "But to arrest Malrik openly will shatter the nobility. He still has allies. The realm could fracture."

My voice was as stern as iron. "If we do nothing, the realm will burn."

King Reynard looked down at his infant sons, asleep in the grass.

Then he nodded. "Tonight. Quietly. You and Sir Worric. Take him without noise. Bring him here."

But Malrik must have been watching us. When I and Sir Worric reached his chambers, he was gone. His robes lay folded on the bed, and a single black feather sat atop them.

The Night of the Attack

The moon hung low, a silver eye half-shuttered behind the clouds, casting the land in a shroud of half-light. The stars above dared not shine, as though the heavens themselves recoiled from what was to come. Beneath that ominous sky, a shadow moved across the hills, fluid, silent, vast. It was not a mere army. It was a legion. At its heart rode a figure clad in blackened steel, jagged like the bones of a dead god. His crimson eyes burned through the visor of his horned helm. Behind him trailed beasts bred in forgotten pits, sorcerers whose veins pulsed with shadow, and soldiers whose oaths had long since cost them their souls. He did not march for conquest. He marched for annihilation.

The Castle of Eldrinth had withstood a hundred sieges. Its alabaster walls gleamed in the daylight like a beacon of hope, and its high towers sang with wind-borne bells that carried peace across the realm. Inside, King Reynard and Queen Elenora ruled with wisdom and strength. Their people adored them, their knights were loyal, and their court was just, but even the brightest flame draws the coldest winds.

No horns announced the enemy's arrival. No scouts returned from the woods. The guard towers, once vigilant, were now manned by lifeless sentries, mouths gaping in final screams, throats slit. The first real warning came from the animals. Horses neighed wildly in their stalls, dogs howled, and the castle's ravens took to the sky in a frenzy, but by then, it was too late. From the shadows of the forest emerged the first wave: Malrik's Legion. Clad in black mail, faces hidden behind emotionless masks, they scaled the walls like spiders. They made no sound, not even as they killed. A sentry turned just in time to see his comrade fall silently, throat spurting red. He reached for his horn. An arrow found his eye before he could blow. Within minutes, the gates were compromised. The great gate groaned under a blast of shadow magic. Behind it, the legion poured in. I stood in the King's Observatory Tower, staring out across the sleeping city. The stars above were pale. The constellations had begun to drift, just slightly, off their eternal paths.

Magic was unraveling. Balance was tipping, and I could feel it in my bones. The end had already begun. It had been two years since the Hollow Flame Order began reporting strange occurrences: missing children from mage bloodlines, tombs disturbed by unseen hands, plagues without cause.

In the throne room, King Reynard donned his armor with shaking hands. His sword shimmered with a light of its own. At his side, Queen Elenora.

"My love," she said, voice calm. "We knew this day would come."

He nodded. "I only hoped it would come after our time."

A knight entered, battered and bloody.

"They've breached the lower halls. We must get you out."

But the King raised a hand. "No. We stand here. The line ends with us, if it must, but the flame... the flame must go on."

The halls of Eldrinth rang with screams and steel. Firelight flickered against stone soaked in blood. The royal guard, though valiant, fell in droves against Malrik's tide. Malrik himself walked through the carnage like a god of death. Knights charged him and were reduced to ash. The Dark Lord reached the base of the central tower and raised a hand. The stones withered, as though the years themselves obeyed him. Cracks spread like veins across the foundation. With a groan of final protest, the great doors shattered inward. The throne room lay ahead.

King Reynard stood tall before the throne, his sword gleaming in his hand. Queen Elenora stood beside him. Malrik stepped into the chamber like a storm given form.

"You've come far, Malrik," King Reynard said. "But you'll not take this throne. Not while we breathe."

Malrik removed his helm. His face was pale, ageless, beautiful and terrible all at once. His hair flowed like ink, and his smile revealed teeth too sharp for any man.

"You breathe only because I allow it," he said.

Then he struck. The duel was like none before. King Reynard's sword met Malrik's sword in a clash of light and shadow that cracked stone and shattered glass. He fought like a demon. King Reynard, to his credit, held him at bay. Their swords clashed and sounds of metal rang out across the room. Once, he even drove a slash across Malrik's chest, but no blood fell. Only darkness. Then, with a motion too fast to follow, Malrik disarmed him. The King's sword clattered to the floor. Elenora screamed. With a flick, Malrik sent her crashing into the marble steps. King Reynard crawled to her, gathered her in his arms. Her breath was faint. Her eyes met his one last time.

"My love," she whispered. "I see the stars." And she was gone.

Malrik watched the King hold his queen with something like curiosity. Then he stepped forward, sword raised. King Reynard stood, trembling, the fire in his eyes guttering but unbroken.

"You will be forgotten," he spat.

Malrik tilted his head. "No," he said. "You will."

Malrik's sword fell. The King of Valebrook died on the throne steps. By dawn, the castle lay in ruins. Towers smoldered, walls crumbled. The royal banners burned on every parapet. Malrik stood at the balcony of the throne room, looking out across the realm.

"It is done," he said.

Malrik and his legion scattered throughout the castle in search of the two princes. While searching Azor found the King where he had fallen, but the Queen was nowhere to be found. He grabbed the King's sword and took it down into the rooms below the castle. He hid the sword for the future. Malrik was unaware of the power that laid in the sword. One day the sword would be found and used to restore the kingdom, Azor thought.

The night the capital fell, Sir Worric, Captain of the Guard and sworn sword to the Flame-Bound King, fought through smoke, blood, and collapsing stone to fulfill his final oath: protect the king's sons. Rayner was only one, Cole just an infant, when Worric found them in the underground crypt where Queen Elenora had hidden them moments before her final stand. The queen had channeled her magic to seal off the chamber, using her life to hold back the cursed tide. Worric bore the children in his arms. They passed through secret tunnels built in King Thalen's time, emerging into the overgrown forest beyond the outer wall. Though wounded and weary, Worric pressed on for three nights without rest, dodging legion scouts and navigating treacherous ground. He knew they could not return to any known road. Instead, he took them west, toward the forgotten deer paths that led to Valebrook. It took eleven days to reach Ashbrook. When they arrived, Sir Worric collapsed at the village edge. He had carried the boys nearly the entire journey, wrapped in mud-soaked cloaks to hide their bloodline. The people of Ashbrook took them in without question. Tomas Hammerline, now the village smith, and Hale, now the elder huntsman.

Azor had once been Archmage of the Veil, a trusted advisor to King Reynard. After the fall of the capital, he vanished, many presumed dead or corrupted. But he had retreated into the northern forest, wounded and grieving. Azor emerged from the forest with a staff of twisted ironwood and robes frayed by time. He looked more a hermit than a mage, but his eyes still glowed with the embers of old power. He arrived in Ashbrook unannounced. The villagers, wary but respectful, took him to Worric.

Upon seeing Cole, Azor said simply, "The Weave has chosen. I must teach him, before others come to twist him."

Both he and Sir Worric agreed to separate the boys for their own protection. Azor then took Cole to the west to the whispering woods. Worric took months to recover, and never fully healed, but his strength of will endure. He built a modest house on the edge of the orchard, and from that day on, trained Rayner each morning before the sun rose.

"If you are to take the crown," he would say, "you must first learn how to stand without it."

At thirteen, Rayner saved the life of a younger child who had fallen into the river that ran past the village. He tied a rope to himself and dove in during a flood. For this, the villagers began calling him "River-Stag." He rejected the name, but it stuck. Worric gave him his first real sword shortly after.

"This," he said, "isn't for ceremony. It's for the day when war returns to find you."

In his eyes, he saw King Reynard, not as a child, but as a quiet echo of the king who stood his ground to the end. And so, the first seeds of return were sown. Hidden in Ashbrook, trained in silence, shaped by love and loss, the true heir was growing.

The morning Azor left Ashbrook with the boy in his arms, the sun was just beginning to rise over the fields. Azor did not raise him as a soldier or a student. He raised him as a question in search of an answer. They settled in a glade beneath an ancient willow where a modest tower stood, half of it reclaimed by vines. The forest around them was dense but not dark, a place of mystery, not menace. Here, Azor taught Cole how to listen before he spoke, to feel before he acted.

The Castle Eldrinth is a place where majesty meets the wild, where the line between civilization and nature is bridged by ancient stone and royal legacy. Tucked between two rivers in the fertile

Vale of Kings, Valebrook is the seat of the old monarchy, the heart of Reynard's realm, and once the jewel of the kingdom.

At the village's crest, atop a rise known as the Dawn hill, sits the castle of the king and queen, a sprawling fortress of gray stone, slate roofs, and ivy-covered battlements. Though imposing, the castle is not one of excess or glittering opulence. It was built not just as a symbol of power, but of protection and wisdom. The castle's towers rise like watchful sentinels. Its great hall, with high-vaulted ceilings and stained-glass windows, once echoed with laughter and song. Banners bearing the stag and flame, Reynard's sigil, fluttered above its gates. Behind the castle, terraced gardens climb the slope, filled with roses, medicinal herbs, and ancient white trees said to bloom year-round. A still pond reflects the sky, and it was here the queen once walked, dreaming of peace. Unlike Malrik's fortress, the royal castle is not a place of darkness or dread, but of legacy, wisdom, and strength. Built with reverence for the natural world and the Weave that binds it, the castle is both sanctuary and symbol.

Approaching the castle, one crosses the Moon water Bridge, a stone span carved with guardian runes and stag motifs. The river below flows clear and cool, fed from mountain snowmelt, passing beneath the bridge with a soothing hush. Lining the entrance road are groves of ash and elder trees, their roots said to be woven into the warding spells that protect the land. Statues of old kings and queens flank the road, worn by time, yet regal still. Beyond the bridge lie the Outer Fields, used for knightly training and harvest festivals. In spring, tents blossom across them during tourneys. In winter, snowball skirmishes and bonfires fill the air with cheer.

The Castle Walls built from pale-gray Vale stone, the castle's walls rise with natural dignity. Ivy climbs their sides in summer, and lanterns line the parapets during the dark months. The main gate bears a carved stag crowned with flame, the royal crest of House Reynard. Inside the walls, three main courtyards serve different functions: The High Courtyard, reserved for royal guests and ceremony, paved in white stone and ringed by flowerbeds. The Garden Court, a lush retreat where nobles take tea and mages contemplate under willows and fountains. The Warrior's Yard, where guards train, squires spar, and banners hang from the barracks.

The Great Hall of Flame or the heart of the castle, this vast hall is where the court gathers, feasts are held, and matters of state are addressed. Pillars carved with legends line the sides, and a vast hearth blazes at the far end. Above the hearth, a mural depicts the founding of the kingdom, mages binding flame and forest, kings kneeling to spirit and balance. Here, King Reynard once sat beside Queen Elinora, holding court with honor. The high windows cast colored light from stained glass, and the hall glows warm even in the bleakest winters. At the head of the Great Hall, the thrones of the King and Queen sit upon a low dais. Not of gold, but carved Ashwood inlaid with silver and sunstone. Above them hangs a tapestry of the Weave, interlocking circles and starlit threads. Behind the alcove lies a hidden passage used in times of siege.

The Royal Library, a circular, domed chamber filled with scrolls, codices, and enchanted tomes. Soft golden light fills the space, and librarians tend the collection with reverence. The library contains lost languages, healing formulas, maps of ancient realms, and memoirs from past queens. The Sunlit Gallery, a long corridor with windows on one side and portraits on the other. The paintings date back three hundred years, each king and queen rendered in oils and magic stasis. The floor is made of polished Ashwood, warm to bare feet. It's said the portraits whisper advice to the royal bloodline when danger nears.

The Mage's Tower, connected by a high arched bridge from the western wall, this tower is where court mages study, experiment, and commune with the Weave. Azor once presided here, mentoring new arcanists and shielding the realm from unseen threats. Its rooms are filled with alchemical devices, scrying bowls, floating lanterns, and arcane seals. The topmost chamber, The Sky room, has no roof, open to stars and moonlight, allowing astral alignment during magical rites. The Queen's Garden, behind the east wing lies a tiered garden filled with medicinal herbs, wind-chimes, and pools of koi. Queen Elinora cultivated this place with her own hands, seeking peace in moments of sorrow. A stone bench under the heart tree bears an inscription: "All things root in love." The Vault of Starlight: Hidden below the castle, guarded by ancestral magic. Here lie ancient relics, Rayner's sword among them. The Sentinel's Walk: A passage along the outer walls, offering sweeping views of the kingdom. The Echo Hall: An old wing where sound lingers longer than it should. It's said that the old kings still speak here.

The Temple of Light and Flame: Built to honor the balance of nature and spirit, this temple is adorned with murals depicting the founding of the kingdom. Inside, a flickering eternal flame burns, protected by the mage order. The Vault of Kings: Deep within the castle lies a sealed chamber where relics, scrolls, and enchanted heirlooms rest. Among them, the Crown of Flame. Valebrook was not just the seat of rule, it was the soul of the kingdom. Even in ruin, it whispers of hope. The Royal Guard, led by the Captain of the Flame, patrol the keep in ceremonial silver-and-crimson armor. The House Steward, Mistress Anwyn, maintains order and tradition with exacting care. The Mage Council, advisors to the king, study beneath the Mage's Tower. Every servant, stable hand, and mason holds quiet pride in serving the realm. Even the cook, Master Bellum, is famed for root stew and honeyed bread.

The castle is not merely stone and spell, it is the embodiment of the kingdom's ideals. Where Malrik's fortress drains, this place inspires. It hums with generational memory, dignity, and the balance of flame and life. Its loss shook the realm. Its restoration signals hope. The Castle of Valebrook is not simply a place where kings rule. It is where they become worthy of ruling. Beneath the castle walls, Valebrook's village winds along cobbled streets and shaded courtyards. The homes here are larger than Ashbrook's, roofed with dark tile and carved with lion-headed beams. Inns and merchant houses line the central square, where trade from across the realm once bustled. The Crown Market, once weekly, featured tapestries from the South Isles, spices from the eastern hills, and the finest blades from Quinn's family's forge. A wide stone bridge spans the Moonwater River, and just beyond it lie the fields that once fed the city in peace.

Present Day

Azor finishing his story, with a tear streaming down his cheeks.

"You see, you both were meant to live on, and bring Malrik to justice".

Rayner and Cole looked at each other with tears welling up in their eyes. They knew that it would take every ounce of strength they have, but in the end, they will destroy Malrik and restore the kingdom back to the gloried days of old.

CHAPTER 6
King Reynard and Queen Elenora

Long before the fall of the Old Kingdom, before Malrik turned to blood, before the towers crumbled and the Veil thinned, there was a young king with fire in his blood and a warrior maiden who would become his heart. His name was Prince Reynard, only son of King Halric. Hers was Elenora of Eiranvale, daughter of the wolf-lord of the northern highlands. They met not in court, but on the battlefield. It was the Siege of Farholde, where raiders from the Eastern Wastes had overrun the border forts. Prince Reynard, just twenty-three and still untested, was given command of a relief force. Among his outriders was a band of northern lancers, mercenaries, fierce and proud. Their leader was a woman with raven-dark hair, bright eyes, and a blade called Elenora. She rode like lightning and fought like a storm. Prince Reynard watched her cleave through three desert raiders to save a wounded squire. He ordered her to his tent the next evening, not out of pride, but out of awe.

"You saved my men," he said.

"I saved your flank," she corrected. "Your men were already broken."

Prince Reynard laughed, a real, surprised laugh.

"I should be insulted," he said.

"You should be grateful," she replied, and just like that, something sparked.

After the siege, Prince Reynard returned to Valebrook. Elenora was offered a place in the Royal Guard. She refused.

"I won't serve," she said. "But I'll stand beside."

Prince Reynard respected that. He invited her to hunt. To train. To dine. She accepted, grudgingly, then curiously, then gladly.

They argued often. She thought his court too soft. He thought her spirit too hard, but she challenged him, he listened, and when his father died suddenly from a fever, and Prince Reynard took the crown, it was Elenora who knelt at his coronation, not as a warrior, but as a woman who believed he might just be the king the realm needed. He asked her to marry him that same day. She made him wait a week before saying yes. She loved and respected him and had belief in his vision of Eldara.

Their union was not of convenience. It was not arranged. It was chosen, and the people felt it. Elenora ruled as queen with a sword on her hip. She walked among the people. Sat with wounded soldiers. Whispered to frightened children. King Reynard rebuilt the roads. Ended old wars. Reformed the mage circle under Azor's guidance. Named Sir Worric as Captain of the Guard, and together, he and Elenora made the kingdom stronger than it had been in generations, and then came Rayner. Rayner was born under the Harvest Moon. Elenora insisted on giving birth in the royal hall, surrounded not by gold and gems, but by banners of every province, symbols of unity. King Reynard wept when he held his son.

"He already looks stubborn," Elenora said.

"He'll be a king," King Reynard said.

She shook her head. "He'll be a warrior first. A leader second. A son always."

A year later came Cole was born during a thunderstorm, screaming and laughing almost at once. He was smaller, lighter, and endlessly curious, but all stories turn. The peace could not last.

Azor the Mage

Azor, the last Archmage of the Hollow Flame and sworn protector of King Reynard, the last true ruler of the Old Kingdom.

This is his story. Azor was born on the distant Ember Isles, a volcanic chain of land surrounded by roiling seas and lightning storms. It was a place where magic bled from the cracks in the earth and fire danced in the sky. Children there were tested by the elements, many were burned, few were chosen. Azor was one of the chosen. At age nine, he conjured flame without flint. At eleven, he silenced a hurricane with a whisper. At fourteen, the Archmages of the Ember Citadel bowed to him in recognition of a power not seen in three generations, but Azor was restless. The islands were his cradle, but not his calling. When he turned eighteen, he crossed the sea to the mainland. He had heard of a king who ruled with justice and wisdom. A man not afraid of magic, but who feared what could happen if it fell into the wrong hands. That man was King Reynard.

The first time Azor met King Reynard, the mage wore sea-stained robes and carried nothing but a staff carved from driftwood. The guards laughed at him. The royal chamberlain refused him entry. Until Azor turned the fountain in the palace square into living flame, and reshaped it into King Reynard's own likeness. King Reynard had him brought inside at once. They spoke for hours. Magic. Power. War. The duty of kings. The frailty of men. By nightfall, King Reynard asked Azor a single question:

"Can you protect what I've built?"

Azor bowed. "Yes, and I will burn the world before I let it fall."

From that day forward, he became the King's Mage, seated at King Reynard's right hand during council, beside him during battle. Azor was more than an advisor, he was a weapon, a shield, and in time… a friend.

King Reynard ruled from the high castle in Valebrook, a city of white towers and stone bridges that glowed in the sun. Trade flourished. The outlands were unified. Bandit kings bowed. Magical study was legalized and regulated under the Order of the Hollow Flame, with Azor as Grandmaster. He trained a new generation of mages. He built towers along the borders to monitor dark magic. He created the Wards of Binding that kept death-magic buried beneath the mountains, and yet, as with all things, the shadow grew in secret.

When Rayner came to his grove, Azor knew fate had circled back. Not as a gift. As a challenge. He saw Sir Worric's teachings in Rayner's stance. He saw sorrow. Strength. Resolve, and he saw the flicker of the old kingdom. So Azor stepped from the trees. Not as a savior, but as a man who still had one duty left unfinished. To keep his promise to a dead king.

CHAPTER 7

The forest was quiet as they left the Grove of Emberroots, west of the Whispering woods, with the fading hum of ancient wards trailing behind them. Rayner led the way, his hand never far from his sword hilt, his eyes constantly scanning the woods ahead. Behind him walked Cole, his younger brother in both blood and spirit, staff slung across his back, mouth rarely closed, and bringing up the rear, leaning slightly on his long wooden staff, walked Azor, the last court mage of the Old Kingdom, eyes haunted by memories no man should carry. They were headed west. To Ashbrook. To Rayner's home.

Cole yawned and stretched as the first rays of sunlight filtered through the trees.

"How far is it again?" he asked, rubbing his eyes.

"Six days' walk," Rayner said without looking back.

"Six days? Rayner, I like you, and all, but I didn't realize we were signing up for a pilgrimage."

Azor chuckled softly.

Cole grinned. "I mean, look at this guy. He's a thousand years old and even he's moving faster than you."

Rayner smirked. "I'm moving at the pace of someone who doesn't waste air with whining."

"Oh, forgive me, Sir Stonejaw," Cole said. "You trained under Sir Worric, not under joy."

Rayner shook his head. "Keep talking, Cole. I'll let a boar sort you out."

As the boys traded jabs and laughter, Azor watched them with quiet fondness. It had been years since he had heard joy spoken so freely. Not in riddles. Not in songs, but in the common banter of brothers. This, he thought, is what Malrik fears. Not swords. Not spells. This bond. This light. By sunset of the sixth day, the trees opened up, revealing the familiar low stone walls, crooked fences, and mist-kissed rooftops of Ashbrook. Rayner slowed. The memories hit fast and sharp. The sound of Quinn's hammer. Tristan's laughter from the woods. Sir Worric's voice, barking at dawn. He clenched his fists.

"It's different," he said quietly.

The village looked older. Sadder. More worn down than he remembered. Cole walked beside him.

"You ever think about staying here?" he asked softly.

Rayner gave a half-smile. "Once. Before everything broke."

"You ever think about what happens after we finish this?"

Rayner stared ahead. "No."

Nestled in the heart of the western lowlands of the old kingdom, Ashbrook is a village forgotten by the crowns of men but remembered in the hearts of those who once called it home. Ashbrook lies in a wide, shallow valley shaped like a cupped hand. A single narrow stream the brook from which the village takes its name winds its way through the center like a silver ribbon. It glistens under the sun and sings during the spring melt, flowing from the distant Emberwood to the west and emptying into the Hallowmere marshes far to the east. The land is fertile, fed by the brook and the rich black soil that generations of farmers have worked with calloused hands. In spring, the valley bursts into color lavender crocuses, golden daffodils, and wild sunflowers in patches along every fence. The fields stretch in gentle waves, dotted by ancient elms, thick oaks, and apple orchards that bloom white and pink in early summer. Beyond the farthest pastures, hills roll up toward the misty edges of the southern pinewoods. The forest, called the

Hollowshade, is quiet and mysterious, often blanketed in fog. Children are warned never to venture too deep. Some say strange lights flicker there at night.

Ashbrook's homes are built from pale Ashwood and gray stone, most with slanted thatched roofs and broad chimneys that puff warm smoke during winter's grasp. The houses are clustered along the brook, divided by mossy stone walls and narrow footpaths worn smooth by generations of boots. Each home has a garden be it of herbs, vegetables, or flowers. A common scent of tilled earth, woodsmoke, and apple cider seems to linger in the air no matter the season.

The center of the village is a circular clearing paved in uneven cobblestones, where a flat slab of ancient granite sits embedded in the ground. Called the Heartstone, it is said to predate the village itself. At Midsummer, dances are held here. Elders tell stories, and traveling minstrels once performed under the stars. On market days, stalls appear around the circle: bread from Millie's ovens, honey and wax from Old Tarmel's bees, and ironworks from the blacksmith's forge. The Blacksmith's Forge, run by Quinn's father, tended for generations by the Hammerline family, the bloodline of Quinn. Their tools and weapons are known for durability and function, not flash. Each blade bears the family's rune: a square-headed hammer over an anvil.

Quinn was raised among fire and steel, taught that a weapon is only as strong as the hand that holds it, and the reason it is drawn. His father, Tomas Hammerline, once served King Reynard's army and was known to say,

"I'll raise a better man with iron and honesty than with gold and armor."

The forge is both workshop and sanctuary. The building itself is larger than most homes, with thick timber beams, wide shuttered windows, and a chimney that smokes through all seasons. Inside, the air is thick with heat and the scent of iron and oil. Here, Quinn learned to swing a hammer before he could lift a sword. Locals say no horse in the vale has worn shoes from another forge.

The Hunter's Roost, built against the edge of the Hollowshade forest is, a half-cabin, half-observation post where Tristan's father, the village's chief hunter and trapper, prepared for his woodland journeys. His father, Hale, taught him to move like wind and think like water. Theirs is a legacy of listening to the forest, reading the tracks of beasts, and protecting the village without applause. The Roost contains racks of pelts, drying herbs, hunting maps, and bows strung above the hearth. Tristan spent more time here than in his own home, learning every birdcall and tree root path that the nearby woods held. It was said that he could walk the forests blindfolded and still find his way. Their home is simple, wooden, unpainted, and half-covered in ivy. But it is from this place that Ashbrook's greatest archers were born. Tristan's aim was spoken of even as a boy. He was quiet, yes, but his silence was the silence of focus, not fear.

Sir Worric's Cottage, the small stone cottage near the brook, but it might as well have been a fortress. Hidden among wild roses and climbing ivy, the cottage has a simple training yard where Rayner practiced day after day his sweat and blood staining the dust. He rebuilt his life training Rayner not just to fight, but to lead, with patience, honor, and grit. Locals recall the rhythmic thud of sword strikes echoing at dawn, and the quiet conversations shared between mentor and student.

The Seasons in Ashbrook, Spring brings songbirds and warm rains. Farmers plant barley and wheat. Children swim in the brook's deeper pools. Fireflies return, dancing in the meadows. In the Summer is golden and still. Days stretch long, filled with chores and laughter. There are midsummer games, archery contests, and music in the square. Autumn brings the cider press and harvest feasts. Leaves turn copper and gold. Nights grow cool. The wind carries stories. Finally, Winter cloaks the village in white. Smoke curls from chimneys. The brook freezes, and footprints line the snow. Tales are told by firelight, and old songs return. The village's strength is its people: The people of Ashbrook are proud but humble, bound by an unspoken code: We protect our own. We honor our word. We work, we watch, we wait. Outsiders often mistake their quiet for coldness, but those who earn an Ashbrook villager's respect will find loyalty sharper than any blade. Ashbrook is not large enough to raise an army, nor wealthy enough to influence the high courts. But it has always provided the kingdom something rarer: men and women of unshakable fiber.

Ashbrook was established during the late years of the Reign of High King Aldeman, by his loyal knight Sir Alric Valen, who had retired after the northern unification wars. He and a group of soldiers-turned-farmers cleared land near the tree line, built stone-walled homes and a long hall, and raised their families on hard work, honor, and silence. The name Ashbrook comes from the brook that winds through the center of the village, its waters cold and clear, and the Valen family, who served the kingdom with unshakable devotion. Generations later, the family's emblem, a stag before a silver river, still hangs above the long hall hearth.

Life in Ashbrook is simple. Rhythmic. The sun wakes the village with the lowing of cattle and the smell of iron and ash from the smithy. By midday, the fields are filled with farmers and hunters preparing the day's work. The evenings are marked by quiet meals, shared stories, and old songs sung under wooden beams worn smooth by time. The village is ringed by hills on three sides and flanked by a dense stretch of forest to the west. No walls guard

Ashbrook, only stone fences and the watchful eyes of those raised to defend without question. Few pass through without notice, and none leave without memory.

They reached the village center just as the last light dipped below the hills. From the forge came the sound of metal, slow, deliberate hammering. Rayner stepped up to the doorway, and there stood Quinn, taller and broader than ever, sweat on his brow, sparks flying. He turned and froze. Rayner smiled.

"You still burn the iron too hot."

Quinn blinked. "Ray?"

And then he dropped the hammer and crushed him in a bear hug.

"I thought you were dead! We heard rumors, demon keepers, talking trees, bounty hunters, gods, I thought they were just stories."

Cole strolled in casually. "Most of them are. Except for the talking tree part. That one's real."

Rayner coughed under Quinn's hug. "You gonna let go or squeeze the breath out of me?"

"Not until you explain why you vanished like smoke," Quinn said, stepping back.

Tristan emerged next, silent as always, crossbow slung over one shoulder, eyes sharp as ever, but he smiled. Just a little.

"You came back," he said simply.

Rayner nodded. "We've got work to do."

That night, they stayed at The Swaying Antler, the local Inn. Many of the villagers reacted strongly to Rayner's return, while other looked on with suspicion. Perhaps they see something in Rayner, compared to the boy they all knew. Azor shared tales from the court. Cole exaggerated their near-death experiences. Rayner mostly listened. Quinn handed out roasted roots and dried venison.

Tristan sharpened his bolts in the corner, always watching. Cole leaned back against a barrel and sighed. Quinn glanced toward the forest.

"You here to stay long?"

"No," Rayner answered. "We leave for the mountain route soon. Tristan looked up.

"Then we should prepare tonight."

Azor nodded.

"We leave at first light. There will be no turning back. First let me tell you a story about King Aldren– The Oath keeper. He was Rayner and Cole's Great Grandfather. King Aldren, known to history as The Oath keeper, was the son of Aldeman the Stone wright and the father of Halric the Unyielding. His reign marked a turning point in Eldara's evolution, a transition from its founding dreams to its more militarized and structured future. Where his father Aldeman saw the world through vision and diplomacy, Aldren inherited a fractured kingdom still reeling from the War of the Rifted Vale. The betrayal of the Hill-Kings had shaken the very idea of alliance. Aldren was not naïve. He loved peace but understood that peace required strength to endure. He reformed the kingdom's law structure, enacting the Oath Charter, which bound lords, soldiers, and even the king himself to a code of conduct and service. Under his watch, the first Royal Sentinels were trained, an elite order of warriors bound by loyalty to the realm, not to land or coin. Aldren also restored the Great Archives of Eldwyre, believing that memory was as vital to a kingdom as its armies. He was a king of balance, firm in justice, but not without mercy. His rule lasted over three decades, marked by relative stability and the construction of the Hall of Accord in Valebrook. His son Halric would carry forward his iron, but not always his temperance. Aldren died in quiet dignity, remembered as a ruler who never broke a vow and never asked of others what he would not do himself. Etched into his tomb are the words: "Where words are sworn, kingdoms stand."

The Swaying Antler was nestled between tall ash trees and flanked by the cobbled village square, The Swaying Antler looks more like a hunter's lodge than a formal inn, and that's precisely how its owner prefers it. Built from thick pine logs and fitted with a wide wraparound porch, the structure leans slightly eastward as if bowing to the forest from which it was born. A massive pair of elk antlers hangs above the entrance, one tine broken, the other glistening with a coating of polished resin. Beneath them swings the carved sign: a crescent moon behind the silhouette of an antlered stag in mid-leap. Locals claim it was modeled after a ghostly creature spotted in the forest during the first moon of winter. Rough-hewn steps lead to a heavy oaken door reinforced with iron bands. The scent of smoke, pine, and roast meat drifts out with every swing of the door, beckoning travelers from the road.

Inside, the inn exudes warmth. It's a single large room divided by thick wooden beams and hanging furs. The walls are paneled in honey-hued ash and carved with simple reliefs, scenes of deer hunts, river crossings, and firelit gatherings. In the center stands a massive stone hearth, blackened by decades of roaring fires, with a stag skull mounted above it, rumored to be the last kill of the inn-keeper's father. The floors are swept but imperfect, with deep grain and worn edges from decades of boots, hooves, and even sword fights. Tables are irregular in shape, some round, some rectangular, many mismatched, as though gathered over generations. Most have nicks or scars from knives, mugs, or the occasional bar brawl. Oil lanterns hang from ceiling hooks, flickering with golden light. Some locals whisper that the hearth's fire never fully dies out, not even in summer, and claim it's blessed by one of the old forest spirits. A side hallway leads to a modest bunk room for travelers: six beds with woolen blankets, and a locked chest under each. Those with coin can rent the Loft Room upstairs, which boasts a small window overlooking the eastern woods.

Brannic, a broad-shouldered man with a tangled beard the color of wet bark, is a former ranger turned innkeeper. He walks with a slight limp, a remnant of a boar hunt gone wrong, and always carries a long carving knife, not for defense, but to whittle wood between orders. Born in Ashbrook, Brannic once served as a scout for King Reynard's father during the Forest Rebellions. After leaving the king's service, he returned home, rebuilt the inn his grandfather founded, and claimed it with pride. He's known for three things: His sharp tongue, his fierce loyalty to Ashbrook's youth (especially Rayner, Quinn, and Tristan, who grew up under his watchful eye) and his famous mead stew, thick with root vegetables, boar fat, and barley. He never charges orphans or the sick for a meal, and keeps a flask of elderberry brandy behind the bar, only served when "the fire dies low and the stories get heavy."

The Swaying Antler isn't just an inn. It's Ashbrook's gathering hall, vigil tower, and lore-keeper's hearth. Weddings are toasted here. The dead are mourned with firelight and drink. Young ones are scolded here, and old ones are honored. Rayner had his first pint here, under Brannic's watchful eye. Tristan learned to skin his first rabbit in Brannic's back kitchen, and Quinn hammered his first horseshoe behind the inn.

Later that night, Cole found Rayner alone, looking out the window.

"You, okay?" Cole asked.

Rayner nodded. "It's strange. Being home. I thought it would give me peace, but all it does is remind me what we're fighting for. I'm glad you're here, he said softly. I couldn't do this alone."

Cole clapped him on the back. "You never have."

The fire crackled warmly as night wrapped its cloak around the forest. Sparks drifted into the dark canopy above like fireflies set loose, and the faint scent of pine and old leaves carried on the breeze. The journey had been long, the dangers many, but tonight, in this clearing lit by flame and moonlight, there was a rare stillness. Azor sat cross-legged beside the fire, his weathered cloak draped over his shoulders, the silver streaks in his beard catching the firelight. His staff lay at his side, and in his gnarled hands, he slowly turned a carved wooden pipe. Rayner leaned back against a log, arms folded, cloak around his shoulders. Quinn was sharpening his hammer's edge with a smooth stone, though his eyes kept drifting toward the mage. Tristan crouched near the fire, carefully roasting a skewer of rabbit. Cole lay on his side with his hood down, head resting on his arm, watching Azor with a tired but amused smirk. Azor puffed the pipe once, let the smoke swirl into the air, and said,

"You boys ever hear about the Battle of Emberholt?"

Tristan perked up. "That the one where the river burned?"

Rayner gave him a sideways look. "Rivers don't burn." Azor grinned. "Unless there's alchemist's fire poured into them. Which there was. Which I told the king not to do, but did he listen? No."

Cole snorted. "That sounds like King Reynard."

"Reynard was young then. Bold. Stubborn. Thought magic was just something flashy to impress diplomats. Until the firestorm turned half the battlefield to cinders and melted two battalions' worth of boots to the ground."

Quinn looked up. "What did you do?"

Azor raised a brow. "Put it out, of course. With a storm spell. That, or it would've spread to Valebrook. Though the horses didn't forgive me for two weeks."

The boys laughed. Azor's gaze softened as he looked into the fire.

"We lost good men that day. But it was the first time the king realized that fire and steel only take you so far. He asked me afterward what real power looked like."

Rayner leaned forward. "And what did you tell him?"

"I told him power is knowing when not to use it. There was a thoughtful silence.

Cole broke it with a grin. "That's why you always let me run my mouth before you stop me."

"Exactly," Azor said dryly.

Azor looked to the stars above, then back to the boys.

"You lot remind me of the Four Blades of Aldrin."

"The who?" Quinn asked.

"They were brothers, not by blood but by bond. A hunter, a hammerman, a fire mage, and a swordsman. Sound familiar?" Azor smirked.

Tristan sat up straighter. "What happened to them?"

"They held the western pass when Malrik first rose. Just four of them. They turned away an entire warband of shadow fiends. No one believed it could be done. They had no banners, no army, just trust in one another."

"Did they survive?" Rayner asked.

Azor's eyes dimmed. "Two did. One was swallowed by the dark. The other... turned against the rest. Power twisted him."

A hush fell again. The fire snapped and popped. Cole sat up, more serious now.

"And the last two?"

Azor looked right at him. "They became legends."

QUINN

The forge always burned hottest in the mornings. Quinn remembered that most of all, the smell of ash and coal clinging to his clothes, the sting of sparks on his skin, and the low, rhythmic clang of his father's hammer against the anvil. Tomas, his father, never said much. He didn't have to. His hands told stories, and his tools taught lessons.

"Metals like people," he'd grumble. "You break it too quick, it shatters., but heat it right, shape it slow... and it lasts."

Quinn learned to shape nails before he learned to read. By ten, he was shoeing horses. By twelve, he was forging blades for hunters, nothing fancy, just strong, straight steel, but it wasn't just the forge that made him who he was. It was the two boys who kept pulling him away from it.

Quinn met Rayner first. Rayner was all edges and fire, already training with Sir Worric by the time other boys were still learning to aim a slingshot. He didn't talk much, didn't laugh easy, but he was brave. Too brave, sometimes. The first time they fought side by side was when a group of older boys started bullying a traveler's child in the village square. Rayner stepped in alone, outnumbered and clearly outmatched. Quinn followed without thinking. He didn't even throw a punch; just swung a metal ladle he'd been carrying for a cooking fire. It rang off a boy's head like a church bell. Later, with scraped knuckles and bloodied lips, they sat behind the stables.

"You didn't have to help," Rayner said.

"Didn't say I was helping you," Quinn replied. "I hate bullies."

Rayner smirked, and that was it. A bond forged in bruises and silent agreement.

Tristan arrived silently, as he always did. The hunter's son, lean, watchful, and always watching the edges of things. He spoke less than even Rayner, but when he did, it was with weight. The kind of words that made you stop and think. The three boys didn't become friends so much as they became orbit drawn to each other like gravity. Quinn brought the humor and food. Rayner brought the edge and direction. Tristan brought the awareness and calm. Together, they built forts, hunted rats, climbed the old trees beyond the village, and dared each other to sleep in the haunted barn at the edge of the woods.

Quinn often brought the other two into the forge when his father was away. Rayner was fascinated by swords, always asking to lift them, test their balance. He'd swing them at straw dummies with far too much intensity for a boy his age. Tristan, meanwhile, stared at the glowing metal like he could hear it whisper. One day, Quinn held up a small dagger he'd just quenched.

"Not perfect," he said. "But it's real. Made it myself."

Rayner held it with awe. "You made this?"

Quinn nodded. Rayner offered it back, but Quinn shook his head.

"It's yours."

Rayner blinked. "You serious?"

"You'll need it more than I will."

From that day on, Rayner never trained without that dagger at his side. They weren't always chasing dreams. Sometimes, life was just hard. The winter the river froze too early, and the crops died under a week of frost, the forge ran low on coal. Tomas worked with cracked fingers, barely eating. Rayner started splitting wood for him. Tristan trapped rabbits and shared the meat. Quinn stoked the forge until his arms shook. They didn't talk about survival like heroes do in stories. They just helped. They endured. That was the way of Ashbrook.

Later that night, as sparks floated up into the stars from his open forge, Quinn looked at the three figures around the fire, Rayner staring into the flames, Tristan oiling his bow, Cole talking too much, and smiled. He remembered their first summer. He remembered when the world was simple, and he knew, when the final battle came, he would not be the strongest, but he would be the last one to fall.

TRISTAN

Tristan always heard things before he saw them. The snap of a twig. The pause in the wind. The way a bird suddenly stopped singing. His father taught him that the world spoke in silences, not in words.

"Anyone can hear noise," he'd say. "Only a good hunter hears what isn't there."

Tristan listened. Not just to the woods, but to people, and in time, he came to know them better than they knew themselves. He grew up on the edge of Ashbrook, in a thatch-roofed cottage with a chimney that leaned left and windows that never quite shut. His father, Hale, was a hunter, one of the best in the region. People paid him in meat, furs, and silence. He tracked things no one else could: ghost deer, marsh wolves, even the occasional bandit trail. Tristan followed in his father's footsteps, barefoot at first, bow too large for his shoulders. He shot his first hare at six. First fox at eight, but the first time he met Rayner; it wasn't with a bow. It was with a fist.

He was nine. Rayner was ten. Both boys were wild in their own way, Rayner all fire and fists, Tristan all silence and stone. Rayner caught him setting a trap in the woods just beyond Sir Worric's training grounds.

"Can't trap here," Rayner said. "It's for drills."

Tristan didn't answer. Rayner tried to move the trap. Tristan knocked him flat with a single punch. Rayner sprang up. They brawled like wolves, rolling in leaves and dirt, bloodying noses and splitting lips. Quinn found them a few minutes later, neither willing to yield. He pulled them apart.

"You two done?" he said, arms crossed.

Rayner and Tristan looked at each other, and laughed. They weren't friends in the beginning. They were rivals. Balanced forces. Rayner was always looking outward, to the horizon. Always charging, fighting, testing. Tristan was always watching, calculating, listening, knowing when to move and when to wait, but over time, something unspoken grew between them. Mutual respect, and then, something deeper: trust. Quinn was the link between them, kindhearted, strong, always able to break tension with a word or a warm meal. Tristan had no siblings, but in time, he found two. By twelve, Tristan could track a boar through river mud. He taught Rayner how to move without snapping branches. Taught Quinn how to follow animal signs. They taught him, too. Rayner taught him sword angles and how to fall without breaking ribs. Quinn taught him how to handle people, how to spot lies, how to bluff, how to speak when you had to. They grew stronger together. Ashbrook wasn't a large village. Most days passed without incident, but they made their own adventures, night hunts, forest games, climbing to the old wind stone cairns and daring each other to stay until the stars blinked out.

The following night, Tristan knelt in the woods outside Ashbrook, sharpening his bolts in the moonlight. He watched the campfire where Rayner sat beside Azor, and where Quinn was turning a rabbit spit. Cole talked too much, as always. Tristan didn't mind. He liked the rhythm of their return, but he knew what was coming. War. He felt it in the way the birds avoided the ridge. In the scent of iron drifting on the night breeze. In Rayner's eyes. He thought about the old days, the wind in the trees, Rayner yelling from a branch,

"Bet you can't hit that crow!" And how he did. Every time.

Rayner walked up beside him, silent for once. Tristan didn't look up.

"You alright?" Rayner asked. Tristan nodded.

"Good," Rayner said. "I'm glad you're still with me."

Tristan finally looked at him. "I always was."

The fire was low now. The logs had burned down to glowing embers, their red light painting flickering shadows across the faces of the four boys. The air had gone still, no wind, no birdsong, only the gentle rhythm of night insects beyond the circle of light. Azor stirred, drawing his cloak tighter around his shoulders. His eyes were distant, gaze fixed not on the fire, but somewhere far beyond it, into memory.

"I once knew a boy," he said quietly, voice low and rough. "He was about Cole's age. Clever. Eager. Too eager. The Weave came easy to him, almost too easy. He could bend light, shape flame, speak to the wind without effort. And like many young mages, he mistook ease for destiny."

The boys were silent. Even Cole sat up straighter.

"I was his mentor," Azor continued. "I taught him the rites. The circles. The ancient tongue. He burned through scrolls in days that took others months. But he grew impatient. He wanted more, to see how deep the Weave ran. One night, he slipped into the Archive and found a sealed grimoire. One meant only for the Archmages."

Azor reached into his satchel and pulled out a charred piece of parchment. The ink had run. The corners were blackened.

"I still keep this," he said, holding it out for the firelight to catch. "It was part of a summoning ritual. Not of flame, or light, or wind… but soulfire."

Rayner frowned. "What's soulfire?"

Azor's face darkened. "It's a flame that burns the soul instead of the flesh. It grants unimaginable power, but it consumes the very thing that makes you, you. Your memories. Your kindness. Your regrets."

Quinn looked uneasy. "What happened to the boy?"

Azor closed his eyes. "He summoned it. Just a flicker. Just to see. It tore through the chamber. Three apprentices died. The boy lived, but when I found him, he didn't know his name. Or mine. He just stared at the fire. And laughed."

The fire snapped, as if reacting to the story.

Tristan swallowed. "Is he still alive?"

Azor's voice turned to gravel. "No. Because power without control leads only to destruction. And mercy… is not always kindness." He leaned forward, staring into the flames. "The Weave is not a sword. It's a river. You must learn to ride it. Not cage it. Not command it. Or it will drown you."

Cole whispered, "You think I'm like him?"

Azor looked at him, not with anger, but with depth. "I think you're better. Because you ask. Because you're afraid of what you could become. That fear? That's wisdom."

Rayner put a hand on his brother's shoulder. "And he's not alone."

Azor smiled faintly. "No. He's not."

"Now let me tell you a story about your grandfather. King Halric, the Iron Stag. King Halric the Unyielding ruled Eldara during an age of turbulence and rebellion. Unlike his son Reynard, Halric was not known for warmth or grace, but for resolve, discipline, and order. His reign was marked by structure, law, and the fortification of the realm's outer provinces following the fracturing of the eastern baronies. He wore a crown of blackened iron and silver, forged in the shape of stag antlers, a symbol of power rooted in ancient northern lore. To his people, he was both protector and judge. To his enemies, he was immovable stone. Halric inherited a fractured kingdom after the death of his father, King Aldren, and spent much of his early rule stamping out dissent. His campaigns were brutal but effective. He raised the Valebrook Legion, built the Citadel of Ashstone, and commissioned the first magical accord with the mages of the Weave College, including a young Azor. Yet, behind his hardened exterior, Halric carried great pain. His wife, Queen Lysena, died giving birth to their only son, Reynard. Halric never remarried. He raised Reynard with stern hands and few words, hoping to instill strength but struggled to show affection. When Halric died, the kingdom mourned a wall of a man who never bowed and never broke. But it was Reynard who brought heart back to the crown."

CHAPTER 8

The storm above Malrik's keep had never ceased. It circled the bone-carved spires day and night, thunder without rain, black clouds stitched with red lightning. A monument to his power. Or, more truthfully, to his limitations. Malrik stood in his sanctum beneath the great hall, surrounded by pillars etched in blood and bone. A massive black brazier glowed faintly in the center, fed not by flame, but by something older. A power that pulsed with pain. Across from him knelt a figure, Vael, his apprentice. Robes of obsidian silk, eyes sunken, face pale as chalk. Vael was not born of darkness. He was shaped by it. The son of a minor noble family in the eastern plains, Vael showed magical talent early, healing sick animals, raising crops, summoning fireflies to light the barn. His parents took pride, but their pride drew fear. When a neighboring lord accused the family of witchcraft, they were dragged before the Crimson Tribunal. Only Vael survived. He was nine. Malrik found him in chains, bloodied and silent. He saw not a broken child, but potential.

"Your grief is power," Malrik whispered. "And I will show you how to wield it."

Vael was brought to the Black Spire. Unlike Elira, he embraced the rituals. Where she asked questions, he demanded results. He memorized blood chants in a week. Learned soul-binding by twelve. Killed his first beast by thirteen. He wore robes of jet-black silk and etched his body with glowing sigils, gifts from Malrik. But he was not just a student. He was the apprentice.

"Rise," Malrik said, voice calm but edged with something sharp. Vael stood. "The sword bearer has entered the forest. The one called Rayner." Malrik turned slowly, hands clasped behind his back.

"Yes," he said. "I know."

Vael hesitated. "They seek the object in the old castle. The one hidden by King Reynard. If they retrieve it…"

"They won't. Not unless I allow it." Malrik's eyes gleamed faintly. "But let them try. It makes the end sweeter."

Malrik moved to a table where ancient tomes lay open, pages written in languages that whispered to anyone foolish enough to read them aloud. He stared at a faded map of the Old Kingdom, once unified under King Reynard, now split and diseased with fear.

"My magic," he said slowly, "was never meant to last forever."

Vael blinked. "Master?"

"Remember, Blood magic is like fire drawn from a dying star. You must feed it constantly. The stronger you become, the more it demands. Sacrifices. Death. Pain."

He gestured toward the walls. Symbols pulsed faintly. The runes that kept his empire bound.

"I have chained the winds. Choked rivers. Reanimated kings, but even now... it slips. That is why they must not succeed."

He leaned in over the map, tapping a spot with a long, clawlike finger: the old castle, nestled in the center of a now-rotted forest.

"The artifact within is not just a weapon. It is a key. A balancing force. Created by the mages of the Hollow Flame. Meant to restore the balance of the Veil."

Vael lowered his head. "Should I send the Shadows?"

"No. Not this time." Malrik turned, and with a gesture, summoned a flame above his palm.

It flickered with faces, images of Rayner, Cole, Quinn, and Tristan.

"I want them hunted like animals. Not destroyed. Not yet." He closed his hand. The flame vanished. "Bring me the bounty hunters."

The tower of Black Thorns stood on a ridge east of the keep, a meeting place where only the most dangerous killers dared tread. It was said that the stone itself had once been flesh and that it still bled when wounded. Malrik stood atop the tower when the first arrived. A shadow rode in on a nightmarish beast half elk, half wolf, all fury. The rider wore a red mask and carried curved daggers etched with screaming runes. His name was, Sark, known for skinning sorcerers alive.

Sark, the Chain-Hunter of Vornholt, Sark was not always a killer. He was born in the shadow of the black spires of Vornholt; the northern stronghold aligned with Malrik. His father was a prison warden, his mother a seamstress who died young, leaving Sark to roam the grim corridors of Vornholt's dungeon halls. While other children learned games, Sark learned silence, cruelty, and how to hear lies in a man's breath.

At seventeen, he joined the Bone Legion, quickly gaining a reputation for capturing more than killing. He wielded hooked chains instead of blades, designed to ensnare legs, disarm foes, and pull them screaming to the dirt. His armor bore no crest, only rusted rings and shackles rattling from his shoulders like a grim bell. His talent for restraint wasn't mercy, it was obsession. Sark believed death was too quick. He found purpose in bringing his prey back alive, watching them squirm, beg, break.

When Malrik rose to power, he saw in Sark not just a bounty hunter, but a collector of despair. Sark hunts without banners, without speech, his face hidden behind a cracked iron mask. The sound of his chains is enough to send entire villages into hiding. He doesn't care about gold. He doesn't care about kingdoms. He cares only about the chase, and about taking trophies from those who think they can't be caught.

The second came from the skies, Maelis, the crow witch, who hovered on leathery wings. Her fingers were long, knotted, ending in talons. She whispered to the dead. Maelis, the Crow Witch, there are tales whispered in roadside inns and around woodland fires about a woman with leathery black wings, who glides through the sky at dusk and lands without a sound. Her name is Maelis, a bounty hunter who needs no blade, for her curses do the cutting.

Maelis was born in the twisted boughs of the Witherfen, a corrupted forest east of the Hollowmere Marsh. Her mother, a hedge witch cast out from Valebrook, was taken by shadow-magic after delving too deep into the dark Weave. Maelis was born of that corruption, touched by magic older than language, her bones hardened by curse, her blood thinned with raven's breath.

She grew wings by the time she was sixteen, torn and ragged at first, until she learned to ride the wind like a specter. Her eyes turned obsidian black, her skin ash-pale. Where she walked, crows followed. They whispered to her in sleep and screamed for her in battle. By thirty, she had taken coin from kings and killers alike. Her targets never saw her coming. She weaves binding charms, shadow hexes, and smoke illusions, using talons carved from blackened bone. Her laughter is said to twist trees and make wolves weep.

The third slithered from beneath the tower itself, Thornjaw, once a man, now a creature of shadow and worm. He had no voice, only hunger. Thornjaw was never given a name at birth. He was born beneath the Wyrwood Hills, in the twisted warrens where blood mages cast off their failed experiments. He was the son of a curse, a child created through ritual sacrifice, intended to house a demon soul. The rite was interrupted, the binding incomplete, and the child survived, part man, part something else. He was raised by the Mireborn, an outlaw cult that worshipped pain as penance and hunted wild beasts with bare hands. From them, he learned to kill not cleanly, but viscerally. He filed his teeth into points. Sewed animal bone into his skin. Masked his face with the lower jaw of a direwolf skull, its fangs curving upward in a permanent sneer, hence the name: Thornjaw. Though many feared him, few ever saw him clearly. Thornjaw moves low and fast through the terrain, covered in mud and bone ash, striking from shadow like a predator. His weapon of choice is a barbed chain-axe, curved and serrated, designed to hook into flesh and drag victims closer. Every kill is a ritual; every hunt, an offering. Malrik didn't summon Thornjaw with gold or threat. He simply left a trail of blood and promised prey worth the chase.

Finally, a fourth stepped into view, Rothar, a silent swordsman clad in armor blacker than night. No face. No voice. Only steel and speed. Before he became one of Malrik's most feared hunters, Rothar was a soldier of Eldara, more precisely, a hero. A decorated captain during the border wars with the Eastmark raiders, Rothar was known for his unshakable discipline and tactical brilliance. But everything changed during the Siege of Hollowmere, when his battalion was cut off and surrounded by Malrik's bloodmages. Rather than retreat, Rothar held the line for three days with no food, fighting through fire and madness. By the time reinforcements arrived, his men were dead, and Rothar had been disfigured by sorcery, his arms and chest branded by blood fire, his mind warped by whispers in the dark. He returned a shell of his former self, haunted, half-mad, and changed. The kingdom no longer had use for him. Stripped of rank, abandoned by the crown he served, Rothar disappeared. But Malrik found him. The dark lord gave Rothar what he craved: purpose. Not as a leader, but as a weapon. With his mind shattered and rebuilt by blood magic, Rothar became a flame-wielding terror, his armor scorched black, his voice a low rasp of embers. Fire no longer burns him, it answers him. Rothar does not hunt for coin. He hunts to burn away weakness, to purge cowardice from the land. Where Sark captures, Rothar annihilates. He leaves no prisoners, only cinders.

They stood before Malrik.

"I offer gold," he began, "but more than that, I offer favor." He let the word echo. "These boys... this Rayner, this Cole... they seek to destroy everything we've built. They believe in honor."

Sark laughed beneath his mask. Malrik held up a hand.

"I want them found. Tracked. Broken, but not killed."

Maelis hissed. "Why not?"

"Because they must witness the fall of hope before they die. They must know that no light will save them."

The bounty hunters exchanged glances. They nodded. Malrik raised his hands. A wave of darkness flowed outward, latching to each of them, a bond. A curse. A promise.

"You will not fail," he said, and they vanished into the night.

After they left, Vael remained behind in the tower. He watched the blood-moon rise through the slit in the stone wall. His fingers trembled slightly. Though loyal, he had begun to feel the cracks in Malrik's power. The endless rituals. The rising cost. The way the keep seemed to groan louder every day. Vael's hesitation did not go unnoticed.

"You're afraid," Malrik said softly, stepping behind him.

"No, master."

"You should be." Malrik placed a cold hand on his shoulder. "If they reach the artifact, the kingdom will burn with light, and light will undo everything. You would fade. So would I."

Vael swallowed hard. "But if they fail,"

Malrik continued, "you will rise. You will take my place one day. I will make sure of it." "Even if… your magic fades?" Malrik's eyes flared. "I will consume the world before I let it fade."

That night, Malrik returned. He stood in the hall, robes streaked with blood, eyes wild with prophecy.

"They will come for the artifact," he said. "But they will fail."

Vael bowed. "Yes, master."

Malrik placed a hand on his shoulder.

"You are my shadow. My dagger in the dark. My last word."

Vael nodded, but inside, something recoiled. He wasn't sure when he stopped believing, but he knew this much: He no longer feared Malrik, and that made him dangerous. In the quiet of his chamber, Vael lit a single candle. He unrolled a map; one he had drawn in secret. It showed the lands beyond the Black Hollow, the mountain passes, and the old road to Eldwyre. He marked a red X where he guessed Rayner's group would travel next. He stared at it a long time. Then whispered to himself: "Maybe the fire isn't gone. Maybe it's just waiting." And for the first time in his life, Vael made a decision without his master's permission.

Far from the keep, Rayner and his companions continued their quest, unaware that shadows were gathering behind them. Sark found their trail first, a broken tree limb, a drop of blood, a footprint not covered by wind. He smiled beneath his mask. Maelis sang to the dead birds in the trees. They told her of fire in the woods and a sword that shone like day. Thornjaw moved through the soil itself, following the scent of Cole's magic, worming through the earth like a serpent, and Rothar watched from above a ridge, eyes black, blade half-drawn. Malrik's plan was in motion, but plans are fragile things, and fate, especially when called by kings and mages, has a will of its own.

CHAPTER 9

Before the sword, before the quest, before the keep of bones and the name Malrik ever reached their ears, there was a village nestled between hills and forest, called Ashbrook. A simple place. A quiet place, and home. This is where Rayner, Quinn, and Tristan were boys, before they became legends. Sir Worric and Rayner lived in a small house on the edge of the village, near the training grounds and the stone circle where travelers once camped. Sir Worric was gruff, weathered, and wore his past like armor visible but never spoken of, but he saw something in Rayner.

"He has eyes that won't flinch," he once told the village elder. "He'll hold a sword before he's nine."

He was right. As a young squire, Rayner swung a wooden sword against a pell every day at dawn. By ten, he could parry blows from grown men. By twelve, he could track movement by sound alone, but Sir Worric trained more than just swordplay.

"Honor is the blade that never dulls," he told Rayner. "Strength fades. Skill rusts, but honor? It endures."

Rayner listened. Even when he didn't fully understand.

Quinn was born to Tomas the Smith, a man with arms like tree trunks and a beard as wild as a bear's mane. Their forge sat at the heart of the village, always hot, always loud. From the time he could walk, Quinn carried coal buckets. As a boy, he was shaping nails. Soon after, he could swing a smithing hammer heavier than most boys' heads. He wasn't as fast as Rayner, nor as quiet as Tristan, but he was dependable as stone. Quinn learned early that metal responds to care.

"You don't beat iron to death," Tomas would say. "You shape it. Listen, lad. Let the steel speak. Steel always speaks if you listen for it"

He did, and when the three boys began to dream of swords and legends, it was Quinn who first built a real weapon crude, short, but true. He gave it to Rayner.

"You'll swing it," he said. "But it's got a bit of me in it too."

Quinn never craved glory. He just wanted to build things that didn't break. Friendships included.

Tristan was always the watcher. His father, Hale, was the village's lead hunter, a man of few words and quiet footsteps. Tristan followed him through the forest from the moment he could walk without tripping on roots. He learned patience before he learned speech. Learned to read wind and shadow. He knew how to move without sound, how to disappear among trees. He never talked much, but when he spoke, it mattered. Unlike Rayner, he didn't fight. Unlike Quinn, he didn't build. He watched, and when trouble came wolves, raiders, sickness it was usually Tristan who saw it first. He had a crossbow at a young age and had taken down his first buck by thirteen. He never missed. Hale always said.

"The world speaks in silence."

Rayner used to say, "Tristan sees what the rest of us ignore."

It was true. They weren't born together, but they grew together. During the seasons of their youth, the three were already inseparable. Rayner brought the fire always climbing trees, challenging older boys, itching to prove himself. Quinn brought the humor quick with a joke, always hungry, always ready to fix what others broke. Tristan brought the silence but also the clarity. When one acted recklessly, the others pulled him back. When one faltered, the others steadied him. They played in the creek, hunted frogs, raced horses when they could sneak them away, but even in childhood, the signs of their paths began to form. Rayner sparred with Sir Worric in the mornings. Quinn forged iron nails and shoe tacks in the afternoons. Tristan walked the forest alone at dusk, listening to the owls.

It wasn't all laughter. When the burned men came from the east exiles who had worshipped dark gods Ashbrook nearly burned. The men tried to raid the village granary, and three villagers were killed before the rest were driven off. Rayner saw his first real death that night. Tristan's father took an arrow through the shoulder defending the west gate. Quinn stood by his father at the forge, melting down tools into makeshift weapons. Sir Worric led the charge, sword flashing like a storm, roaring like war was still in his blood. When the fires died, the boys were different. Quieter. Sharper. The world had changed. So did their dreams.

One winter, just before Rayner turned sixteen, Hale, the hunter invited all three boys on a hunt into the northern woodlands. He called it a trial not of manhood, but of purpose. They tracked a great white stag rumored to live only during the coldest seasons. The hunt lasted four days. They built shelters. Cooked what they caught. Faced snow wolves. Watched the aurora bleed across the sky. On the fifth day, they found the stag. It stood on a ridge of frost-covered stone, antlers like a crown of ice, staring directly at them. Rayner lifted his bow but didn't fire. Tristan lowered his crossbow.

Quinn whispered, "We're not meant to take it."

And they let the stag go. Years later, they would speak of that moment often. It had been a choice. Mercy over might. Balance over blood.

CHAPTER 10

The forest deepened as Rayner, Cole, Quinn, and Tristan followed Azor along the moss-covered path. The air grew older here thick with memory. Sunlight broke through the high canopy in golden shafts, illuminating the ground like a cathedral floor. Birdsong fell silent. The wind slowed.

Cole stopped first. "Uh… anyone else notice the trees are breathing?"

Indeed, the trunks were subtly shifting creaking softly, as if stretching in slow thought. The path narrowed into a glade framed by four enormous trees whose roots twisted together into a spiral knot. Azor halted. He bowed his head. Then a low groan filled the air. Not hostile. Not angry. Ancient. From the center of the glade, a figure stirred. A towering sentinel, bark-skinned and leaf-crowned, rose slowly from the ground. It stood twice as tall as any man, with eyes like glowing amber coals. Its voice was a rumble of earth itself:

"You who walk with Weave-light… why do you disturb my trees?"

Rayner stepped forward, placing a hand on the hilt of his sword but not drawing it.

"We seek to destroy Malrik. The object that can undo his darkness is buried in the ruins of the Old Kingdom."

The guardian studied him, bark folding and shifting like stone under pressure.

"So many came before you, warriors, kings, and wolves in crowns. They bled upon the roots of this world. What makes you worthy of the forest's guidance?"

Rayner opened his mouth, but Cole beat him to it. "I don't think we are worthy."

The tree's eyes blinked slowly. Quinn stepped beside Cole.

"We don't fight for power. We fight because people still have hope in us, and if we fall... we want to fall standing."

Tristan said nothing. He simply nodded, gaze steady. The sentinel bent slightly forward, vines curling through the air like fingers

"Then listen, Children of Men. Malrik's darkness is not born of strength, it is born of imbalance. He rips from the Weave but offers no thread in return. He wounds the land without tending its roots. The object you seek will not save you unless you understand this truth."

Rayner frowned. "What truth?"

The guardian stepped back and gestured with a branch-like arm to the center of the grove, where a tiny flower bloomed alone in the spiral roots.

"The Weave does not yield to those who conquer. It yields to those who remember. Only by anchoring your purpose in memory, mercy, and meaning... can you survive what lies ahead."

Azor bowed again. "We thank you, guardian of the forest."

The guardian began to sink back into the forest floor, vines folding over its limbs like a blanket.

"Go now, but plant no hatred in your hearts. For even the tallest tree can fall... when its roots rot in rage."

Silence returned. Rayner looked to his friends.

Cole gave a low whistle. "Well," he muttered, "I think I just got lectured by a tree, and honestly? That was better than anything Azor's ever said."

Azor snorted.

Rayner looked back at the spiral flower. "Let's keep walking, but remember what he said. We don't just fight to win. We fight to heal."

moved through the forest cautiously now. Rayner led the way, sword on his back and eyes sharp. Beside him walked Cole, hands gloved, staff ready. Quinn brought up the rear with his heavy hammer slung across his shoulder, and Tristan moved through the brush like a shadow silent, alert, already scouting two steps ahead. They had passed into the Blackpine Grove, the trees tighter and darker than the others, where sun barely touched the moss-covered ground.

Cole suddenly stopped. "They're near," he whispered.

Rayner glanced back. "How near?"

Cole looked up. "Watching us already."

It began with a sound like a distant scream animal and wrong. Above, dark shapes circled the treetops. Maelis.

"Crows!" Tristan hissed, already nocking a bolt.

Rayner drew his sword, and light flared from its edge, casting shadows through the forest.

"Positions!"

Too late. From the shadows, Sark lunged. The masked bounty hunter struck fast curved daggers flashing in both hands. He came at Rayner like a whip of smoke, silent, deathly fast. Rayner barely raised his blade in time to block, metal ringing in the gloom. Quinn roared, hammer raised, but Sark danced away before he could strike. Above them, crows screamed and Maelis descended in a whirl of wings and wind. Her voice crackled like dead leaves as she chanted in the old tongue, summoning black flame in her skeletal hands. Cole raised a shield of magic, just in time to block her blast.

"Get back!" he shouted.

Sark darted through the trees, blades flashing, slashing at Rayner and Tristan. He moved like a shadoweach blow almost too fast to follow. Rayner met him strike for strike, but the bounty hunter was trained, vicious, and unpredictable. Quinn bellowed and charged, forcing Sark back with sheer force. His hammer cracked a tree in two trying to connect. Meanwhile, Maelis swooped down again. Cole turned and hurled a bolt of pure fire into the air only for Maelis to vanish into a cloud of feathers, reappearing ten feet away. She screeched, and the crow's dove.

"Cover your eyes!" Cole shouted and with a word of power, unleashed a blinding burst of white light.

Feathers and birds exploded in all directions. Maelis screamed and retreated to the branches. In the chaos, Tristan disappeared into the brush. Rayner and Quinn kept Sark at bay, each swing and counter taking everything they had. Sark was bleeding from a shoulder wound but smiling beneath his mask. He liked this. Suddenly, a bolt flew from the woods and buried itself deep in Sark's thigh. He screamed, stumbling.

"Now!" shouted Tristan from the shadows.

Rayner struck first blade flashing, cutting across Sark's arm. Quinn followed with a hammer blow that broke the bounty hunter's ribs and sent him crashing into the underbrush. He didn't get up. Maelis shrieked again, higher now more animal than human. The trees twisted. The light faded.

"She's summoning something," Cole warned. "We can't fight her and what's coming!"

"Retreat?" Rayner asked.

"No lure," Cole corrected. "She's tied to the birds. If we get far enough into the open, she loses control."

Rayner nodded. "Tristan, flank right. Quinn, with me. Cole, hold her attention."

They broke into a run. Maelis dived again, but her attacks missed scattering bark and leaves, forcing the trees to bend as if screaming. Cole turned at the edge of the clearing and chanted. Flames spiraled around his hands this time golden, not black. The witch hesitated. Cole hurled the fireball skyward. Light burst through the canopy. The birds scattered, and Maelis vanished with them, screaming as the forest rejected her presence.

The grove fell still. Sark lay unconscious, bleeding heavily. Rayner checked his pulse. Still alive, but barely.

"We can't keep him," said Quinn. "He'll wake, and if he follows again..."

Rayner stood. "Tie him. Strip him. Leave him."

Tristan nodded, already removing Sark's blades and mask. Beneath it was a man with sharp eyes and dozens of scars. Rayner looked down at him for a long moment.

"What kind of coin pays a man to kill for sport?" he muttered.

Cole answered quietly. "The kind Malrik offers."

They left Sark bound to a tree and vanished into the woods before Maelis could return.

That night, they camped in silence. The fire was small. Cole set wards around the perimeter. Rayner sat with the sword in his lap, watching it glow, softly in the dark.

"We're being hunted," Quinn said.

"Of course we are," Cole replied. "We carry the last hope of the kingdom."

Rayner didn't speak. Not for a long while. Then: "Next time, we end it faster."

The moon had crested higher, bathing the clearing in soft silver light. The fire had been stoked again, and the boys huddled close, wrapped in their cloaks. Cole was chewing dried apple slices. Quinn rubbed oil into his gauntlets. Tristan picked his teeth with a sliver of wood, and Rayner rested his arms on his knees, chin low, listening intently. Azor leaned back on a stump, pipe in hand, watching the sparks drift. Then, without prompting, he began:

"Before he was king, Reynard was, how should I put it? A menace."

Rayner lifted an eyebrow. Azor smirked.

"A walking storm of charm and idiocy in equal measure. Bold as brass, reckless as a fox in a henhouse. And one spring festival in Valebrook, he nearly caused a riot... over a painted sword."

Cole's eyes lit up. "Oh, I have to hear this."

Azor took a puff from his pipe and continued. "There was an old smith, retired from the wars, who made ceremonial blades for parades and nobles. Beautiful work, painted hilts, inlaid with gems, but the blades themselves were dull. Decorative. Harmless. Well, Reynard, seventeen at the time, decided he needed to prove himself during the festival's dueling exhibition. But instead of drawing his training blade, he stole one of the painted ceremonial swords. Didn't realize it had been lacquered that morning."

Tristan chuckled. "Oh no..."

"Oh yes," Azor nodded. He walked into the square, raised the thing high like some hero from the old songs, and it slipped clean out of his hand."

Cole burst out laughing.

"Hit a nobleman's goose in mid-strut. Feathers everywhere. Goose survived. Nobleman nearly didn't."

Rayner groaned. "Please tell me that's not true."

Azor grinned. "True as the stars. I spent the next three hours casting apologies in every language I knew. And do you know what your father said?"

"What?"

"He looked at the goose, then the sword, then the nobleman, and said, 'Well, at least my aim is improving.'"

Laughter echoed through the trees. Quinn wiped tears from his eyes.

"Did the nobleman forgive him?"

Azor shrugged. "Eventually. Once Reynard bought him a new goose. And a new hat."

Tristan leaned in. "You ever duel with the king?"

Azor chuckled. "Once. He challenged me to a spar using brooms. Claimed he could beat me 'with the handle end of destiny.'"

Cole laughed so hard he nearly choked.

Azor's gaze softened again. "He was bold, your father. Reckless, yes, but always with heart. He believed in people. He believed the kingdom could be more than swords and banners. That's why he named me his mage. Not for power. But for trust."

Rayner looked into the fire. "I hope I live up to him."

Azor nodded. "You already do. But don't try to be your father. Be better."

He tapped the side of his pipe with a grin.

"And maybe don't duel with geese."

The Village of Brevenhall, nestled deep in the southern foothills of the Duskbar Range, Brevenhall lay hidden where forest met fire. It was a village of iron-colored roofs and copper-toned earth, a settlement where heat rose not just from hearths but from beneath the ground itself. Long ago, Brevenhall had been a mining town, tapping the shallow magma veins that pulsed under the cracked rock, but the mines had long since been sealed. In their place, the village had become a place of trade, secrecy, and forgotten firelore.

Approaching Brevenhall from the north, the land sloped into a steaming basin where sulfur-laced mist hung low over the fields. Dark pine and ash trees ringed the outskirts, their black-needled boughs brushing low against timeworn fences. Birds rarely sang here. The earth was warm to the touch, even in the early morning. The village was built in an oval around a central gathering space, but instead of a typical market square or chapel, Brevenhall revolved around The Emberhall, a long, low stone structure with a split chimney and stained-glass skylights above a central flame. There was no formal inn in Brevenhall. Travelers found lodging in homes or bunkhouses, and strangers often camped along the cliffs or near the steaming ponds that bubbled gently to the south. Homes in Brevenhall were carved from reddish stone and timber, with wide, slanted roofs layered with slate tiles. Chimneys were stout and always smoking, venting the dense warmth from firepits that had been burning for generations. Every home had a fire altar, and every child was taught the names of the old fire spirits, Ashenel, Bryntor, Elaria Flame, and Maek the Cinderwatcher.

At night, Brevenhall glowed softly from within, like a coal ember tucked into the forest's hand. The streets were lit not by oil lanterns, but by glowglass orbs, globes filled with heated river crystals that pulsed with amber and red hues. They were mined from the ancient riverbed deep below the village, an old trade that still fed Brevenhall's modest economy.

Where most villages had an inn or temple as a social hub, Brevenhall had the Emberhall, a half-buried hall of volcanic stone and dragon-iron beams. It was built atop the oldest known vent in the region, a sealed lava fissure said to be protected by elemental wards. The villagers claimed it was once the sanctum of the Firekeepers, a now-forgotten order that had walked the balance between fire magic and its destructive chaos. Inside the Emberhall, a massive sunken hearth dominated the floor. It burned without fuel, fed by the unseen warmth of the vent below. Around this fire were thick benches of darkwood, often full of residents during the long evenings. Children practiced fire chants in low tones. Elders smoked rootleaf and whispered stories. Conflicts were settled here by vote or flame-casting, rituals where truths were told by how quickly a coal turned white. The hall also served as the town archive, storing scrolls, etched copper plates, and wooden sigils bearing the lineage of Brevenhall's oldest families. An ancient bell, forged from obsidian and lined with silver, hung over the northern hearth and was only rung in dire times.

The people of Brevenhall were quiet but not unkind. They moved with the caution of those who knew the earth could shift beneath their feet. Most were artisans, glassblowers, charmwrights, or tenders of the heated fields. Fire-milling, the practice of shaping metal using earth-heated forges, was a trade born in Brevenhall, and it was said a sword from its forges never dulled, and a kettle never rusted. Children were taught early to read heat and shadow, to sense when the earth grew restless, and to honor the fire gods even in silence. Superstition ran deep. Villagers placed rune-carved stones in doorways to ward off misfortune. They left cinderfruit, small, fiery-red apples, on the old Firekeeper shrines to appease ancient spirits. Those born with red-hued hair or fire marks on their skin were considered touched by the flame and either revered or feared, depending on the decade. Despite the volcanic warmth, winters were still harsh, with smoke hanging low in the valley and snow curling against the heated stones like steam.

The wind howled low as the four travelers stepped into the steaming vale of Brevenhall. Their cloaks hung heavy with dust from the trail, and their boots, stained with the ochre-red mud of the south, bore the weight of a dozen days' journey. The skies overhead hung like smoke, thick with cloud, and the scent of sulfur, pine ash, and damp stone clung to the air like memory. Rayner led the way, hand resting on the pommel of his sword, his brow drawn. He had known quiet villages before, Ashbrook, with its golden fields, and Stonebrook with its story-laced paths, but this place... it felt different. The land beneath his feet was warm, almost pulsing. It was like stepping onto the chest of a slumbering beast. Cole grunted and glanced up at the rooftops as they passed under the shadow of black-tiled eaves.

"Well, this is a cheerful place," he said. "Are we sure we haven't wandered into the backend of a volcano?"

Tristan, always alert, scanned the tree lines for movement.

"I've never seen mist move like that," he murmured, gesturing to the swirls rolling across the heated fields. "It's like the village is breathing."

Quinn nodded in agreement. "Feels like the forge back home, just bigger. A lot bigger."

They passed rows of low stone homes, most with obsidian-carved totems by their doors and runes etched into lintels. Villagers glanced up from their chores, quiet and unsmiling, but not unkind. A child darted behind a stairwell; her face marked with soot and curiosity. An old man adjusted his walking stick and muttered a fire-chant under his breath as they passed. The boys followed the narrow stone path that coiled like a snake toward the center of the village. The strange mist thickened near the basin, where they found the Emberhall, half-sunken in the earth and radiating a faint heat.

"I thought we'd find an inn," Tristan muttered, eyes narrowing. "Not a cave with windows."

"No inn here," Rayner said. "Only fire."

A figure waited for them near the Emberhall's threshold. She was lean and cloaked in brown, with an orange sash tied about her waist. Her hair was gray but her posture unbent, and her eyes burned with a flame that had long refused to go out.

Fayla Nern, lorekeeper of Brevenhall.

"I saw your approach in the fire's sleep," she said. "Strangers, but not without purpose. Come inside. The flame won't judge, but it will see you clearly."

Inside the Emberhall, the boys sat on low stone benches around the fire pit. Its blue-white flame cast no shadows and gave off no smoke, only a strange warmth that seemed to stir the ache in their bones from travel. Fayla poured them each a bowl of soot tea, earthy and strong They drank in silence, listening to the crackling flame. Around them, a few villagers watched from the edges, whispering.

"So, what brings four boys to Brevenhall?" Fayla finally asked.

Rayner shared little, only that they sought rest and direction. Cole added a few jokes, lightening the mood, while Quinn and Tristan listened quietly, watching the way villagers cast sideways glances toward a young girl standing just beyond the benches. She had flame-red hair and wore a scarf over her shoulders despite the heat. A swirling mark peeked from beneath her collarbone, the birth-scorch they would later learn about.

"Who's that?" Tristan asked in a hushed tone.

Fayla's smile faded. "That is Marna. She was born during the last Ash storm. The fire marked her, and some say she brings it too close to the surface. The crops have withered this season. The goats won't breed. Some believe she's the reason."

"But she's just a child," Rayner said. "Not to those who fear what they don't understand."

Before anyone could speak again, a loud crack echoed from outside, a shudder in the earth. The fire in the pit flickered once, then steadied. Cole's hand moved instinctively to the leather pouch at his belt, where old runes hummed faintly.

"What was that?" Quinn asked.

"An echo," Fayla replied. But her voice lacked certainty.

Rayner stood. "I think we arrived at the right time after all."

The tremor faded, but its presence lingered, like a half-forgotten song humming beneath the floor of the Emberhall. As the fire steadied and returned to its quiet flicker, the villagers in the room exchanged wary looks. Fayla leaned heavily on her staff.

"The fire beneath is stirring again. And Brevenhall remembers what that means."

Over the following day, the boys learned quickly that Marna, the girl with the birth-scorch, was both pitied and feared. Her family lived on the outer edge of the village, near the glass ponds, in a cottage blackened by soot. Only her father remained with her, her mother had vanished during the last flame season, swallowed by a sudden sinkhole outside the farmstead.

The village had long endured a delicate balance between flame and field. The fire-fed crops grew fast but withered if the heat pulsed wrong. The glowglass orbs needed steady temperatures to be harvested without cracking. And in the last season, everything had begun to falter. Crops rotted in the soil. Steam vents dried or belched foul gas. Children fell sick from strange fevers that left their skin hot and dry. Some whispered it was the earth retaliating. Others blamed Marna. She was not allowed in the Emberhall anymore. Cole saw her outside it that evening, seated on the stone steps, sketching runes in the dirt with a stick. The shapes were fire-call sigils, though poorly formed.

"Who taught you those?" Cole asked, kneeling.

Marna didn't look up. "No one. I saw them once when the wind pushed open the library scrolls."

"Those are dangerous symbols, you know."

She shrugged. "Everything about me is dangerous, they say."

Cole frowned. "They're wrong. But you should let someone teach you the right way to draw them."

She looked at him for the first time. "Would you?"

Later that night, Rayner and Quinn followed Fayla beneath the Emberhall, through an iron door bolted with six runes and sealed with a twisted flame sigil. Inside was a long, curved staircase descending into old fire-chambers, where the walls sweated heat and the air thrummed with ancient magic.

"This is the oldest place in Brevenhall," Fayla said. "Built by the Firekeepers. They shaped the flame, but they also knew it needed balance. That's what most forget."

They entered a round vault, its floor etched with a massive rune, a circle broken by three lines, surrounded by ash runes.

"This was a binding seal," she said, "meant to hold the imbalance deep beneath the village. Long ago, a fire-spirit was wounded here in a battle with an ice mage, and the wound festered. The Firekeepers buried its anger here, beneath this seal. But now something is weakening the bindings."

Quinn stepped closer, brow furrowed. "Could it be the girl?"

"No. But it might be calling to her. Her mark connects her to the fire-spirit's bloodline. She doesn't bring the imbalance, she senses it."

That same night, another tremor hit Brevenhall, stronger this time. A vent near the goat fields burst open, spewing ash and molten rock. Several villagers were burned, and blame came swiftly. A group gathered outside Marna's home, torches in hand, eyes wide with fear. Mayor Tellen did nothing to stop them.

"She's cursed!" someone cried.

"She needs to leave the village, take her to the hills!"

"She'll bring Brevenhall to ruin!"

Rayner, Quinn, and Tristan stood in their path.

"No one is banishing a child," Rayner said. "We don't exile our own because the ground shakes."

"She's not our own," said a woman with streaks of soot on her cheeks. "She's something else."

Then, from the tree line, a voice broke through. "Enough." Azor had arrived.

The old mage strode through the crowd like a gust of wind, his cloak ash-grey, his staff wrapped with smoldering sigils. His eyes were alight, not with wrath, but with clarity.

"I have walked through cursed forests and fire-scarred ruins. I have seen true corruption. And I tell you now, this girl is no source of evil. She is a key."

He turned to Marna, who clung to her father's side.

"Come with me, child. We have work to do."

With Rayner and Cole's help, Azor led her and the boys back into the Emberhall and down to the vault. Azor studied the seal with a grim face.

"The fire-spirit's binding is breaking. Its rage burns through the cracks in the seal and twists the heat in Brevenhall."

"And how do we stop it?" Rayner asked.

"With fire, and one who hears it."

At dawn, Azor, Cole, and Marna descended into the sealed chamber. Cole helped her draw the proper runes this time, not to summon, but to listen. As the final glyph lit up, a deep growl rolled through the stone. The spirit stirred. Flame burst upward in a spire, but Marna stood firm. The heat didn't touch her. She whispered. Her words were not in the tongue of men but ancient flame-speech, a fragment of the firekeeper language Azor hadn't heard in decades. The flame quivered... then dimmed. The pressure in the chamber lifted. The air cleared. Above ground, vents sealed, the earth settled. The sky opened to reveal the sun for the first time in weeks. Brevenhall exhaled.

That night, the villagers gathered in the Emberhall for the first time with Marna present. Mayor Tellen, still reluctant, offered her a small flame-apple in silence, a symbol of welcome. Rayner clapped Quinn on the back.

"Well, not the worst village we've saved." Cole grinned.

"Speak for yourself. I got bit by a goat."

Marna sat beside Azor, who leaned close and whispered

"Your path is just beginning, flameborn. You carry a torch that may one day light the darkest places in this realm."

The skies above Brevenhall opened the next morning, casting light across the basin for the first time in a fortnight. The clouds, once low and brooding, broke into thin rays of gold and blue, spilling warmth onto the slate roofs and red stone paths. Steam still rose from the vents, but it was softer now, more natural, like the land itself was breathing easier. The change was subtle, but undeniable. Rayner stood at the edge of the Emberhall, arms crossed, watching children play in the now-dry courtyard. They chased each other with wooden sticks and kicked a bundle of cloth down the lane. A week earlier, those same children had huddled in doorways, afraid of the earth cracking under their feet. He heard footsteps behind him.

"Not bad," said Azor, his voice gravel and wisdom. "You handled that with a knight's heart."

Rayner turned. "You were the one who knew what to do."

Azor chuckled. "Aye. But knowledge doesn't mean much without someone willing to stand in front of a mob. That took courage. You reminded them who they were, before the fear set in."

Rayner looked at the Emberhall's twin chimneys, both rising with clean smoke now.

"So, the fire-spirit is healed?"

Azor's gaze drifted to the horizon. "Healed? No. But no longer angry. No longer twisted.

Marna helped him remember what he was, before war, before wounding. That's what children can do, sometimes. Reach the things old men forget."

That evening, a feast was held. Not a lavish one, but simple and sincere. Bowls of roasted cinderfruit and stonepot stew, bread blackened at the edges but warm inside, ashwine passed in wooden mugs. Cole sat with Marna near the fire, showing her how to trace runework with a coal-tip.

"You ever wonder what your flame would look like if you weren't so angry all the time?" he teased, gesturing to the spark still flickering in her palm.

She smirked. "You're one to talk. You mutter to your belt pouch like it's a friend."

"It is a friend," Cole said, patting the pouch. "You think the runes scribe themselves?"

Quinn clinked mugs with Tristan and let out a rare laugh.

"I'll take this over being chased by that crow-thing any day."

"Don't jinx it," Tristan muttered.

Rayner joined them after helping an elderly woman carry wood to her door. He sat quietly for a moment, watching the fire. Then he looked to Azor, seated across from him, the glowglass light reflecting in his aged eyes.

"What's next?" Rayner asked.

Azor stirred his mug with a carved iron stick. "South, through the glade roads. Then to the foothills. Malrik's lands grow closer with every step."

"And the thing in the castle? You still think it's still there?"

Azor didn't answer right away. When he did, it was with a measured tone. "I know it is. The object that can unmake Malrik's blood magic lies there, but only if you reach it before he does."

CHAPTER 11

The fire had burned low again, now more ember than flame. A hush had fallen over the clearing. The trees whispered softly, and the moon hung pale and full above them. Azor sat still for a long time, as if listening to something only he could hear. Then he said,

"Your mother, Rayner... your mother never needed a sword."

Rayner straightened. Even Cole grew quiet, sensing the shift in Azor's tone.

"Elenora of Valebrook. A name that rings like silver and settles like still water. She was no warrior, not in the way your father was, or even Sir Worric. But she could quiet a room with a look. She knew what words to use when steel would fail, and when silence spoke louder than any cry of war."

He rubbed a thumb along his pipe but didn't smoke it.

"Did you ever hear about the Winter Garden?" he asked.

Tristan shook his head. Quinn leaned in.

Rayner answered, "She tended it, didn't she? Behind the east wing of the castle?"

"She built it," Azor said. "Every flower, every tree. She had it grown from seeds carried from across Eldara. Thorned roses from Eldwyre. Starblooms from Ashbrook. Moonvine from the Eroded Mountains. It became her place of peace. And the only one she would allow no guards to follow her into."

Cole's brow furrowed. "Why?"

Azor's eyes grew distant. "Because she listened to the Weave there. Elenora... she was touched by magic, though she never cast a spell. The wind would shift around her. Birds would land on her hand. The dying flowers would bloom again in her wake. She was

117

never taught the Art, but I believe the Weave spoke to her all the same."

Rayner's voice was soft. "Did she know?"

Azor nodded. "Oh, yes. But she feared what it might cost if she used it. Her strength was in restraint. Her power was choice."

He smiled faintly, not with joy, but reverence.

"There was a day King Reynard came back from battle, wounded, broken in spirit. His men had turned on each other. Brothers lost to suspicion and fear. He told her, I feel like I command shadows."

And she said…" Azor looked to Rayner. "Do you know what she said?"

Rayner shook his head.

"Then be the light they need to remember."

The fire popped.

"She healed him that day. Not with spells or salves. But with the reminder of what a king was meant to be. She was the one who gave him the words that carried through his reign. She was the crown before the crown was forged."

Cole whispered, "What happened to the Winter Garden?"

Azor was quiet for a long time. "It withered… after she passed. No one could keep it alive. Not even the castle mages. The flowers refused to bloom. As though the Weave itself mourned her."

The boys sat silently, the image of the Queen, gentle, wise, full of quiet magic, forming clearly in their minds. Azor looked around at them, then added with a half-smile,

"She would've liked all of you. Even you, Cole."

Cole grinned. "That's high praise, old man." Azor chuckled softly. "Indeed, it is."

At dawn the next day, the four boys stood at the village's western edge, bags packed, weapons cleaned, boots patched with fresh leather by Brevenhall's charmwright. Marna walked up to them, still wearing her scarf but now with rune-thread woven through it, a gift from Cole.

"Do you have to go?" she asked.

Rayner knelt to her level. "We do. But we'll remember this place, and what you did."

She looked at Cole, then at Azor. "Will I see you again?"

Azor stepped forward and placed a small obsidian pendant in her palm. "When the time comes, and the fire inside you need direction, use this. Speak the word Kel'narath into the flame. I'll hear it."

"Even from far away?"

Azor smiled. "Especially from far away."

The journey west took them along the stone-hollow path, a route that wound through gnarled forests and steaming cliffs. The land still bore the heat of the mountains behind them, but now it felt different, less hostile, more like the breath of something living and ancient. Rayner walked at the front, eyes steady. Behind him, Cole muttered a rune and sparked a wisp of fire to float in front of him like a lazy star.

"Still practicing?" Quinn asked.

"Trying to remember the one Azor showed me. The one that twists back on itself."

Tristan chuckled. "The one that blew your hair off your brow?"

Cole frowned. "It was experimental."

Rayner grinned. It felt good. The road was hard, but they were still together. That night, as they camped under a sky split by stars, Azor sat with Cole a distance from the others. The fire crackled low, embers dancing in the dark. Azor looked to his student.

"There will come a moment, when you're alone. Truly alone. And the choice you make then will echo far louder than any spell you've ever learned."

Cole nodded. "I know."

"You are ready," Azor said. "I won't be with you in the end. But you won't need me then."

"Where will you go?"

Azor looked to the North. "To speak with the stonefolk. To gather old debts. The war ahead needs more than swords and spells, it needs reminders. He placed a hand on Cole's shoulder. "Be that reminder."

Azor did not tell them everything. There are truths too heavy to place on the backs of young warriors. Even Cole, so bright, so fierce in spirit, would not yet understand the weight of what I must carry alone, and so, as the fire died low that night beneath the whispering trees, Azor told them only this:

"There is a relic in the North, older than any of us, even the wind. If we are to defeat Malrik, Cole must have it. I am the only one who knows the way."

Rayner gave a slow nod, his eyes hard with worry. Elira looked away. Cole opened his mouth twice, then closed it, gripping the hilt of his staff. Cole wanted to come with Azor. Azor knew it, but this was his road. So, before dawn, he left them sleeping.

The Northern Mountains are not a place of maps. They are not drawn or charted. They do not want to be. Men have tried, of course, scribes and soldiers with compasses and charcoal. Their bones still sit in the hollows beneath the shale, picked clean by silence. The cold of the north wrapped itself around Azor like an old friend, familiar and harsh. The wind howled like the lost voices of those who had come before him, their warnings and wisdom etched into the very stones of the Northern Mountains, but Azor was no stranger to the weight of ancient magic, nor to the harsh call of the mountains that demanded respect from all who dared approach. It had been decided. He would retrieve the Codex of Binding, not for himself, but for Cole. The young mage had shown promise, far more than Azor had expected. Perhaps it was time for the boy to understand the truth of his origins, the depth of the power he wielded, and the responsibilities that came with it.

Azor had never intended to return to the Northern Mountains. He had left them behind years ago, his reasons known only to the old stones and the winds that whispered through their peaks, but the Codex had been hidden there long ago, buried beneath layers of enchantment, its power too dangerous to remain in the hands of any one person. The Weave had sealed it there, and for good reason, but now, the world needed it. He had told Rayner and the others that they would not follow. The journey was his, and his alone. For what they sought could not be understood in the same way that Cole might understand it. The boy's destiny was intertwined with the Codex, and Azor was the key to unlocking that fate.

Standing at the edge of the forest where the trees grew sparse and the sky was nothing but grey, Azor gathered his belongings. The Codex was no simple book. It was an ancient tome, bound in the skins of creatures long forgotten, etched with runes that could bend the very fabric of reality. It held the secrets of binding magic, of sealing and unsealing, and of binding one's soul to the weave of life itself. The journey ahead would be long and perilous, and Azor was no fool. He knew that the mountains were not a welcoming place. They had changed in the years since he had last walked their icy paths. Darker magic had taken root. He had felt it in the air, a chill that did not come from the biting winds but from the land itself. The path ahead was obscured by mist. It swirled around him, wrapping itself like a veil between him and the world beyond. His breath came in steady clouds, his every movement deliberate, every step measured. There was no turning back now.

The road to the Codex of Binding led deeper into the mountains, through cliffs that rose like giants and valleys where the sun barely touched the ground. Azor had heard tales of the ancient guardians that once roamed these peaks, stone giants who protected the secrets of the Codex, bound by an oath to prevent its power from falling into the wrong hands, but Azor was no stranger to guardians or their oaths. The Weave itself was his ally, and with its power, he could unravel any binding, challenge any ward. As he climbed higher, the air grew thin, the pressure heavy on his chest. The mountain trail twisted and turned like a serpent, winding its way through jagged rock formations and deep ravines. A cold mist curled around his feet, rising from unseen crevices, and the shadows seemed to lengthen with each passing step. The feeling of being watched, always a lingering sensation in the back of his mind, grew stronger.

Azor paused at the crest of a ridge, his breath ragged from the exertion. Below him, the valley spread out like a tapestry of grey and white, the peaks rising sharply around it. The mountains were silent now; the eerie hum of magic ever present beneath the surface. He could feel it, like a pulse, calling to him, guiding his steps. The first obstacle came soon after. A barrier of energy rippled across his path, a shimmering veil that seemed to pulse with an ancient, forbidden power. It was a ward, woven by the Weave itself to keep intruders from crossing. Azor smiled wryly, reaching into the depths of his magical reserves. He could feel the threads of the ward, felt them pushing against him, resisting his every effort, but he was no stranger to unraveling the complex layers of magic. His hands moved in a dance of forgotten gestures, each one pulling at the threads of the ward, loosening the bindings until the veil of energy shimmered and fell away. The path ahead was open, but Azor knew this was only the beginning. The journey was far from over.

As he continued, the wind began to pick up, howling through the crags and sweeping across the path. He knew that the Codex of Binding was not just hidden by enchantments, it was protected by ancient forces, guardians who had sworn to keep it safe. He had been warned of the trials ahead, trials that would test not only his strength but his mind, his will, and his very soul. The first trial would be one of strength. The mountain itself would demand it. The second, a test of wisdom, the Codex would not reveal itself easily to the unworthy, and the final trial... Azor could not know for sure. He had heard only whispers, dark rumors of those who had tried before him and failed, but Azor was not one to fail.

With a deep breath, he pushed forward, moving into the heart of the mountain. The path grew steeper, and the shadows deepened. The air was thick with magic, the very earth beneath his feet vibrating with an ancient power, and with every step, Azor felt the presence of the Codex growing stronger, its pull more insistent, its secrets beckoning to him. Azor pressed deeper into the mountains, his fingers brushing against the stone walls of the narrow pass. They hummed with ancient energy, vibrations that pulsed in tune with the Weave itself. He whispered an incantation under his breath, more for focus than necessity, a low thrum of syllables in the Old Tongue. Light shimmered faintly around him, a ward of protection he'd learned from the Magisters of Vaelmore long ago. The wind rose to a scream. Snow flurried sideways in slicing gusts, and the path narrowed further until Azor found himself standing at the edge of a crevasse. There was no bridge. No visible means of crossing. Yet he could sense the Codex beyond, its echo in the ether unmistakable. The first trial was nearby. Across the chasm stood a stone figure, unmoving. A sentinel. It was a golem of the old world, taller than any man, crafted from basalt and etched with glowing runes. It stirred as Azor approached, its eyes flaring with blue fire. With a groaning shift, it stepped forward.

"WHO SEEKS THE CODEX?"

Azor did not flinch. "One bound to the Weave. One chosen to awaken what sleeps."

The golem's voice boomed again, like avalanche thunder. "THEN PROVE YOUR RIGHT. STRENGTH AGAINST STONE."

The earth beneath Azor trembled. From the ground rose another form, an elemental born of the mountain itself. Its body was jagged, its arms heavy with malice. Azor rolled his shoulders back and prepared. He didn't fight with brute force. He never had. Instead, he channeled the Weave, drawing power through his staff, tracing sigils in the air that crackled with energy. The elemental lunged, and Azor sidestepped, driving a shockwave of light into its midsection. Stone cracked. Magic flared. The fight was long, brutal. Azor took blows that bruised ribs and seared flesh, but he endured. With a final surge of power, he summoned a lance of crystalline energy and drove it through the elemental's core. It shattered in a storm of rock and dust. The sentinel bowed its head. The path opened. Azor stumbled forward, drained but alive. The Weave whispered approval. One trial passed.

The second trial lay within a cave, deeper still in the mountain's marrow. The entrance was carved in ancient script, almost illegible. A riddle was etched above the arch: "He who sees without eyes and knows without name, shall enter." Azor breathed in. This was a test of insight. He stepped into darkness. The moment he did, the light from the world vanished. No stars. No moon. Not even the shimmer of his staff. There was nothing. He walked forward, carefully, slowly, listening. Then, whispers. They came from all sides. They weren't in any language he knew. The voices overlapped, crescendo 'ed, faded, returned. Memories? Illusions? Spirits of those who failed before him?

"Who are you?" a voice hissed.

Azor answered with silence.

"What do you seek?" Again, silence.

Finally, he said, "Not power. Not glory. Knowledge for the one who follows."

The voices quieted. A light flared. Before him appeared a spectral form, his younger self, full of arrogance and pride. The mirror image spoke:

"You came here once before. You sought the Codex then, too."

Azor nodded. "But I was not ready. I would have misused it."

"And now?"

"I am the vessel, not the master. It is not for me."

The spectral form smiled, then faded into dust. The cave opened. Azor stepped into a chamber bathed in blue light. A pedestal rose from the ground. Upon it lay the Codex of Binding, wrapped in chains of light, but one final guardian remained.

The third trial was not of strength or wisdom, but of fear. As Azor reached for the Codex, the chamber warped. Walls closed in. The air grew still, and from the shadows, a figure emerged. Not a beast. Not a demon. Vael. His old apprentice. The one he had failed. Vael's eyes were hollow. Blood dripped from his fingertips. His voice was a whisper, yet it thundered in Azor's ears.

"You let me fall."

Azor trembled. "I tried to save you."

"You left me to rot."

The illusion circled him.

"You chose another. You chose Cole."

Azor fell to his knees. Not from weakness, but grief.

"Yes," he whispered. "I did, but I will not fail him."

The illusion hissed, struck, and vanished. The Codex unchained itself. Light swelled. Azor reached out and took it. He collapsed, holding the tome to his chest, and the Weave sang. He had passed. He would return, but not as the same man, and Cole... Cole would be ready.

The Codex of Binding is no ordinary scroll. It is a relic of another age, older than kingdoms, older even than the rise of blood magic itself. When unrolled, it measures just over three feet in length, but its aura makes it feel vast, like something more lived within it than on it. The codex is housed in a cylindrical case made of blackened ironwood, veined with glowing runes inlaid with dawnstone, a long-lost mineral said to react to truth, pulsing when held by a worthy bearer. It is bound by a silver-threaded chain, soft as silk, strong as forged steel. The thread is enchanted with protective magic, only one attuned to the Weave can unwind it. Inside, the scroll's parchment is dark cream, smooth and cold to the touch, etched with living glyphs, symbols that shimmer in shifting hues of copper, emerald, and violet. They don't remain static, almost like they breathe, rearranging based on the reader's intention or magical affinity. At the center of the scroll is a single golden seal, bearing the sigil of the Weave: a spiraling knot of flame and water, wind and stone, a symbol representing balance across all elements.

The Codex of Binding is not a book of spells. It is a foundational artifact, a record and channel of the Weave itself. It doesn't teach magic so much as reveal it, allowing the mage to connect to the underlying truth of all things. The Codex is believed to be the last surviving relic from the First Weavers, who served not as rulers, but as guardians of balance during the Time Before Crowns. It represents a covenant: magic must serve the world, not master it. To hold the Codex is not merely to wield power, but to carry a burden. It is said that: "He who holds the Codex binds himself to the fate of the world."

As dawn broke once more, and the first birdsong pierced the mist beyond the trees, the group continued their journey, leaving behind the strange, warm village of Brevenhall. Behind them, a girl with fire in her blood stood watching from the cliffs, the emberlight at her throat beginning to glow. The fire in Brevenhall had been rekindled. And soon, so would the flame across the kingdom.

CHAPTER 12

The village of Stonebrook, lay nestled against a ridge of moss-covered hills, its cottages built from dark river stone and its narrow lanes coiled like roots beneath a heavy canopy of trees. From a distance, it looked safe. Too safe. It was a place born of river and rock, framed by the slow-moving current of the Stonebrook River, from which the village drew its name, and the craggy shoulders of the Eroded Hills, where winds never ceased their whispering. Stonebrook was not large, no more than thirty homes, a market square, two mills, a smithy, a granary, a riverside chapel, and the inn that served as its warm heart. But what it lacked in size, it made up for in stonework that could have withstood a siege. Every home, wall, and well was built from smooth gray riverstone, fitted without mortar by craftsmen whose trade had passed from father to son for generations. Roofs were mostly slate and lichen-covered wood, dark and muted, the color of clouds before a storm. It rained often in Stonebrook, and so everything seemed damp and alive, stone darkened with mist, moss creeping over walls, water droplets clinging to windowpanes like tiny beads of glass. But the village never felt dreary. No, there was a quiet strength to Stonebrook, as though its very foundation hummed with age and memory.

The villagers themselves were hardy folk with calloused hands and shoulders made broad by honest labor. Most were masons or stonecutters, and the surrounding hills bore deep scars from generations of quarrying. Yet the people carried themselves with the dignity of artisans, proud of what they shaped from earth and mountain. Their stone was used across the realm, from the castle walls of Valebrook to the arched bridges of Hollowmere. When royalty needed foundations that would outlast dynasties, they sent for Stonebrook masons. The Stonebrook River, wide and swift in the spring thaw, curved along the eastern edge of the village. It ran shallow in summer but always cold, fed by the snowmelt from distant peaks. Children played along its banks in the warmer months, and elders set fishing lines from the polished boulders that rose like sleeping giants just beneath the surface.

A simple wooden bridge, one of the few pieces in the village not made of stone, spanned the river near the northern edge of town. It creaked underfoot, but never failed. Beyond it, a narrow path led into the Verdant Pines, a forest thick with mushrooms, deer, and old secrets. The air in Stonebrook always smelled faintly of stone dust, wet earth, and woodsmoke. There were no grand towers, no temples of gilded spires, only squat buildings, low walls, and chimneys puffing gentle coils of gray against a sky that rarely turned blue but always seemed vast. In the center of the village stood the Market Ring, a circular open-air space bordered by merchant stalls, a sundial mounted on a carved pillar, and stone benches worn smooth by decades of sitting. On market days, the square came alive with traders from neighboring valleys, spices from Eldwyre, wool from Hollowmere, and finely wrought iron-work from the north. But even on quiet days, children played underfoot while old men carved whittling figures from cedar, and women exchanged herbs or gossip. And always, at the very heart of it all, stood the Shattered Anvil Inn.

The Shattered Anvil Inn stood just off the Market Ring, nestled between the old bell tower and a merchant row of cobblers and potters. It was the largest structure in Stonebrook aside from the granary and chapel, and certainly the most storied. Locals said the inn had been there since before the first mason set a foundation stone in the village. Whether that was true or just the sort of myth every old place earned, no one could say. The building itself was a marvel of rustic craftsmanship, an oblong, two-story structure made entirely of pale riverstone, chiseled smooth and stacked in meticulous rows. The lower level bore deep carvings of tools, chisels, hammers, tongs, and anvils, etched into the stone. Above the doorway was a circular wooden sign, stained with age and soot, displaying a cracked blacksmith's anvil cleft nearly in two, with flames licking around it. Beneath the image was written, in broad dwarven runes: "Tempered Through Fire." That was the inn's motto, and most believed it described both the building and its keeper.

A short stone stoop led up to the thick wooden door, oak banded in black iron, with a brass handle polished smooth by decades of use. The lintel above was carved with the names of generations of stonecutters who had stayed within the inn's walls, and each name bore a tiny emblem next to it, some a hammer, others a crest, one even a mountain. The moment one stepped inside, warmth wrapped around them like an old wool cloak. The main taproom was broad and low, the ceiling of dark timber beams so close that taller men had to duck near the hearth. The walls were a deep gray but glowed amber from the light of half a dozen lanterns and the great central fireplace. That fireplace, arched in stone and massive enough to roast a boar, burned constantly, its flames always fed by thick pine logs, crackling and scenting the room with the spicy tang of sap. The floors were made of dark plank wood, slightly uneven in spots, worn smooth by generations of boots. Dozens of round tables filled the space, some scarred with initials, others ringed with the stains of decades of mugs and spills. On the far side of the room, a narrow stone bar curved like a smile beneath shelves of clay jugs, glass bottles, and wooden mugs. A thick iron bell hung over the bar, used not to call attention, but to announce meals.

Above the hearth hung the Shattered Anvil itself, a real anvil, cleft down the center by a mysterious crack that, according to legend, appeared during a fierce lightning storm nearly two centuries ago. The inn's founder, a retired smith named Barlo Hendrick, took it as a sign that his days of forging steel were over, and his new forge would be in food and fire, not iron. The inn's current owner was Mira Hendrick, Barlo's great-granddaughter. A woman in her late forties with strong shoulders, crows' feet at her eyes, and a booming laugh that could stop an argument at thirty paces. She wore her graying hair in a thick braid down her back and always had a leather apron slung over her dress, regardless of whether she was cooking, cleaning, or pouring ale. Mira was the inn. Her presence filled it. She knew every creak in the floorboards, every chip in every mug. She had opinions about everyone and everything, and a sharp tongue to go with her sharper wit. But beneath her hard edge was a heart bigger than most barns. She took in orphans. Fed beggars without charge. And if a traveler walked in cold and coinless, Mira would find them a spot by the hearth and a bowl of stew before asking any questions. The food at the Shattered Anvil was legendary across three valleys. Stews so thick you could stand a spoon upright in them. Buttered rolls baked fresh each morning in the clay oven out back. Smoked river trout. Pickled vegetables in jars that lined the back shelf like colorful soldiers. And the infamous "Stonebrew," a dark, frothy ale that Mira claimed was strong enough to make a dwarf sing opera. Upstairs, a creaky staircase led to the guest quarters, seven rooms total, each with its own small stone hearth, woolen blankets, and sturdy beds. The walls were decorated with carvings and paintings donated by passing artists, landscapes, river scenes, the occasional portrait of someone important Mira couldn't name. Downstairs, behind the bar, was a small door that led to Mira's private quarters, as well as a supply cellar stacked with barrels, kegs, and salted meats. She kept the key to the cellar around her neck, and the joke among locals was that she'd trust someone with her life before she trusted them with her smoked sausages. But perhaps the most unique feature of the Shattered Anvil was its story wall.

At the far end of the taproom, between two tall lantern sconces, stood a bare patch of smooth, chiseled stone roughly ten feet wide and six high. Upon it were etched names, messages, poems, oaths, and short verses, left by travelers, soldiers, mages, and even a few nobles over the decades. Mira allowed anyone to carve into it, so long as the words were respectful and not foolish. Mira had the wall cleaned weekly and treated with special oil to keep it from weathering. When asked why she did it, she would shrug and say, "Stone remembers. Might as well help it speak." Stonebrook and the Shattered Anvil Inn, focusing on village life, the inn's cultural role, and its connection to the greater world.

In Stonebrook, the Shattered Anvil Inn was more than just a rest stop for weary travelers. It was a sanctuary, a courthouse, a theater, a storyteller's pulpit, and sometimes, a battlefield for stubborn arguments. Mira Hendrick often joked that it had survived five generations, two storms, a flooding river, and one unfortunate goat fire, and would outlast them all. Life in Stonebrook moved with the slow grace of an old river. Mornings began with the smell of fresh bread wafting from Mira's ovens, blending with the smoke of early hearth fires and the crisp sting of morning dew. Stonecutters would trudge off toward the quarries just past the eastern hillocks, their picks and hammers glinting in the rising light. Children walked to the chapel school near the southern glade, satchels bouncing, laughter echoing down narrow lanes of cobbled stone. The inn served as the daily heart of village rhythm. At midday, workers returned for Mira's barley soup or her fried rootcakes dipped in honey butter. In the evenings, the benches and stools filled with exhausted laborers, wandering traders, traveling peddlers, and the occasional bard or mage passing through on business unspoken.

On most nights, stories filled the taproom like smoke, soft and curling, catching in the rafters. Mira encouraged storytelling. She claimed that when people stopped telling stories, they started forgetting what they were fighting for. And so, travelers told of haunted rivers beyond the eastern cliffs. Elders whispered of a time before Malrik's rise. Some spoke of the Old Kingdom, of ruins swallowed by forest and magic. A few dared even speak of the Dark Expanse, and the things that moved in its shadows. Mira kept a small tin bell behind the bar. Whenever someone told a tale worth remembering, she rang it once, clear and sharp. That sound became known as the "Anvil's Echo," and it was considered a mark of pride to earn one. Occasionally, riders would gallop in from the west, bearing news of royal decrees or border skirmishes. Mira would hang the parchment beside the bar and pour an extra round on the house. But even then, the inn remained a sanctuary. A place untouched, if only briefly, by the claws of politics and war.

One winter, a knight came wounded to the village, claiming to have escaped one of Malrik's black-armored legions. Mira nursed him back to health herself, never asking his name. When he left, he carved only this into the story wall: "In fire, I was forged. In stone, I was saved."

Beyond the stone walls of the village and the curling path of the Stonebrook River, the land opened into fields of dry yellow grass and thyme scrub. The soil here was hard, not easily tilled, and so most villagers raised goats or traded quarried stone for grain. To the south rose a gentle hill called Bellman's Rise, where old oaks grew, and ravens nested in the hollow limbs. Eastward lay the

Stonecutters' Reach, a series of terraced quarries cut into the sides of the Eroded Hills. These were ancient scars in the earth, gray, sloped, echoing with the clinks of chisels and the rumble of stone carts. It was said the oldest quarry, Whisper's Pit, had reached low enough to disturb veins of silver and deepstone. Rumors claimed strange dreams haunted any man who stayed too long beneath the surface. North of the village lay a forgotten path, now little more than a game trail, that once led to a ruined watchtower from the Old Kingdom. Overgrown and half-collapsed, only a few children ever dared to explore it, and even they spoke of strange lights within. To the west, across the Stonebrook bridge, the land fell into dense woodland and the mists of the Verdant Pines, where the trees whispered too loudly and the moss grew thick enough to swallow footprints. Despite the dangers beyond, Stonebrook endured. Not because of fortifications, or armies, or some arcane protection, but because of its people. And because of places like the Shattered Anvil, where people found shelter and memory.

Rayner, Cole, Quinn, and Tristan approached just after dusk. Smoke drifted lazily from chimneys. Lanterns glowed amber behind shutters. A woman drew water from a well without glancing toward them, but Tristan's voice was tight.

"Something's wrong."

Rayner gripped the hilt of his sword. "We've seen 'wrong' before."

"This is quieter." Cole muttered, "It's emptier. Too quiet. No laughter. No dogs. No shouting. No life."

The group passed through the front gates and the hair on Rayner's arms stood on end. They were being watched. Not from above. From below. They reached the village square and found the elder, an old man with eyes ringed in gray and fingers that trembled when he spoke.

"You should leave," he warned them. "This place is not safe for your kind."

Rayner raised an eyebrow. "Our kind?"

The elder leaned close. "You carry magic. You carry purpose. That is the scent the earth now follows."

Cole stiffened. "You've seen something."

The elder's voice dropped to a whisper. "Not seen. Felt. The ground moves. Children vanish. Our strongest men go missing during the night, their beds left cold. Something crawls through the old tunnels beneath the village. Something called by your enemy."

Rayner's jaw clenched. "Thornjaw."

They took a room in the old tavern, though none of them expected to sleep. Quinn reinforced the doors. Tristan mapped out the rooftops and wells. Cole set magical wards around the foundation stones. Rayner sat with his back to the wall, sword across his lap.

"If he comes tonight," he said, "we kill him."

Cole didn't disagree. "But he doesn't come like the others. He doesn't fly or charge. He burrows. He stalks."

"Then we smoke him out," said Quinn.

Tristan nodded. "Or trap him above ground."

"Either way," Rayner said, "we don't run this time."

The village fell into that eerie stillness that only exists in the hours before violence. A fog rolled in from the hills. Dogs, those that remained, whined under porches. The wind carried the scent of wet stone. Then it began. A rumble. Soft at first. Then stronger. The ground beneath the tavern trembled. Dust fell from the rafters. Glass clinked. Cole stood suddenly.

"He's here."

The floorboards buckled.

Rayner shouted, "Out, now!"

They dove through the door just as a section of the floor exploded upward stone and wood shattering as a monstrous form burst through from below. What once was a man had been remade into something grotesque. His limbs were twisted with sinew and root. His lower body resembled the body of a centipede, covered in plated bone. His skin was leprous, patched with moss and rot. His mouth stretched wider than a man's should, filled with jagged, blackened teeth. He screamed and the air went cold. Villagers screamed and scattered.

Rayner drew his sword, "Face me!"

Thornjaw lunged not toward Rayner, but toward Cole. Tristan fired a bolt that struck Thornjaw's back, but the beast barely flinched.

"Quinn, cut him off!"

Quinn charged, hammer crashing against Thornjaw's side. Bone cracked, but Thornjaw's tail snapped and sent Quinn flying into a cart of barrels. Rayner dashed forward, blade flashing. He cut deep across Thornjaw's chest and black fluid hissed from the wound. Still the creature fought on. Cole raised his staff. His voice echoed with ancient words. A ring of fire erupted around the square, forcing Thornjaw inward. The beast hissed, enraged. Rayner and Tristan struck in tandem sword and bolt, steel and precision. The crossbow bolt hit one of Thornjaw's many legs, pinning it momentarily to the earth. Rayner drove his sword into the creature's shoulder, but Thornjaw twisted and slammed him to the ground with a blow from his gnarled limb. Rayner gasped. Pain lanced through his ribs. Quinn returned then bleeding, bruised, but roaring. He raised his hammer and brought it down with everything he had on Thornjaw's head. The sound cracked like thunder. The beast staggered. Rayner rolled to his feet, blade raised. Cole stepped forward, his staff burning now with white flame.

"For the Hollow Flame," he whispered and unleashed a blast of focused fire directly into Thornjaw's gaping mouth.

The creature screamed and began to burn from the inside out. It collapsed, convulsing, and then lay still smoke curling from its ruinous form. The fog lifted. The villagers emerged slowly, wide-eyed, trembling.

The elder approached, his voice barely more than breath. "You've saved us."

"No," said Rayner, still watching the smoldering corpse.

"We survived."

Quinn sat against the well, clutching his ribs. Tristan cleaned his crossbow with shaking hands. Cole stared into the fire.

"We're being hunted," he said. "Like prey, and they're sending stronger ones now."

Rayner nodded. "Then we'll get stronger too."

CHAPTER 13

The mountain path narrowed as the sun dipped low, casting long shadows that spilled over jagged rocks and twisted pine. The wind howled down the slope, carrying with it the scent of snow and stone, old as the world itself. Rayner led the group, his sword strapped to his back, cloak snapping in the chill. Cole followed close, his staff now etched with newer sigils from their last encounter with the forest wraiths. Quinn trudged behind them with the slow, deliberate steps of a man bearing a war hammer twice the weight of reason, while Tristan, ever nimble, kept eyes and ears sharp for trouble. They were four days into the Greyspike Mountains, seeking a hidden pass said to lead into the Old Kingdom. The object they needed, the ancient key to Malrik's defeat, was locked deep within its ruined castle, veiled in mystery and guarded by more than mere stone. Rayner paused on a ledge overlooking a narrow ravine. The wind dropped, and all sound with it. He raised a hand. The others stopped.

"You hear that?" Rayner asked.

Tristan tilted his head, his crossbow ready. "Nothing."

"Exactly." Rayner whispered.

Cole stepped forward, brows furrowed. "Too quiet."

Then the ground rumbled. It was faint, like the heartbeat of the mountain. But growing. Rayner braced himself as a cluster of loose pebbles tumbled past their boots and vanished into the abyss. A sharp whistle split the air. Rayner turned, too late. The ledge beneath them gave way. With a deafening crack, the rock crumbled. Quinn roared as the ground dropped from beneath him. They fell, not far, but violently, into a hidden crevice, landing in a tangle of limbs and curses on a sloped tunnel of ice and rock. The cold scraped their skin as they slid deeper, the light behind them fading until only darkness remained. Then, abruptly, the tunnel leveled. Rayner landed in a roll and came up with his sword drawn. The others staggered to their feet, coughing and blinking in the faint blue glow of Cole's magic.

A long, stone corridor stretched ahead, clearly carved, too clean, too straight. The air smelled of earth, iron, and old fires. Along the walls, runes flickered to life in response to the mage's presence.

"This isn't natural," Tristan said quietly, lowering his crossbow.

"No," Cole agreed.

"It's dwarven." Rayner stepped forward.

"We've stumbled into a stronghold." "Or a tomb," Quinn muttered, inspecting the stonework with a surprising familiarity. "The craftsmanship is old. Very old. Pre-Collapse."

"Then let's hope they're friendly," Tristan said, though his hand didn't leave his weapon.

As they moved deeper, the passage opened into a vast underground hall, lined with pillars carved in the likeness of bearded warriors bearing axes and shields. Dust hung in the air like mist. On the far end stood a great stone gate, sealed and covered in script.

Rayner approached it, then stopped. A faint clicking echoed through the hall.

"Form up," he ordered.

From the shadows, a dozen figures emerged, short, broad, and armored in overlapping plates of bronze and black iron. Their eyes gleamed like gems in the dimness. Dwarves. The Dwarves of Eldara claim their birthright from the Heartfire, the molten core of the world. According to their own myths, preserved in carved stone annals beneath the mountains, the first dwarves were forged by

139

Thragmun Flamebeard, a divine smith who struck sparks from the bedrock itself, forming the ancestors of their race from molten iron, gold, and obsidian cooled by mountain wind. Dwarves average between 4.5 to 5 feet tall, with broad shoulders and limbs like compact tree trunks. Their skin ranges from stone-brown to deep ash-grey. Most have thick hair and beards, often intricately braided and adorned with rings, clasps, or runes.

They are hardy, enduring cold, heat, and physical hardship with little complaint. Their lifespan stretches 250 to 300 years, with many not considered elders until their second century.

Dwarves value craft, memory, and loyalty. Every tool, weapon, or building they create is part of a lineage, with crafts signed by rune and marked in clan record. They remember debts, betrayals, and oaths for generations. Dwarves do not draw upon the Weave like mages do. Instead, their magic is embedded into the world itself, Rune Magic and Forgecraft, passed down from smith to apprentice. Runes are their oldest and most sacred art. Carved into metal, stone, or even bone, runes bind magic to material, granting weapons strength, armor resilience, and doorways protection. The lead dwarf stepped forward, helmet under one arm, a braided beard falling to his belt. His voice, when he spoke, was gravel and thunder.

"You walk unbidden in Khaz-Grim's bones. Speak your names, or perish in silence."

Rayner lowered his blade, but not fully. "I am Rayner of Valebrook. These are my companions, Cole, mage of the Whispering Woodlands; Quinn of Ashbrook; and Tristan of the Ashbrook. We mean no harm. The mountain… brought us here."

The dwarf squinted at Quinn. "Of the Ashbrook, you say?"

Quinn nodded. "My grandfather served beside the Ironborn clans during the Siege of Hollowdeep."

The dwarf grunted. "Then your blood may speak for you."

Cole stepped forward, staff glowing faintly. "We seek passage through the mountains to the Old Kingdom. The pass is hidden. Perhaps even lost. But we were told the dwarves might know its path."

A murmur passed through the dwarves. The lead dwarf regarded them for a long moment, then turned to his kin and barked a command in their language, deep, consonant-heavy, and full of age.

"Follow, if you value truth," he said.

They were led through twisting halls deeper into the mountain, past ancient forges, collapsed mines, and a bridge that spanned a subterranean chasm filled with glowing crystal. The dwarves said little, but the lookouts posted along every passage told the companions that this stronghold, though buried, was far from abandoned. Finally, they arrived at a chamber where a great anvil sat atop a dais. A brazier burned beside it, though no one had tended it. A carved throne stood at the back, upon which sat a dwarf even older than the rest, beard silver as moonlight, eyes cloudy but unblinking. He regarded the newcomers with a gaze like stone.

"Why do surface folk seek what lies buried?" he asked.

Rayner stepped forward. "Because darkness rises above. Malrik, the Black Legion's commander, hunts an object hidden in the Old Kingdom, one that may end the war."

The old dwarf said nothing.

Cole added, "We believe it is a relic forged by your kind. Something ancient. Sacred."

That earned a flicker of interest. "Many relics were forged. Most were lost. Others... buried with purpose."

Rayner met the dwarf's eyes. "Then we ask not for theft, but for guidance. Help us stop him. And the world will not forget the dwarves stood with us."

A long silence passed. Then the elder nodded once.

"You may have the path. But know this: the mountain does not forget its debts."

He clapped his hands once, and a stone door behind him rumbled open. The Deep Road lay beyond. The dwarves allowed the party to rest in a side chamber, where they were given food, tough bread, root stew, and a thick drink that left even Quinn blinking. The walls were covered in carvings that told the history of Khaz-Grim, its founding, its battles, its fall. Later, as they made their way down the Deep Road, their dwarf guide, a younger warrior named Solem, walked beside Rayner.

"Your fight," Solem said, "is ours, in part. Malrik's armies broke into the lower tunnels of Mount Faldor last winter. Took a hundred lives before we sealed the breach."

"Then you know his strength," Rayner said.

Solem nodded grimly. "Aye. And his cunning."

They descended into a lower passage where the air grew colder, the walls damp with old water and lichen. Strange shapes lined the walls, reliefs of eyes, mouths, and beasts with too many limbs. Cole paused.

"This wasn't built by dwarves."

"No," Solem said. "It was carved long ago. Before even our kind set foot in these halls."

Rayner frowned. "Then what lies ahead?" "Trial."

As if summoned by the word, the ground shook. A great roar echoed down the tunnel. From the dark ahead, a massive form emerged, a guardian wrought from stone and fire, shaped like a bear with glowing runes along its flanks. Its eyes burned orange, and its breath came in puffs of steam. Solem backed away.

"You must face it."

Rayner stepped forward, sword drawn. "Then we stand together."

The bear charged. The battle was fierce, a test not only of strength, but coordination. Quinn moved first, striking the beast's flank with a two-handed blow that sent a shockwave through the air. The bear reared back, but not before swinging a massive paw that clipped Quinn's shoulder, sending him crashing into the wall. Rayner darted in, his blade flashing as he slashed at the creature's legs, drawing sparks but little blood, if it had any. Tristan circled, firing a bolt into its eye, which exploded in a burst of molten rock. Cole chanted from the back, his staff erupting with light as he sent arcs of magic into the bear's chest, charring stone and burning away runes. Still, the guardian fought, relentless and ancient. Rayner finally saw the pattern: the runes on its chest pulsed in rhythm, a heartbeat. He timed his strike, shouted to Cole.

"Now!"

Cole sent a beam of raw energy at the center of the beast's chest just as Rayner drove his sword in from the opposite side. The bear froze, shuddered, and with a rumble, collapsed into rubble. The mountain was still again. Solem stepped forward, visibly impressed.

"You have the mountain's blessing." Solem said.

At the tunnel's end stood a gate, ancient, massive, and silent. It bore the seal of the Old Kingdom and the mark of the dwarves. Cole stepped forward, hands raised.

"It's sealed with a blood key."

Solem unsheathed a small dagger and offered it to Rayner.

"You carry the legacy of men. If the mountain accepts you, it will open."

Rayner hesitated, then took the blade and cut his palm, pressing it to the stone. For a moment nothing. Then the gate glowed faintly, and the stone pulled back with a grinding moan, revealing the first rays of morning spilling through the far exit. They had passed through. As the companions stepped into the sunlight, Rayner looked back once. Solem stood in the shadows, watching.

"You walk the path of kings," the dwarf said. "Do not stumble. Or we all fall with you."

Rayner nodded once, then turned forward, toward the ruins of the Old Kingdom, where destiny awaited. Rayner, Cole, Quinn, and Tristan have passed through the dwarven gate onto the road to Valebrook.

The road to the Valebrook was cloaked in mist and silence. Trees lined the broken cobblestone path like ancient sentinels, their branches skeletal against the twilight sky. Rayner went at the head of the party, his hand never far from the hilt of his sword. Cole followed close behind, a flicker of arcane light pulsing faintly from the crystal embedded in his staff. Quinn and Tristan went side by side, the former with his massive hammer strapped to his back and the latter adjusting the scope on his crossbow every few minutes.

They walked until the village lights glimmered through the trees. A crooked sign creaked in the wind The Golden Chalice. Situated just off the grand marble promenade that leads to the castle gates, The Golden Chalice gleams with quiet nobility. Unlike the timbered inns of the outer villages, the Chalice is built of polished stone and rosewood. Ivy climbs its sun-warmed facade, carefully trimmed into the shape of royal sigils, eagles, flames, and a flowering crown. An ornate wrought-iron sign bearing a gilded goblet swing from a silver bracket. The goblet overflows with etched stars and vines, a symbol of hospitality, wealth, and ancient knowledge. Locals whisper that the inn was once a noble's manor house during King Reynard's grandfather's reign. It's three stories high with slate-blue rooftops, flowering window boxes, and a covered balcony on the second floor where musicians often play for passersby. Gold-inlaid lanterns line the steps and arch over the doorway, lighting it every night with a soft celestial glow, mage-light fueled by the city's Weave lanterns.

The inside of the Golden Chalice is opulent, but not gaudy. The floors are polished oak with rugs imported from Duskvale. The entry hall features a full mural of Valebrook's skyline and the river that loops beneath the castle. Guests are welcomed by a carved wood panel displaying a quote from King Aldren the Wise: "Let every cup shared beneath this roof be a peace forged in the flame of kinship." To the left, a grand dining room stretches toward a massive hearth flanked by two lion statues, carved from river-stone and enchanted to purr contentedly when the fire is well-fed. Tables of polished yew and velvet-backed chairs sit beneath chandeliers made of hanging quartz and mageglass that flickers with color as if responding to music. To the right is the taproom, a cozier, more informal space for travelers, soldiers, bards, and mages to mingle. The walls are filled with portraits of past kings, innkeepers, and even mages who once stayed during times of war or celebration. A spiral staircase near the back leads to twenty private guest rooms, each one named after a constellation and featuring velvet linens, stained glass windows, and bronze basins filled with steaming lavender water upon check-in.

Meriel Carvane is unlike any innkeeper in the realm. A once-disgraced noblewoman from the eastern isles, she arrived in Valebrook with little more than a coat of arms and a debt to the crown. Over the decades, she rebuilt her name not through war or court politics, but through refined hospitality. With silver-streaked hair coiled in braids and eyes sharp as falcon steel, Meriel rules the Chalice with quiet dignity. She wears black velvet gowns, a silver ring bearing her family crest, and always carries a ledger bound in dragonhide, recording every guest of interest. She speaks in measured tones, never raises her voice, and wields silence as a weapon. But behind that poise is a fierce loyalty to the city, and a sharp tongue for fools who disrespect her staff. It's rumored she once turned away a prince for poor manners and a stained doublet.

The Golden Chalice is the bridge between crown and commoner. If the castle is the heart of Valebrook, the Chalice is the soul. It offers refuge to mages who've come to teach, warriors with wounds that need quiet, and heirs with questions too heavy for court. It is where: Sir Worric and King Reynard once plotted the resistance against Malrik's growing power. Azor once performed a private ritual, blending tea and memory, to see echoes of what was to come.

Inside the inn, warmth and noise clashed with the chill outside. A hearth fire crackled, casting flickering light on old wooden beams. Locals nursed their mugs and looked up as the four travelers entered. Rayner pushed back his hood.

"We need rooms, and ale."

The innkeeper, a plump woman with a tired face and kind eyes, nodded. "Four silvers for the night, and the drinks on the house if you've got news."

Tristan flipped her five. "We've got questions."

"Seems fair."

She poured dark ale into four mugs and motioned them to a corner table. The room grew quiet as the villagers leaned in to listen.

"We're headed for the castle," Cole said. "We're looking for something. Something that belonged to the Old King."

The innkeeper paled slightly. "Then you're not the first. Malrik's men came last week, black armor, cruel eyes. They're tearing the place apart, and they don't ask nicely. You'd do well to turn around."

"Can't," Rayner replied. "We need what's in there."

An old man near the fire grunted. "If you're lookin' for what I think you are, you'll find more than steel waiting for you in that ruin. Magic guards the heart of the castle still, and the dead don't rest easy."

The innkeeper lowered her voice. "They say the King forged a relic in secret a weapon of light to counter darkness. Malrik feared it, even as a young man. Some say it's still hidden in the throne chamber, beneath the stones."

Quinn leaned in. "Why didn't Malrik take it when he conquered?"

"He tried," said the old man. "But the castle closed itself to him. Traps. Ghosts. Walls that shift. The King's Mage was a master of enchantments. Only those who are worthy will find the weapon."

Rayner drained his mug. "Then we'll be the ones."

That night, they took turns sleeping. Cole meditated in the corner, murmuring to the flickering candlelight. Rayner stared into the hearth, haunted by dreams of fire and blood. Malrik's shadow loomed over his thoughts like a storm cloud. By dawn, they rode to the foot of the castle.

The sunlight that greeted them was thin and cold, as if the very land mourned what once stood here. Beyond the gate lay the Old Kingdom or what remained of it. Stone ruins stretched across a frost-laced valley, surrounded by the broken ribs of fallen towers and crumbling walls. Moss covered the bones of the past. A collapsed citadel stood at the center, its spires shattered and leaning, but unmistakably regal even in ruin. Rayner stepped forward, his boots crunching over gravel and snow. The others followed in silence, each feeling the weight of history pressing down on them like a mantle.

"We're walking through legend," Cole said quietly.

Quinn nodded. "Can feel it in my gut. Like the whole place is watching."

Tristan paused beside a toppled statue, a knight with wings carved into his armor. The head had broken off, lying nearby in the grass.

"Whatever happened here… it wasn't just time that brought this down."

Rayner knelt by the base of the statue and brushed away dust. A single word remained etched into the stone: "Drachen."

Cole inhaled sharply. "That was the name of the last royal guardian. The blade-ward of the king."

Rayner stood. "Then we're close."

They made their way through what had once been the castle courtyard. The wind carried faint whispers, not voices, but echoes, like memory trapped in the stone. Inside the keep, they found the remnants of the royal hall. A grand staircase rose up toward collapsed balconies, and black banners hung in tatters from the rafters. Dust motes danced in the shafts of light pouring through the holes in the roof.

Cole's staff pulsed. "The relic is here."

"Where?" Rayner asked.

The mage closed his eyes. "Below."

They descended into the crypt through a spiraling stair behind the throne, the air growing colder with every step. The torches along the wall lit themselves as they passed, as if the place still remembered its purpose. At the base, they found a sealed chamber. A heavy iron door stood before them, untouched for centuries. Carved into its face was the image of a sword plunged into a crown, surrounded by fire. Rayner stepped forward, hand on the hilt of his blade.

"Let me."

He pushed the door, and it opened without a sound. Inside was a circular chamber. At the center, atop a stone pedestal, rested a long black case bound in silver filigree. Around it was statues, six in total, knights in different armor, their eyes downcast as if mourning. Rayner approached and unlatched the case. Inside lay a sword. It was unlike any he had seen, long, straight, forged of silver-steel with veins of gold, and etched with runes along the blade. The hilt bore the mark of the First King; a lion crowned in flame. Cole whispered,

"That's it." "The King blade," Quinn murmured.

Rayner reached out and gripped the hilt. It was cold, then warm. His heart raced. Visions flashed through his mind, battles fought on ancient fields, a king standing against a monstrous host, a blade raised in defiance. When he opened his eyes again, the sword glowed faintly in his hand. Cole stepped forward.

"The blade was bound to the royal line. Only a rightful heir could awaken it."

Rayner looked down at the weapon. "...What are you saying?"

"You have royal blood," Cole said. "You always have."

The silence that followed was heavy. Quinn let out a breath. "Well. That explains a few things."

Before Rayner could respond, a deep horn echoed across the valley. A second blast followed, closer. Then a third, behind them.

Tristan turned toward the stair. "We're not alone."

They raced back through the crypt, sword in hand, emerging into the great hall just as black-armored soldiers poured through the castle's front gate. The Black Legion had found them. The four companions backed into the hall, facing the oncoming threat.

Malrik's troops were unlike regular soldiers, these were bred for war, their eyes hollow, their movements too precise. A dozen of them filed in, and behind them came a man clad in armor darker than night. His face was hidden behind a helm carved like a skull.

"The sword," he said. "Hand it over, and I will grant you a swift death."

Rayner stepped forward, blade in hand, defiance in his voice. "Come take it."

The warrior raised a hand, and the legion charged. The fight was brutal. Quinn met them head-on, swinging his hammer with the fury of a siege engine, breaking shields and helmets in bone-crushing arcs. Tristan darted between pillars, loosing bolts with deadly precision. Cole stood behind them, summoning shields of light and fire that danced across the battlefield. Rayner clashed with the skull-helmed warrior. Their blades met in a flash of sparks, ancient magic singing in steel. The King blade pulsed in Rayner's grip, guiding his hand.

"Who are you?" Rayner demanded.

The warrior answered with a backhand strike that sent him skidding across the hall floor.

"I am Drachen."

Rayner froze. "What...?"

Cole's voice rang out. "He's been bound! That's not a man, it's a revenant! A guardian turned against his oath!"

The skull helm turned toward Cole. "I serve the true king now. Malrik has risen, and he will rule."

Rayner stood, rage burning in his chest. "Then I'll free you from his chains."

They fought again, harder, faster. This time, Rayner held nothing back. The King blade sang, striking runed armor, carving through wards, deflecting the cursed weapon Drachen wielded.

150

Finally, with a cry, Rayner swept low and drove the blade up through the revenant's chest. Drachen staggered, dropping his sword. His eyes flickered, for just a moment, and he whispered,

"Thank you…"

Then the light faded from them, and he collapsed to the floor. The remaining legionnaires fell with him, as if their will had been tied to his. Silence returned. Rayner stood in the center of the ruined hall, chest heaving, sword dripping dark ichor. His friends gathered around him, bloodied but alive.

"We have what we came for," Cole said.

Rayner nodded, his voice hoarse. "Then let's finish what we started."

They made camp in the castle that night. Though ruined, the walls still offered shelter from the wind. A fire crackled in a hearth that hadn't been lit in centuries. The shadows danced on the walls as they sat in silence, each lost in their own thoughts.

Tristan broke it first. "So. You're a king now?"

Rayner looked up. "I don't know what I am."

"A man with a sword that glows when he touches it," Quinn said.

"And an army of the dead trying to kill him." Cole smiled faintly. "Sounds like royalty to me."

Rayner sighed, looking down at the King blade. "I never wanted a crown. I just wanted to protect my people."

"That," said Cole, "is why you deserve it."

Outside, the mountain winds howled, but they were warm, now. As if the land itself recognized the change. Cole stood and began to draw sigils around the fire, protective wards.

"Malrik will know we have the blade. He'll move fast."

"We'll move faster," Rayner said.

Quinn cracked his knuckles.

Rayner rose, holding the sword aloft. Its light bathed the chamber in silver fire. "The age of darkness ends now."

The Sword of King Reynard, also called: Virellian, King Reynard's Flame, The Last Flame. Forged in the First Age by the mage-smiths of Eldwyre, Virellian was not made in fire alone, but in memory and sacrifice. It is the only weapon known to have been woven directly into the Aetheric Weave itself. The sword was gifted to King Reynard by Azor, who bound it with an oath to protect the realm, not conquer it. Inscription (in Vaetraan). Engraved along the fuller in Aetheric Tongue: "Solas Tharan Mira Vorr or "Let light endure beyond pain, and steel stand for the forgotten."

CHAPTER 14

The sword still glowed in Rayner's hand when the second wave of Malrik's legion arrived. From the eastern tower, a horn blasted a deep, hungry sound that rattled the bones of the castle. Shadows spilled into the broken throne room as dozens of soldiers in black armor swarmed through shattered archways and crumbling stairwells.

"We're out of time!" Cole shouted, hurling a bolt of searing flame down the hall.

It lit the corridor in brilliant orange, scattering the front line of Malrik's men. Quinn planted his hammer into the stone floor.

"That sword better be worth the trouble, Ray."

"It is," Rayner said, eyes locked on the soldiers closing in.

The blade of the Old King shimmered with a golden light that repelled the creeping darkness, but even its brilliance couldn't hold off a legion alone. Tristan lost an arrow from the far balcony, dropping a soldier before he could raise a horn.

"They'll keep coming. No end to them. We need another way out." Tristen shouted.

Rayner pointed to a shattered arch at the far end of the throne room.

"That way leads to the catacombs. There's an old tunnel beneath the king's chapel. It might take us beyond the inner wall."

Cole's face hardened. "Then move. I'll hold them."

Rayner grabbed his shoulder. "Together."

They fled through the archway, boots thudding against ancient stone. Behind them, the throne room trembled as Malrik's soldiers poured in, blades drawn, eyes cold with unnatural purpose. Down twisting stairs they ran, deeper into the bowels of the castle, where torchlight died and the walls grew damp with centuries of silence. Here, the dust of kings and priests rested in long-forgotten crypts. Bones lay undisturbed beneath shattered murals and collapsed statues. The echo of their footsteps stirred whispers that had no mouths. They passed a sealed tomb. On its face: Aelan, Son of the Flame. Rest eternal.

"I think we're trespassing," Quinn muttered.

"Better a ghost's wrath than a soldier's sword," Cole replied.

At last, they reached a gate of rusted iron. Rayner shoved his shoulder against it. It groaned, splintered, then collapsed outward into a mossy tunnel, lined with root-covered stone. The air stank of water and rot but it was free of footsteps. They crawled through it until light greeted them ahead. The tunnel ended at a bramble covered slope overlooking a gorge. Below, a river raged wide, dark, and swollen with mountain melt. Across the water, nestled between trees and mist, lay a village: Elrowen.

Elrowen huddled within the outer skirts of the Moonshade Forest, Elrowen is a quiet, mist-kissed village where twilight seems to linger longer, and the trees whisper names no one has spoken in generations. It is a place both enchanting and somber, known across the region for its moonlit glades, silver-leafed trees, and a deep-rooted tradition of lore, herbalism, and song. Elrowen is not large, fewer than two hundred villagers live there, but it is one of the oldest settlements in Eldara, built atop ruins said to predate even King Reynard's ancestors. Some say it was once an elven outpost. Others believe it rests over a ley line where the Weave runs closest to the surface.

Elrowen is surrounded on three sides by ancient forest, where tall silverbark trees stretch like cathedral spires and faint blue fungi glow at night. A narrow river, called the Lanthel Stream, cuts through the village, feeding the Mirepond, a shallow, fog-laced pool on the village's eastern edge. Houses are mostly timber and stone, their rooftops draped with moss or carved in soft peaks. Many buildings feature small shrines carved into their doorposts, offerings to old forest spirits, not gods. The village square is modest, with a sunken firepit surrounded by carved benches and windchimes made from antler, bone, and polished glass. Instead of an inn, Elrowen's travelers sleep in the Moon Hall, a communal structure open to any who seek safe rest, as long as they respect the silence.

Elrowen holds to old ways, its people value stillness, dreams, and memory. Every full moon, the villagers light floating candles and send them down the Lanthel Stream. It's a tradition known as the Night Drift, where people whisper wishes to the candles, hoping the water carries them to the stars. Children are taught not to speak the names of the dead aloud after the sun has set, lest their spirits mistake it as a call to return. Instead, names are sung into the wind, or carved into the bark of memorial trees.

Smoke rose from chimneys. Lights flickered in windows. Freedom, but behind them, the horn sounded again closer now. Rayner turned. Black figures appeared at the edge of the tunnel. Arrows whistled. One scraped Tristan's shoulder, another grazed Quinn's arm.

"They're too close!" Cole shouted.

Rayner scanned the riverbank. "We swim."

Tristan's eyes widened. "That current will kill us."

Rayner looked down at the glowing sword in his hand. "Or we die here. Move!"

They raced down the slope, crashing through thickets, leaping over roots and rocks as arrows chased them like angry wasps. One struck the ground beside Cole's boot. The river roared like a beast. Rayner plunged in first. The cold stole his breath, wrapped around his limbs like chains. The current ripped at him, dragged him side-ways, slammed him into a jagged rock. He held the sword above water, its light dimming in the mist.

Behind him, Quinn bellowed as he jumped. Cole followed, shouting a spell to heat his skin as he hit the water. Tristan came last, already bleeding from the arrow wound in his shoulder. The legion reached the shore too late. Arrows hissed into the water but missed. Rayner kicked, clawed forward, keeping his head above the surface. Beside him, Quinn roared with every stroke, swimming like a warhorse. Cole drifted fast, riding the current with magical bursts. Tristan was falling behind.

"Tristan!" Rayner shouted.

A dark shape loomed behind the archer a sharp current pulling him toward a cluster of rocks. Rayner turned, ignoring the pain in his arms, and paddled hard. The sword in his hand began to hum, then glow brighter, as if sensing death near. He reached Tristan, grabbed his collar, and kicked away from the rocks just as they passed them, missing the stone by inches.

Tristan gasped, choking, but alive. "I owe you," he coughed.

"Buy me an ale in Elrowen," Rayner growled.

They crashed against the far bank, sprawling into mud and moss. Cole pulled himself onto shore, panting.

"I'll take freezing water over being skewered." Quinn col-lapsed on his back. "Remind me never to trust your escape plans again."

Rayner stood, sword still gleaming. "But we're alive."

Behind them, across the river, the black-armored soldiers lined the bank, watching. One raised a horn but didn't blow it. They knew the current wouldn't let them cross easily. For now, the four were safe. Elrowen was quiet. A village of woodcutters and goat herders, nestled deep in the folds of forest and fog. The people stared as the four dripping, wounded travelers approached from the trees covered in river muck, blood, and ash.

An old woman gasped. "You came from the castle."

A boy pointed at the sword in Rayner's hand. "That's... that's the light!"

A dozen voices began whispering at once. They were taken to the hearth of the town's hall, where the village elder, a gray-bearded man named Eldric, offered them blankets and warm broth.

"You crossed the River of Ghosts," Eldric said, awe in his voice. "Many think it cursed."

Rayner stared into the flames. "It's not ghosts we fear."

Cole unrolled a cloth and began tending to Tristan's wound from the arrow. "Malrik's soldiers are in the castle. They'll come this way."

"Then we'll hide you," Eldric said. "No one who carries the Old King's light will be turned away in Elrowen."

Rayner's grip tightened on the sword. "We need a healer, and a way to the mountains."

Eldric nodded slowly. "There's a path. A forgotten road used by smugglers, through the hollow hills, but the road is dangerous, and not marked on any map."

"Nothing's ever simple," Quinn muttered.

The village gave them shelter for the night. While the others slept, Rayner sat outside beneath the stars, sword across his knees. The blade pulsed softly, like a heartbeat. Cole joined him.

"You feel it too?" the Cole asked.

Rayner nodded. "It's guiding me. Pulling me somewhere."

"Toward Malrik?" Cole looked east. "Then we follow it."

They left Elrowen at first light, with the village elder's blessing and packs full of food and poultices. The air was crisp. Mist drifted between trees. Birds called from high branches, and somewhere far off, the river still roared. They followed a narrow trail through the woods, past stone markers half-buried in moss. The land grew wilder, older. Trees twisted into shapes that didn't follow natural law. Cole muttered protective wards under his breath. By midday, they reached a ridge overlooking a series of caves carved into a cliffside.

"This is the start of the hollow hills," Eldric had warned. "Things live in those caves that the world forgot."

Rayner took a breath. "Then let's not wake them."

They pressed on wounded, hunted, but unbroken. The sword of the Old King glowed brighter with every step.

CHAPTER 15

The boy who would become Malrik was not born of shadow, but of dust and forgotten names. Long before his name drew whispers from frightened lips, he was Marek Valen, third son of a minor noble in the eastern reaches of the Old Kingdom. His house had no wealth, no land worth fighting over, and no future beyond the thin illusion of courtly courtesy. From the start, Marek was different. Quiet. Observant. While his brothers practiced with blades or charmed the daughters of greater lords, Marek wandered the edges of the estate, always watching. Always listening. He spoke often with the servants, the woodsmen, even the old crone who lived in the swamp beyond the fields. The others mocked him. They stopped mocking him when his father died. A sickness swept through House Valen. One by one, they succumbed, first his mother, then his brothers. Only Marek remained untouched. He never wept. The estate passed to distant cousins, and Marek was cast out. They gave him a horse, a pouch of coin, and a sneering farewell. He rode east, into the mountains, where no maps dared go.

For three years, Marek lived in isolation. He took refuge in the ruins of Serrow's Hollow, a collapsed monastery near the bloodwood trees that locals believed cursed. He hunted by bow, studied old scrolls scavenged from the ruin, and lit fires beneath the moons, whispering names no one had spoken in centuries. One night, a traveler came. Old, hunched, blind in one eye, he introduced himself as Calreg the Binder, though it was doubtful the name was real. Calreg laughed at Marek's spells.

"You twist your tongue like a drunk mimicking priests," he rasped. "But you have intent. That's what blood magic needs."

Marek followed him into the catacombs beneath the hollow. There, Calreg revealed the truth: the Old Kingdom had once used blood magic, not for power, but for knowledge, to pierce the Veil between worlds and bind themselves to truth itself. The practice was outlawed when its darker uses were revealed, control, possession, undeath.

"Truth bends easily when flesh feeds the spell," Calreg said.

Under the old man's tutelage, Marek learned the First Binding: pain for insight. He offered drops of blood to the bone etched bowl and asked questions of the spirits that lingered between realms. They whispered back. He learned the Second Binding: life for strength. A fox. A hawk. A deer. With each offering, Marek grew stronger. His eyes sharpened. His voice took on a weight that bent the air around it. Calreg warned him:

"Third Binding is the path of no return. That is where your soul becomes clay."

Marek had already chosen. The prisoner was a brigand, dragged from the forest by a patrol and offered to the magistrate of Karron's Post. Marek posed as a scholar; said he needed a subject for "anatomical study." They handed the man over gladly. In the Hollow, Marek drew the circle, carved the sigils into bone, and slit the brigand's throat under a waxing moon. The power that came was no trickle. It was a storm. Visions. Voices. Strength beyond reason. He saw through the eyes of a crow and spoke a word that split a boulder. He carved the Third Binding into his own flesh, a spiral of jagged runes down his spine, and became more than human. Calreg fled that night.

"You've stepped into the dark," he said. "It will not let go."

Years passed. The Old King grew old. Whispers of civil unrest stirred in the south, banditry, cults, rogue sorcery. Marek, now calling himself Malrik, walked among them in secret. He did not conquer by sword. He conquered by fear. He raised the first of his blood-bound, men and women bound to his will through ritual. With their blood in his goblet, he could hear their thoughts, see through their eyes, control their limbs. They became his spies, his assassins, his army. One night, in the fortress of Draymere, he stood before a rebel lord who dared oppose him. The man laughed, until Malrik spoke his daughter's name and made her walk into the fire, eyes blank and mouth silent. The fortress surrendered without a fight. Malrik took the lands, razed the temples, and built his Sanctum of Bone, a fortress carved from the remains of the slain. Inside, a throne made of white ribcages. Above it, a chandelier of skulls.

Blood magic demands escalation. The Fourth Binding, known only to a few, was the Binding of Memory. To truly control men, Malrik needed more than obedience. He needed belief. So, he crafted a ritual that fed on blood and shadow, consuming the memories of those around him and replacing them with his own version of truth. He performed it first on an entire village. Every man, woman, and child forgotten their own names. He gave them new ones. Gave them a new god to worship him. They sang his praises in a language he taught them in a single night. His legend spread like plague. Peasants whispered of the Lord of Bone and Blood, whose eyes could steal your name. Soldiers feared the red mist that rolled into camps at night, leaving only silence behind. The Old King sent emissaries. They never returned. Finally, he sent an army. Malrik met them in the Black Valley. There were no banners. No battle cries. Just a wall of bone-bound warriors, eyes blank, armor etched with blood-sigils. Malrik raised a hand. Rivers of crimson erupted from the soil, forming tendrils that tore men from their horses and crushed them like dolls. By nightfall, ten thousand lay dead. Malrik walked among them and breathed in the blood-soaked earth. The land remembered him now.

The High Circle of Mages convened in secret. They had outlawed blood magic for centuries, fearing its lure. Now they saw its
full horror. Together, they crafted a sealing ritual, the Accord of
White Flame, to bind Malrik's essence and strip him of magic, but
Malrik had spies. On the night of the binding, he walked into the
Circle's sanctum with the severed heads of two Archmages and
burned the Accord to ash. He did not kill the rest. He took their
blood, one by one, and made them his Seers, sorcerers bound to
his will, who could see across time and speak lies into truth. The
age of prophecy ended that night.

Malrik's rise seemed unstoppable, until he found the Gate of
Morryn, buried beneath the Old Kingdom's capital. There, he
learned of the Fifth Binding. Sacrifice of Self. To complete it, he
had to kill the last part of his humanity. He performed it on the day
the Old King died. In front of a great mirror, he carved away the
last remnants of Marek Valen. Piece by piece, memories, love, guilt,
hope. He fed them to the mirror. What stared back was no longer
mortal. His body became a vessel. His blood burned with runes.
His soul, such as it was, became unbound from flesh. He could
walk the dream world. Possess others. Warp reality through the
bloodlines of those who carried even a hint of his magic. He needed
no longer to kill to bind. A drop of blood would do. The Old Kingdom fell in three days. The capital burned. The royal family vanished. The castle sealed itself by its own enchantments, as if sensing
the corruption at its gates, but the object of the Old King's magic,
the weapon meant to end Malrik, remained hidden. Malrik tried to
take it, but the castle rejected him. Only those untouched by his
bindings, by fear, by power, by corruption, could claim it, and so,
Malrik turned to war. He built a legion. He sent them into the castle
in waves, and he waits, now, in the east. Watching. Searching.

Because he knows: One day, someone will reach the weapon, and he must be ready.

CHAPTER 16

The village of Dunmar, sat nestled between high ridges and black pines, a forgotten place choked with fog and shadow. Dunmar was not a place one stumbled upon by chance. Paths to the village were narrow, treacherous, and often disappeared beneath snow or landslide in the winter months. Yet the people of Dunmar endured. They always had. The village itself was an unlikely bloom of life among scorched stone. Houses were squat and triangular, built from thick beams of blackened cedar and stone bricks cut from old volcanic slabs. The roofs were steeply pitched and covered in overlapping tiles of shale or ironwood shingles, resistant to the biting snows and embers that sometimes drifted from deeper faults. Most chimneys belched a continuous stream of pale smoke that clung low to the valley like a second ceiling.

At night, the village glowed faintly from within, like coals resting beneath ash. Lanterns burned with an orange hue thanks to the local slag-oil, a mineral-laced extract found in pockets underground. It gave off a faint metallic smell and a warmth that lasted through storms, though it left thin black soot on the stone sills. The people of Dunmar were pale-skinned and stoic, with dark hair and broad shoulders. Their eyes were keen from long years spent navigating stone paths and hunting in low visibility. Their speech was quiet and efficient, their humor dry and as sharp as the obsidian used to craft their ceremonial blades. Work in Dunmar centered around forging, mining, and weathercraft, an old mountain tradition of reading wind and snow patterns to predict storms. The forges of Dunmar were modest in size but fierce in output. Using fire pits fed with slag-coal and bellows carved from the hide of upland aurochs, the blacksmiths of Dunmar forged weapons and tools that were prized for their density and balance.

Children in Dunmar were raised with an eye toward survival. From an early age they were taught to trap, climb, and carry weight uphill. Education included old runes, rock lore, and the stories of the Fire Sages, long-vanished mystics said to have once inhabited the nearby ridges before vanishing into the smoke. At the northern edge of the village, perched atop a black plateau overlooking the river-cut gorge, stood a weatherworn bell tower built from red basalt. It rang only once a season, to mark the arrival of the thaw or the first frost. Beside it was a shrine of stone pillars wrapped in leather cords and bone fetishes, where people still left offerings for unseen spirits of mountain and ash. In the center of Dunmar lay the Ember Square, an open-air gathering space marked by a mosaic of obsidian chips and copper filings in the shape of a great flame. This was where messages were delivered, disputes resolved, and stories traded. During the seasonal market, stalls of smoked meat, rare herbs, horn-carvings, and polished ores were arranged around the edges, and strange visitors would arrive, often shrouded, sometimes silent. Yet even here, above the cold flame and shadowed cliffs, the Inn of Dunmar burned like a beacon.

In a village chiseled from shadow and stone, the Emberrest Inn stood like a story half-remembered: carved into the side of a black rock bluff near the southern edge of Dunmar, where the cliffs sloped down into a steep gorge. Unlike most inns that rose above the land, the Emberrest seemed to have emerged from it, as if the mountain itself had chosen to open its heart and offer warmth. The inn's entrance was a tall, arched mouth of basalt, rimmed with iron sconces that burned with slag-oil torches night and day. Above the entry was a relief carved directly into the rock, a spiral of flame embracing a single, downward-facing sword. Beneath it, etched in runes that shimmered with flecks of quartz, was a simple phrase: "Rest Through Flame, Rise Through Ash."

Stepping into the Emberrest was like walking into the heart of a dormant volcano. The main chamber, hollowed from volcanic stone, was low and wide, lit by hanging lanterns and a central fire pit sunk into the floor, ringed with copper stones. The fire burned hot and blue from a mix of coal and slag-oil, casting strange shadows that danced like spirits against the walls. Walls were etched with petroglyphs: flame-spirits, storm-goats, hunters, and mountain beasts. Some were ancient, others recently added by travelers who paid a small fee to mark their presence. One panel was dedicated solely to the memory of those who had died in the Eroded Peaks. Locals called it the Wall of Smoke. Seating came in the form of stone benches cushioned with thick leathers and furs. Several alcoves, natural hollows in the rock, were fitted with low tables for small groups. Each had its own small brazier, its own quiet privacy.

A stone bar ran along the left side, polished to a dusky sheen, with grooves worn by the sliding of mugs. Behind it stood shelves lined with clay jugs, smoked glass bottles, and polished horn containers. Most contained ironroot ale, black honey mead, and bitter mint cider, all brewed in Dunmar and as strong as the mountains themselves. At the back of the chamber, stairs carved from obsidian led up to a loft carved into the stone wall, guest rooms tucked like burrows above the taproom. There were only five, each with a heavy wool curtain for a door, soft pelts on the bed, and a fire basin made of pumice stone in the corner. They bore no numbers, only glyphs: antler, flame, fang, moon, storm, symbols for protection during sleep. A tunnel led deeper into the cliff where the kitchen and private quarters were located. It was said that during winter storms or avalanches, when the outer paths were sealed by snow, the Emberrest remained warm and open, its fire never going out, not once in five generations. That fire was the pride of the inn-keeper, Dhenna Mardel.

Dhenna was not a woman easily described. In her mid-fifties, she had the posture of a ranger and the calloused hands of a smith. Her skin bore the gray-brown hue of cliffstone and her black hair was always tied with a strip of crimson cloth. Her voice was low, scratchy, and often amused, as if she found the entire world's strug-gle a little ironic. Her eyes, however, were precise as a blade's edge. When Dhenna looked at someone, they felt weighed, measured, and not always found wanting. She had inherited the inn from her father, who had carved it with his own hands before falling into the gorge in a fogstorm. She rarely spoke of him, save when the embers burned low and ale was flowing. Dhenna had never married, never left Dunmar. Some whispered she had once been a mercenary or a fire-dancer from the southern courts. Others claimed she had dwa-rven blood. All she ever said was:

"I outdrink bears and outlive storms. That's enough."

She brewed the inn's charred root stew, a thick, smoky con-coction made from black carrots, bone broth, wild onion, and her own spice blend that could make a man sweat through his boots. Her ember bread, baked over hot stones and coated in ash-salt, was dense, filling, and highly addictive. She served it with strips of pep-pered boar and root pickles that made the eyes water. Dhenna ran the inn with a strict hand. Fights were rare, and when they hap-pened, she ended them with a hammer she kept behind the bar, not to strike, but to slam once on the counter. The sound echoed like thunder, and all arguments died instantly.

In a place where wind screamed like beasts and stone cracked from age and frost, the people of Dunmar endured not because of luxury or might, but because of rhythm. Life here had a pulse, an-cient and slow, timed to the clinking of hammer against forge, the howl of wind against slate roofs, and the soft thrum of fire behind every door. They called it "the Fire Beneath," a phrase passed from tongue to tongue like an inheritance. It meant many things: the warmth of family, the memory of fallen kin, the hunger to outlast another winter. It meant the will to survive, and nowhere was that Fire more evident than in the Emberrest Inn. Each night, the Emberrest filled with soft murmurings and songs hummed low. The fire pit glowed blue in the center of the room, and its heat gathered stories like moths to flame. Miners, storm-watchers, and night-foragers would drift in from the cold, stomping snow from their boots, steam rising off their shoulders. They'd take the same seats every night, sip the same ale, and listen to whatever tale passed between the arches.

Sometimes it was travelers, lost on the high passes or fleeing Malrik's influence, bringing news from the kingdoms below. Occasionally, it was a bard from the valley, singing in a cracked voice about love under frost moons or betrayal among smoke. Storytelling was sacred here. Dhenna would not let tales be interrupted. If someone tried, she would snap, "Let the fire speak," and silence would return like snowfall. Every week on Restday, a ritual was held at the inn's fire. Locals would gather with small firestones, bits of red jasper or obsidian warmed in hand, and place them in the fire pit. With it, they offered thanks, hopes, or farewells. It was said the fire heard all and carried the messages through the veins of the mountain to where the Old Gods waited. Whether anyone still believed in those gods was beside the point, the tradition bound the village together.

Beyond Dunmar's high ridge lines and shadowed cliffs stretched the Ashvale Reaches, a series of dry valleys filled with wind-sculpted boulders and fireroot thickets. The terrain was deceptively beautiful, black-and-red stone kissed with lichen and pine needles, veins of copper glinting in sunlight. But it was treacherous. Avalanches could come with little warning. So could flamequakes, minor tremors born of slumbering magma. The old dwarven roads once carved into the mountains had long since crumbled, but echoes remained: a bridge made of fused black glass, a tower's stone base half-swallowed by moss. Some said there were vaults buried deep under Dunmar, sealed since the Fire Sages vanished. Others whispered of ashwraiths, spirits of fire-bound ancestors, seen drifting in the mist above cracked ravines. To the west lay the Fissure Fields, a cracked terrain of sulfur pools and warm geysers. No one built there, but hunters sometimes ventured into the steam-choked valleys to seek rare herbs or glimmering minerals that grew along the fissures, valuable to alchemists and mages. To the east, if one climbed the Ashbreak Rise and descended into the gorge beyond, they would find the ruined edges of the Old Kingdom's northern outposts, long since abandoned. From there, one could follow forgotten roads to Malrik's corrupted lands, or to even deeper ancient places, where the land remembered the time of dragons.

Because of Dunmar's location and the Emberrest's position along the old northern routes, it became a silent sentinel on the edge of forgotten kingdoms. When travelers came from Eldwyre or Valebrook, they always found shelter. Dhenna took in messengers bearing news to mountain outposts, wardens patrolling for signs of Malrik's legions, and even the occasional mage on pilgrimage to the fire-shrines etched into higher ridges. All found food, fire, and peace under her roof. And those with no name, runaways, hunted men, or lost souls, were often given a warm place and no questions, so long as they respected the flame. As time went on, the Emberrest became more than an inn. It became a repository of memory. Names of fallen kin were carved into the wall beside the bar; prayers folded into parchment and sealed with wax were placed in the cracks of the stone hearth. There were whispers that Dhenna herself had memorized every tale told within her walls, and if the time came, she could tell them again.

Dunmar was not for the faint-hearted. But those who stayed came to understand a quiet truth: the greatest strength came not from steel or spell, but from endurance, from shelter, and from the choice to carry on even when the world froze around you. And so, it stood, Dunmar, carved from mountain and memory. And at its heart, the Emberrest, an inn where even the coldest night gave way to the warmth of old flame.

Rayner didn't like it. "No guards on the gate. No smoke from the chimneys. Too quiet."

"Or maybe everyone's napping," said Tristan, his crossbow slung over his back.

He ran a hand through his windswept blond hair and squinted toward the tavern.

"You're always so cheerful, Rayner." "We shouldn't stay long," Cole muttered.

His cloak was drawn tight around him, concealing the arcane runes burned into his skin.

"The sky doesn't like this place. Neither do I."

Quinn just grunted, resting his Warhammer on his shoulder like it weighed no more than a loaf of bread. His thick arms were scarred from years of smithy work.

"Let's just get ale and be on our way."

They walked into town in a diamond formation Rayner in front, Cole beside him, Tristan covering the rear, and Quinn scanning the alleys. The village looked half-abandoned. Shutters were closed. A single cart sat overturned by a well, but the tavern, The Broken Boar, was open. Lanterns flickered behind the fogged windows. Inside, a half-dozen locals drank in silence, their eyes flicking up as the four entered. They sat at the corner table. A pale serving girl brought ale without a word.

"I don't like this," Rayner whispered, resting his sword against the table leg. "Feels wrong."

"Because it is," Cole said softly.

"There's a bounty hunter here." Rayner tensed.

"Are you sure?"

"I can feel it. Someone's cloaked in arcane shadow. Watching. Waiting."

Tristan's eyes scanned the room. "Where?"

Before Cole could answer, the tavern door creaked open. A tall figure stepped through, wrapped in black leather and fur, a long-handled axe on his back and a short blade gleaming at his hip. His face was hidden beneath a mask of hammered iron no eyes visible, only darkness. The room went silent.

"Little Princes," the bounty hunter said. His voice was like gravel and smoke.

"Rayner. Cole. You're worth a lot of coin."

"Friend of yours?" Tristan muttered.

Rayner stood slowly, drawing his sword. "Who sent you?"

"Does it matter?" the hunter replied. "Walk out now in chains, and maybe I leave you breathing." "Maybe,"

Quinn growled, rising to his feet, "we'll break your damn jaw and see how much gold that gets you."

The hunter smiled at least, the mask tilted like a grin. "So be it."

He snapped his fingers. The tavern windows exploded inward, and half a dozen crossbow bolts flew in from the shadows outside. One grazed Tristan's arm. Quinn flipped the table as a shield, while Cole raised both hands and shouted,

"Virel'shahn!"

A wave of blue flame burst from his palms and rolled across the floor, sending the hunter and two thugs flying backward. The villagers screamed and scattered as chaos erupted. Rayner was already moving, blade flashing. He slashed down a charging mercenary, ducked a club swing, and rammed his shoulder into another. Cole hurled lightning at a pair of bowmen who tried to block the stairs.

"Up!" he shouted. "Second floor! Go!"

Tristan rolled behind the overturned table. "Go, I've got this covered!"

Quinn nodded and charged with his hammer, smashing a thug straight through a support beam.

"You always say that!"

The four burst through the tavern's narrow stairwell into a storage loft above. A shattered window offered their only escape. Rayner pointed.

"We leap, run for the woods. Quinn, take the rear."

Tristan peeked through the gap. "We've got at least three on the rooftops with crossbows."

Cole's eyes glowed faintly. "I'll cover the leap." "Go on my mark now!"

Cole raised his hand and unleashed a blast of arcane wind. It shattered the window and flung glass and arrows wide. Rayner leapt through, rolled over a thatch roof, and landed in the muddy street. Tristan followed, then Quinn with a grunt, his hammer knocking loose roof tiles. Cole dropped last, twisting midair and landing in a crouch, robes smoking from magic residue. The village was awake now more thugs poured from alleys, and the bounty hunter stalked from the tavern's back exit like death incarnate.

"There!" Rayner pointed toward the forest edge, where an old cart path led out of the village.

They ran for it. Dunmar's outer woods were thick and slick with mud. Pine needles carpeted the forest floor, and thick mist clung to every branch. They sprinted as best they could, dodging roots and vaulting fallen logs. Behind them, the bounty hunter's men followed fast.

"He's summoning something," Cole said, panting.

"Then we need to lose him now," Rayner barked.

Quinn turned and skidded to a stop. "Keep going. I'll slow 'em down."

"Quinn" Rayner shouted.

"Go!" Quinn barked back.

Rayner hesitated only a moment. Then nodded.

"We'll meet at the Black Ravine."

Quinn grinned, hefted his hammer, and charged back down the path roaring like a beast. The others vanished into the trees. The forest grew darker, the mist thicker. Cole muttered words of concealment, wrapping them in a veil of shadow and silence. Still, the hunter was gaining.

"Up ahead," Tristan said, pointing. "Cliff drop."

The ground fell away to a deep ravine fifty feet across and filled with jagged rocks and old bones.

"There's no bridge," Rayner said.

"There was," Cole murmured. "But it's gone."

"Now what?" Tristan asked.

Cole stepped forward. "Give me time."

He raised his hands, chanting in a forgotten tongue. The runes on his arms blazed white, and wind howled around him.

"Rayner, guard him! Tristan yelled.

The bounty hunter appeared from the woods, stepping out like a phantom. Two arrows thudded into the ground near Rayner's feet Tristan took out one of the rooftop marksmen before ducking back.

"Come, then!" Rayner shouted, raising his sword.

The hunter accepted. They clashed like titan's steel on steel, axe against blade. Rayner moved like a hurricane, but the hunter blocked each strike with brutal efficiency. Sparks flew. Trees splintered. Blood spilled. Behind them, Cole screamed the final word. A bridge of glowing stone formed arcane and unstable, barely wide enough to walk.

"Go!" he yelled.

Rayner broke free and ran, blood trailing from his side. Tristan followed, loosing a final bolt into the woods. Cole stumbled onto the bridge last, just as the hunter reached the edge. The bounty hunter did not pursue. He simply watched, and vanished into mist. They ran until their lungs burned and the trees thinned into jagged rock. The ravine was behind them now, and the hunter somehow had not followed. Rayner staggered to a stop beneath a broken stone archway, gasping. Blood soaked the side of his tunic, but he stayed on his feet.

"Cole… how far…?" he panted.

Cole collapsed against the stone, his face pale, eyes glowing faintly. "Far enough… for now."

Tristan dropped his quiver and counted the bolts left. "Three. Not enough."

Rayner turned, his voice low and tense. "We need to find Quinn. We said the Black Ravine, and we're here. He should've"

A low grunt echoed from deeper in the rocks. Then a boulder rolled aside, and Quinn stepped out, his face bruised, hammer stained red.

"Late," he growled. "You owe me drinks."

Rayner exhaled. "You're alive."

"Barely." Quinn spat blood.

Cole rose shakily. "We need shelter."

"We need answers," Rayner said. "Who is this hunter? Why now?"

"I think we were set up," Cole replied. "I felt a spell woven into the tavern's hearth. Like a beacon. Someone knew we'd stop there."

Rayner's face hardened. "We find out who, but first we get out of these hills."

They moved again, deeper into the canyons, toward a cave, but the air grew thick too thick.

Cole suddenly stopped. "Wait," he whispered. "Don't take another step."

The others froze. He knelt, placing his hand against the dirt. The earth hummed.

"There's magic beneath us," he murmured. "Buried deep."

Tristan raised a brow. "What kind?"

Cole's face turned grim. "The kind that kills mages."

Suddenly, runes flared across the rocks in a ring around them golden and jagged like lightning scars. The stone beneath their feet cracked.

"It's a trap!" Cole shouted.

From the cliffs above, a voice rang out: "Very good, little mage."

The bounty hunter stepped from the shadows atop the cliff, flanked by two masked spellcasters in grey robes. His voice was amused.

"I wondered which of you would spot it. You're faster than the others I've buried here."

Rayner snarled. "You don't fight fair."

"I don't get paid to be fair." He raised a hand.

The earth beneath Cole lit up with golden fire. Cole screamed and fell to one knee, clutching his chest. The runes burned brighter.

"It's leeching my magic!" he gasped.

Tristan aimed his crossbow at the hunter but the mage next to him raised a hand and summoned a wall of shimmering air. The bolt bounced off, spinning into the abyss. Rayner made a decision. He sprinted toward Cole and plunged his sword deep into the runes. The earth howled. The light flared. The ground exploded, flinging them all backward in a shockwave of dust and flame. When the smoke cleared, the trap was broken but Rayner's hand bled freely, and Cole looked half-dead.

Quinn stood, shaking off dirt, and roared, "I'm going up there!" He charged the slope, hammer in both hands.

Rayner turned to Tristan. "Can you take one of the mages?"

"Give me a clean shot."

Rayner grabbed a rock and hurled it to the side. The mage's head turned slightly. That was all Tristan needed. Thwip. The bolt punched through the mage's eye and dropped him like a sack.

Cole struggled to his feet, eyes burning with wrath. "Help me up."

"You need rest" Rayner began.

"NO," Cole snarled. "He tried to kill me with my own blood."

He raised both hands and his voice was not his own. It was deep, echoing, ancient. The sky screamed. Thunder cracked, and a storm of blue fire rained from above, engulfing the second mage and the hunter's ledge in a pillar of burning air. When the fire faded, the second mage was ash, but the bounty hunter still stood. Armor blackened. Mask cracked. Unburned. He looked down at them, then turned, and disappeared into the mist.

They reached the cave just before dusk. It was narrow and jagged, but dry. Cole collapsed into a corner and passed out. Rayner bound his own bleeding hand with cloth. Quinn stood at the entrance, silent, while Tristan watched the path below.

"I've seen a lot of killers," Quinn said at last. "But this one… he's not hunting for coin. He's hunting for pleasure."

Tristan added, "He didn't finish us. He could have, and he didn't. Why?"

Rayner stared into the dark. "To watch us run."

Night fell hard in the mountains. Fog slid through the peaks like a serpent. Inside the cave, the fire burned low, casting flickering shadows across stone walls. Tristan sat at the entrance, crossbow across his lap, eyes sharp. Rayner couldn't sleep. His hand throbbed. His mind returned again and again to the hunter's mask, the way he had stood in the fire untouched.

"He's not a man," Rayner muttered.

Across the fire, Cole stirred. His skin was pale, lips cracked, breath shallow. He looked at Rayner with a strange light in his eyes.

"He's more than that. He's bound to something. Old. Dangerous. I've seen mages twist their bodies with shadow magic before… but this is deeper. The mask holds it in."

Rayner stared at the coals. "You're not strong enough to fight him again."

Cole's lips curled into a weak smile. "I'll fight him with ash if I have to."

Quinn returned from his watch; a length of chain wrapped over one shoulder.

"There's a narrow ledge we can push him toward. It drops a hundred feet. Rocks at the bottom. Not even a cursed bastard like him could survive it."

Rayner nodded. "Then we end this tonight."

Tristan glanced out into the darkness. "Too late."

The fog moved wrong. It didn't drift it curled, coiled, reached like fingers through the trees. Then came the sound. Chains dragging. The bounty hunter stepped into view, mist parting around him. No backup. No archers. Just him. He came alone to finish what he started. The cave entrance exploded inwards. Rayner barely rolled aside in time as a spiked chain tore into the stone where his head had been. The bounty hunter lunged forward, a second chain flying out from beneath his cloak like a serpent. It wrapped around Tristan's arm and yanked him off his feet.

"Tristan!" Rayner roared.

Quinn intercepted the next strike, swinging his hammer into the chain with a metallic clang that echoed through the cliffs. Sparks flew. The chain snapped but the bounty hunter was already in the air. He landed in the center of the cave, and hell broke loose.

Rayner grabbed a fallen iron bar from the fire and swung it like a blade. It hissed against the hunter's axe, barely holding the strike. The heat singed his fingers, but he held firm. Cole rose, eyes blazing with blue light, shouting a spell older than the mountain itself. The cave trembled. Runes shimmered across the walls. The hunter snarled the first real sound from his mouth and flung one of his chains toward Cole. It pierced the boy's shoulder. Cole screamed and fell, twitching, his magic fizzling into sparks. Rayner broke free and charged. No sword. Just rage and instinct. He slammed into the bounty hunter with all his strength, driving him back against the stone. The mask cracked again under the force. For a split second, Rayner saw eyes behind it. Human eyes. Terrified eyes. The bounty hunter shoved Rayner off and raised his axe to finish him, but Quinn tackled him from the side, both of them crashing through the cave mouth and out into the open night.

Outside, the wind howled. The cliff ledge was narrow, no more than six feet across, with nothing but air and jagged rock below. Quinn wrestled with the bounty hunter in silence, neither man speaking, only grunting like beasts. Quinn's Warhammer lay discarded. Now it was brute strength against unnatural fury. Rayner stumbled out after them, grabbing a fallen chunk of stone to use as a club.

"Quinn, move!"

But Quinn had his arms locked around the hunter's waist in a bear hug. "Go... NOW!"

"Don't" Quinn smiled over his shoulder, blood streaming down his cheek.

"Tell Cole... I said he's not allowed to die."

Then he hurled both himself and the bounty hunter off the cliff. Rayner screamed. Their bodies vanished into the mist. Rayner knelt by the edge, breath shaking. Tristan limped out of the cave, dragging Cole unconscious but breathing.

"He's alive," Tristan said. "Barely."

Rayner rose, fists clenched, blood drying on his face. He couldn't feel anything. No rage. No grief. Just hollow. They built a cairn of stones on the cliff, right where Quinn had fallen. They left his hammer there, resting upright in the rock. A marker for a warrior who died standing. Cole awoke later that night, groggy.

"Where's Quinn?" he whispered.

Rayner didn't answer. He only put a hand on his brother's shoulder. Cole understood. He wept silently. Suddenly, they heard a stir from the bushes and Quinn appeared, hammer in hand.

"You were just going to leave my Hammer?"

"Quinn" they all shouted.

"How did you survive?" "Not sure" Quinn sighed.

The next morning, they reached the borders of Eldwyre. Rayner walked with his sword across his back. Tristan beside him, one arm in a sling.

"We should find whoever sent that monster."

"We will," Rayner said.

Cole looked toward the rising sun. The mark on his shoulder from the chain still glowed faintly, but he had strength in his eyes again.

"We're not done," he said. "Whoever controls hunters like that... whoever built those traps... they're still out there."

"And they'll come again," Rayner added.

"But next time," said Tristan, "we'll be ready."

They marched on. South of the kingdom of Valebrook lies Eldwyre, a town known not for its wealth or position, but for its crossroads. It is where the great forest paths meet the road to the mountains. Eldwyre's buildings are crafted of dark oak and timbered brick, with wide eaves and storm-shuttered windows. The roofs pitch steeply, as if bracing against old winds. A wide central road divides the town in half, marked by hanging lanterns and old iron posts. Eldwyre is a town where everyone watches, and no one speaks first. There's a quiet tension to its streets, as if the town holds its breath in anticipation of something. Eldwyre sits in the shadow of greater places but has always been a place where choices are made, and where masks are tested. Windrest Hearth – The Inn of Eldwyre tucked between two ridgelines on the eastern edge of the Wyrdwood, Eldwyre is a village defined by breezes, blooms, and secrets, and at its very heart stands its most beloved structure. Unlike the stone-carved elegance of Valebrook's inns or the timber-lodged familiarity of Ashbrook's, Windrest Hearth seems to have grown out of the land itself. Its walls are built from pale driftwood and wisteria-laced sandstone. Thin banners hang from the roofline, each one catching the wind and fluttering with the village's symbol: a sleeping leaf beneath a crescent moon. The inn's roof is steep and tiled with uneven, hand-shaped shingles painted soft greens and sky blues, giving it a dreamlike patchwork appearance. Aromatic herbs grow in bundles around the base of the inn, thyme, mint, sage, and lend a soothing scent to the air.

Walking inside Windrest Hearth feels like entering a dream forged of comfort and natural magic. The common room is wide, with high ceilings supported by beams carved with symbols of the Weave, sigils of balance, healing, and renewal. No two tables match in shape or design, but all are carved from the same flowering ash. Colorful tapestries hang along the walls, depicting local legends, moonscapes, and scenes of animals sleeping in peace beside humans. A fire pit rests in the center of the room, encircled by a ring of cushions and wooden benches. Unlike traditional hearths, Windrest's fire is blue-white and whispering, dancing on stones enchanted to never scorch nor smoke. Eldwyre folk say it was gifted by a passing mage whose life was saved here after a storm nearly drowned him. Glass lanterns glow with trapped firelight, floating gently above patrons, casting cool light rather than warmth. Wind chimes line the ceiling beams, faintly echoing the breeze outside, as if the wind itself were part of the building's breath. Every room smells like wildflowers, old parchment, and fresh bread. Talla Brindlefenn is not just an innkeeper, she is the soul of Eldwyre. Once a traveling herbalist and healer, she returned to her home village when her twin brother died in the war against Malrik's earliest forces. She rebuilt the inn from his broken study and began a new life, quietly tending the weary who passed through Eldwyre's borderlands. Talla is tall and soft-spoken, with long silvered auburn hair braided with sprigs of dried lavender and tiny silver leaves. She wears layered skirts and a cloak of patchworked green and gold, and always carries a satchel of pouches filled with remedies, poultices, and little bits of wisdom. She speaks slowly, often in metaphors, and listens more than she talks. Her hands are always busy, kneading dough, grinding herbs, or gently tending to wounded birds brought in by village children. Her kindness is legendary, but she will not suffer cruelty. The last man to draw a blade in her inn found his sword warped into a shepherd's crook the next morning.

Windrest Hearth is not just a stopover; it's a threshold. It's the place where characters catch their breath before fate moves again. Where doubt can be whispered without judgment. Where pain is acknowledged without shame. The people of Eldwyre believe it was built where a convergence of Weave-threads meets the breath of the sky, and as such, healing and clarity come easier here. Mages say the wind is older in Eldwyre, full of memory and warning. Many kings, including Reynard, once stayed here in disguise, just to hear stories from travelers and feel the pulse of the land.

CHAPTER 17

In the highest chamber of Black Hollow Keep, where the stone bled red and shadows moved on their own, Malrik stood before the ancient mirror of Anek'Thur. The blood magic pulsed along his veins, each beat echoing in the vaulted hall like a war drum. His power had grown but not enough. Not without the relic. Not without the Veil torn open completely. He clenched his fist.

"They move toward the mountain pass," he murmured. "Rayner leads them... the fool."

Behind him, the doors creaked open. A voice, sharp as frost, spoke.

"You summoned me, father?" Elira stepped into the room.

She wore a gown of black and crimson, her long braid woven with obsidian threads. Her eyes cool, calculating met Malrik's without fear. Elira was Malrik's only child. Not born, but made shaped by sorcery and forged in the rituals of blood and fire. Her mother, a noblewoman of the Eastern Range, had perished years ago sacrificed in one of Malrik's earliest rites. Elira never wept. She had been raised to command. Raised to manipulate, and most importantly raised to wear any mask needed to survive.

"You will go to Eldwyre," Malrik said. "They will arrive there soon. Rayner. Cole. Quinn. Tristan."

Elira raised an eyebrow. "And I'm to kill them?"

"No," Malrik replied, stepping down from the dais. "You are to deceive them."

She said nothing. He continued: You will claim you were meant to marry Rayner. That it was arranged by King Reynard before his fall. Say you were hidden away. That you've only now learned of his return."

She gave a soft, mocking laugh. "And you think he'll believe that?"

"He's a soldier," Malrik said. "Soldiers want to believe in duty. In oaths. In the past."

"And the mage?" she asked.

"Distract him," Malrik said. "Or kill him, if you must, but earn their trust. Walk with them. Smile when needed. Cry when useful, but most of all learn where the artifact is."

Elira turned, cloak swaying. "And if I do?"

"Then I will grant you power greater than any sorcerer or queen, and when they kneel, it will be you who wears the crown beside me."

Elira's first memories were of wind shrieking through tall, dark towers. The halls of Black Spire were cold, lit only by green flames and lined with whispers. Her caretakers were masked, their voices thin and joyless. No lullabies, no stories, only scrolls and symbols. She was taught the old tongue before she could speak her own name. Magic was not shown to her with wonder, but drilled into her with ritual. They made her copy blood sigils until her fingers bled. When she cried, the candles dimmed, and she was locked in silence. Despite this, she was not bitter. She watched the skies. Birds fascinated her, especially those that dared fly near the tower. She named them. She whispered poems to them when alone. Something gentle lived in her, protected by a quiet defiance.

Malrik visited her only sparingly. When he did, he appeared in flowing black robes, his eyes like dying coals. He would test her, not for affection, but power. He demanded results.

"Break this stone with thought." "Lift the dagger." "Repeat the invocation. Do not falter."

She obeyed. Not because she feared him, but because she sensed a game within the game. Power granted freedom, and she longed to be free. It was in the Mirror Halls of the Spire that she saw something new: a flicker of her future. The mirrors, enchanted to reveal one's potential, once showed her not in black robes, but in white and gold, standing beside someone with a crown of fire. She never told anyone what she saw. But from that day, she began to resist.

When Elira was ten, a young apprentice named Vael was brought to the Spire. He was older, sharper, and already twisted by Malrik's teachings. Where Elira sought understanding, Vael sought dominance. He bullied the lesser students. Elira ignored him, until he mocked the birds she kept feeding from her window. That night, she lured him into the Mirror Hall, cast a rune of binding, and locked him in his own reflection for hours. She was punished severely. Days in the Shadow Vaults. Whispers in her ears that bent her mind. But when she returned, she was not broken. She was determined.

Among her many handlers was an old servant named Mara, once a mage of the Old Kingdom who had been captured during the wars. Mara never revealed her past, but she taught Elira small things in secret: healing salves, names of flowers, and old lullabies from the south.

"Elira," she once whispered, "you are not the cage you were born in."

Mara's kindness became her anchor. When Malrik began to mold Elira into a weapon, it was Mara who reminded her that power must serve the living, not the throne. Mara was executed when Elira was thirteen, burned for treason. That night, Elira wrote her name into the old stones of the Spire. A spell of remembrance. It still glows faintly, defying Malrik's darkness. At fifteen, Malrik summoned her for the Rite of Binding, a blood ritual that would seal her as his magical heir. He offered her a blade and a bound stag.

"Spill its blood. Seal your place in my line."

Elira stood silently. Then, instead of killing the stag, she turned the blade on herself, just enough to draw her own blood.

"I choose my own line," she said.

Malrik watched in silence. He did not punish her. Nor did he praise her.

He only said, "You will walk a harder path." But from that day forward, he no longer tried to bend her will.

Malrik grew desperate. He sought the Object of Balance, hidden deep in the Old Kingdom's ruins, and he knew four young warriors sought it, one of whom was Rayner, son of Reynard. So Malrik sent Elira, not as a weapon, but as a whisper. He gave her a false past, a sealed letter claiming she was Rayner's betrothed from long ago. Her mission: infiltrate the group, mislead them, and deliver their location to Vael and the Bounty Circle. She agreed. But her heart had other plans.

Vael had always disliked Elira. She was too sharp. Too pretty. Too good at lying. She called him a ghost. A pet. "Malrik's blade," she liked to whisper. They were rivals in all but title, but he watched her with curiosity. Especially now, as she departed for Eldwyre on Malrik's orders. Pretending to be someone she wasn't. Sent to deceive Rayner and his friends. Vael didn't trust her, but he didn't trust anyone, and yet… A thought lingered: What if she doesn't come back? What if she doesn't want to? He began to wonder: Was she pretending so well… she might forget it was pretend? One night, when Malrik was away performing rites beneath the Keep, Vael entered the Forbidden Chamber, a sealed vault lined with old banners, broken crowns, and bones too large to be human. At the center sat a pedestal, and on it, a crystal sphere, black as pitch, swirling with shadows. Vael approached. He didn't touch it, but the sphere pulsed, and inside it, he saw visions: Rayner, holding a sword wreathed in golden flame. Cole, chanting ancient words, tears in his eyes. Quinn, forging something beneath the mountain. Tristan, loosing an arrow at a serpent's eye. Elira... choosing. Vael stumbled back. The sphere cracked. The vision vanished, and he knew. Something in him was shifting.

Elira traveled alone, dressed not in royal robes but in traveler's leather, her face modestly covered, her hair braided in the common style of plains folk. She passed through ruins and outposts, her words always measured, her gaze always observing. In villages, she listened to rumors.

"They say the boy Rayner carries the sword of King Reynard..."

"I heard the mage Azor walks again..."

"Quinn the blacksmith's son? With them?"

Elira collected every whisper. She learned what made people talk, and what made them afraid. Eldwyre was a wind-beaten village nestled near the edge of the eastern grasslands, halfway to the mountain pass. It smelled of dust and coal smoke, and its people kept their eyes down. Elira arrived two days before the four heroes. She found lodging at the inn and began weaving her tale quietly, carefully.

The summer sun cast a golden sheen across the rolling fields of Eldwyre, and the scent of heather carried on the wind. Four horses rode fast along the dirt road that snaked toward the village of Brookmere, hooves thundering, laughter rising. The four went on a hunt for the Talla the Inn Keeper. Talla had given them four horses to quicken their hunt.

Rayner led, tall and broad-shouldered, and the cold blue eyes of a northern hawk. Behind him galloped his younger brother Cole, leaner, quicker, with a boyish grin that never quite left his face. Followed by Quinn and Tristan.

"First one to the bridge drinks for free!" Cole shouted.

"Your coin's as light as your blade!" Rayner barked, through his smile.

They walked hard until they reached the edge of Brookmere, where a wooden bridge crossed a narrow stream. Cole reached it first and raised a fist in triumph.

"Ha! You owe me an ale."

Rayner approached, clapping his brother on the back.

"I'll buy it."

The village of Brookmere was quiet but pleasant stone cottages covered in ivy, a central square lined with merchant carts, and the ever-present ring of hammers from the smithy, but what caught both brothers' eyes was not iron or coin, but a girl tending a flower stall near the well. She was no more than twenty, with chestnut hair braided in ribbons, a face kissed by sun, and eyes the color of green glass. She moved gracefully, laughing with an elderly woman, adjusting a bundle of lilies with delicate fingers. Rayner and Cole slowed.

"Who is she?" Cole asked, though his voice dropped unconsciously.

Rayner didn't answer. He was to busy staring.

"Not someone we've met before."

"She's..." Cole trailed off. "Something else."

They approached her together. She looked up, and her expression shifted to polite curiosity. The elderly woman excused herself, limping away with a bunch of daisies.

"Good day, my lady," Rayner said, bowing slightly.

Cole did the same, though with a flash of a grin.

"Good day, sirs," she replied. Her voice was soft, lilting with the local accent. "You must be knights. You look it."

Rayner chuckled. "Near enough. I am Rayner. This is my brother, Cole."

She curtsied. "A pleasure. I am Elira. My father is the village reeve."

"A reeve's daughter?" Cole said. "I should buy every flower you have, to honor so fair a lady."

She laughed. "They wilt too fast for that, but your kind to say so." Rayner smiled.

"Might we escort you to the tavern? My brother owes me an ale." Cole glanced at him, eyebrows raised, but said nothing.

Elira tilted her head. "I suppose I could walk with you."

Over the next few days, the brothers found excuses to remain in Eldwyre. The pretense was preparing for a journey to the next village, but everyone saw through it, especially Elira.

CHAPTER 18

The campfire crackled low, casting flickers of orange light on the old stones of the ruined outpost where they'd stopped to rest. The wind carried the scent of pine and frost from the approaching mountains. Elira sat near the edge of the firelight, sharpening her dagger with steady, practiced strokes. The rhythmic scrape of steel on stone soothed her nerves, but did nothing to still the storm inside. Across from her, Rayner leaned against a boulder, arms folded, eyes closed but clearly awake. Not asleep. Never completely asleep. He didn't trust her. Not fully. Not yet. That should've made her job easier, but it didn't. Five days had passed since she'd joined the group in Eldwyre. Five days of pretending to be the long-lost betrothed of the son of a dead king. It had been simple at first. She'd told the lie a hundred times before she ever opened her mouth. Her father, Malrik, had rehearsed it with her like a stage play: every expression, every pause, every tear, but nothing in that training had prepared her for how human Rayner was. He wasn't the vengeful knight Malrik had described. He was scarred. Controlled, but kind, and loyal to a fault. He tended to Quinn's bruised ribs after a skirmish without being asked. He carried Cole's gear when his brother twisted an ankle. He stood watch two shifts instead of one. He didn't boast. He didn't brood. He simply carried the weight, and Elira hated that it impressed her.

She approached Rayner after a long day of travel, when most of the group was settling in.

"I never said thank you," she said, voice quiet.

Rayner opened one eye. "For what?"

"For letting me join you," she said. "For trusting me... even if you don't."

190

He gave a slight nod. "I trust actions."

"And mine?"

"Still waiting to see."

Elira smirked. "Fair enough."

They sat in silence for a moment, the fire between them. Then she asked,

"Did you ever think of marriage? Before all this?"

Rayner looked over at her, eyes serious. "Once, but I am not sure where my path will lead."

Elira didn't say what she was thinking that her whole life had been a promise she never made, handed to her in a blood-soaked crown by a father who used her like a pawn.

Instead, she smiled. "I understand."

Later that night, Cole plopped down beside her without warning.

"So," he said, chewing on a dried apple, "you're the mysterious future wife of my brooding older brother. Mind if I ask a few questions?"

She raised an eyebrow. "Go on."

"What's your favorite animal?"

She blinked. "What?"

"Just answer it."

She thought for a moment. "Hawk."

"Okay, solid choice," he said. Cole gave an approving nod. "You'll fit in just fine."

She couldn't help but laugh, an actual, unguarded laugh. Cole grinned. She shared night watch with Tristan, whose silence was unsettling even for her. He didn't speak for the first hour. Then, suddenly, he said:

"I don't believe you're who you say you are."

Elira's heart jumped, but her face stayed calm. "What makes you say that?"

Tristan didn't look at her. "You move like someone who's had training. Royal training, but not from the West. You speak with two accents. Your boots are Eastern-cut but worn deliberately. Your dagger isn't ceremonial. It's been used recently."

She said nothing. Tristan finally turned to her.

"But Rayner sees something in you. So, I'm giving you time."

"To prove myself?"

"No," he said. "To choose."

That night, she dreamed of her father. She was small again, walking the black corridors of Black Hollow Keep. Malrik sat on his throne of bone and ash, whispering spells she couldn't understand.

"You are my greatest spell," he said once. "Made flesh."

But now... the words made her skin crawl. What was she, truly? A weapon? A daughter? Or something else entirely? The next evening, near a stream beneath the stars, Elira found Rayner alone again. He looked up as she approached, then returned to whittling a branch into a rough-pointed spear. She sat nearby.

"Do you think it's possible," she asked quietly, "to come from darkness... and still choose the light?"

Rayner didn't answer at first. Then: "Sir Worric once told me, 'A man is not his blood. He's, his breath. Every breath, a choice.'"

She looked at him. "Then what if someone's whole life was built on a lie?"

"Then maybe the next part doesn't have to be."

They sat in silence again, the air between them warmer than before. Later, as the others slept and the stars wheeled overhead, Elira walked alone into the woods and pulled a small stone from her pouch, a communication charm, tied to her father's sigil. She hesitated. Then whispered:

"They trust me."

Malrik's voice crackled from the stone, low and harsh. "Good. Keep it that way."

Elira's fingers tightened., and she didn't respond. Not yet. Not tonight. Instead, she buried the stone beneath the roots of an ash tree. The next morning, as they broke camp, Elira passed Rayner. He looked at her and said,

"You're not the same woman we met days ago."

She looked at him carefully. "Neither are you the boy from the stories."

He nodded once. "Good."

For the first time in years, perhaps ever, Elira smiled without pretending. By morning, Eldwyre had settled into a quiet tension. Word had spread of the glowing sword, of the four who fled the ruined castle, of Malrik's legion that might soon follow. Smoke drifted lazily from the chimneys, and villagers went about their routines with hushed voices and wary eyes. Rayner, Cole, Quinn and Tristan stood over a hand-drawn map in the village hall, lit by shafts of sunlight and the low flicker of lanterns, weighing their next move.

"The Keep lies beyond the Iron Teeth," said Eldric, the village elder. "Mountains as old as the world. No road passes clean through anymore. Not since Malrik claimed the northern passes, but if you reach them, you'll be close to his kingdom."

Rayner nodded. "And to him."

Cole traced a finger along the grasslands south of the hills. "Three routes," he muttered. "One follows the old road, too exposed, especially with Malrik's eyes in the skies."

"The second cuts through the black pines," Quinn added.

"But if we take that, we'll be fighting more than terrain. Bandits. Worse things."

Rayner's gaze settled on the third option a faded trail, barely more than a line between open plains and the highlands.

"This one," he said. "The shepherd's path. No settlements, no patrols. Just wild land and stars."

"It's risky," Eldric warned. "No cover. If the sky-walkers are out"

"Then we move at night," Rayner said.

"We'll rest during the day. Stay low. No fires." Cole sighed.

"Night marching. My favorite kind." Quinn grinned.

"At least it's not raining." Eldric nodded gravely. "I'll outfit you with what little we can spare. A hunter's cloak, a quiver of black-fletched arrows, dried meat, herbs, and this"

He handed Rayner a small wooden token, carved with a circle of flame.

"What is it?" Rayner asked.

"The mark of the Hollow Flame. A symbol of the old resistance. If any loyalists remain beyond the grasslands, this may keep them from killing you on sight."

Rayner bowed his head. "Thank you."

"You carry the sword," Eldric said. "That means the Old Kings chose you. It also means you'll die if you're not careful."

They spent the rest of the day preparing. Rayner sharpened his blade, though the sword of the Old King never seemed to dull. Still, it brought him peace, tracing the stone across its radiant edge, as if the motion reminded him who he was. Cole packed bundles of dried roots and glowing mushrooms into his satchel, whispering soft spells to conceal their scent. He carried no spellbook anymore, his knowledge was etched into memory, into bone, into the runes he had tattooed into the leather of his gloves. Quinn helped the village blacksmith reinforce their gear. His hammer was newly wrapped in steel bands, its handle reinforced.

"They call this ironfire," the smith had said. "Pulled it from the heart of a fallen star."

Quinn nodded in appreciation; he liked simple tools with a purpose. By sundown, they were ready. They set out under a crescent moon. The air smelled of dew and distant thunder. Ahead, the grasslands stretched like a silver sea, waist-high and windblown. No trees, no rocks. Just rolling fields that rustled with unseen life. Coyotes howled in the distance. Somewhere behind, in the direction of the castle, a different sound stirred, the long, low call of Malrik's horn.

"His scouts are still looking for us," Cole said.

"Let them look," Rayner replied. "We're already gone."

They moved like shadows. Wrapped in hunter's cloaks, crouched low, avoiding the crests of the hills. Rayner led the way, sword strapped to his back, senses sharp. He could feel the blade's pull always east, always forward. Every few hours, they paused to drink or check the sky. Once, they heard wings. All five dropped flat into the grass. A dark shape passed overhead. Massive. Silent. Its wings beat with unnatural rhythm too slow, too deliberate for any normal beast. Cole shivered as it vanished behind a cloud.

"Sky-walker," he whispered. "Carries sorcerers. Or worse."

They waited ten full minutes before moving again. Near midnight, they found a low depression in the ground sheltered by a cluster of boulders so ancient they were half buried in earth and vine. One of the stones bore a carved face worn smooth but still grim. An old god, forgotten even by name. They made camp there. No fire. Just silence and cold food. Cole ran his hands across the face of the stone.

"This used to be a shrine." "To what?" Quinn asked.

"Judgment. Mercy. Balance. It's hard to tell anymore. Even the gods go quiet when Malrik grows strong."

Rayner sat with his back to the stone, sword across his knees.

"We'll reach the foothills tomorrow night," he said. "Then the Teeth. We'll have to find a pass through, and fast. Malrik won't wait forever."

Quinn nodded. "And after that?"

Rayner stared into the dark. "Then we enter his kingdom."

"You ever think we won't make it?" Quinn asked softly.

Rayner's voice was steady. "I assume we won't. That's what keeps me sharp."

Cole looked up. "But you think the sword is enough?"

Rayner hesitated, then said, "I don't know."

For a while, none of them spoke. Then the wind shifted, and the grass hissed. Something moved. Rayner was the first to stand. Shapes flickered at the edge of the hills too smooth to be animals, too quiet to be men. Shadows gliding between the blades of grass.

Quinn raised his hammer. "Company?"

"Not Malrik's soldiers," Cole said. "Too fluid. Spirits?"

Rayner narrowed his eyes. "No. Blood-born."

He stepped forward, drawing the sword. A shriek pierced the night. Three creatures burst from the grass half-men, half-shadow. Their bodies were twisted, limbs too long, teeth too sharp. Eyes like dying stars. They moved faster than anything should have, drawn by the scent of the sword. Rayner raised it, and the light flared. One of the creatures shrieked, turned to smoke, and vanished. The others leapt. Quinn swung his hammer into one's chest, crushing bone and driving it into the dirt. It spasmed, then stilled. The last lunged for Cole but the mage thrust out his palm and spoke a word in the old tongue. Fire burst forth, catching the creature midair and setting it ablaze. Its scream echoed across the plains.

Then silence. The grass whispered again, but only the wind returned.

"What were those?" Quinn asked, breathing heavy.

"Scouts," Cole said. "Spawned from blood and nightmare. Malrik's messengers."

Rayner sheathed the sword. "He knows we're coming."

By dawn, the hills of the Iron Teeth loomed ahead jagged silhouettes rising from the horizon like fangs. They stood at the edge of the grasslands, wind blowing through cloaks and hair, and stared at the mountains. Cole lowered his hood.

"That's where the stories always say the heroes die."

Rayner looked at the sword. Its light was dimmer now but steadier. Focused. As if it knew its purpose.

"We're not heroes," Rayner said.

Quinn smiled. "That's probably why we'll win."

They turned east, toward the Teeth., and walked on.

CHAPTER 19

The mountains did not welcome them. From the moment the five, stepped onto the foothills of the Iron Teeth, the world seemed to grow heavier. The wind, once sharp and clean across the grass-lands, became stale. The sky dimmed, even though clouds did not cover the sun. Sound traveled strangely sometimes echoing too far, sometimes vanishing entirely.

"The mountains remember pain," Cole murmured as they climbed a narrow trail. That's why they're called the Iron Teeth. The old tales say giants fought gods here, and their bones formed the peaks."

Quinn snorted. "I'll believe it. Everything here looks like it wants to kill us."

Rayner led in silence. The sword of the Old King remained strapped to his back, wrapped in cloth. Its light was a beacon but also a signal. They couldn't afford to draw attention in land where Malrik's eyes and ears bent with the wind. Their route followed an ancient smugglers' trail known as the Gray Spine. It twisted through steep ravines and narrow ledges, passing old shrines carved into the cliffs and bridges of cracked stone that spanned bottomless gorges. The first day of climbing left them breathless and bruised. The sec-ond day nearly claimed them.

It began with a whisper of falling stones. Rayner halted.

"Hold."

They stood on a ridge no wider than a cart's axle, sheer cliff above and below. The rocks beneath their boots trembled. Quinn looked up and cursed. A wall of loose shale and snow broke free from a high ledge.

"Down!" he shouted.

They scrambled for shelter. Cole dove beneath an outcropping, clutching his satchel. Rayner wrapped an arm around Quinn and leapt into a shallow hollow beneath a fallen pillar of stone. The avalanche roared past like a dragon's breath, deafening and violent. Dust filled the air. Stones pelted their backs. The mountain screamed. When it passed, silence returned except for the wheezing of breath and the slow crackle of shifting rock. Cole emerged, covered in dust, blood trailing from a cut above his eye.

"We were lucky," he muttered.

Rayner scanned the path. It was gone buried beneath tons of debris.

"No way forward that way," Quinn said. "We'll have to find a new route."

Rayner pointed to a nearby ridge where a crumbling staircase led up to a narrow ledge.

"There. That was a priest's path. If it's still stable, it'll take us to the high pass."

That night, they camped beneath an overhang where ancient statues lined the wall warriors, judges, kings long dead. One of the statues had no head, but its hand held a broken blade. Cole studied the runes beneath it.

"This was part of the Trial of Echoes. A pilgrimage route. The priests believed the mountains judged the worth of a soul."

Quinn leaned back, chewing on a strip of dried meat. "Let's hope they judge quietly."

Rayner stared into the fireless camp light, a small orb Cole conjured to avoid revealing their location.

"Malrik's kingdom lies just beyond the pass," he said. "Once we cross, the land belongs to him. Every tree, every stone. We'll need to be faster. Smarter."

Cole nodded. "And ready for the Wards."

Quinn raised an eyebrow. "Wards?"

Cole drew a circle in the dirt. "Malrik's kingdom is laced with blood-sorcery. Glyphs and binding spells written into the land. Some are warnings. Others are traps. Step wrong, and your soul becomes a whisper."

Quinn swallowed. "Good to know."

They slept in turns. Rayner dreamed of a castle on fire, of screams echoing through marble halls. He awoke with his sword humming in his grip. On the third day, they reached the high pass. The air grew thin. Snow dusted the ground. Wind howled between the rocks like a thing alive. The path narrowed to little more than a ledge clinging to a mountain's side. Below, cliffs dropped into fog-covered abysses. Rayner moved first, each step deliberate. Cole came second; his staff pressed to the rock for balance. Quinn followed last, silent for once. Finally, Tristan, crouched and looking around. Halfway across, they heard the voice. It came from the wind not words, but sound shaped like meaning. Cold and mocking.

"You come to die."

Rayner stopped. The sword on his back pulsed once, a flare of warmth in the cold.

"You think light will save you? Light burns. Light dies."

Cole's eyes went wide. "It's a ward. A sentient one."

Rayner kept walking. The voice hissed.

"Rayner. Son of nothing. You bear a king's sword but you are no king."

Rayner didn't stop.

Quinn gritted his teeth. "Ignore it."

Rayner turned. "Don't listen."

The wind laughed. Rayner gripped the hilt of the sword and unsheathed it slowly. Light burst from the blade like a sunrise. The wind screamed, truly screamed, like a wounded thing, and then the silence returned. Rayner sheathed the sword.

"Come on," he said.

They passed the final ledge in silence. The air in the Shadowvale Peaks was thin and sharp, like a blade pressed to the skin. Snow clung to the higher crags, and the path below wound like a scar through the ancient mountains, carved by wind, time, and war. High above the trail, on a jagged cliff where no man should have stood, Vael crouched in silence. Cloaked in ash-grey, eyes fixed on the distant figures below Rayner, Cole, Quinn, Tristan, and... Elira. For the last few days Elira had barely spoken a word. They moved slowly through the pass. Tired. Focused. Unaware that the wind itself carried eyes. Vael had followed them from Eldwyre, silent, unseen. He had not told Malrik. The last time he used the communication stone, he had only said:

"They travel east. Elira walks with them."

That had been enough to satisfy his master, but inside, Vael's thoughts churned. Why was he following them? To steal the sword? To ensure Elira did her part? Or... to understand them? He watched Cole, laughing too loud, speaking too much, casting sparks from his fingers without precision or fear. Vael should have hated him, but instead, he envied him. He had never been allowed laughter. Never had a brother. Never read by candlelight for pleasure. Then there was Quinn, strong and grounded, who never questioned his place. Tristan, whose silence was not born from fear, but from calm, and Rayner, who led not because of power, but because others believed in him. Vael had never seen belief like that. Not in Black Hollow, and not in Malrik.

That night, as the group camped near a frozen stream, Vael slipped into a forgotten stone ruin, a shrine long buried beneath snow and rock. He lit a small flame with a whisper of magic. Inside, etched into the stone walls, were words of the old kings.

"Light is not born in gold, but in sacrifice."

He stared at it. For a long time. Then he sat, placed his dagger beside him, and for the first time in years, wept silently into the cold. He had always known Elira to be like him, sharp, cruel when needed, a mask worn over steel, but watching her walk beside Rayner, helping Cole clean a wound, laughing with Quinn... It didn't match what he'd known. She was changing, and change was dangerous, but also... beautiful. Vael began to fear what would happen when Malrik found out, and what he himself might be forced to do. Vael descended from the ridge in silence. He wouldn't confront them. Not yet, but he would follow.

At midday, the path dropped into a basin walled by sheer cliffs and crowned with jagged teeth of rock. A great archway stood at the center, formed from black stone and veined with red crystal. Beneath it, the land changed. The sky darkened. Grass wilted. Trees leaned like broken men. The soil turned gray. Mist hung low, and the air smelled faintly of copper and ash. They had reached the border of Malrik's kingdom. Cole muttered a spell beneath his breath, a shimmer forming over his eyes.

"It's layered," he said. "Multiple bindings. Time, space, mind. Everything here is under his command."

Rayner stepped forward. The sword trembled in his grip, but held. He passed under the arch. The others followed. The world beyond was quiet. Too quiet. They walked for an hour and saw no movement, no animals, no birds. Just twisted woods and dying fields. Craters in the ground where old magic had scorched the earth. Then they saw the marker. A stone pillar, freshly carved. On it, the symbol of Malrik's legion: a skull wrapped in chains, and beside it, three heads on pikes. A warning.

Quinn looked away. "This is what he does to villagers that resist."

Rayner stared at the heads. One was barely more than a child. That night, they made camp in a hollow surrounded by ash trees. The leaves were black, the bark pale and cracked. Even the fire Cole conjured flickered oddly, as if afraid to burn too bright. Rayner sat apart from the others, the sword across his knees. He could feel it now, pulling harder. Drawing him somewhere deep in the east. Toward Malrik. Toward the keep. Cole joined him.

"He knows we're here," Cole said.

"I know."

"He'll send more than scouts this time."

"I know that too."

Cole looked at him, eyes hollow but steady. "You still believe we can kill him?"

Rayner didn't answer right away. "I believe we have to try."

Cole nodded slowly. "Then I'm with you. Until the end."

From behind them, Quinn called out, "Stop making dramatic speeches and get some sleep. I'm not carrying both your corpses."

They laughed, just a little. It was enough. The sky the color of rust and a low rumble in the distance. Thunder or something worse. The land ahead stretched like a scar dead soil, twisted trees, the ruins of forgotten outposts. Somewhere beyond, Malrik's keep waited. A fortress of bone and fire, shrouded in endless night. They broke camp. Rayner looked once more at the blade in his hand. It shimmered brighter now. Alive. He nodded.

"Let's finish this."

And together, they marched into the heart of shadow.

CHAPTER 20

From the base of the Ever-Reaching Mountains to the looming gates of Malrik's Keep, the land stretches in a blackened blur, a
place known as the Dark Expanse. It is a forsaken no-man's-land
of shifting mists, drowned ruins, and lifeless bogs, where even time
seems to lose its grip. No map charts it fully. No birds fly over it.
Travelers call it cursed, and the wise do not speak its name after
nightfall. The mountain pass that leads down from the Ever-Reaching winds through jagged crags and frostbitten cliffs. As one de-
scends, the snow fades, but not the cold. The chill seeps deeper,
not of temperature, but of dread. The first step into the Expanse is
marked by the Shatterbridge, a broken span of black stone. Once
part of a trade route in ancient times, now it arches uselessly over
a chasm that breathes mist. Below, a faint rumbling echoes like the
groans of a buried beast. Past the chasm, a tangled copse of dead
trees, called the Wraithwood, greets the wary. Their branches never
bear leaves, and bark peels like old skin. Some say the trees whisper
names. Others say they bleed.

The Sunken Fields, the trail slopes downward into the Sunken
Fields, a wide basin of rotted farmland and half-submerged struc-
tures. Homes once stood here, long ago, before Malrik's rise. Now,
black water floods the fields, and scarecrows still stand, twisted,
bloated, and nailed to crooked poles. Crows never land here. Frogs
do not croak. Only the wind moves. Sometimes, shapes move beneath the water. Footsteps make no splash. Even the dead soil
seems to drink light. Beyond the fields lie the Bleeding Mire, a
stretch of wetlands where red moss grows thick over mud that
oozes crimson when disturbed. Some believe the ground here remembers battle, perhaps a great war of the Old Kingdom, where

blood soaked the land until it stained it forever. Small knolls rise from the mire, each holding remnants of broken statues or fallen watchtowers. Many leaned at odd angles, half-swallowed by the bog. The fog here is especially thick, curling around ankles and clinging to cloaks. Travelers risk becoming turned around. Paths vanish. Strange lights flicker in the distance, lures, perhaps, or spirits.

At the heart of the mire rise the Mirewatch Pillars, four enormous obsidian obelisks, smooth and angular, with no marks or joints. They emit a low hum, almost imperceptible, and interfere with magical senses. Local legend says the pillars were driven into the earth by an ancient mage to hold something beneath. Others claim they mark the edge of Malrik's true domain. Past the Mirewatch is a stretch of eroded valleys and sinkholes known as the Howling Hollows. Here, the wind never stops. It screams through crevices, moans through cracks, and whistles across the bones of old creatures left in the open. These hollows shift constantly. New ridges rise overnight. Paths collapse. Echoes disorient even the cleverest trackers.

Near the final stretch of the Expanse lies the River of Dusk, a sluggish, black river that winds like a coiled serpent. Its waters reflect nothing, not stars, not torches, not the moon. Crossings are few. A ruined bridge spans the narrowest gap. It is called the Gate of Silence, named not for its quiet, but because those who speak while crossing it are said to be cursed. Many believe the bridge itself listens. On the far side lies the final stretch of land before Malrik's keep. Here, the terrain becomes rocky, broken by veins of red glass and twisted trees.

The last stretch of the Expanse is called the Ashen Rise, a steep, fire-scarred hill leading to the cliff where Malrik's keep waits. Ash coats everything. Burned remains of wagons, armor, and corpses litter the slope. Lightning strikes here often, but no storms roll in. The air crackles with static, and the sky darkens unnaturally. At the summit of Ashen Rise, one sees the Black Bastion in full, its towers jagged, its gates shut like a clenched jaw. The smell of smoke and iron permeates the air. The Dark Expanse is not just a terrain; it is a threshold. A veil between life and death, memory and forgetting. Magic twists here. The Weave thins, and reality itself warps in places. Spells misfire or change meaning. Time folds or stutters. Dreams bleed into waking. The Dark Expanse is the price of reaching Malrik's keep. It is the graveyard of kingdoms, the echo of failure, and the crucible of heroes. It does not forget, and it does not forgive.

No road marked the way. The map they carried was little more than a guess inked from memory, scattered rumors, and the warnings of dying men. Still, Rayner knew where to go. The sword guided him. Its glow had grown dimmer since they entered the heart of Malrik's kingdom, but now it pulsed with certainty, like a heartbeat echoing toward the throne of darkness. They crossed the Dark Expanse in silence, each step slower than the last. Time bent in strange ways here. Sometimes the sun hovered overhead for hours without moving. Other times it vanished mid-step, plunging the land into cold twilight without warning. The land had flattened, no hills, no trees. Only black soil, cracked and lifeless. Strange bones jutted from the ground like spears. Here and there, pillars of stone stood half-buried in ash, carved with glyphs that twisted when stared at too long. Nothing lived. Not even crows.

As they approached, they found a man walking toward them. He was barefoot, skin pale and stretched thin across his bones. His eyes were milky white, mouth hanging slightly open as though mid-sentence. No blood. No wounds. Rayner raised his sword, which flickered weakly. The man kept walking.

"Don't move," Cole whispered, but Quinn had already stepped forward.

"Who are you?" he asked.

The man didn't stop. He opened his mouth. A chorus of voices spilled out hundreds, all screaming the same word.

"RUN." Quinn leapt back.

Cole shouted "Another ward."

A blast of light struck the figure and knocked it flat but it didn't bleed. Its flesh peeled open like paper, revealing more faces beneath the skin. Eyes. Mouths. Rayner stepped forward and drove the sword down into its chest. The light surged. The thing screamed once and then collapsed into dust. None of them spoke.

"Malrik's creation," Cole muttered finally. "Souls fused to a single body. He uses them as warnings. Or bait."

Quinn wiped his brow. "That's the second worst thing I've seen this week."

"Don't ask what's first," Rayner said, already moving.

Elira continued the journey beside the others. The entire time questioning what she was doing. That night, they made camp beneath a collapsed archway that once belonged to a temple. Even the stones here whispered. They slept in shifts. During Rayner's watch, the sword began to hum again. He rose and looked ahead. Then he saw them. Figures faint, shimmering like reflections in water. Dozens, maybe hundreds. Walking through the mist, heads bowed. Some bore swords. Others held torches. A few carried nothing at all. They made no sound. Ghosts, Rayner thought, but not just ghosts. They were memories. He stepped closer and felt it a pull on his thoughts, like hands digging into his skull. Suddenly, he saw himself. A boy. Standing in a field of green. A woman with long dark hair reaching down to ruffle his hair. Her voice warm.

"You're stronger than all your fathers before you."

Rayner blinked. The field was gone. The woman too. He stumbled back.

"It's a trap," He thought to himself. "A field of memory. If we go in, we might not come out."

Quinn looked out at the mist. "There's no way around it, is there?"

Rayner shook his head. "No, but the sword might get us through."

He stepped forward again, the others close behind. The blade glowed brighter as they entered the field. Whispers closed in on them like fog. Names. Faces. Fears. The sword parted the mist like a flame through cobwebs, and then, suddenly, the whispers ceased. They had crossed. Behind them, the field swirled and vanished.

Midway through the third day, they found a ruin. A tower once tall, now broken in half. Black stone. A beacon long extinguished. They climbed its shattered stairs and looked east, and there it was. Malrik's Keep. A monolith of bone and iron. It rose like a mountain out of the land, surrounded by swirling mists and veins of red fire that pulsed across the black ground. Spires pierced the sky like knives. Chains hung from the walls, swaying though no wind blew.

Rayner felt his breath catch. "That's it," he said.

"There is no cover between us and the wall," Cole added.

"We'll need to wait for nightfall." Rayner said. "We need to rest, and then we find a way in."

They made camp beneath the tower's shadow. None of them spoke. They all knew what came next. The final approach. The stars above blinked faintly through a layer of thin cloud, veiled like the world itself held its breath. Rayner sat sharpening his blade, the steel whispering against the whetstone. His eyes raised now and then to the distance, where the shadow of Malrik's keep loomed on the horizon. Across from him, Quinn was hunched over rummaging through his satchel.

"Dinner's ready," he muttered. "It's all we have left."

"I swear, if that's more dead swamp beetles," Cole said, "I'm letting them take me at dawn."

Quinn snorted. "No bugs. It's dried meat."

He passed small pieces to everyone. Rayner sniffed his. Tristan took a slow bite and smiled faintly.

"It tastes like home."

Elira curled her knees beneath her cloak. Her dark braid was wind-tossed, and a thin layer of grime dulled the shine in her eyes, but she still looked more regal than any of them.

"This might be the last meal we eat."

"Don't say that," Rayner said quietly.

Cole took a bite and gagged. "Whether it is or isn't, this meat deserves to be our last."

Laughter rippled. Even Rayner smiled.

"I miss my father's roast boar," said Quinn. "He'd let me sneak pieces off the spit while it turned."

"Do you remember the honey apples from Fall harvest?" said Tristan.

"The ones they roasted in cinnamon bark?" Rayner nodded. "And the bread your mother made. The crust so thick you needed a dagger to get through it."

Quinn smiled. "She called it 'soldier's bread.' Said it could stop an arrow."

"You should've brought some for Malrik," Cole offered. "End this war without lifting a sword."

Elira laughed softly, head tilting back. "You all act like children."

"We were children," Rayner said. "Until all this began."

They sat in silence a moment. Rayner looked around the circle. A blacksmith's son. A hunter's boy. His little brother, grown into a mage. A girl he was growing fond of. He'd trained for battle. But he'd never trained for this kind of family.

"Tomorrow," he said, "we cross the breach. After that, we either bring light back to the kingdom… or we don't come back at all."

No one answered right away. Then Elira lifted her cup.

"To whatever comes next."

"To the Weave," said Cole.

"To the fire that waits," Quinn added.

"To the hunt," Tristan said.

Rayner raised his cup last. "To all the meals we'll have again… once this is done."

They drank the last of the water in silence, the fire burning lower, its warmth stretching only so far into the darkness. But it was enough, for now.

Rayner's Memory "The Last Night"

I remember the taste of that meat. Not because it was good, it wasn't. Gods, it was awful. But I remember it all the same. Because it was ours. We were camped at the edge of the Tower, just before the rise of the keep. We sat in a small circle, cloaks drawn tight around our shoulders. Even then, with the sky stretched black above us and the stench of rotting marsh in our lungs, it felt… safe.

Strange, that feeling. Safety. It had nothing to do with walls or even weapons. It came from them, Quinn with his callused hands and tired eyes, cracking jokes. Tristan, quiet, watching the night like he could already hear danger crawling through it. Cole, my brother, mage robes frayed at the hem, quoting

Azor and pretending not to be afraid. And Elira... her voice a calm I didn't know I needed. They were laughing. Just for a moment. Quinn said something about soldier's bread being strong enough to stop arrows, and Cole nearly choked. Even Elira smiled. It was the first time I'd seen her laugh without something behind it. Not a mask. Just her. I didn't laugh. I wanted to, but I felt it like a stone in my chest, that this might be the last time we'd all be together. That one of us might not make it through the next stretch. The Keep lay ahead, and beyond it, Malrik. And no matter how many times I told myself we'd survive it, that I'd protect them.

I remember the sound of Quinn's laugh, the way Elira leaned closer to me without realizing it. I remember how Tristan's gaze never left the dark. We toasted. Not to victory. Not even to survival. Just... to whatever came next. That memory is the ember I hold onto. The last fire. The last quiet.

Cole's Memory "The Night We Were Just Us"

You'd think I'd remember the magic. The spells. The incantations Azor whispered to me under moonlight, or the feel of the Weave trembling beneath my fingers before a battle. But what I remember most that night was, for a few fleeting hours, we weren't soldiers or spell-slingers or the last desperate hope of a kingdom on the brink, we were just five tired people, huddled around each other. We were at the edge of the Keep, and the ground squelched when you shifted your weight wrong. The air smelled like something had died there a century ago and never quite finished decomposing. Rayner was quiet that night. That kind of quiet where you can feel thoughts piling up behind his eyes like storm clouds. He sharpened his sword as if it could hold back the weight of what was coming. And maybe it could. He was always the one who bore more than he let on.

Tristan watched the dark like he expected it to watch back. It probably was. And Elira... she was curled into herself, silent. I remember saying something dumb. They all laughed. Not because it was particularly funny, but

211

because they wanted to. Needed to. That was our last normal moment. No crowns. No blood magic. No last stands or echoes of ancient kings whispering from stone. Just Rayner looking older than he was, Quinn pretending the world was still simple, Tristan keeping watch like it mattered, Elira finding her way closer to Rayner. We were just five weary souls.

That night, under a blood-colored moon, they made their way through the final stretch of the Expanse. The sword stayed sheathed, its glow hidden. Cole wore runes painted in ash and silver across his arms and face wards of silence, sightlessness. Quinn carried a dagger now, in addition to his hammer. They crept through twisted ravines and dried-out canals once used for blood rituals. No birds. No beasts. Only the hum of power in the ground. Then they found it. A breach in the Keep's base a shattered servant tunnel, long forgotten and buried beneath rubble. A crevice big enough to crawl through. Rayner knelt beside it.

"So, what now?" Rayner looked at them all. "We go in."

CHAPTER 21

On the southern edge of the known world, where mountains rise like the jagged spines of a sleeping beast and the sun hesitates to shine, there lies Malrik's Keep, an ancient stronghold swallowed by darkness. Perched upon the cliffs of Dreadspire Ridge, its towers claw at the sky, veiled always in shadow and storm. This fortress, also called The Black Bastion, was not built, but reborn. Once a ruin from a forgotten age, it was resurrected by Malrik using blood magic, iron, and hatred. Every stone in its walls hums with cold intent, as if the keep itself remembers its master's cruelty.

The Surrounding Land, nothing green grows here. The mountains encase the keep in a ring of stone, leaving only one narrow pass open, The Serpent's Wound, a winding trail of shale and cursed runes. No birds sing, and the wind howls through broken peaks like the moaning of ghosts. Below the cliff, the ocean crashes violently. From above, one can see wreckage strewn along the jagged rocks, ships shattered and swallowed by black waves. This place is one where the world ends.

The keep's walls are blackened granite, towering and thick. They glisten with a sheen that is not water, but the dried residue of spells. Runes etched into the stone shimmer faintly red at night, warding off intruders and trapping spirits within. Massive iron gates, engraved with skulls and serpents, guard the entrance. Above them, perched in alcoves, are statues of faceless sentinels, some say they move. The courtyard within is vast and cracked, paved with stone slabs where no moss grows. It once housed barracks and stables, now reduced to ruins or overtaken by shadow vines that feed on blood.

The Hall of Chains, this is the central gathering place of the keep. Unlike a great hall of feasts and banners, this chamber is long, cold, and echoing. Chains hang from the high ceiling like iron vines, some broken, others adorned with bones. Here, Malrik meets with his generals and creatures. The room is dimly lit by blue flame sconces, and murals along the wall depict the fall of the old kingdom, twisted versions meant to reinforce Malrik's rule.

The Throne of Bone and Ember, at the far end of the Hall of Chains stands Malrik's throne, crafted from fused bone, black obsidian, and scorched iron. It sits atop a raised dais, behind which a massive stained-glass window filters crimson light into the room.

Each piece of bone in the throne is said to have belonged to a fallen enemy, kings, rebels, even mages. When Malrik sits upon it, whispers rise like smoke.

The Chamber of Flame and Blood, this secret chamber lies deep beneath the keep. It is the source of Malrik's power, the heart of his blood magic. The room is circular, with veins of molten energy coursing through the stone floor. In its center floats the Crimson Font, a basin of churning, glowing blood drawn from dark rituals. Here, Malrik binds souls, creates wards, and channels his ancient power. The air is thick and metallic; the walls lined with incantations and ancient symbols carved so deep they bleed. The Hall of Mirrors, a long corridor filled with tall, warped mirrors that reflect not what one is, but what one fears. The glass ripples, sometimes showing alternate pasts or futures. Only Malrik walks here freely. Many who enter never emerge, their minds shattered by visions. It is said Vael, his apprentice, was born again in this hall.

The Spire of Sorrows, a narrow tower that juts highest into the sky. It houses Malrik's study and personal quarters. Books bound in skin, scrolls inked in ash, and tomes of lost lore fill every shelf. The view from the top reveals all the lands below, Ashbrook to the

Northwest, the ruins of Valebrook to the west, and the black sea to the north. Elira, his daughter, was kept here before she was sent to the villages.

The Silent Cells, beneath the keep lies a labyrinth of dungeons, cells of jagged stone, sealed with blood wards and bone locks. No torch burns here. Screams are swallowed by silence.

Some cells contain creatures from the old wars, half-men, shadow spawn, failed experiments. Others hold prisoners, trapped in slumber by enchantment. Even Malrik fears to walk too long in these halls. The Hall of Statues, a forgotten hall lined with statues of former kings, mages, and warriors, all turned to stone. They stand mid-motion, faces frozen in agony. Whether they were turned by curse or craft remains unknown. At the far end is a statue of Malrik himself, twice life-sized, one hand outstretched as if to grasp the world.

The War Chamber: A room filled with ancient maps, banners, and enchanted war tables that show troop movements. The Vault of Unmaking: Locked behind seven seals, this vault holds Malrik's most dangerous artifacts, daggers that sing, masks that whisper, books that write themselves. The Gallery of Regret: A hall of portraits painted in blood and shadow, showing moments from Malrik's past, many believe this is where his humanity once tried to speak.

Elira's Wing, hidden behind a false wall in the western tower is a small, sunless suite meant for Elira. Unlike the rest of the keep, it is quiet, dust-covered books, a mirror never used, and a bed never slept in. Here she read tales of kingdoms and stars, secretly learning magic by candlelight. Her escape began here.

The Living Magic of the Keep, the fortress itself is alive in ways not understood. Walls shift subtly. Echoes carry secrets. Shadows lengthen where none should be. The keep rejects the weak and feeds on pain. At night, eyes glow in the halls. Sometimes doors open by themselves. Other times they never open again.

The stone of the breach pulsed faintly beneath Rayner's fingers warm and alive, like flesh stretched too thin. He didn't speak. He didn't need to. He unsheathed the sword. Its golden light flared in the darkness, casting shadows along the collapsed tunnel. The Old King's blade trembled now not from fear, but anticipation. It wanted to be here. This was where it belonged. Cole and Quinn flanked him, crouched low. Behind them, the wastelands and the Dark Expanse stretched into black stillness. Ahead, the unknown. They entered Malrik's Keep. The breach led into a forgotten service corridor, half-collapsed and choked with debris. Rats or things like rats scurried along the walls, eyes glowing blue. The floor was slick with something black and tar-like, and the walls pulsed faintly as though veins ran through the stone. Cole cast a minor light spell, its flame hovering near his shoulder. Even so, the darkness pressed close, greedy and hungry.

"This place is alive," Cole muttered. "Not metaphorically. Blood magic runs through its walls."

"I can feel it," Rayner said, gripping the sword tighter.

The deeper they went, the more wrong the air became thicker, hotter, full of distant whispers. The kind you couldn't understand but still felt. The kind that left a residue behind your eyes. Quinn glanced down a branching hallway, where chains hung from the ceiling like vines.

"Dungeons?" Quinn whispered.

Cole nodded. "Torture pits. Sacrificial halls. Malrik doesn't just punish people. He feeds on them. Their fear. Their pain. It sustains the keep."

"Let's not visit, then," Quinn said, voice low.

Rayner led them onward, guided not by maps, but by the pull of the sword. Every turn, every stairwell, the blade grew hotter, more eager. It was seeking its opposite drawn to the black heart at the keep's core. They passed through a hall filled with carved stone tablets thousands of them; each etched with a name. Most were in languages none of them knew. A few were recognizable. All radiated sorrow. Cole stopped at one.

"This is Elenra," he said quietly. "She was a priestess. She tried to fight him with the binding songs."

He pointed to the line beneath her name. "Burned. Forgotten. Bound."

Rayner read another: "Jorun of the Flame Guard. Soul shattered. Bones offered." Quinn said nothing, but he touched one stone gently.

"Tera of the White Hills. Vanished beneath the black sun." Cole read.

They moved on in silence. They came to a great circular chamber; its walls etched with spirals that spun when you stared too long. In the center sat a throne carved from obsidian and bone, layered in chains and dried blood. It was empty, but it wasn't abandoned. Rayner stepped forward and felt a sudden pull, like the gravity of a mountain. He staggered.

Cole caught him. "You feel it?"

Rayner nodded. "It's... watching me."

A voice whispered not aloud, but within. "You came at last, little flame."

Rayner turned. No one stood there, but the room grew darker.

Quinn raised his hammer. "Something's coming."

From the walls, the spirals began to rotate faster and then things stepped out. Figures wrapped in red cloaks. No faces. No limbs. Just cloaks, floating, drifting forward with blades of smoke in their hands.

"The Bound," Cole spat. "Souls sacrificed to defend the keep."

Rayner raised the sword. The blade ignited. The first Bound rushed Quinn, blade flashing. He ducked, countered with a crushing swing, and the thing exploded into ash. Rayner clashed with another its weapon struck his shoulder, and cold shot through him like venom, but he retaliated with a sweeping arc of the sword. The golden light cut through the creature like paper. Cole chanted in the old tongue, casting a wall of fire to block more from entering.

"They're not endless," he shouted. "But they're close!"

More came. From the walls, from cracks in the ceiling. Dozens now. Quinn fought like a man possessed, keeping their flank clear. Rayner pushed forward, cutting down two, then three more. Each fell with a high scream that shattered into wind, but then a shadow fell over them all. From the far side of the room, something massive descended. A figure in black armor, ten feet tall, cloaked in rusted chainmail. Its face was a hollow void, its weapon a blade fused to its arm.

Cole's face turned white. "That's a Hollow Warden."

It roared a sound like a bell cracked in half. Rayner rushed it. They clashed in the center of the throne room. The Warden's blade met the Old King's sword with a shockwave that shook the walls. Blow after blow. Sparks flew. The Warden moved like stone slow but unstoppable. Rayner ducked one slash, rolled beneath another, then stabbed upward. The blade pierced the Warden's chest. The light flared. The Warden screamed and burst into shards. The Bound scattered. The throne room went still. After the battle, they limped deeper into the keep. The sword glowed steadily now. It knew where it was going. At last, they reached a spiraling staircase, descending into the earth. The walls were smooth and red. They felt like skin. At the bottom, a door waited massive, metallic, carved with thousands of screaming faces. It pulsed. Like a heartbeat.

Cole touched it. "The threshold. This leads to the heart of the keep."

"Where he waits," Rayner said.

They rested only briefly. When they rose, Rayner placed his hand on the door. It opened with a sigh.

CHAPTER 22

The air inside Malrik's keep was thicker than smoke, heavier than ash. It hummed with a low vibration, like a scream buried under stone. With every step forward, Rayner felt it pressing against his skin, the presence of blood magic, woven into the very bones of the fortress. He gripped the hilt of the Sword of Reynard, the ancient steel humming with its own energy, resonating against the weight of the fortress. At his back, his companions moved in silence. Cole, his brother, moved beside him, robes tattered from days of travel and battle. His fingers twitched, spell-light clinging to his knuckles like dying embers Quinn, stalwart and grim, held his hammer over one shoulder. The weight did not seem to slow him, only ground him Tristan, arrow already nocked, scanned every shadowed crevice in the stone walls, his movements sharp as instinct, and Elira, wrapped in twilight leathers and silver thread, moved like a phantom beside them, her dagger flashing with a flicker of pale light.

They had come through fire and ruin. Crossed the Dark Expanse. Watched comrades fall, seen villages burn, and still, still, they stood. For this. Before them loomed the Iron Door, carved with Malrik's sigil: a spiral of thorns surrounding a bleeding eye. The magic woven into it was pulsing, not locked but alive, waiting to consume.

Rayner stepped forward, placed his hand against the cold metal, and said quietly, "This is it."

Cole was already murmuring beneath his breath; ancient syllables shaped from the Codex of Binding. His eyes glowed faintly blue as he raised both hands.

"The magic in this door... It's fed by blood echoes. Trapped memories. We'll hear them."

"We've heard worse," Quinn muttered.

With a flash, Cole pressed his palm to the center of the eye. The sigil screamed. It wasn't a noise so much as a rush of every voice ever slain in this keep. Screaming in agony. Begging for release. Accusing. Cursing. The door peeled open like stone exhaling flame. Beyond lay a corridor of twisted black stone, illuminated by dim red veins running through the walls, veins pulsing like the beat of a dying heart. In the distance, the faint rhythm of chanting echoed, along with the stench of sulfur and burnt metal. They stepped inside. The corridor narrowed, the walls closing in. Every few steps, faces flickered across the stone, some screaming, others laughing, all distorted by blood magic. Elira moved silently ahead, pressing one hand to the walls.

"They're drawn to fear," she whispered. "If we don't give it to them... they pass by."

But the corridor tested them. Whispers filled the air. Rayner heard his mother calling his name. Then Sir Worric's voice, broken and afraid. You failed me, boy. The sword's not yours. He clenched his jaw and kept walking. Tristan nearly broke when he heard a child's cry echo off the wall.

"It's not real," he hissed, lowering his bow. But his hand shook.

Cole whispered a calming charm. "Breathe. Let it pass through you."

Quinn alone growled at the voices. "I don't care what you show me. I have a hammer. You don't."

He slammed it into the wall for good measure, cracking the face of a snarling illusion. Eventually, the voices faded. Ahead, a spiral staircase of blackened stone wound upward into a tower of twisted iron and glass.

At the top, Cole turned. "This is where it begins."

The staircase opened into a wide circular chamber, the Antechamber of Flame. At its center burned a brazier of green fire, surrounded by four statues: one of a knight, one of a child, one of a queen, and one of a chained beast.

"They're echoes of Malrik's power," Elira said. "Anchors."

Rayner moved toward the brazier. "Destroy them?"

"No," Cole murmured. "We face them."

The statues came to life. The knight's armor split open, revealing empty black within as it raised a sword of molten bone. The child floated, eyes glowing with crimson flame, giggling and weeping. The queen stepped forward, her face a shattered mirror, every reflection showing a different kind of grief, and the chained beast roared, its eyes blind but its claws glowing with cursed runes. Rayner went for the knight. Their blades met with a clash that echoed through the tower. The molten sword hissed against Reynard's steel, but Rayner's resolve burned hotter. With a spinning strike, he knocked the creature's head from its shoulders, and it dissolved into ash. Quinn met the chained beast with a snarl. His hammer cracked against runed limbs, breaking curses with brute force. The beast knocked him back once, but only once. On the second swing, Quinn's hammer shattered the creature's spine.

Elira and Tristan flanked the queen. Her illusions tried to twist their memories, but Elira whispered words of light, a spell taught to her by Azor. It burned through the falsehoods. Tristan fired a silver-tipped arrow through the queen's chest. She dissolved in a mist of sobs and silence. Only the child remained. Cole stepped forward alone. He dropped to one knee, looked at the child, and whispered:

"I forgive you." Cole said.

The flame flickered. The child blinked, looked down, and vanished in a burst of silver mist. The brazier flared and died. The chamber fell silent. A new door opened behind the statues. No sigil this time. No guards. Only darkness.

Rayner gripped his sword. "He's waiting."

The door closed behind them with the sound of a tomb sealing. Ahead stretched the Throne Hall, a wide, circular chamber of jagged black stone and crimson crystal. The floor was carved with spiral glyphs, glowing with a dull red pulse that beat like a heart. High above, thin slits in the ceiling let in shafts of broken moonlight, scattering pale beams over what remained of the Old Throne.

Rayner was thrown backward by a concussive blast. Cole's shield spell saved them from being incinerated outright but his nose bled from the strain. From the smoke stepped armored guards with pitch-black blades and empty eyes. Deathbound. Malrik's personal creations. Tristan dropped one with a bolt to the throat, but it didn't die. It kept walking.

"Not natural," he spat, reloading.

Cole raised both hands. "Trellath Vornan!"

A surge of white light blasted the nearest Deathbound apart. Rayner staggered to Elira,

"Elira, we're getting you out."

She looked at him, face pale. "Rayner, listen to me"

"No. No talking. We're getting out."

"You don't understand" She fell into his arms, and whispered: "He's, my father."

Time stopped.

"What?" Rayner breathed.

Elira looked up, eyes full of pain. "Malrik. The Dark Lord. I am his daughter."

Rayner staggered back, as if struck.

Tristan froze. "You're joking."

"I wish I was," Elira said. "He took me when I was a child. Raised me in secret. There's something in me. A seed of his power. He was going to use it. Claim the lands through bloodline and magic."

Tristan's voice was hollow. "You're his vessel."

"I didn't choose this," she snapped. "I chose you."

Rayner didn't know whether to believe her or kill her, but then Cole grabbed his shoulder.

"We don't have time."

The air vibrated. Footsteps echoed through the stone.

"He's coming," Elira whispered. "My father. Malrik."

Malrik sat atop it, cloaked in a mantle of shadow stitched with threads of living flame. His eyes, one blind and white, the other burning with inner fire, watched them as if he had known their faces since birth.

"You took your time," he said, voice echoing through the chamber like a funeral bell.

Rayner stepped forward, sword drawn. "We came to end this."

Malrik rose. He towered above them, taller than any man should be, his presence warping the air. Tendrils of blood magic writhed from beneath his sleeves, coiling like snakes of smoke.

"And do you understand what you're ending?" he said. "I built this realm from ruin. I forged peace from fire. You, you are children of fools."

"No," Cole said softly. "We are the end of your story."

Malrik snarled. "Then let me show you what your end looks like."

With a single motion, he raised both arms. The runes on the floor flared bright, and the room exploded with force. The blast threw them apart like leaves in a storm. Quinn slammed into a pillar with a grunt. Tristan rolled beneath a cascade of falling stone. Elira hit the ground hard, knives spinning from her hands. Cole tumbled backwards, blood on his lip. Rayner stood his ground, sword planted, as a wave of shadow crashed over him. Malrik descended from the throne like a storm incarnate. He swept his hand toward Quinn. The runes lit, and chains of searing energy erupted from the ground, binding his limbs. The hammer fell from his grasp.

"Elira, flank him!" Rayner shouted.

She was already moving. Spinning between runes, dodging bursts of fire and lightning. Her daggers flashed, slicing a line across Malrik's leg, but he didn't even flinch. Cole staggered to his feet, chanting.

"Bind him... Vora'thal. Sel'nar. Kaelthrin!"

Blue sigils burst around Malrik, but he raised his hand and shattered them with a snarl.

"You have your mother's voice," Malrik said to Cole. "And her weakness."

He lifted him into the air with a gesture, choking him with invisible force. His feet kicked.

"Let him go!" Rayner roared, and charged.

He met Malrik's blade with his own, Reynard's sword, forged in the fires of the first crown. The moment their blades touched, the air howled. Sparks erupted. Malrik snarled. Rayner drove forward, fury in every blow. He remembered every village that had burned. Every cry. Every loss. Worric. His father. The silence in Ashbrook.

"You'll never rule this realm again!"

Malrik pushed him back with a blast of dark energy.

"I am this realm!"

But the sword of Reynard shimmered, bright silver light pouring from its runes. Malrik staggered, just for a heartbeat. That was enough.

Cole shouted a spell "Thalarae ve'sennath!"

The chains binding Quinn shattered. The blacksmith's son leapt to his feet, caught his hammer, and charged with a roar.

"You want fire?! HERE IT IS!"

He swung, and Malrik caught the blow with a gauntleted hand. But then Tristan lost an arrow. The shaft glowed with silver fire, aimed for Malrik's blind eye. It struck. The dark lord screamed. Malrik staggered. The arrow lodged in his temple, bleeding black ichor. Elira ran beside Rayner. Cole's hands flared blue. He called the Weave again.

"Hold him," he gasped. "I need a clear circle!"

Rayner met his eyes. "Do it."

"Elira, cover Cole!"

She rolled to her feet, knives in hand, cutting down two summoned shades that leapt from Malrik's cloak. Quinn and Tristan flanked Rayner as they pressed the attack. Rayner's sword glowed brighter with each strike. Malrik reeled, still powerful, still ancient, but for the first time, mortal. Then Cole stepped into the center of the runic floor. He raised both hands.

"By the Codex. By the Light Beyond. By the Weave's Eye... I BIND THE BLOOD THAT BROKE THIS WORLD!"

The runes on the floor changed color, from red to gold. Malrik screamed as golden chains erupted from the ground and wrapped around his limbs, his throat, his burning core. He thrashed. Shadows poured from his mouth.

"No!" he bellowed. "I am eternal! I AM THE FLAME!"

Rayner raised the Sword of Reynard. It burned white now, brighter than the torches, brighter than the sun. He looked at his brother.

Cole nodded once. "Do it."

Rayner leapt forward, sword raised high. "This is for Eldara."

He plunged the blade through Malrik's chest. Malrik screamed, not just in pain, but as something old being torn from time. His body exploded in flame and ash. The chains shattered. The walls cracked. Rayner was thrown backward. Cole caught him. Malrik was gone. Only a burned mark remained shaped like a broken crown. Silence followed. The kind of silence that feels unnatural after war. The kind that doesn't quite feel like peace, only the absence of pain, the sudden relief of stillness after the last scream.

Rayner lay still, his breath shallow, his eyes staring upward at the cracked ceiling of Malrik's throne chamber. A single thread of smoke curled skyward where Malrik had stood. His armor was scorched, his knuckles torn, his heart thundering, but he was alive.

Beside him, Cole sank to his knees, exhaustion bleeding from every limb. His fingers were raw from the spellcasting, blue veins glowing faintly beneath the skin where the Weave had burned through him.

"That... was too close."

"You held him," Rayner whispered.

"I bought you three seconds. You used them better than I would have." Cole laughed dryly, coughing soot.

"I told you... never let the younger brother show you up." Rayner chuckled, then winced at the pain in his ribs.

"We'll argue about that later."

Across the chamber, Quinn dragged himself upright, wiping blood from his brow. His hammer was cracked down the center, but still intact. He looked around slowly, eyes squinting in disbelief.

"Is it... over?"

Tristan appeared beside him, limping but alert, scanning the shadows for any last flicker of sorcery. He lowered his bow, exhaled sharply, then walked to the mark on the floor where Malrik had burned away.

"Gone," he said. "Not hiding. Not waiting. Just... gone."

Elira approached last, blades still in hand, eyes rimmed with tears, not of grief, but of something deeper.

"He was my father," she said quietly.

Rayner stood, walked to her. The Sword of Reynard still shimmered faintly in his hand. He looked at her not with suspicion, not with pity, but with shared understanding.

"I know," he said.

She looked up at him. "You saw it too, didn't you? In the moment the blade struck."

Rayner nodded slowly. "There was still something human in him. But it was buried beneath too much."

They stood in silence, surrounded by ruin. Then came the quake. At first it was just a groan in the walls, a settling of stone. But it grew. The blood-woven runes across the chamber cracked, leaking red light, then bursting into arcs of flame.

"The fortress is unraveling!" Cole shouted. "Malrik's magic was the only thing holding this place together!"

Chunks of stone began falling from above. One of the high pillars split in half and crashed down onto the black floor, smashing it into molten shards. Smoke poured from the walls. Fire erupted along the spiral staircase behind them.

"Move!" Rayner shouted. "We head back through the Antechamber!"

They sprinted together, wounded, breathless, but alive. The tower was collapsing around them, every floor crumbling, every spell faltering. In the Antechamber of Flame, the four statues they'd defeated earlier had reformed, but lifeless now, drained of power, crumbling to dust as they passed. The brazier guttered out. Tristan led them through the whispering corridor. This time, the faces on the wall did not scream. They watched silently. One of them, a knight's face with a scar, whispered,

"Well done."

Then silence again. When they burst through the final door and out into the light, the sky was red and gold. The storm clouds above Malrik's keep had begun to break. Sunlight pierced through in beams, shining on the black spires and melted towers. All around the keep, the fields of the Dark Expanse had begun to smoke and shift. The swamps and marshes were receding. The blood-slicked grass had begun to wither, and pale green buds emerged from ash. Rayner turned back and looked at the fortress one last time. It trembled. And then. It collapsed. The central spire of Malrik's keep split in half and crumbled like rotted bone. The rest followed, falling into a heap of shattered stone, molten iron, and fading light. The final echo of Malrik's reign… was silence. They stood on a ridge overlooking the remains. No legions. No banners. No monsters. Only the five of them. Elira wrapped her arms around herself, still trembling. Quinn let out a long breath.

"We did it."

"No," said Cole. "Rayner did."

Rayner shook his head. "We all did. Together."

Tristan walked to the edge of the hill, peering toward the horizon.

"There'll be people coming soon. From the other villages. From the coast. Word will spread."

"And they'll look to you," Cole said.

Rayner stared down at the Sword of Reynard in his hand.

"I'm not ready."

"Neither was our father," Cole replied gently. "But he learned. So will you."

Quinn grunted. "At least now we can sleep without shadows clawing at the door."

"Do we rebuild?" Tristan asked. "What happens next?"

Rayner looked to the east, toward the sun rising above the ruined keep. He felt the sword pulse one final time, then grow still. Its work was done.

"We return to Valebrook," he said. "There's a kingdom to heal."

CHAPTER 23

The wind howled across the ruined battlements of Black Hollow Keep, carrying with it the scent of ash, steel, and freedom. Malrik was dead. His blood magic shattered. His armies broken. His shadow lifted, but the cost was heavy. The final blow had been struck by Rayner, the sword of King Reynard burning with light as it pierced the chest of the tyrant who had twisted the world for too long. Malrik's death wasn't the end. It was the beginning. The land didn't heal instantly. The skies didn't suddenly clear, but across the realm, the Veil sealed, the dead ceased to whisper, and the storms finally quieted. The kingdom had no king, and so, the people looked to the one who had brought them hope.

The bells of Valebrook tolled low and slow, their sound rolling like thunder over the riverbanks and orchards that stretched beneath the high, battered walls of the castle. A soft breeze stirred the torn banners overhead, gold threads catching sunlight like strands of memory. Inside the eastern courtyard, the survivors gathered, nobles and farmers alike, scarred soldiers standing beside children who now knew war. Rayner stood at the center of it all. Elira stood to his right, hand in his, silent and steady. Quinn behind them, wrapped in a captain's cloak. Tristan, crossbow slung but at ease. And Cole... the youngest of them, but eyes older now. He leaned on his staff not from weakness, but weight. The kind that didn't touch the body, but pressed upon the soul. Then the gate creaked open. But none moved to stop the cloaked figure who stepped beneath the arch. His staff struck softly against the stone, his beard a nest of silver caught in the wind. His robes, once sky-blue, were frayed and scorched at the edges. But his eyes were bright as stars.

"Azor," Cole breathed.

Rayner took one slow step forward. "We thought"

"That I was dead?" the old mage said, voice soft as dusk. "So, did I. For a time."

Azor stopped before them, and though his face was lined, and the weight of years hung about his shoulders, he stood tall. Taller than Cole remembered.

"I knew you'd return," Cole said. "You said you'd watch the end from afar."

"I did." Azor's eyes drifted upward.

They gathered later in the inner chamber; the war room now emptied of swords and maps. Just a hearth, a circle of chairs, and the fire that still burned, quiet and steady. Azor sat near it, his gnarled fingers tracing the warmth like an old friend.

"I felt it the moment Malrik crossed the threshold of forbidden power, he said. The Weave, our world's thread of life and balance, bent. And in bending, it broke. When the veil shattered, Azor continued, I felt it.

The following day, they stepped into the outer courtyard where a quiet ceremony was to begin. The crown would finally rise. The banners would fly again. But Azor stopped Cole at the edge of the stone arch, near a shaded alcove where the sun carved gold through ivy.

"I have something for you," the old mage said.

He reached into his cloak and withdrew a scroll; a narrow spindle bound in iron thread. Cole recognized it instantly.

"The Codex of Binding," he whispered.

Azor nodded. "The last relic of the First Weavers. Kept from Malrik. Hidden even from the royal vaults. It belongs to the one who will defend the realm with magic, not rule it."

Cole stared at it, then slowly took the scroll. It pulsed faintly in his hands.

"I'm not ready," he said.

Azor raised a brow. "You're not supposed to be."

Cole laughed, a short, nervous sound. Azor rested a hand on his shoulder.

"You'll be many things, Cole. A friend. A protector. A guardian of the Weave. But never perfect. And that's why you'll succeed where others failed."

He looked toward the gathering ahead, where Rayner stood waiting, crown in hand, firelight dancing across his armor.

"He will rule in daylight," Azor said. "But you... you will watch the shadows."

Rayner stood atop the walls of Valebrook, the ancient capital once thought lost. It had taken years to reclaim it. To clear the rot. To restore the flags of the old line. The people began to gather. Nobles, farmers, former soldiers. They called him King. And so, in the Great Hall of Valebrook, Rayner knelt where his father once had. Azor placed the crown of gold and stone upon his head, and the people roared:

"Long live King Rayner."

Later that night, as the castle slept and the new age began, Cole sat in the old observatory atop the mage's tower. The Codex of Binding sat before him, its scroll unfurled just slightly. He traced one of the symbols with his finger.

"I'll guard this kingdom," he said quietly. "Not with fire. But with light."

Outside, the Weave pulsed softly in the stars above, alive again. And below, in the heart of Valebrook, the world held its breath no longer. Held in the Sun-Garden of Valebrook, beneath the Crown Tree.

The sun rose slowly that next morning, as if Eldara herself was holding her breath. Morning mist curled like silk around the stones of Valebrook, weaving between the columns and hedgerows of the royal Sun-Garden. The ancient Crown Tree, tall and silver-leaved, stood at the garden's heart, its bark etched with glyphs no one living could translate, and its roots whispering into the Weave. It had witnessed the rise of kings, the fall of kingdoms, and now, the beginning of something entirely new.

Rayner stood looking out among the people. Quinn stood beside him, clean-shaven and radiant in a royal tabard trimmed with gold. Tristan was behind them in forest leathers, one hand resting lightly on the pommel of a ceremonial blade, and Cole, Rayner's younger brother, now the king's mage, was in formal robes of midnight blue. The ends of his sleeves shimmered faintly with spell-thread, and his grin, slightly crooked, ever irreverent, offered quiet support. The guests gathered in quiet rows, warriors, villagers, nobles, and those who had simply survived. Knights once bound to the Balance Charter, refugees from Stonebrook and Dunmar, mages and apprentices, and even the last elders of Ashbrook's circle. They carried no banners. Instead, they carried wildflowers from every village in Eldara. Together, they lined the path with petals: scarlet mountain lilies from Dunmar, pale blossom vines from Eldwyre, moonbuds from Hollowmere. Then came the music. It was not grand fanfare or military drum. It was a single flute, played by a boy from Ashbrook, soft and high like birdsong at the edge of spring. As the notes floated over the crowd, the garden hushed and turned.

Elira emerged from the eastern gate. Her gown was stitched from the silks of Eldwyre and the mist-wool of Valebrook's highlands. It shimmered pale gold, as if woven from the first light of morning. A braid of starlight vines wound through her dark hair, and her veil was bound by a circlet that had once belonged to her mother, a woman she scarcely remembered, but carried in every step. She walked not with pomp, but with grace earned through fire. The daughter of Malrik, raised in secrets and taught deception, now revealed, redeemed, and beloved. As she walked, the villagers did not flinch. They bowed.

Azor stood near the Crown Tree, hands clasped, robes layered and ceremonial. The elder mage had returned to Valebrook for this purpose, saying only,

"The threads of the realm demand closure... and blessing. His voice carried over the hush: Let this union be more than peace. Let it be promise. Let it be the stillness after the storm. Let it be the moment the sword is placed upon the stone."

Rayner stepped forward to meet her. When their eyes met, the silence was absolute. There had been so many reasons to fear this moment. Elira's lineage, the pain left in the kingdom, the wounds not yet fully healed, but here, in this place, none of that mattered. Because the truth of them, the truth born in a ruined keep, sealed with sword and blood and choice, was stronger than the past.

"I should warn you," Elira whispered, her voice soft enough only for Rayner to hear. "I snore like a dire wolf."

Rayner smiled. "Then I'll never sleep again, but I'll die happy."

Azor's arms lifted, and the Weave stirred. Not magic in force, but presence, a subtle shift in the air, as though the world was adjusting itself to witness this binding. A ring of low wind stirred the petals on the ground, swirling them around the couple in spirals. Then Azor spoke again.

"Rayner, son of King Reynard and Queen Elenora, sworn of the Balance Charter, bearer of the Crown of Flame, do you offer your heart and will to Elira, not as king to subject, but as man to woman?"

"I do," Rayner said, voice strong.

"Elira, daughter of Malrik, child of shadow turned to light, do you offer your spirit and strength to Rayner, not as penance, but as promise?"

"I do," she said, and the garden breathed.

They turned toward each other. No rings were exchanged. Instead, they each drew a single ribbon, Rayner's was silver, Elira's deep blue. They bound their hands together at the wrist and spoke, in unison:

"Let our pasts be fuel. Let our bond be fire. Let our kingdom rise not from blood, but from what we choose, together."

Azor's staff struck the earth once, a low chime sounding in the Weave. The Crown Tree rustled, though no wind blew, and the realm, at last, had its King and Queen.

Azor slipped quietly into the edge of the square, unnoticed by most, save for a few elders who remembered him. Cole found him later near the old well behind the library tower.

"Where will you go?" the young mage asked.

Azor looked up at the stars. "Somewhere quiet," he said. "Magic is healing. Slowly. But it will take time. And time is what I have left to offer. Perhaps I will find where the threads are thinnest and begin mending what's frayed."

Cole nodded, eyes shining. "Will I ever see you again?"

Azor smiled. "You'll hear me in your spellwork. In the silence before the storm. In the whisper of flame and wind. Mages never truly leave, Cole."

He turned then, walking slowly toward the outer path, staff tapping against stone.

"Azor?" Cole called. The old mage stopped, glancing back. "Thank you," Cole said.

Azor gave him a long look. Pride. Peace. And then he was gone.

The Crown of Ash and Flame

CHAPTER 24

In the following months, Rayner would not rule from a throne, but from among the people. He rebuilt the kingdom not to resemble what it had been but what it should have been all along. He traveled to villages, dined with farmers, sat with grieving widows. He outlawed blood rites. He banned the hoarding of magical relics. He raised statues not of kings, but of those who fought and bled beside him. Rayner had been a friend, a brother, and a leader, but becoming king was another matter entirely. Rayner faced a kingdom broken by war: Roads had crumbled. Villages had been razed or abandoned. Entire provinces once loyal to the crown now operated under their own laws, or worse, under no laws at all, but he did not rebuild it alone.

Elira wore the crown with grace. Her compassion earned her the loyalty of those who had once feared her, and in time, even the noble houses began to bow more easily. Cole rebuilt the mage circles, and began teaching new mages to balance power with compassion. He still made bad jokes. Still left books lying open, but his eyes saw the threads of magic more clearly than anyone since the old age, and when the new Keep was built, a tower was raised at its heart. Cole called it the Ember Spire. For knowledge. For wonder. For the spark that starts all things.

Quinn was named Captain of the Royal Guard. He protested at first, muttering about

"Noble nonsense" and "shiny boots," but he wore the mantle well.

He turned the disbanded remnants of the old guard into a true brotherhood. Blacksmiths and woodsmen. Farmers and hunters. He trained them all. Under Quinn, the Wardens of the Crown became more than soldiers, they became protectors of the realm, patrolling the roads between Valebrook, Ashbrook, Dunmar, and the northern routes. Still, he never gave up the forge. Every month, like clockwork, Quinn could be found in the Valebrook smithy, sleeves rolled, crafting a new blade or hammer. It grounded him.

Tristan vanished for three months after the war. Tristan had gone into the wilds, past the Eroded Mountains, into the high forests near Eldara's eastern cliffs. When he returned, he brought maps. Knowledge. Treaties with the cliff-dwelling falcon tribes and word of strange lights on the sea. He was appointed Chief Ranger of the Realm, with the responsibility of keeping Eldara's borders protected and its trade routes secure. But he often traveled alone, with only his longbow.

He was the silent edge of the kingdom, the shadow in the trees that watched so the others could rest. Across Eldara, the work of peace was slow but steady. Stonebrook, once a border village razed by Malrik's legion, became a center for grain and horse trade. Dunmar, aided by its innkeeper's efforts, became a hub for trade caravans passing into the highlands. The river nymphs were once again seen near the banks of Hollowmere, no longer fleeing, but singing. Rayner reopened diplomatic channels with the dwarves in the north, sending emissaries to rebuild the alliance broken in his grandfather's time. Eldwyre, under Elira's stewardship, began producing ink and rare herbs again, essential for mage work and healing. Valebrook was rebuilt stone by stone. New homes were constructed. The castle's spires were repaired. The great library, once burned, was restored with help from Cole and a wandering scholar named Renn.

Not all was calm. Cole began having visions, not of the past, but the future. They came with pain now. Searing, sudden, and worse than anything he'd felt before. He told no one at first, but they came every time he touched the Codex or dreamt too deeply in the Weave. They showed him: A girl with silver eyes, crying alone in a field of ash. Snow swallowing villages whole. A broken tower in the far north, pulsing with light, and one night, a whisper: She waits. Cole didn't know who she was, but he knew it was beginning again.

The clang of hammer against steel had been Quinn's first language. Long before he learned the weight of a blade in his hand, he learned the weight of one across an anvil, how steel groaned when overworked, how it sang when tempered right. Now, that same discipline echoed not in the forge, but across the southern courtyard of Valebrook's keep. Morning light cast a golden sheen over the frost-dusted stones as Quinn surveyed the row of would-be guards before him. Thirty men and women, no two alike. Some fresh from villages. Others, scarred, grim, had seen war.

None of them were ready. Quinn crossed his arms, boots crunching on the frozen ground. Behind him, the castle's banners hung heavy with morning dew, blue and silver, the mark of the new reign.

"Raise your weapons," he said, voice level but sharp.

A rustle of motion. Spears, swords, axes, shields, awkward, uneven. One lad dropped his buckler. Another blinked sweat from his eyes though the air was cold. Quinn shook his head.

"You're not soldiers," he said. "Not yet. But you will be."

He walked slowly down the line, his gaze hard but not cruel.

"I don't need brutes who swing like tavern brawlers. I don't need nobles looking to puff their chest. I need protectors. Guards. The ones who take the hit so others don't have to."

He stopped in front of a girl no older than seventeen. Her knuckles were white on the grip of a longsword.

"Name?"

240

"Lira," she answered.

"Ever been in a fight?"

"Once. A wolf."

He nodded. "And did you win?"

"It bled more than I did."

A faint smile touched Quinn's lips. "Good. You'll fit in fine."

He turned back to the group. "This isn't just about drills or pretty formations. You'll learn to track, to guard, to ride. To fight beside a king. That means trust. That means silence. That means giving everything, even when it hurts. Especially when it hurts."

The yard fell quiet. Then, with a nod, Quinn drew his sword, not the ceremonial one Rayner gave him at the coronation, but the blade he forged himself in Valebrook. Its steel was dark, balanced, notched at the hilt from years of use.

"Form lines. Five paces apart. Blunted edges today. We start with endurance. If your arms don't ache by midday, you're not swinging hard enough."

A few groaned. One cursed under his breath.

Quinn just smiled. "Welcome to the Wardens of the Crown."

By the end of the first week, ten had quit. The rest remained, some through pride, others through desperation, a few because they'd begun to believe in the man who led them. Quinn was not a yeller. He barked commands when needed, but more often he showed than shouted. He taught formations by standing in them. Showed sword grips by letting them feel the flex in his wrists. Demonstrated counters by sparring with recruits until they found the movement for themselves. In the evenings, when drills ended, he sat with them by the fire. Cooked with them. Listened. He heard the fears they whispered when they thought he'd left: That they'd never live up to Rayner's legend. That they'd freeze the first time they faced a blade. That they weren't soldiers, they were bakers and farmers, tanners and thieves, and Quinn, sharpening his blade or oiling his boots, would sometimes answer:

"I wasn't a soldier either."

They would look at him. He would just nod.

"I was a blacksmith's son. No one asked me to fight. I chose to."

That always quieted them. By midwinter, Quinn's recruits had callused hands and clearer eyes. The weak had fallen away, not by dismissal, but by choice. The ones who remained had something else in them now: resilience, but grit wasn't enough. Quinn knew battle did not wait on even ground, under the neat rows of castle flags. War came in the dark. In confusion. In cold and mud and silence. And so, he took them into the woods. They marched northeast of Valebrook, into the twisted pines beyond the River Farroth. Snow fell in lazy sheets. Boots sank in frost-hardened dirt. The trees whispered like old ghosts. Here, they would undergo the Trial in the Pines, a three-day test with no orders, no fires, and only what they carried. Quinn led them in silence. At dusk, he vanished into the trees, leaving behind a single message:

"You will not be found until you prove you can move as one."

At first, they panicked. Lira argued with the barrel-chested man, now known as Darron. Two others wandered off to scout. A third tried to take charge but failed to inspire anything but confusion. By morning, one was missing, and the others were soaked, cold, and silent, but then something changed.

Darron, once loud and boastful, quietly took up point. Lira, who had learned to listen more than speak, suggested signals, two bird calls, a stone toss, a blade tap. The group began to move. Not perfectly, but as a unit. On the second night, as frost rimmed their cloaks and a distant howl rose from the hills, they set a silent camp in a hollow beneath pine boughs. No fire. No chatter. Just shared warmth, and eyes that watched for threats beyond the dark. Quinn, from his perch in the branches above, nodded to himself. They were learning.

When the guard returned to Valebrook, they were no longer recruits. Not warriors yet, but close. Quinn gathered them in the northern courtyard, where stone columns ringed the edges and the ancient fountain of the First King ran again, freshly restored with water from the mountain springs. Rayner was there. Cole, too. Even Elira, cloaked against the cold, watched with quiet approval. One by one, the guards approached the stone dais. Each laid their hand upon a shield, Quinn's shield, forged in Valebrook, painted with the Crown sigil, and spoke the oath Quinn had written in the quiet hours of dusk.

"By breath and blade,
I stand for those who cannot.
I guard not only the throne,
But the soul of Eldara.
No darkness shall pass me.
No fear shall root me.
I am Warden,
In flame or frost,
In life or death
I endure."

They did not cheer afterward. They simply stood taller. The King nodded his approval.

"These are not just guards," Rayner said. "They are the shield between peace and ruin. And their captain is one I would trust with my life."

Quinn tried not to look too proud. But Cole elbowed him as they passed, grinning.

"Not bad for a blacksmith."

Quinn just snorted. "Says the kid with a talking book and a fireball problem."

Quinn's greatest lesson came not in battle, but from a slip of a girl named Merren. She was eleven. Too young for service. But she followed the guards every day, mimicking their movements with a stick for a sword and a rusted cooking pot for a helmet. One afternoon, as they practiced maneuvers, Merren shouted from the edge of the yard.

"You turned wrong! Foot was late! You'll lose your balance!"

The guards paused. Quinn raised a brow. And then smiled.

"Alright, Commander Merren. Show us."

She blinked. Then marched out, demonstrating the move, with better form than half the squad. Quinn knelt.

"You want to train?"

"Yes," she said, fierce. "I want to protect people."

He stood. "Then come. You'll help drill footwork."

They laughed. But she came back the next day. And the next. Merren reminded them what they were protecting. Not just a king. Not even just a kingdom. But the small ones. The quiet ones. The future. It was spring when the test came. A caravan from Dunmar, carrying grain and blackroot, was ambushed outside the hills. Bandits, not remnants of Malrik's forces, just desperate men in desperate times, but the guards responded in hours. Under Quinn's command, a squad of six intercepted the raiders. Darron took a spear to the leg defending a merchant. Lira saved two children by shielding them behind a fallen cart. The fight was short but brutal. When it ended, and the bandits fled, Quinn ordered the wounded carried back, no glory talk, no celebration, but that night, as the caravan was secured, the fire burned warm. Quinn passed around a flask of blackberry whiskey from Ashbrook. Lira laughed for the first time in weeks. Darron limped, but smiled like a wolf. These weren't just soldiers anymore. They were Wardens.

Later that year, on the anniversary of Rayner's coronation, the Wardens stood in full regalia on the steps of the castle. Their armor was not polished gold, but brushed steel-etched with mountain runes, painted with blue and ash-gray. Quinn refused capes.

"Too easy to grab."

Rayner approached Quinn as the sun set behind them.

"You've done well," he said.

"They did the work," Quinn replied.

Rayner clapped a hand on his friend's shoulder. "You gave them reason to."

He handed Quinn a small token, a coin of obsidian and silver, marked with the Crown's symbol on one side and a hammer on the other.

"A new emblem," Rayner said. "For the forge you built. And the flame you carry."

Quinn looked down at the coin, silent for a long moment. Then he nodded. "We're ready."

Rayner looked out at the horizon. "Then I hope peace holds. But if it doesn't... I'm glad they have you."

The next day, Quinn headed back to Ashbrook to visit his father. The forge was colder than he remembered. The walls were soot-streaked stone, patched where time had chipped them. The roof sagged a little more than it had when he was a boy, and the woodpile was lower, softer, slowly surrendering to moss, but the anvil stood exactly where it always had, centered, solid, unyielding. A monument not to metal, but to memory. Quinn stepped inside, the scent of ash and oil hitting him like a blow. He closed his eyes for a breath and let it wash over him. Here, his father had stood, hammer in hand, humming low songs no one remembered. Here, Quinn had burned his fingers, learned balance by accident, and shaped his first crude knife. Here, he had looked out the window and watched Rayner sparring with Sir Worric in the field, the boy laughing as he was knocked into the mud. That boy was a king now, and Quinn... he was Captain of the Royal Guard. He let out a slow breath and stepped closer to the anvil. He ran his fingers across the worn edge, remembering the day he forged his own blade. It wasn't perfect. The handle was uneven. The edge needed work, but it was his. He'd brought it with him the first day he marched behind Rayner into battle. It had never left his side. Now he carried a new one, still his, but tempered by more than flame. By failure. By duty. By the trust of those who followed him into storm and shadow.

He turned to the workbench. Dust covered it, but beneath that dust lay his father's final hammer. He picked it up. Heavy. Warm, somehow, even in the chill. Quinn smiled. He wasn't just a blacksmith's son anymore. He was a Warden. A leader, but this place, this fire-blackened forge, would always be the start of it all. He set the hammer down gently, like placing a memory back where it belonged. Then he turned toward the door, stepping into the afternoon sun that painted Ashbrook gold. Ahead lay duty. Behind, roots. He walked on, steady and sure.

The wind whispered through the high grass of the eastern ridge, carrying the scent of pine and old rain. Tristan crouched low in the brush, bow in hand, his breath shallow, his heartbeat still. The world around him pulsed with life, birdsong, the rustle of rodents, the distant crack of a branch, and the recruit blundering toward him like a drunken bear. Tristan sighed.

"Again," he said without rising.

His voice was quiet, like wind through reeds, but the trainee heard it. He froze mid-step, face flushing.

"I moved like you said, heel first, knees soft"

"You moved like you were trying not to die. That's different than moving like you belong here."

The recruit opened his mouth to argue, but Tristan was already gone. He reappeared ten feet to the left, silent as mist, crouching beneath a low branch, bow still in hand.

"There's no path," he said. "No formation. You're not knights. You're not soldiers. You're watchers. Listeners. Hunters. You move when the trees say move, and stop when the rocks whisper stop."

A second recruit, hidden nearby, blinked in surprise. She hadn't seen him either. That was the point. Tristan's Rangers trained far from the stone walls of Valebrook. Tristan's trainees slept in lean-tos, ate what they foraged, and spoke rarely. Their base was little more than a ring of trees and a cave nestled in the Vale of Morn, where mist clung to the ground like old sorrow. He accepted twelve to begin. All volunteers. Five were hunters from the northern hills. Two had served in Rayner's army during the Siege of Hollowmere. One, silent, sharp-eyed, was a reformed thief from Dunmar who could climb like a squirrel and vanish between shadows, and the rest?

They were the ones no one noticed. The ones who had spent their lives listening. Tristan didn't teach them to fight. Not first. He taught them to disappear. They learned how to step without sound, how to spot a rabbit's nest from fifty paces, how to track a boot print in wet moss. They trained their ears to detect breath across bark, their eyes to read broken twigs like a map.

"Your bow is only as good as your patience," Tristan said as they waited motionless for hours in the rain. "If you can't sit with the wind and listen, you don't deserve to strike."

It was two weeks before he let them carry weapons. Even then, he gave them wood-knobbed staves and dulled training knives.

"Steel is a lie," he said. "Steel thinks it wins because it's sharp. But in the wild, silence wins. Distance wins. Not being seen wins."

One recruit, a burly trapper named Fen, scoffed. "A knife in the gut wins too."

Tristan didn't answer. That night, he crept into Fen's bedroll and pressed the cold flat of a blade against his throat before vanishing into the dark. The lesson stuck, but Tristan wasn't cruel. He didn't mock failure. When a recruit tripped a wire, he helped them reset it. When they missed a shot, he made them fletch new arrows until they learned the rhythm of the string and wind. He shared food, too. Taught them the difference between bitterroot and whisperleaf. Showed them how to boil bark into tea that warmed the bones. It wasn't comfort, but it was survival, and when the first snow fell, he had them map the forest by memory, by stars, by the way the wind curled through the oaks. The wild was their home now. And he was its ghost.

It came on a blue morning, sky clear, frost biting the trees, silence deep and glass like. Tristan and his trainees were returning from a week's trek along the riverbound edges of the forest when the crows began to circle. Not one. A dozen. Black flecks in an otherwise unblemished sky, wheeling above the snowdrifts near the northern slope. He held up a fist, the signal to halt. Helena, small, agile, the best tracker of the group, slipped beside him.

"Dead animal?" she whispered.

"Maybe." His tone said otherwise.

They moved with caution, not as one body, but as a scattered web, each Ranger flowing through the trees, bows slung, eyes sharp. Tristan found the boot prints first. Heavy. Clumsy. No attempt to mask them. Five men, maybe six. Heading south with haste. Blood, too, trailing in the snow like red threads across white cloth. Not far ahead, a merchant's cart lay overturned. A man and woman, farmers from the look of it, lay slumped beside the wheel. The man's chest was still. The woman breathed shallow, lips blue. Tristan knelt and pressed two fingers to her wrist.

"She's alive."

No one spoke. No one needed to. The bandits had come from the north. Malrik was gone, but chaos still festered in the cracks of the realm. These weren't soldiers. Just wolves with blades. Tristan stood.

"You know the path," he said. "Don't engage unless I say. Stay above them. Watch. We track until dusk. Then we hunt."

They followed the bandits for two days. Snow gave them a trail easy to read, but hard to chase. Each footfall had to be tested, each branch avoided. The Rangers fanned out across ridgelines, hidden behind tree trunks, never letting the prey know it was being stalked. Tristan's commands were minimal: hand signals, bird calls, glances. The reformed thief, called Jett, got within twenty paces of the camp by the second night. He reported back under starlight.

"Six men. Two sleeping. One on watch. Drinking. Sloppy."

Tristan nodded. "Positions?"

"Backs to the slope. Good vantage, but no eyes overhead."

That was their mistake. At dawn, the Rangers moved. It wasn't war. It wasn't even a proper fight. It was precision. A snare pulled the watchman into the trees. A second fell to a silent arrow. The third ran, only to vanish in the mists and not return. By sunrise, four of the bandits lay bound or bleeding. Two escaped, but not without wounds. The woman from the cart survived. She was brought to Valebrook with supplies and silver. She remembered nothing, save for the ghostlike eyes in the woods who carried her to safety. The Rangers returned to their cave in silence. It was Jett who spoke first.

"Was that... what it's always like?"

Tristan met his eyes. "No. Sometimes it's worse." He smiled. "You did well."

They were Rangers now. In oath. In blood. Tristan called them together beneath the boughs of an ancient blackpine, the one he used to sleep beneath when he was just a hunter's son with a bow too big for his arms.

"We don't wear crests," he told them. "We don't get parades. We don't ride with banners or shout in halls. What we do, no one sees." He looked around at them. "But the people sleep safely because of it."

He unslung the carved bone totem from his belt. It had once been his father's. He drove it into the earth like a marker.

"No flame. No fanfare. Just watch. Listen. Guard."

They circled around the totem and placed their blades against it.

"Speak your oath," Tristan said. "Not to me. To the wild. To the land."

Each of them did. Soft voices in the trees. They called themselves the Eyes of Eldara. That spring, news reached them of raiders gathering near the edges of the Dark Expanse. Tristan and the Eyes moved quietly, sending word to Quinn and Rayner, who prepared the guard. The Rangers did not march to war. They disappeared into it. For weeks, they harassed the enemy's scouts, led them into bogs, stole supplies in the night. One raider was found tied to a tree with a single arrow in his boot, no wound, just a message: "Go back." Tristan became legend to the enemy. They called him the Wolf of the Pines. He never sought the title. He only wanted the silence of the woods, the strength of his team, and the peace he knew was never permanent.

Summer came slowly to the northern woods, as if the land itself had not yet decided whether it was safe to bloom. Wildflowers crept through thawed soil. The pine boughs were lush again, casting long green shadows over the slopes where snow had once slept. Yet, the Eyes of Eldara did not relax. Peace was a thing always balanced on the edge of a blade. Tristan stood at the edge of a high ridge, the canopy stretching beneath him like a living sea. His cloak fluttered lightly behind him, his longbow resting against a rock. His eyes sharp. Behind him, Perren stepped softly, a younger recruit, maybe sixteen winters old, with quiet feet and bright eyes. The boy reminded Tristan of himself. Of a time before legend.

"Captain?" Perren asked.

Tristan didn't turn. "Just call me Tristan."

"They said you took down ten raiders with a single arrow."

Tristan chuckled. "They said that, did they?"

The boy nodded. "At Hollowmere. And that you vanished before anyone saw you."

"Funny," Tristan said, "I seem to remember it took most of the night and a lot of crawling through wet roots."

Perren grinned. "Still sounds like magic."

"No magic. Just listening. Watching. Knowing where to be, and when not to be seen."

He handed the boy his spyglass. "Look there, past the ridge. See the twin pines? What's in the gap between them?"

Perren squinted. "A broken cart."

"Good. And to the left?"

The boy paused. "A glint. Metal?"

"Sunlight off a helmet," Tristan said. "You're learning."

They stood for a while in silence. The forest buzzed with insects and drifting songbirds. Peaceful, but never empty. Tristan finally spoke.

"One day, I'll step back. This ridge will belong to someone else. But the land never stops needing eyes."

Perren nodded. "I want to be ready."

"You will be. As long as you remember the first truth."

"What's that?"

Tristan looked to the wind. "That quiet saves more lives than any sword."

That night, the Rangers sat around a low fire under a pine canopy, smoke curling lazily upward. Jett sharpened a blade in silence. Helena braided a new bowstring. Perren sat beside Tristan, scribbling notes on a scrap of leather parchment. There were no songs. No toasts. No loud victories. Just the hush of wind through branches, and the slow rhythm of breathing earned by survival. When the fire dimmed and the stars blinked awake, Tristan rose and stepped away from the camp. He walked a dozen paces and vanished into the trees, his form swallowed by the forest's embrace. A shadow among shadows. A ghost among leaves. The Eyes of Eldara were watching, and the realm slept safer for it.

That night back in Valebrook, Cole had a headache. This wasn't unusual, he'd found that being Crown Mage came with a daily migraine the size of a war horse, but today it had a particular flavor: the scent of scorched eyebrows, three different dialects of shouting, and someone conjuring goats in the hallway. Again. Across the granite floor of the Arcane Atrium in Valebrook, fourteen would-be mages from all corners of Eldara stood (or, more accurately, fidgeted) in various states of anxiety, pride, and confusion. They had come from Ashbrook, Hollowmere, Stonebrook, and even the mist-veiled highlands of Wyrvale. Some were talented. A few had potentials. One was chewing a candle. Cole clapped his hands once.

"All right," he said, "Welcome to Mage Instruction. You may be here because your village sent you, or because someone told you you're special, or because you accidentally lit your aunt on fire during a temper tantrum."

One girl from Hollowmere looked sheepish.

"Let's begin with ground rules, Cole continued, pacing like a hawk that had been forced to teach ducks how to fly. Rule one: No summoning anything with more legs than you. Rule two: If you must explode, do it outside. Rule three: If you even think about enchanting anything in the kitchen again, I will personally relocate your eyebrows to your feet."

Cole had once told Azor, half-joking, that he wasn't the "teacher type." Azor had laughed. Not the warm, belly kind of laugh, more the quiet, knowing sort that echoed behind the eyes of someone who'd taught a thousand students and seen two survive it with their minds intact, and now Cole understood why. He stood at the head of a long, rune-carved table in the Hall of Weaving Light, watching fourteen different shades of disaster unfold. Nimira of Dunmar had turned her spellbook into a chicken. Again. Darin from Wyrvale was locked in a staring contest with a floating ember he accidentally conjured three hours ago and was now too afraid to put out, and somewhere in the corner, one of the twins from Hollowmere, he still couldn't tell which, was actively trying to flirt with a mirror that had developed sentience. Cole pinched the bridge of his nose.

"Okay," he muttered, "Time for fire drills." The class froze. "Not literal drills made of fire, obviously," Cole added. "Though now that I've said that out loud, someone is going to try it." He waved a hand. "Out to the courtyard. Bring your minds, your focus, and none of whatever cursed nonsense Darin has trapped in that bottle."

Darin looked guilty. The bottle blinked. The courtyard was wide, open, and mostly stone for good reason. The grass had died the first week after someone tried to grow a walking tree. The walking tree had then grown fangs. Cole gathered the group in a semi-circle.

"You'll take turns. One element at a time. Controlled bursts only. No summoning, no transformation, and absolutely no fireballs the size of wagons."

The first student, Arlen from Ashbrook, stepped forward. Tall, awkward, and painfully sincere, he extended both hands, furrowed his brow, and summoned a flame. It was a perfect sphere. It hovered, humming softly, radiating warmth.

Cole blinked. "That... was actually good."

Arlen smiled. Then sneezed. The fireball flew sideways and singed Nimira's sleeve. She shrieked, spun, and accidentally cast an ice bolt that froze Darin's boots to the ground. Darin panicked, dropped his bottle, and the blinking smoke creature finally escaped, cackling into the sky like a child's nightmare on holiday. Cole watched it all with an expression of tired acceptance.

"Remind me," he said flatly, "Did I volunteer for this? Or was this punishment for existing?"

After several constructive disasters, Cole called a break. The mages sprawled in the shade, eating bread and apples, while Cole sat alone with a small, battered journal, Azor's old notes.

"You're thinking of the staff lesson," said a voice behind him. Cole turned to see Elira approaching, arms folded, a smirk on her face.

"I'm thinking of buying a boat and sailing away," he replied.

"Mm. Rayner would miss you."

Elira sat beside him. "They're not that bad."

"They set the hall on fire last week."

Elira raised an eyebrow. "Impressive."

A long silence passed between them. Cole finally sighed, snapping the journal shut.

"I don't want to be Azor."

"You're not," she said. "But you are the Mage of the Crown. And whether you like it or not, they're looking to you like you once looked to him."

Cole frowned. "I looked to him like he was an endless source of wisdom."

Elira smiled gently. It was inevitable. The students began to argue. About who was strongest. About whose spell was better. About whether turning a goat into a teapot was technically transmutation. Cole, exhausted finally said:

"Fine. Duel. They stared at him. You want to test skill? We'll host a mock duel. Pairs. Illusions only. I'll moderate. No injuries, no actual elements, no accidental portals to screaming voids. We all walk away with eyebrows intact."

Kira and Jett went first. It was... not graceful. Jett tripped on his own illusion. Kira conjured a laughing fox wearing pants. Cole gave them both points for creativity and none for strategy. Next came Arlen and Darin. Arlen tried a clever illusion of a three-headed snake. Darin panicked and summoned a literal wall of fog so thick no one could see. For five minutes. Cole clapped when the smoke cleared.

"And that, children, is how kingdoms fall."

The final match, shockingly, went well. Nimira, the girl who had once set her own boots on fire, faced off against Della, a soft-spoken mage from the coast. Their duel was elegant. Controlled illusions. Measured responses. Creativity. Flow. For a moment, Cole saw what Azor once saw in him, raw magic tempered by effort. When it ended, he nodded.

"Finally. Hope."

Then the ground cracked beneath them and someone accidentally summoned a thundercloud indoors. Weeks passed. The chaos lessened. Slightly. Spells stabilized. Students worked together. Laughter filled the hall. Even Darin learned to speak to animals without creating an army of resentful squirrels. One morning, Cole sat at the long table, quill in hand, drafting a letter for the royal records.

To His Grace, King Rayner of Eldara,

Crown Defender, Bearer of the Sword of Reynard, Bringer of Mild Headaches,

Re: Mage Training Progress

The good news: No one has exploded today.

The better news: I believe we have the beginnings of a proper Arcane Cohort.

They are unfocused, overconfident, and constantly hungry. They argue. They cheat. One of them named a fireball.

But they care.

They're learning.

And I... I think I am too.

Do not tell Quinn, or I'll never hear the end of it.

- Cole

Mage of the Crown

He signed it, folded it, and sealed it with wax. Just as he stood, the hallway outside erupted in shouts. Something about flying chairs. Again. Cole sighed, grabbed his staff, and muttered:

"Another beautiful day in Valebrook."

The River Lysenne had never frozen in Rayner's lifetime. Not in the hardest winters of his youth, not even during the cold-snap siege of Garan Hold, where Sir Worric once spoke of frost creeping into the cracks of men's bones. Now, as Rayner stood at the balcony of the eastern watchtower of Valebrook Castle, wrapped in a thick fur cloak, he looked down at the river below and saw ice, thick, dark, and spreading.

"Spring's not yet gone, and we're locking into winter again." Rayner muttered.

He narrowed his eyes at the way the ice seemed to claw upstream rather than downstream, as though fighting the natural flow. Across the glistening sheet, the morning sun bounced dull silver, no warmth in it. Villagers were already gathering at the banks, some pointing, some kneeling to touch the strange frost with reverence, or fear.

"This isn't weather," Rayner said finally. "Something's wrong with the Weave."

Tharic grunted in agreement, but it was not his place to speak of magic. Not in the King's presence. Not with the Mage of the Crown involved. Rayner turned from the view and descended the inner stairs of the watchtower, boots clinking on the stone. He passed guards who saluted stiffly and young pages carrying baskets of fresh scrolls and court correspondence. Even now, Rayner still walked his halls like a soldier, fast, purposeful, always slightly too alert. As if waiting for the floor to give out from under him. He found Cole in the lower observatory, surrounded by shards of blue crystal and curling pages of the Codex of Binding. The room smelled of burned parchment and frost-scorched air. A single orb of light floated above Cole's shoulder, flickering irregularly, like a candle in a storm.

"You felt it too?" Rayner asked.

Cole didn't look up. He was hunched over a runic circle etched into the floor, fingers stained with ink, eyes bloodshot and unfocused, but when he spoke, his voice was steady.

"Worse than felt. I saw it."

Rayner stepped closer, the cold intensifying the nearer he got to the circle. Frost feathered out from the edges, reaching toward the stones like roots. Cole slowly stood and turned toward him. His left sleeve was rolled back. Across his forearm, pale skin had darkened into a faint sigil, not a wound, not ink, but something in between. Like a brand burned by moonlight.

"A girl," Cole said. "In chains. Alone. Somewhere in the North."

Rayner frowned. "You've been seeing her for weeks."

"This was different," Cole said. "This time she saw me back."

In the Royal Garden, Elira stood among the blossom ash trees, watching the petals fall like pale embers. She had not worn a crown today, she seldom did unless court demanded it, but she still carried the air of a queen. In her hand was a letter from the harbor-town of Aewynne, sealed in red wax and marked urgent. Something about missing traders, weather turned wild, snow in the sails. She didn't read it again. She was watching the birds when Quinn approached. His armor shone only slightly in the dappled sun, muted like all things lately. Being the Captain of the Royal Guard had hardened him into a man of vigilance rather than brawn. His hammer still hung at his back, but he'd grown sharper in court, quieter in movement.

"More strange weather," he said. "And three scouts from Hollowmere haven't returned. Tristan's already gone to track them."

Elira sighed. "The realm is colder than it should be, and colder still when Rayner's dreams are full of fire, and Cole's are full of ice."

"You trust Cole?" Quinn asked softly.

She turned to him with a calm, clear gaze. "I trust his pain."

Tristan crouched low at the edge of a tree hollow in the Whispering Woods, fingers pressed to the earth. The scout's trail had vanished halfway into the glade, and the usual chirps of wood sparrows had fallen silent. Only the wind remained, and even that moved strangely, curling instead of cutting. He drew his dagger slowly. Around the next tree, he found frost. Not winter snow, not morning dew, real, old-world frost, the kind the forest did not allow. Trees had cracked beneath its touch, bark bleeding white sap. In the center of the glade, a sigil had been burned into the roots, the same mark Cole had described in private weeks ago. Tristan rose. No bandit had made this. No beast. He turned toward his horse, and toward Valebrook. That night, Rayner summoned the four to the King's Hall, now repurposed as a private chamber of war, warmed by a low fire and framed by shadowy banners bearing the stag of his line. Tristan reported what he'd seen. Cole added what he'd felt. Quinn stood silent until Rayner spoke.

"I can't ignore this," the King said. "Something is stirring in the North, and we all feel it. It's more than magic. It's... old."

Elira entered then, interrupting nothing, merely joining. She took Rayner's hand, her expression unreadable.

"I'm not asking you to stay," she said. "But don't pretend this is just a rescue. Whatever's there, it's calling you."

To Cole, she added, "Do you know her name?"

Cole hesitated. "Aelin."

Quinn looked up at that. "You're sure?"

Cole nodded. "She whispered it. Through the Weave. Through pain. I didn't dream her, Quinn. I heard her."

The following morning, the forges in Valebrook roared to life. Though the season should have heralded spring planting and blooming groves along the outer vales, the city moved with a hush, as if nature itself held its breath. Word of the frozen river had traveled faster than any rider, and already, villagers murmured of curses and omens. The hammering of iron and steel echoed off stone walls, not for market wares or harvest tools, but for travel gear, weapons, armor. At the western edge of the citadel, Quinn stood at the Royal Armory, inspecting the team's traveling kit. His hammer had been reforged with layered runes after the last war, and now he strapped it across his back as he watched the blacksmiths work. Their faces were grim, not merely from soot. Behind him, Tristan arrived with a bundle of rolled parchment, maps of the northern territories, barely charted since the age of King Halric. He tossed them onto the workbench and frowned.

"Not a clear road past the Wyrmspine Range. Just old hunter trails and rumors."

"Just how we like it," Quinn muttered, checking the edge of his blade.

In the scrying chamber, Cole stood before the Codex of Binding, its enchanted pages still open on the northern spread. Ink moved on its own, rearranging itself every few minutes like starlight shifting patterns in the sky. The lines of text glowed faintly in places, runes for frost, shadow, and grief. Azor had once told him that grief is the oldest magic. Now Cole understood why. He traced the outline of the runes on the page, letting his fingers brush the spell-etched text, and again, without warning, the vision struck. The room vanished. In its place, ice, stretching far, a flat expanse beneath a blackened sky. In the center stood a tower of twisted spires, rising from within a glacier that groaned with unnatural life. Lightning crawled through the clouds above, casting pale light on a balcony of black stone.

There she was, Aelin. Chained to an altar of bone and crystal, her eyes closed, her body still, but as Cole's vision locked onto her, she opened her eyes.

"Please," she whispered.

Her voice didn't echo across the frozen wind; it echoed inside his bones. Then came another voice, darker and colder than any storm.

"You've touched the Codex too long, apprentice." Vael.

Cole gasped, eyes flying open as blood dripped from his nose. The Codex snapped shut with a bang, and every torch in the chamber went out at once. That night, they convened in the sanctum hall, normally reserved for sacred rituals and royal ceremonies. Only five stood within: Rayner, Cole, Quinn, Tristan, and Elira. Rayner had dismissed all advisors and guards. What they were about to do had not been spoken aloud before a court.

"The visions are worsening," Cole said. His voice was quiet, but sharp. "I saw her again. The place is real. A glacier with a black spire. North of Wyrvale, past the Spined Crags. It's colder than any map records."

"And Vael?" Elira asked, her fingers tightening on the sleeve of her cloak.

Cole nodded slowly. "He spoke to me. Through the vision. I don't think he's trying to kill me yet... I think he wants something."

Tristan raised a brow. "Doesn't sound like good company."

Rayner didn't smile. "We can't risk waiting. If he's alive, and has this girl, he's after something older than Malrik's blood magic. Something worse."

"What if it's a trap?" Elira asked, her voice calm but strong. "You're the king now."

Rayner stepped forward. "Then it's a trap I walk into. Because I won't leave anyone, especially not someone crying out through the Weave, chained in a wasteland."

Quinn looked at them both. "Then we ride at dawn."

Before dawn broke, Rayner visited the tomb of Sir Worric. It stood beneath the Chapel of the Stag, carved into the roots of the castle itself. A simple stone slab marked the grave. Upon it lay the Sword of Reynard, sheathed in worn leather. Not magical, only memory-bound. He knelt.

"Another road," he murmured, eyes lowered. "Another shadow. I thought peace would last longer. I thought I'd grown beyond the sword."

No voice answered, only the faint breath of wind that came from the chapel's upper vents, but Rayner stood, took the sword in both hands, and strapped it to his back. As they gathered in the castle yard, their packs full and weapons ready, Elira stepped forward. She held a small token in her hand, a woven ring of frost-birch and river nymph cord.

"For luck," she said, slipping it onto Cole's wrist.

"Thank you," he said, not quite able to meet her eyes.

Rayner embraced her. "If anything happens"

"You come back," she said, not allowing the rest. "You always come back."

Then, as the gates opened, the four riders turned north, hooves striking hard stone, heading into a land that no chart dared name. The road out of Valebrook was veiled in a hush more solemn than any they had known. The old trade route bent northeast toward Ashbrook, then diverged into the Hollowmere Wilds, brushing the edge of known maps before vanishing altogether into unclaimed lands. It was a lonely road, cobbled only in parts, flanked by leafless trees and watchful ravens. None of the four spoke much that first day. Tristan rode at the front, eyes always scanning the ridgelines, fingers never far from the fletching of his arrows. Quinn rode beside him, his hammer resting across his saddle, a storm always building in his chest when silence stretched too long. Cole stayed at the rear, his horse slower, steps deliberate. He'd grown pale again, visions tugging at him like hooks beneath the skin, but his mind stayed sharp, and his staff rested across his back like a second spine, warm with dormant runes. Rayner rode at the center, his face set like stone. A king now, but more a soldier again, as if the north had pulled the crown off his brow and handed him a sword once more.

They made camp beneath a crooked sycamore, the bark stripped bare by northern winds. There were no inns this far, no patrols, only the brittle hush of a land that had grown colder than it remembered. Quinn started a fire. Tristan returned with two wild pheasants and a handful of juniper root. Cole carved runes into the logs to keep frost spirits away. Rayner sat quiet, watching sparks climb into the trees.

"Do you think she's real?" Tristan asked eventually, spitting a pheasant leg into the coals.

"The girl." "She's real," Cole said before Rayner could answer. "But I don't think she remembers what real means anymore."

By morning, the frost had spread again. They passed through Hollowmere by dawn, a scattering of homesteads wrapped in fog. Even in its smallness, Hollowmere had been home once to Rayner and the others during their march to war, but now it stood quiet, shutters closed, chimneys cold. A hollow wind rolled through the fields like breath from an unseen mouth. Rayner saw a child staring from a window, wide-eyed and unblinking. He raised a hand in greeting. The child didn't respond.

Cole spoke softly. "The Weave is unraveling here. I can feel it. Like threads torn from a tapestry."

That night, the storm found them. It came not from the sky, but from the earth, winds bursting up from cracks between hills, from forgotten caves and chasms. Ice whipped sideways, horizontal like blades. The fire refused to catch, no matter what runes Cole scrawled or how many sparks Quinn struck from his flint. They took shelter in a ruined waystone, a circular shell of ancient stone that bore carvings of kings older than memory. The walls were cracked, frost blooming across the sigils like veins. Rayner sat with his back against the stone, sword across his knees.

"Do you think this is Vael?" he asked quietly.

Cole shook his head. "Not directly. This is the Weave reacting to him. He's breaking things. Pulling at seams."

"Like Malrik did?" Quinn asked.

Cole met his eyes. "Worse. Malrik drew blood, but Vael… Vael knows where to cut."

As the storm howled and frost crept under their cloaks, Rayner remembered another storm, not of wind and ice, but of fire and war. The siege of Malrik's keep. The moment he took the sword of his father and stood against a legion of horrors. That memory still lived behind his eyes, and now it stirred again, not as triumph, but as warning. He looked at his friends. Tristan asleep, bow wrapped in a fur skin. Quinn resting upright, arms folded, one eye always half-open. Cole hunched in the corner, scribbling new runes even in half-sleep. They were older now. More scarred, and once again, they were walking toward something none of them understood.

By the fourth day, they reached the Wyrmspine Pass, the jagged mountain ridge that marked the boundary of the old realm.

Few dared cross it in any season, let alone one stolen by frost. Here, the land grew sharp, like it had grown teeth. Trees leaned inward, their trunks twisted. The snow didn't fall, it gathered, like it had always been there, waiting, and standing at the edge of the pass, blocking the path forward, was a figure. Wrapped in a wolf-hide cloak, antlers rising from his helm, silver eyes gleaming through a painted mask.

Quinn stood. "Friend or foe?"

The figure raised a hand, and the snow around his boots receded. Then he spoke.

"You cross into the high north. Tread carefully. The Weave is wounded here, and it bleeds poison."

Rayner stepped forward. "Who are you?"

"I am Elvarn. Last of the Watchers."

Cole's eyes widened. "The Weave-bound sentinels… They were said to have died out with the old empires."

Elvarn nodded. "Not dead. Dormant. Until now."

Tristan circled behind. "Why show yourself to us?"

"Because one of you bears the Codex's mark." Elvarn looked directly at Cole. "And you are being hunted."

The wind screamed down from the Wyrmspine Peaks as if the mountains themselves had breath. Rayner, Cole, Quinn, and Tristan followed Elvarn, the masked Watcher, along the narrow trail that clung to the cliffside like a scar. The path had once been carved by dwarves, broad enough for carts and caravans, but time and frost had eaten at its edges. Chunks of stone had fallen into the foggy abyss below, leaving only a crumbling shelf and the occasional frost-laced chain embedded into the rock.

"Keep your hands on the wall," Elvarn called, voice unshaken by the cold. "The winds are not natural here. They'll pull your thoughts before your body."

Tristan snorted behind his scarf. "That's comforting."

Cole barely heard him. The Codex's mark on his arm had begun to burn again, the sigils glowing faintly beneath his sleeve. Every step up the pass felt like walking against a current, the Weave thick with resistance. Ahead, Elvarn stopped at a cairn of black stone, shaped like a flame. He placed his palm upon it, and the runes engraved on its surface pulsed faint gold.

"The gate holds," he said. "But just barely."

"What gate?" Rayner asked, drawing closer.

Elvarn stepped aside, and there, through the swirling mist, loomed an arch of ancient stone, half buried in the snow, veined with ice. Within it, a shimmer like liquid moonlight. Not a doorway, not a cave, something in between. A passage through the folds of the Weave itself.

"A threshold," Cole murmured. "A crossing point."

"To what?" Quinn asked.

Elvarn turned his masked face toward them. "To the part of the world that was forgotten when Malrik rose. Where old magic still dreams, and where your answers lie."

Crossing the threshold felt like falling sideways. No sensation of movement, only sudden weightlessness, a drop in the stomach, and then, Silence. The world they emerged into was not merely colder, it was quieter. The wind was gone. Even their footsteps sounded muffled. The snow here had a bluish sheen, and the sky, though cloudless, glowed with a false twilight. They stood in a wide basin, surrounded by jagged stone and bent pines. The trees grew at strange angles, like they had twisted to escape something beneath the ground.

"This is the edge of the Shivering Plateau," Elvarn said. "And we are no longer in Eldara as you know it. We're in the mirror that lies beneath it."

Cole stepped forward and looked at the horizon. Far in the distance, a black tower pierced the sky, barely more than a needle from here.

"That's where she is," he said.

Rayner followed his gaze. "That's where we go."

They did not get far. As they descended into the basin, they found the remnants of a hunting camp, tents torn open, bones scattered in the snow, blood frozen into sharp flakes across the canvas. Tristan crouched near the firepit.

"Not a beast. No claw marks." Quinn inspected the weapons left behind. "Whoever it was, they left in a hurry. Or died fast."

Then came a whisper. Just a thread of sound on the air, curling between the trees. Cole's eyes glazed over. He took a step toward the woods.

"Cole?" Rayner grabbed his arm. "Don't."

But the mage's lips were moving. "She's calling again."

Tristan spun, bow already raised. "We're not alone."

From the tree line, a shadow moved. No, not a shadow. A figure made of bark and frost, with antlers like spears and eyes glowing faint blue. It moved without sound, gliding across the snow. Behind it came two more.

"They were hunters once," Elvarn said grimly. "Now they serve the Deep Ice."

Quinn didn't wait. He charged. His hammer struck the first creature's chest, sending a wave of frost splintering outward. The creature staggered, then burst into powder, reforming its shape around him like a swarm of snow. Tristan's arrow struck another between the eyes, but it didn't slow. Rayner drew his sword, the Sword of Reynard, humming with old enchantment, and stepped between Cole and the third creature. Steel met frost. The blow echoed like thunder. They fought not for victory, but to escape.

Rayner's blade sliced clean, but each creature dissolved into mist and reformed. Quinn smashed limbs apart only for them to crawl back together. Cole, regaining his senses, slammed his staff into the snow, shouting an incantation that shimmered like heat in winter:

"Ves'thra nilum varen!"

A pulse of force burst outward, sending the frost creatures into shatters, but they would not die.

"Run!" Elvarn barked. "They feed on the Weave. You can't kill them here."

They fled toward a crag of stone, where a low tunnel opened beneath the cliffs. Elvarn led them in, sealing the entrance with a rune that crackled with gold and fire. Only then did the snow fall still again. Inside the cave, the air was warmer, barely. They lit a fire from dried mushrooms and lichen, and for a while, just breathed. Cole sat shaking, staring at his hands.

"She was there," he whispered. "In the mist. I saw her again."

"Could it be a trick?" Rayner asked.

Cole met his eyes, steady now. "Maybe, but it doesn't change what I'm going to do."

Rayner nodded. "Then we keep going."

Tristan sighed. "Into worse places than this."

Quinn grinned. "Wouldn't be a proper quest otherwise."

Elvarn sat beside the fire. "You are not the first to seek the girl."

Rayner turned. "Others?"

"One. Long ago. A warrior-prince with a broken oath. He failed, but he left something behind, a blade touched by starlight. If we find it, it may be enough to fight what lies at the tower's heart."

Cole tilted his head. "And what lies there?"

Elvarn whispered, "Something that remembers what you were before the world forgot."

The tunnel beneath the crag led them down through narrow corridors of black rock slick with frozen veins. Every echo returned strangely, doubled, or speaking back in unfamiliar tones. Even Elvarn grew cautious, running his hand along the ancient glyphs that lined the walls.

"This is old ground," he said. "Older than Malrik, older than the Weave as your people know it."

Tristan whispered, "How can anything be older than the Weave?"

Elvarn didn't answer at first. When he did, his voice was grave.

"The Weave is a river, but something had to carve the bed it flows through."

They passed beneath a broken archway, and the walls opened suddenly into a cavern as wide as a fortress keep. Stalactites glistened overhead like frozen swords, and an ancient light, moon-pale and unexplainable, poured in from nowhere, casting faint halos on the ice. At the center of the cavern stood a pool, frozen into a perfect mirror. Cole stepped toward it, stopping just at the edge. The surface reflected all of them, but the versions looking back were wrong. Older. Worn. Some with scars that hadn't yet been earned, and one, with Cole's face, wore black robes and eyes devoid of light. Rayner drew in a breath.

"What is this place?"

"The Mirror of Ice," Elvarn replied. "It shows not what is, but what may become."

Cole stared at his reflection. "Is this... where she's being held?"

"No," Elvarn said, his gaze fixed on the center of the pool. "But this is where the path splits."

The group circled the mirror cautiously. As they passed it, the light shifted, and the temperature dropped again, unnatural cold, biting through furs and skin. Frost crept along their boots with every step. Then, a sound, metal striking stone. Quinn spun, hammer raised. A figure emerged from the shadows at the far end of the cavern. Clad in gray armor etched with glyphs, a hood pulled over the face. Not a creature. Not a beast. A man. He removed his hood slowly, revealing silver hair, long and wind-matted. A scar cut across his cheek like a brand, and his eyes, glacier-blue, seemed too still.

"I thought I'd never see another soul here," he said, voice even.

Elvarn's body tensed. "He's not alive." The man smiled faintly. "Not entirely."

Rayner stepped forward. "Who are you?"

"I was called Theran. Once."

Cole blinked. "Theran? Azor spoke of you. You were one of the Starbound Mages. You disappeared in the Wars of Shattered Snow."

Theran nodded. "I died, but not fully. The Mirror holds echoes. I am one of them."

Rayner narrowed his eyes. "Are you here to stop us?"

Theran's gaze fixed on Cole. "No. I'm here to warn you."

Theran walked slowly along the mirror's edge, trailing one hand over the frost.

"She is real, the girl in your visions, and she is held in the tower beyond the northern glacier, but the one who holds her, Vael, is no longer just a man."

Cole's grip on his staff tightened. "What do you mean?"

"Vael drank too deeply from the well Azor once sealed," Theran said. "He's opened a wound in the Weave, and through it, something else stirs."

Rayner remembered Malrik's fortress. The shadows that whispered. The flesh that didn't bleed.

"Like Malrik?"

"No," Theran said grimly.

"Malrik borrowed power. Vael is letting something through."

The cavern trembled slightly, just for a moment, as if the world itself didn't like those words. Tristan moved to the far edge of the chamber and pointed to an archway carved into the far wall, partly collapsed but passable.

"This the way forward?"

Theran nodded. "Yes. Through there lies the Glacier of Chains, and beyond that, the gate to Vael's hold."

Quinn lowered his hammer. "Then that's where we go."

Theran stepped in front of them. "You cannot pass without leaving something behind."

Rayner frowned. "What?"

"A memory," Theran said. "A moment you hold dear. The Mirror must take it before you can move forward."

The group exchanged uneasy glances. Elvarn was first. He stepped before the mirror, bowed his head, and placed a hand upon the ice. His mask glowed briefly, and then dimmed. He stepped back, saying nothing.

Quinn muttered, "Fine. If it's what it takes."

He stepped forward, placed his hand on the mirror, and closed his eyes. A heartbeat passed. Then two. When he returned, his face was pale. Rayner went next. The ice was colder than anything he'd touched. He felt it crawl up his fingers, behind his eyes, into his chest, and then he saw her. His mother. The Queen. Elenora, standing in the Valebrook garden, brushing snow from a rose. And then, she was gone.

The memory pulled from him like a thread cut loose. He stumbled back, hand clutching his chest. Tristan followed. Then Cole. Each of them gave something. Each returned changed. Theran stepped aside.

"Now you may go."

They passed through the final arch and into the narrowing gorge. Cold pressed down like stone, but ahead, beyond the icy ridgeline, the skies began to shift. The Tower of Vael now rose clearer in the distance, and Cole could feel her again. Not calling. Not screaming. Just waiting. The path twisted between walls of frozen stone, narrowing to a corridor of sharp ice ridges. The wind howled again, this time laced with whispers that didn't belong to the weather. Above them, icy cliffs shimmered with a faint violet light as if the stars themselves had bled into the ice. Rayner led the way now, sword drawn, not for battle, but for comfort. Behind him, Cole walked with his staff alight in blue flame, casting just enough light to make the shadows flee. Every now and then he would pause, shiver, and press a hand to the Codex symbol branded into his forearm. The pulses were growing stronger.

"She's close," he whispered.

They crested a ridge, and then the world opened up. The Glacier of Chains stretched out before them like a prison forged from winter. A lake of ice, solid and blue, with iron chains the width of tree trunks sunken beneath its surface, some broken, some taut, all glowing faintly from within. Rising at the far end of the glacier stood a jagged obsidian spire. A watchtower or an old beacon, but ruined and leaning slightly as if even the ice couldn't hold its weight.

"What is this place?" Tristan asked, his voice a breath in the air.

Elvarn, who had grown ever quieter, replied, "This is where Vael bound the Forgotten. Those he tested blood magic on. The chains were meant to hold their souls, but some..." His masked face turned slightly. "...do not rest easy."

No one spoke for a moment. Then Cole pointed to the tower.

"She's near there. I can feel her. If we cross quickly"

The glacier sang. A low hum vibrated beneath their boots. The chains began to tremble, and from beneath the ice, shapes stirred.

"Move," Rayner ordered.

They stepped lightly across the frozen surface, each of them gripping weapon or staff, eyes darting beneath their feet. Shadows moved below, some slow, some like lightning. Faces flickered in the deep, pale and screaming, mouths open as if they still cried out. One chain snapped. A geyser of frost shot up, and from the rupture emerged a creature half-formed, a woman once, twisted now into a shape of frost and tendons, her face a frozen rictus of pain. Rayner stepped forward, sword flashing. The creature screamed, not aloud, but directly into their minds. It clawed across the ice, dragging itself forward on one massive hand while the other remained bound to a chain sunk deep in the glacier. Quinn leapt between her and Cole, hammer raised. THOOM. The hammer crashed down, shattering the creature's reaching limb, but the frost-mist reformed it almost instantly.

"We need to move faster!" Tristan called, loosing arrows into the mist.

Each arrow hit its mark, but the ice bled no blood. More ruptures opened. More creatures rose. Cole raised his staff and spoke words that felt like thunder beneath his tongue.

"Suvorin tal'venesh!"

A ring of blue fire erupted outward, pushing back the twisted souls, but they kept reforming, crawling through cracks like water through stone. Then Rayner turned and saw him. Not a spirit. Not a bound soul. But a man. Vael. Or what remained of him. He stood atop the leaning tower at the glacier's end, his cloak billowing like a torn banner in the storm. His face was mostly shadow, but his eyes were unmistakable, white with slits, glowing faintly like dying embers. One hand held a crooked staff made of black iron. The other, outstretched, made a simple gesture. The creatures froze, and then withdrew. As if called back. The chain-wraiths sank beneath the glacier once more. The glacier went still. Only the wind remained.

Rayner stepped forward. "Vael!" he shouted.

The figure raised its head slightly, and smiled.

"Rayner," came the voice, clear despite the distance. "Son of the golden king. Brother of the marked mage. I wondered when you'd come."

Cole moved beside Rayner, face pale. "You have her."

"I guard her," Vael said calmly. "As one guards a candle in the storm. She is... delicate. Touched by the Weave in ways even Azor feared."

"She calls to me," Cole said, fists clenched. "You're hurting her."

Vael tilted his head. "I am not the danger. You are. What you carry is not salvation. Its hunger wrapped in parchment and spell."

The Codex burned beneath Cole's sleeve, reacting to Vael's voice.

Rayner narrowed his eyes. "Let her go."

"You'll have to climb to ask," Vael said, turning from the glacier. "And pray your courage does not freeze before the summit."

With that, he vanished. They made for the glacier's far edge at a sprint. The ice remained still this time, as if Vael's presence had calmed the spirits. Or perhaps warned them. Either way, they reached the craggy slope beneath the black tower without further attack. The air grew heavier as they climbed, and the sky, once full of stars, began to darken. They found a small alcove near the base of the tower, tucked beneath a frozen outcropping. A place to rest. Cole collapsed against the wall, breathing hard, the Codex still burning beneath his skin.

"It reacts to him," he said. "To Vael. The book hates him."

Tristan offered him water. "That makes two of us."

Quinn sat sharpening the edge of his hammer. "He doesn't look like Malrik, but he feels worse."

Rayner stared at the tower's peak through the storm. "He's still human. There's a way to reach him. Or end him."

Elvarn, who had remained eerily silent since the encounter, finally spoke. "Vael is not just a sorcerer. He's a gate. A bridge between the Weave and whatever lies in the frost beyond. He looked at Cole. If he breaks, something comes through, and the girl, whoever she is, may be the only thing holding that back."

Cole didn't sleep that night. Neither did Rayner. They sat near the edge of the alcove, watching the dark tower above them.

Rayner spoke first. "You're sure she's real?"

Cole nodded. "I feel her when I close my eyes. Not like a dream. Like she's reaching out. A name... I think her name is Aelin."

Rayner rested a hand on his shoulder. "We'll get her."

Cole didn't smile. He just stared up at the looming tower. and whispered, "We have to."

They began the climb before dawn. The storm had quieted, but cold still gripped the mountain like a clenched fist. The black tower, jagged and rising out of the frost, was no ordinary stronghold. It had no doors, no battlements. only spiraling steps carved directly into the obsidian stone, slick with wind-swept ice. Quinn led first, hammer slung across his back. He tested each step with caution, for some crumbled beneath his boots. Behind him came Rayner and Cole, followed by Tristan and Elvarn, who said little and moved like a shadow. The sky overhead swirled with grey. No sun. No moon. Only cold light, as if the world had forgotten how to burn. They climbed for hours. Twice, the wind almost pulled Tristan over the edge. Once, a shard of ice fell from above and shattered beside Rayner's foot. Still, they climbed. At last, near the top, they found the first sign of what lay within. A door, seamless with the wall, etched with a sigil of interlocked stars. It pulsed faintly in Cole's presence. The Codex inside his satchel glowed softly, like a heartbeat.

"It's waiting for you," Elvarn murmured.

Cole stepped forward and placed a palm on the sigil. It shivered under his touch. Not a resistance, more a recognition. Then the wall split apart silently, revealing a narrow corridor lit by a strange silver flame. The group entered without a word. Inside, the air changed. It no longer smelled of snow or stone, but of old paper, burnt incense, and faint metal. The hallway curved unnaturally, bending up and to the side, with no clear architecture. As if the tower had been built by someone who had heard of halls but never walked one. After several turns, they emerged into a chamber of mirrors. Seven great mirrors, each reaching from floor to ceiling, stood in a ring. Their surfaces shimmered not with reflections, but with scenes, flashes of memory and moments stolen from other times. In one, Rayner saw his mother holding a newborn Cole beneath the castle's rose arch. In another, Tristan saw himself laughing with his father in the woods, before the War of the Pines. In the third, Quinn saw the forge where his father had taught him to strike true, but Cole, he saw a mirror that showed only her. Aelin. She sat in a room of moonlight, her hands bound, eyes closed. A faint glow surrounded her head, pulsing with each breath. She whispered something he could not hear. Then her eyes opened, and looked directly at him.

"She's real," he gasped. "She saw me."

Rayner stepped beside him. "Then we know she's alive."

"No," Elvarn warned. "This is a trap." They turned to him. "The mirrors draw you in. They feed on memory, twist it. If you walk into one, you may never return."

"But if it's the only path" Cole started.

Elvarn raised a hand. "There's another way. Watch."

He walked to the center of the room and drew a sigil in the air. A simple circle with three lines, the mark of the old Arcanum. One mirror, the seventh, shattered. Behind it was a spiral staircase, descending into blackness.

"That is where Vael waits," Elvarn said. "And the girl."

The descent was harder than the climb. The stairs grew narrower the deeper they went, until they were nearly shoulder-width. The walls whispered with faint spells, unspoken and ancient, half-prayers to the things Vael now worshiped. Cole's head pounded. The Codex glowed again. and then they reached the bottom. The chamber was vast and hollowed out of black ice. Pillars shaped like kneeling men circled the walls, their hands holding up an invisible ceiling. In the center was a raised platform, and atop it, a silver cage. Within that cage sat Aelin. Pale. Silent, but alive. Vael stood behind her, his eyes like storm glass, one hand on the cage, the other holding a thread of violet light that pulsed from her heart to his.

"I wondered how long it would take," he said softly. "But you came."

Rayner stepped forward, sword raised. "Let her go."

Vael smiled. "If I do, the ice breaks, and something… wakes."

Cole raised his staff. "Then I'll make you."

Vael's expression changed. "Azor was right to fear you."

He released the thread of light and turned fully toward them. With his free hand, he summoned fire, but not like Cole's. This flame was black, and did not cast light. It devoured it. The battle began. Rayner charged, swinging the Sword of Reynard. It clashed with Vael's staff, and the shockwave blew back frost from the floor. Quinn followed, slamming down with his hammer, missed, but shattered one of the kneeling pillars. Tristan circled, loosing arrows. Elvarn chanted an ancient word, summoning four masks of stone to orbit his head. They shimmered with protective runes, slowing Vael's magic, but it was Cole who moved for Aelin. He reached the cage, raised his staff, and began unraveling the binding sigils. Vael saw. He screamed, not in rage, but in fear.

"NO. You'll tear the seam!"

Cole didn't stop. He pressed his palm to the final rune, shouted:

"Verenos kel-tai!"

The cage shattered. Aelin collapsed into his arms. Light exploded from her skin, not white, but woven, like threads of gold and silver and blue, rising into the air and knotting around her and Cole. Vael stumbled back. The shadows he had drawn to himself began to flee, as if fearing her touch.

Rayner struck again, sword glowing with the runes of his father. "NOW!" he shouted.

Cole nodded. Together, they spoke the words Azor had taught in secret. Words from the Codex of Binding.

"Sol'karan, the thread shall end."

Cole raised his staff. Rayner drove the blade forward. Vael screamed. The spell struck as the sword pierced, and everything fell silent. The ice cracked, but it did not shatter. The spell had sealed the wound. Vael collapsed, silent, unmoving. Aelin breathed once more. Rayner lowered his sword. Cole held her, and outside, the sky began to clear. The ground trembled. Hairline fractures spread beneath their feet, winding outward from Vael's broken body like a spider's web of doom. The pillars of black ice cracked at their bases, groaning as if mourning the unraveling of the tower's enchantments. Cole tightened his grip on Aelin, who stirred faintly in his arms. Her breath was shallow but steady, her skin warmer now that the cage was gone. The light surrounding her had dimmed, yet its threads lingered around Cole's shoulders, a lingering bond, woven in spell craft deeper than he yet understood.

"Rayner!"

Quinn shouted from across the chamber, helping Tristan steady Elvarn, who was bleeding from the mouth, his stone masks shattered at his feet.

"The whole tower's coming down!"

Rayner stood over Vael's body, eyes narrowed. The former apprentice of Malrik looked peaceful now, no longer twisted by madness, just… still. His staff, broken in half, had rolled away into a crack. His face, once shadowed and lined with the glow of unnatural magic, now looked younger. Tired.

Rayner knelt beside him. "You could've chosen differently."

The walls groaned. He stood and turned.

"Get to the stairs!" he ordered.

They ran. The spiral steps they had descended only hours before were collapsing behind them, stone snapping off into the dark. The tower moaned with each tremor, like a beast dying by inches. Tristan led now, light on his feet, bow across his back, guiding them through the smoke and falling shards of obsidian. Quinn carried Elvarn, grunting with each step but never faltering. Cole ran at Rayner's side; Aelin cradled in his arms.

"She's fading," he said between breaths.

Rayner looked back. "We'll get her out."

They reached the mirror chamber. Or what was left of it. Six of the mirrors had shattered, scattering illusion-glass across the floor. The seventh still pulsed faintly, showing the forest near Ashbrook, warm and green.

"Don't look at them!" Rayner barked. "Keep moving!"

The exit loomed ahead, nearly blocked by fallen stone. Quinn dropped Elvarn gently and shoved his shoulder against the rubble.

"I got it," he growled. "Just go!"

Rayner joined him, sword sheathed, and together they heaved until the stone rolled aside with a crack. Daylight spilled in. They burst from the tower just as the top caved inward. The black spire folded like a dying tree, crashing down into itself and sending shards of frost and obsidian skyward. The ground shook violently, and the glacier moaned in protest, as if it too had been wounded by Vael's fall. They ran for the ridge overlooking the Glacier of Chains. When they finally stopped, gasping, the ruined tower was gone, only a ring of scorched ice and faint magical ash marked where it had stood.

Rayner turned to Cole. "How is she?"

Cole was on his knees in the snow, holding Aelin in his lap. Her eyes were open now, barely, but she was awake.

"She's alive," he said softly.

Aelin lifted a trembling hand to touch his cheek.

Her voice was a whisper. "Cole." He froze. "You know me?" She nodded. "I've always known you."

They made camp just below the ridge that night, using a sheltered hollow beneath an overhang of ice to escape the cutting winds. Quinn built a fire from frozen driftwood and bits of dried root they'd gathered during the climb, and Tristan set wards at the perimeter in case any of Vael's remnants still lingered. Rayner sat sharpening his sword, watching the sparks jump. The silence was heavy. Not mournful, exactly, more like breath held after a storm. Cole sat beside Aelin, who now lay on a fur blanket wrapped in Rayner's spare cloak. Her color was returning. She had eaten a few bites of hard bread soaked in warmed broth, and had begun to sit up with effort.

"I dreamed of you," she said, voice faint. "Even when I couldn't speak. Even when he had me trapped. I saw you... coming."

Cole looked down. "You saved me as much as I saved you."

They shared a silence that needed no explanation. Later, as stars pricked the frozen sky, Rayner pulled Cole aside.

"She's more than she seems."

Cole nodded. "I know. Whatever power Vael feared in her, it wasn't dark. It was something else. A light. Something the Codex recognizes."

Rayner looked at the open satchel where the Codex of Binding lay. It didn't pulse now. It rested.

"As if it's satisfied," Rayner said.

Cole frowned. "Or waiting."

CHAPTER 25

The next morning, Elvarn was gone. He left only a trail of soot footprints and a single note written on a torn strip of linen. "The Weave breathes again. My time among you, ends. Watch the northern stars." Elvarn Rayner folded the note, unsure whether to be angry or thankful. He'd grown used to the masked sorcerer's presence, but trusted him no more than the frost beneath his feet. They turned their backs on the glacier, and began the long descent south.

By the time they reached the northern slopes, the snows had thinned, but the wind remained cruel. Aelin traveled on horseback now, wrapped in Quinn's spare cloak and a woolen scarf. Her strength was returning, but slowly. Each hour, she asked more questions, about the road ahead, about the kingdom, about Cole. He answered them all patiently, though his heart twisted each time she smiled. It felt like a blessing that might vanish again in the mist. Rayner rode ahead, quiet. The sword of Reynard rested across his back, still faintly humming from the battle. Tristan scouted along the ridgelines, vanishing into trees like smoke. Quinn brought up the rear, whistling tunelessly, hammer slung over his shoulder. They traveled toward Wyrvale, an old farming village nestled in a valley known for its mead, its orchards, and its hard-headed people. But even from a mile away, something felt wrong. There was no smoke from hearth fires. No laughter in the wind. No smell of bread or roasting fowl. Only stillness, and a single plume of black smoke, rising from the village square. They reached the outer fields just past dusk. The apple orchards, once famed for fruit sweeter than honey, were withered. Trees stripped bare, roots blackened. Fences were broken, and carts lay overturned in the frost.

Quinn dismounted. "This looks like plague, but there's no burn pits."

Tristan crouched beside a sheep carcass, examining the wounds. "These weren't wolves. The entrails were drained, like something drew out the blood."

Cole dismounted to steady Aelin as she slipped from her horse. Rayner drew his sword.

"Wyrvale's been cursed."

The village square was deserted. Shutters banged open in the wind. Signs creaked. A weathered post with the village sigil, a tree in bloom, was half-burned. Chickens pecked at ash near a cold forge. Then a door opened. A boy, no older than ten, peered out with hollow eyes. He didn't speak, only gestured for them to follow. They entered a building once known as the Longfire Hall, a communal meeting house for feasts and stories. Now it smelled of sickness and smoke. Inside, a few survivors huddled near the hearth. An old man coughed into a blanket. A woman wept beside a cot where her husband lay unmoving, his chest rising only faintly. A priestess sat near the fire, robes tattered, eyes sunken.

"You're too late," she rasped.

Rayner stepped forward. "What happened here?"

She turned her eyes on them. "The wind came down from the dark mountains. And with it came a man in silver. He cursed our trees. Our wells. He took our sons as tithe."

"A man?" Cole asked.

She nodded. "He said he served the one who fell. Said he would finish what Vael began."

Rayner's jaw clenched. "So, he was one of Vael's disciples?"

"Or something worse."

The priestess held up a cracked charm: a twisted bone carved with a crescent and a bleeding eye.

"He gave these to our elders as a 'blessing.' Within three nights, the dead no longer stayed buried."

Aelin shivered.

Rayner turned to the others. "We can't leave them like this."

They stayed the night in Wyrvale. Cole used what magic he could to burn out the corruption from the village wells. Quinn and Tristan helped fortify the meeting hall. Rayner stood watch until dawn, the sword glowing faintly in the fog. Aelin sat beside the fire, her hand in Cole's.

"I dreamed of this place," she whispered. "Before the cage. I saw the trees rotting, the black wind."

Cole looked at her, eyebrows furrowed. "Your visions... they weren't just dreams, were they?"

She shook her head. "I think I was born from the Weave."

He didn't know what to say to that. Only that he believed her. In the morning, the sky cleared. Birdsong returned to the trees, and the people of Wyrvale, though still mourning, found the strength to bury their dead with dignity. They gave the travelers bread, dried meat, and a small bottle of honeyed wine from the last barrel left unspoiled. Rayner, standing at the village gate, placed a hand over his heart.

"You're not alone. If Valebrook can rise again, so will Wyrvale."

The priestess nodded. "Then go, knights of the fire. We will sing of your coming in the days ahead."

So, with hearts heavier but hands steadier, the five left Wyrvale behind, riding south toward the edge of the known world. Where the frost ends. and the truth of Aelin's origin waits. They crossed the ash plain two days later. What had once been forest and glade now stretched black and barren. The trees were long gone, burned to stumps that still wept tar. The soil cracked beneath their horses' hooves like old leather. Here, no birds sang. No wind moved. The silence of ruin hung like a veil. Rayner rode at the head, sword across his back, eyes fixed to the horizon. They followed a fading trail that had once been a road, cobbled stones buried beneath dust and cinder. Tristan scouted ahead in widening arcs, returning only to whisper warnings of old bones and disturbed graves.

"Something walked through here," Tristan muttered, eyes narrowed. "And it wasn't alone."

Cole said nothing. He was reading the Codex of Binding, open across his lap even while he rode. The book's pages shifted now on their own, like a living thing, revealing fragments in languages he didn't fully understand, but that Aelin seemed to. At night, they spoke in hushed tones.

"The Arcanum guarded the Weave," she explained, tracing a glyph with her fingertip. "They believed magic was balance. When that balance was broken, they disappeared."

"Disappeared?" Cole asked.

"Or hid," she said. "In a place no one remembers."

On the fourth morning, they found the temple. It stood beneath a cliff's shadow, partially collapsed, half-buried in rubble and vine. Not a true structure anymore, but a circle of columns, blackened and scorched, rising like teeth from the earth. At its center was a stone dais, engraved with the sigil of the Arcanum: three stars bound in a spiral, with a line struck through the center.

"It's real," Aelin whispered. Cole stepped forward. "It was here the Arcanum cast their last spell."

The air above the dais shimmered. Without warning, the Codex pulsed in Cole's hands. A beam of light, thin as thread, shot from the pages and touched the sigil. The stone groaned. A hidden door opened in the dais.

Rayner gripped his sword. "Do we enter?"

Aelin nodded. "If the Arcanum left anything behind... this is where it lives."

Beneath the earth, the Circle waited. They descended narrow stairs carved by hands older than kingdoms. The air smelled of dust and ink, of magic gone to sleep. As they passed through a low arch of obsidian, torches flared to life one by one, unlit for a hundred years, but still remembering their purpose. The chamber they entered was round, domed, and vast. Twelve chairs formed a circle. Each one carved from a different stone, onyx, sapphire, obsidian, jade, each marked with a rune of power, but the chairs were empty. A massive book sat in the center. Closed. Chained. Surrounding the chamber stood twelve armored statues, cloaked and headless.

Quinn whistled softly. "Cozy place."

Cole stepped closer to the book. "This is the Weave heart," he whispered.

"The ledger of all spells once spoken by the Arcanum."

Aelin reached for the chains, and the statues moved. The first drew a blade of black fire. The second raised a staff wreathed in gold flame. A voice rang from every wall, echoing and distant.

"Who seeks the Weave?"

Rayner stepped forward. "I am Rayner, son of Reynard, King of Eldara. I seek nothing but truth."

The voice shifted. "Who speaks for the Arcanum?"

Cole stepped up beside Rayner. "I do. I carry the Codex. I walk in Azor's path."

The statues paused. One stepped forward, blade lowered.

"Then the trial begins."

They were separated. Each dragged into a different chamber by illusion and light. Rayner found himself standing in the ruined hall of Valebrook, his crown burning in his hands. Ghosts of fallen warriors surrounded him, whispering of betrayal and weakness. He had to walk through them, past them, carrying his father's sword. Cole stood before a mirror of himself, but aged, corrupted, power-drunk. The reflection offered him mastery over all magic... at the cost of Aelin's life. He refused. The glass shattered. Quinn was placed in a forge where every hammer blow echoed the screams of those he couldn't save. He endured, sweat and tears falling on molten steel, until his hammer rang true. Tristan walked through a forest of shadows, each tree whispering doubts, fears, regrets. He followed the sound of his father's whistle to emerge into the light. Aelin walked through fire, and was not burned. When they awoke, they were back in the Circle. The book was unchained. The statues bowed.

The voice whispered: "You are chosen."

Cole opened the Weave heart. Within its pages were spells long thought lost, incantations to bind storms, to unmake illusions, to speak with spirits of the air. But more than that, there was a warning. At the back of the book, scrawled in trembling hand: If the Circle fails, the Weave tears. And from the tear, something ancient stirs. Not Vael. Not Malrik. But the First Fire unbound... Rayner read the words aloud. Then he looked at the others.

"We may have defeated Vael," he said. "But we've only torn open the veil."

Aelin closed the book. "And what waits behind it... is watching."

The banners of war flew once more above Valebrook, but they were not the proud gold and crimson of House Reynard. From the northern rise where the five travelers stood, the capital below looked bruised, its walls blackened with smoke, the outer farmlands trampled. A siege camp ringed the city like a collar of iron. Fires crackled across the eastern quarter. The enemy's banners, silver on black, with a single red eye, snapped in the wind. Malrik was dead. Vael was dust, but his legion lived on.

"They've been preparing," Rayner said darkly, peering through the spyglass. "At least four companies. Siege towers. Ballistas. Some warlocks still walking."

"How long since they arrived?" Quinn asked.

Tristan knelt beside them, scanning the enemy lines. "Three days. Maybe four. Looks like they pushed through the northern trade road."

"A coordinated strike," Aelin murmured, gripping her cloak. "They must have waited for Vael's fall."

Cole closed the Codex and tucked it beneath his robes. "They're here for one reason. The book, or her."

Rayner lowered the glass. "Then we don't let them take either."

They descended through a ravine known only to the Royal Guard, a goat trail Sir Worric had once shown Rayner, long ago, for emergencies exactly like this. It wound through cedar trees and crossed beneath a streambed before emerging into the old stone tunnels beneath Valebrook's walls.

Quinn grunted as they pushed a hidden gate open. "Still smells like Worric's socks."

Rayner smiled faintly. "That means no one's used it since."

They moved swiftly through the shadows of the undercity, past crumbled foundations, sleeping rats, old wine barrels. At last, they emerged into the lower stables, behind the castle's inner wall, and found it held. Flags of House Reynard still flew. The city's great bells, though silent, remained whole. They were not too late. The throne room was no longer a place of ceremony. It was a war chamber. Maps covered the marble table where Queen Elenora now stood in armor, her hair braided tight with gold thread. At her side stood General Eredas, leaning on a cane, his other hand resting on a sheathed blade. When Rayner entered, her eyes lifted.

"Rayner."

She didn't smile. She stepped forward and embraced him, brief, fierce.

"How?" Rayner said.

"I was released once Vael fell. It was an old type of magic. After your father was killed, Vael cast a spell and I was placed into the Weave". Queen Elenora said.

"We thought you lost." Rayner nodded.

"Nearly."

He gestured to Cole, Aelin, Quinn, and Tristan. "But we found what we needed."

Cole placed the Weave Heart on the table. A ripple of awe passed through the room. Even General Eredas bowed his head slightly.

"This is what they're after?" the Queen asked.

"Yes," Cole said. "But it's more than knowledge. It's a key. It opens what's hidden, and seals what should never wake."

Aelin spoke next. "And I am what they seek to bind."

Her words silenced the room. She stepped forward, lowering her hood. The flickering torches caught her hair, her eyes, the glow of the Weave running faintly along her skin.

"Malrik kept me to harness the Weave's thread. Vael sought to turn me into a weapon. But I am neither."

Elenora met her gaze. "What are you?"

Aelin answered softly. "A guide."

The first drumbeat came with the mist. It was faint, almost like thunder, but carried with it the deep, resonant weight of war. Valebrook, still half-asleep beneath the blush of false dawn, stirred uneasily. Birds scattered from the pine tops. The river stilled. The banners hanging from the outer towers snapped once, then held motionless, as though the air itself had turned cold in anticipation.

A horn sounded. Then another. Soon the castle bells began to toll. Rayner was already in his armor.

He stood atop the highest parapet of Valebrook Keep, watching shadows shift beyond the tree line. His sword, the heirloom of his line, the Sword of Reynard, rested sheathed at his back, humming faintly as it often did in the presence of danger. To his left, Elira adjusted her gauntlets, braid tight, eyes fixed on the horizon.

"Rangers say the enemy crested the far ridge an hour before dawn," she said.

"A thousand. Maybe more." Rayner nodded.

"They waited until the fog rolled in. They think it'll help them hide."

He turned toward her, eyes sharp. "It will help them die quietly."

Below, the gates of Valebrook groaned open as Captain Quinn and his Royal Wardens poured onto the outer wall and battlements, armor clinking, boots hammering on stone. He shouted orders over the bells, his deep voice clear even above the alarm.

"Shields forward! Archers, positions! I want torches along the rampart! If you can't see what you're stabbing, neither can the man behind you!"

Wardens scrambled into place, disciplined, fast. These were not fresh conscripts. These were the finest fighters Eldara had forged since the War of the Broken Pines. At the rear of the outer grounds, Tristan, cloaked in forest green, leaned beside his lead ranger atop the western wall, where a gap in the cliffs allowed a hidden path to wind down through the tree-covered slope.

"They'll flank us," his Ranger whispered.

"They'll try," Tristan replied, slipping a thin-bladed dagger into his bracer. "We'll be waiting."

When the first enemy standard rose from the mist, it came like a ghost. A black banner, stitched with red symbols, unfurled behind a rank of armored soldiers clad in bone-colored plates. At their head rode a towering brute of a man, his helmet crowned with spikes, his great axe already slick with something dark. Malrik's generals had come. Quinn raised a fist. The archers along the wall drew in unison.

"Hold," he growled.

The enemy did not charge. Not yet. Instead, behind them, war drums resumed their rhythm, deep, slow, like a heart preparing to stop. Rayner stepped to the battlement and drew the Sword of Reynard. Its blade burst into light. The radiance cut through the mist in a cone, illuminating the enemies' front line. It made them hesitate.

"Now," Quinn barked.

The first volley of arrows sang across the field. Dozens of shadowy figures crumpled, some instantly, others twisting in pain. The enemies surged forward then, roaring, smashing against the first defense lines like a tide of metal and rage. Siege ladders slammed against stone. Grappling hooks soared. Spears clattered, and the war for Valebrook began.

Quinn was a hammer among hammers. As the ladders rose and enemy soldiers scrambled up them, he moved with brutal efficiency, sweeping them down with a war hammer nearly as tall as a man, its steel head carved with runes of warding. Every strike cracked ribs, split shields, or sent invaders flying off the parapets into the mud below.

"Wardens!" he shouted. "Repel them! Do not let them breach the archway!"

His second-in-command, a seasoned knight named Kellin, fought beside him. The two made a wall of iron and fury. Enemies surged, screaming, some corrupted by blood magic, eyes glowing with false power. Quinn met them all. An axe clanged off his pauldron. He responded by burying his hammer into the wielder's chest. Another tried to vault over the battlement; Quinn caught him mid-leap with a backhand swing and flung the body into the spearmen below. The gate trembled with the first blow of a battering ram. It wouldn't hold forever.

"Brace it!" Quinn yelled. "Get me fire barrels on the flanks! And tell Cole we need a spell on that gate!"

While the full force of Malrik's army pressed the walls, Tristan and his Rangers watched from the northern ridge above the field, hidden by years of overgrowth and magic-enhanced camouflage. Tristan knelt and drew a rough map in the dirt.

"They're pouring everything into the front," he murmured.

"But look there, flank columns, breaking off to move around through the creek bed. Likely think we don't see them." His lead ranger, Jora, grinned.

"Bad assumption." Tristan rose. "Wait until they're halfway through the choke point. Then we hit them hard. Smoke, blades, then vanish."

"And if they summon reinforcements?"

"We'll kill them faster."

He gave the signal. Three short whistles. From the trees, dozens of cloaked figures emerged, bows drawn, swords low, faces painted with ash. They moved like ghosts. When the first wave of enemy flankers entered the dry creek, they were met with silence. Then, chaos. Arrows fell like rain. Smoke bombs exploded among the enemy, throwing their lines into disarray. Then came the blades, Rangers charging from the trees, cutting fast and vanishing before they could be hit. It was a whispering slaughter. One ranger, perched high in the trees, lit an oil trail along the rocks, fire raced through the flanking column. Screams rose. Tristan himself waded in, twin daggers flashing, moving like a shadow unbound. By the time the flames cleared, the flanking column was gone, and the northern ridge belonged to Eldara.

In the highest tower of Valebrook's eastern wing, Cole stood in a circle of silver glyphs, sweat pouring down his brow. Beside him, Aelin, her fingers glowing with azure flame, completed a spell that rippled through the skies. Below, the battlefield was alive with fire and fury. Cole could see Rayner, gold and crimson cloak trailing, blade shining like a beacon, holding the wall with Elira at his side.

"Third wave coming," Aelin said, her voice tight with effort.

"Then we better start getting creative," Cole replied.

He raised his staff. From the tower's peak, a circle of arcane fire erupted outward. Where it passed, enemy enchantments unraveled, blood magic sigils on the soldiers' armor dimmed, some even cried out as their dark blessings were stripped away. Aelin lifted her hand and twisted her wrist, summoning a dome of ice that dropped onto a siege tower mid-roll, freezing the wood so fast it cracked and splintered into rubble.

"Five left," she said, breathless.

"I've got something for that," Cole replied.

He reached into his robes and pulled forth the Codex of Binding, its pages thrumming with raw power. He flipped to a page he hadn't dared touch since the Dark Expanse.

"Aelin. Cover me."

He began to chant. From the sky, blue-white meteors streaked down, each one crashing into siege engines and enemy clusters with devastating force. Screams echoed. The sky turned gold and violet.

Aelin grinned. "Now that's a spell."

The thunder of war swallowed everything, bellows of beasts, screams of men, and the shattering ring of steel against steel. Rayner leapt down the final stone steps of the tower and landed hard on the lower parapet, sword flashing in the pale morning light. He moved with grim purpose, each strike precise, devastating. Elira was a storm at his side, her twin blades spinning in arcs of silver light, severing limbs and spilling enemy blood without hesitation.

"East wall is holding," she called. "But the gate"

A distant boom shook the stones beneath their feet. The gates of Valebrook had just buckled under the ram.

Rayner growled. "We go now."

They vaulted from the battlements, sliding down the inner wall's ramp and crashing into the enemy's flanking force before they could regroup. Elira cut through the neck of a blood maddened berserker, even as Rayner plunged his sword into the gut of another, then used his boot to hurl the corpse off his blade.

He shouted, "With me!"

A knot of remaining wardens fell in behind them. Elira gave no quarter, slicing her way through to the inner courtyard like a reaper in firelight. Everywhere around them, chaos. Enemy soldiers poured into the courtyard through the shattered gates. Flames licked at banners. Smoke curled up through the rooftops. Screams rang out, but so too did the clash of resistance, Quinn's wardens were not yielding.

Rayner turned to Elira. "We end this in the courtyard. Cole's buying us time, now we give it back."

Quinn's war hammer shattered the chest plate of the man in front of him. He turned. Another came at his flank, and he caught the blow with his shield, twisting to slam the man's head into the wall beside him. His arm ached, and blood from a deep gash in his thigh soaked into his greaves, but still he stood, unyielding. Behind him, a small unit of wardens braced for another wave. The court-yard gate had cracked apart, splinters scattered like bone through the air, and the enemy surged in as one monstrous tide.

Quinn gritted his teeth. "Form circle! You give one step, and I swear I'll haunt your sleep!"

They obeyed. Then the enemy came, and the circle met them with roars of defiance. Quinn fought like a force of nature. He pivoted between strikes, hammer swinging in great arcs that sent enemies flying into walls and columns. A sword slashed across his back. He turned and broke its wielder's jaw with the butt of his weapon. Too many. He could feel it. Then, light. Golden, blinding. Rayner and Elira tore through the enemy's left flank, carving a bloody path to Quinn's side.

"You took long enough," Quinn panted, blocking another blow.

Rayner grinned, blood on his brow. "Had to let you warm them up."

Elira slammed her blade through a hulking brute's knee, then finished him with a stab to the throat.

"The gate's gone. We fall back to the inner keep doors. Make our stand there."

Quinn shook his head. "We fall back; we give them the ground."

Rayner stepped forward. "We don't fall back. We hold. Here."

He raised the Sword of Reynard to the sky. Its light pulsed, throwing back the mist and sending a shockwave of warmth and force across the battlefield, and that's when they saw him. The enemy parted before him as he stepped through the shattered gate like death come walking. His armor was not steel; it was black iron etched in crimson veins of pulsing magic. A horned helm rested atop his head, hiding his features save for the cruel gleam of burning red eyes. He carried a glaive longer than a man, forged in ancient blood. The moment he stepped onto Valebrook's sacred stone, the sky darkened as if recoiling from him.

"Malrik's elite," Elira whispered.

"No," Rayner muttered. "That is his elite. His commander. The one they call, The Dreadhand."

The Dreadhand raised his weapon and pointed it toward Rayner. A voice like cracking tombstone rolled out across the courtyard.

"By my master's will, I will deliver your death."

Rayner stepped forward. "Then come earn it."

The Dreadhand charged. The collision was thunder. Rayner met the glaive's sweep with his sword, sparks exploding as enchanted metal struck enchanted metal. The force of the blow knocked him back a step, but he held firm, spinning and slashing low. The Dreadhand pivoted unnaturally fast for someone so large, blocking and retaliating with a flurry of jabs that would have skewered any lesser man. Elira tried to flank him, her blades catching his side, but the Dreadhand spun with a roar and caught her mid-strike, flinging her back with an arcane blast from his off-hand. She crashed into the side of the well and didn't rise.

Rayner growled. "You'll regret that."

The Sword of Reynard burned brighter, its runes flaring in celestial gold. Rayner struck. Steel sang. They clashed again and again, the courtyard became a blur of motion around them as others fought, but this was the center. This was where the battle's fate would be decided.

The Dreadhand laughed. "You are nothing but a boy playing king."

Rayner answered with a slash that split the Dreadhand's pauldron and carved a line into his chest. Blood, not red but black, spilled onto the stones.

"You bleed," Rayner spat. "And if you bleed, you fall."

Above the battlefield, the tower trembled. Cole staggered as a surge of dark magic pulsed up through the stones.

"Aelin, he's here," he said. "Malrik sent his right hand."

"I felt it," she said, brushing blood from her lip. "If he kills Rayner"

"He won't." Cole gritted his teeth.

He flipped open the Codex of Binding once more. Pages turned of their own accord. Spells whispered from the parchment like voices from the dead.

"Cover me," he said again.

Aelin extended both hands to the sky, summoning wind and storm clouds. Arcane energy crackled around her like a halo.

Cole began to speak. "By the weave that binds all fate... By light forgotten and shadow undone... Let the storm fall. Let the chains break. Let the fire consume."

A ring of white fire erupted from the tower and descended like a dome over the courtyard. It passed through friend and foe alike, but only the enemy screamed. Their blood magic hissed and unraveled. The Dreadhand froze. Rayner took his chance. He drove the Sword of Reynard deep into the Dreadhand's chest. The blade's light flared, pure, ancient, righteous. The Dreadhand staggered back, gasping, black smoke pouring from his mouth and eyes.

"For Eldara," Rayner said.

Then he cleaved the Dreadhand's head from his shoulders. Smoke rolled through the shattered gates, thick and bitter, masking the enemy's renewed assault. Even without their commander, Malrik's horde surged again, like a beast in death throes, more dangerous than ever. They screamed for vengeance, for chaos, for conquest. Frenzied War Priests in blood-smeared robes lifted their hands and hurled blasts of dark magic into the courtyard. Twisted siege-beasts, misshapen creatures stitched together with sorcery, charged the walls with bone-crushing force. Rayner stood at the base of the steps, bloodied, chest heaving. Elira was at his side once more, bruised and cut but unbowed. Her blades dripped crimson. Around them, the wardens held what little ground they could. Quinn limped to their side, his hammer cracked but still clenched in white-knuckled fists.

"We won't hold another charge," he said through broken breath. "They'll overrun us."

Rayner looked at the firestorm spreading across the courtyard. The enemy had been wounded, but not broken.

"We don't fall here," he said. "Not while we still breathe."

Then, a sound, sharp and high. A horn, long and keening, echoing from the western streets of Valebrook. Quinn's eyes lit with disbelief.

"That's Tristan's call."

From the smoke and ruin of the alleyways came swift movement, shadows slipping between buildings, boots silent on scorched stone. Tristan and his Rangers had returned. Camouflaged in ash-gray cloaks and gliding like ghosts, they struck the enemy's flank with surgical precision. Arrows whistled through the air, embedding in eyes, necks, and joints. Knives flashed in the dim light as they slid between ribs and into spines. The enemy turned to face them, and found no one. For every Ranger that appeared, another vanished behind smoke, stone, and shadow. Tristan emerged behind a broken column near Rayner, his bow already nocked again.

"Sorry we're late," he said, notched arrow whistling into the neck of a beast man. "Had to burn through a war camp on the south ridge."

Rayner's eyes widened. "You what?"

"Long story. Fire everywhere. Tents don't hold up well."

Elira laughed, short and breathless. "I'll take your madness if it keeps us alive."

Tristan turned, eyes narrowing as he assessed the chaos.

"We'll take the rooftops and harass the line. You hold this ground. He looked at Rayner. This is where it ends, isn't it?"

Rayner nodded. "Or begins again."

In the highest spire of Valebrook's castle, the wind howled. Cole stood in the middle of a glowing circle, carved into the stone with salt, ash, and starlight. The Codex of Binding hovered before him, its pages turning faster now, words whispering across the void. Beside him, Aelin floated inches above the ground, her eyes pure white with arcane power. Runes shimmered along her skin like living silver. Below, he could feel the pull of hundreds of lives. Soldiers. Friends. Rayner. Elira. Quinn. Tristan.

"Now?" Aelin asked.

Cole nodded. "Now."

They spoke in unison.

"By the will of the First Flame... By the laws etched in the Vault of Weave... By the breath of the Bound Star... Let all that was unmade... Be undone."

The Codex opened to its final page. A single word, Unbind. The tower trembled. Light exploded across the sky. Not firelight or sunlight, but pure weave-born brilliance, threads of blue, gold, and white racing through the air like lightning spun into silk. From the circle beneath Cole's feet, tendrils of light poured out into Valebrook, slipping into cracks, curling down stairwells, diving beneath stones and banners and blood-soaked earth. Everywhere it touched, the world changed. The enchantments Malrik had embedded into his soldiers, the blood-binding spells and death-pacts, shattered. Enemy warriors screamed and clutched their skulls as power turned against them. Some collapsed in agony. Others dropped their weapons, confused, disoriented, free of the madness that had driven them. The siege beasts withered, their twisted enchantments reversing until they crumbled into dust and bone, and atop the castle, Cole dropped to one knee, gasping. Aelin caught him before he could fall.

"You did it." He shook his head, smiling faintly.

"We did."

Down in the courtyard, Rayner watched as the enemy line faltered. Men staggered. War Priests looked around in disbelief. The black tide had begun to collapse.

He raised the Sword of Reynard. "Push!" he roared.

Quinn, Elira, and the remaining wardens surged forward. Tristan's Rangers rained arrows from above, cutting down retreating foes. The sound of steel rang truer now, louder, cleaner. Rayner reached the broken gate. A War Priest stepped in front of him, eyes wild with betrayal.

"You were never meant to wield the light"

Rayner cleaved through him without pause. Beyond the walls, enemy soldiers dropped their weapons and fled. A moment later, horns of Valebrook sounded, true and strong. Victory. The sun broke through the clouds for the first time in days. Smoke still rose in thin curls from the battlements. The once-gleaming stones of the inner courtyard were blackened with soot and stained with blood. The banners of Eldara hung tattered, but still aloft, defiant even in ruin. Rayner stood in the middle of it all, the Sword of Reynard still in his grip, its light finally dimmed. He swayed slightly, exhaustion pulling at every muscle. The battle had bled him, tested him, tried to break him, but it had not. They had won. He lifted his gaze slowly. The battlefield was scattered with bodies, friend and foe, but the enemy was gone. Fled or fallen. The final echoes of steel had died away, replaced by the murmurs of survivors and the soft flutter of wind through torn banners. A shadow approached, limping.

"Next time," said Quinn, wiping blood from his temple, "I vote we build a second wall. Or a moat. Or maybe both."

Rayner gave a tired chuckle and embraced him. "You held the gate."

Quinn grimaced. "Barely. I thought we'd lose everything."

"You didn't," said Elira, approaching from the side.

Her blades were sheathed, her long red cloak torn in half, but she smiled.

"We lost much... but not everything."

Behind her, Tristan approached, Rangers fanning out to collect arrows and tend to the wounded.

"No sign of any more resistance in the city," he reported. "We've secured the walls. I'd say they're in full retreat."

He glanced toward the horizon.

"Cowards ran toward the lowlands. Should be the last we see of them for now."

Rayner nodded slowly, then turned his gaze to the tower. "Cole?"

The air inside the upper tower crackled with the scent of ozone and burned parchment. Cole sat on the floor, legs sprawled out before him, cloak singed, eyes closed. The Codex of Binding lay open beside him, its last page blank now, the magic drained. Aelin knelt beside him, brushing his hair back with one hand.

"You didn't need to kill yourself," she said softly.

"Just... mostly," Cole whispered, coughing.

"Wasn't in the instructions, but seemed necessary."

The door groaned open. Rayner entered first, followed by Elira and the others.

"Nice fireworks," Rayner said, leaning against the wall.

Cole opened one eye. "Nice sword swing. You drop the guy with the antlers?"

Rayner raised an eyebrow. "Clean off."

"Good," Cole said. "He had a really punchable aura."

Aelin stood and gave them room as Elira crossed to Cole and knelt beside him.

"You saved all of us," she said.

He smiled faintly. "You sound surprised."

Quinn clapped him on the shoulder hard enough to rattle his ribs.

"You ever think about sticking to library work?"

"Every day."

They all laughed then, weak, weary laughter, but real. By the second day, smoke no longer choked the skies. The dead were honored. The wounded tended. Fires were smothered and stone was cleared. For every ruin, someone began stacking bricks to rebuild. Rayner stood atop the parapets with Elira, their cloaks fluttering gently in the breeze. Below, the people of Valebrook moved through the courtyards with buckets, stretchers, ropes. Some wept. Others sang. Rebirth, painful but true.

"This place nearly fell," Elira said, brushing dust from her armor.

"But it didn't." Rayner nodded. "Not because of walls. Or swords, but because we stood. Together."

She looked at him, then down to the field beyond the walls where the wind stirred the grass.

"Do you think... this is the end of it?"

Rayner didn't answer right away. His thoughts drifted north, to colder lands, to whispers yet heard.

"It's the end of this battle," he said. "But the world is wide, and evil never sleeps forever."

She touched his hand. "Then we'll be ready."

The sun broke over the hills like a whispered promise. Its first rays spilled across the scorched fields beyond Valebrook, catching on the broken spears and shattered shields, gilding the ruins with light. Smoke still rose in gentle spirals from the city's walls, but the fires had ceased. The enemy was gone. The banners of the Reynard line still flew, tattered but proud. The war was over. Rayner stood on the battlements, staring at the dawn. He hadn't removed his armor. Blood crusted the edges of the plates. The Sword of Reynard hung across his back, the runes along its fuller still glowing faintly with Weavefire. Below, the city stirred. Survivors emerged from cellars. Families wept. Soldiers limped through the streets, offering water, food, and silence to those who had none. The bells of the cathedral rang for the first time in weeks, not in warning, but in mourning and in hope. Footsteps behind him. Cole.

"I thought you might be here," the mage said softly.

Rayner didn't turn. "They fought for this place. Died for it."

"They did."

Cole moved beside him, the morning wind tugging at his dark robes. The Codex was gone, sealed again by his hand, hidden deep in the Sanctum Vault, where only the Mage of the Crown could reach it.

"You are ready. You proved it with every step since we left Ashbrook."

Rayner exhaled. "I never wanted this."

"Neither did Worric," Cole said. "But he rose to it. So did our father."

That made Rayner turn. Cole gave him a sad smile.

"You're not alone, brother."

They stood in silence for a time. Then a voice called from the stairs.

"They're ready."

The Hall of Thrones was not whole. But it was clean, swept of blood and dust, the great chandelier rehung, the sun falling through the high arched windows in streams of gold. The nobles had gathered in simple robes. Knights of the realm, both old and new, lined the columns. Survivors stood behind them, farmers, blacksmiths, servants, and healers. The people of Eldara. Queen Elenora stood beside the throne. Her armor was gone, replaced by a white gown lined in silver thread. A small circlet rested upon her brow. As Rayner entered, every voice fell silent. He walked the long marble floor alone. His sword remained sheathed. His stride was sure, if heavy. He stopped before the throne.

"By right of blood and deed," she said, her voice steady, "you are Rayner, son of Reynard, heir of Eldara, and true King of this realm."

A pause. Rayner turned around, and the hall roared. That night, the five gathered around a fire in the central courtyard, no longer warriors, just friends. Rayner leaned back on a crate, sipping wine. Elira rested beside him; legs stretched toward the warmth. Tristan sharpened a blade. Quinn poked at the fire with a stick. Cole leaned on his staff like an old man, his head against Aelin's shoulder, already snoring. The flames danced. No words came for a long time. Then Rayner lifted his cup.

"To the fallen."

They raised theirs in solemn reply. Then Elira added, "To the future."

Quinn raised his. "To rest. Please, rest."

Tristan chuckled. "To friendship, and maybe, maybe no more cursed fortresses."

Aelin lifted her cup last. "To the ones who believed we'd make it."

They drank. Above them, for the first time in weeks, the stars emerged from behind the clouds, watching, silent, eternal. The celebration lasted three days. Food poured in from the surrounding villages, carts of spiced mutton, barley bread, honeyed apples, and smoked fish from the harbor towns. Music returned to the squares. Children danced in the streets. Songs were sung not just of the war, but of the new King, the Mage who bound the storm, the brave hammer of the guard, the hawk-eyed scout, and the Weave born girl who saved them all.

Rayner spent much of it listening. Quiet, watchful. He sat with the wounded. He walked the lower quarters. He held the hands of those who had lost fathers, brothers, daughters. He did not smile often, but they loved him for that, too. Cole found Aelin in the inner garden on the second night. She stood by the white tree, its blossoms faintly glowing in the moonlight, petals falling slowly like snow. Her hands were bare, fingers trailing along the bark.

"You always find the places the Weave lingers," he said.

"I don't find them," she replied. "They call."

He stepped beside her. Neither spoke for a time. Then he said, "I sealed the Codex. But I left one page open." She turned.

"For me?"

"For us," he corrected.

"There's something in you, Aelin. Something older than Malrik ever understood."

She touched his hand. He flinched, just once, from the echo. The pull he had always felt, a kind of thrum in his bones, returned. But this time, it didn't hurt. It calmed.

"I'm staying," she said.

"Here?"

"With you."

He exhaled. For the first time in a long time, the burden on his shoulders lessened. On the final day of celebration, in the Cathedral of Dawn, Cole and Aelin were to be married. The crowd was so large that even the surrounding fields were filled. From as far as Dunmar and Wyrvale, the people came to see. She wore a gown of river-silk, her dark hair crowned in white blossoms. When the priest asked if they would walk the road together, Aelin looked up at Cole and said,

"Even through flame."

His answer: "Even through ash."

Their kiss was greeted by thunderous cheers, and in that moment, Eldara began again. That night, beneath the stars, the five friends gathered on the castle balcony. Tristan passed around a bottle of strongberry wine. Quinn toasted the sword, the realm, and the goats of Ashbrook in the same breath. Aelin teased Cole about his robes being wrinkled. Rayner just sat back, watching them all. His family. His future. The wind carried the scent of burning cedar and distant rain. Cole raised his cup.

"To the oath."

They all echoed it.

"To the oath."

Somewhere in the distance, beyond the reaches of the city, the land of Eldara breathed. Alive. Months passed. The banners of war faded from the walls, and the scars of battle became stories told in taverns and whispered in ballads sung by firelight. Eldara, once trembling on the edge of ruin, grew strong again, rising like a phoenix from ash. In the royal gardens of Valebrook, the white tree bloomed year-round now. No one quite understood why. Some said it was a gift from the Weave. Others claimed it was Aelin's touch. Children played beneath its glowing branches. Lovers carved initials into its bark. The world, at last, had time to breathe.

Rayner ruled not as a conqueror, but as a guardian. He rebuilt the roads between the villages, reestablished trade with the harbors of Dunwyn and Fallowreach, and brought together once-fractured kingdoms under banners of unity, not fear. He remained a warrior at heart, often sparring in the courtyard with Quinn, or slipping away on quiet rides through Ashbrook. Yet he was also a father, and a husband, and in time, a king people sang about not for his sword... but for his fairness. His father's crown sat upon his brow. But it was the weight of his people's hope he carried most carefully.

Cole became one of the most revered Mages in Eldaran history, not for his power alone, but for how he wielded it. He rewrote the mage trials with Azor's final lessons in mind: character, will, and restraint. The Codex of Binding remained sealed in the deepest chamber of the sanctum. Some feared it. Others wanted it studied. But Cole knew better. He had seen what it did to Vael. What it nearly did to him. He and Aelin lived in the tower above the old library, where laughter and candlelight always warmed the halls. Their bond was more than love; it was a shared echo of the Weave itself. The world whispered through them, and they listened.

Quinn became Captain of the Royal Guard. He still preferred a mug of ale to a noble's dinner, and still fixed his own armor in the forge behind the barracks. He trained young knights not just to fight, but to stand, the way Sir Worric once taught them. Tristan led the Rangers, roaming the far reaches of the kingdom. He mapped the forgotten trails, brokered peace with the mountain dwarves, and sent word of strange things stirring beyond the sea cliffs. Though often gone, he always returned, with new arrows, and better stories.

Queen Elira, once the daughter of darkness, became a symbol of redemption and grace. She forged alliances with lands that once feared her father. She spoke to orphans, walked among villagers, and established a sanctuary in Eldwyre for those lost between worlds. Her voice in court became one of wisdom and mercy. She was the heart beside Rayner's shield.

The name of Azor the Mage was carved into the highest stone of the sanctum. Not as a relic of the past, but as a beginning. He had taught them all to choose the right path when the Weave twisted into shadow. His memory lingered not in books, but in every candle lit in his honor. A new generation of mages studied under Cole now, many of them from villages once forgotten or feared. Some whispered that a boy born with silver eyes had begun showing signs of great power, and that he too, might one day carry Azor's flame.

Eldara thrived. Far to the north, in the broken lands beyond the Dark Expanse, something moved beneath the ice. In the eastern mountains, old runes began to glow again, and deep below the ruined fortress of Malrik, a heartbeat stirred, slow, cold, waiting. Legends do not die. They sleep. For now... peace reigned.

A year later, Rayner received a letter written in trembling hand, sealed in wax. From Azor.

"The land remembers pain, but it also remembers those who heal it. You were not born to be your father. You became something greater. You gave the broken a name again: home."

Rayner and Elira had a son. They named him Worric. On his tenth birthday, he held a wooden sword, and Cole set the air glowing with harmless sparks. Quinn watched from the gate with folded arms, and Rayner? He simply smiled and whispered to Elira:

"Let's make sure his world never needs the sword we did."

And beyond the walls of the new Valebrook, green fields stretched far under peaceful skies.

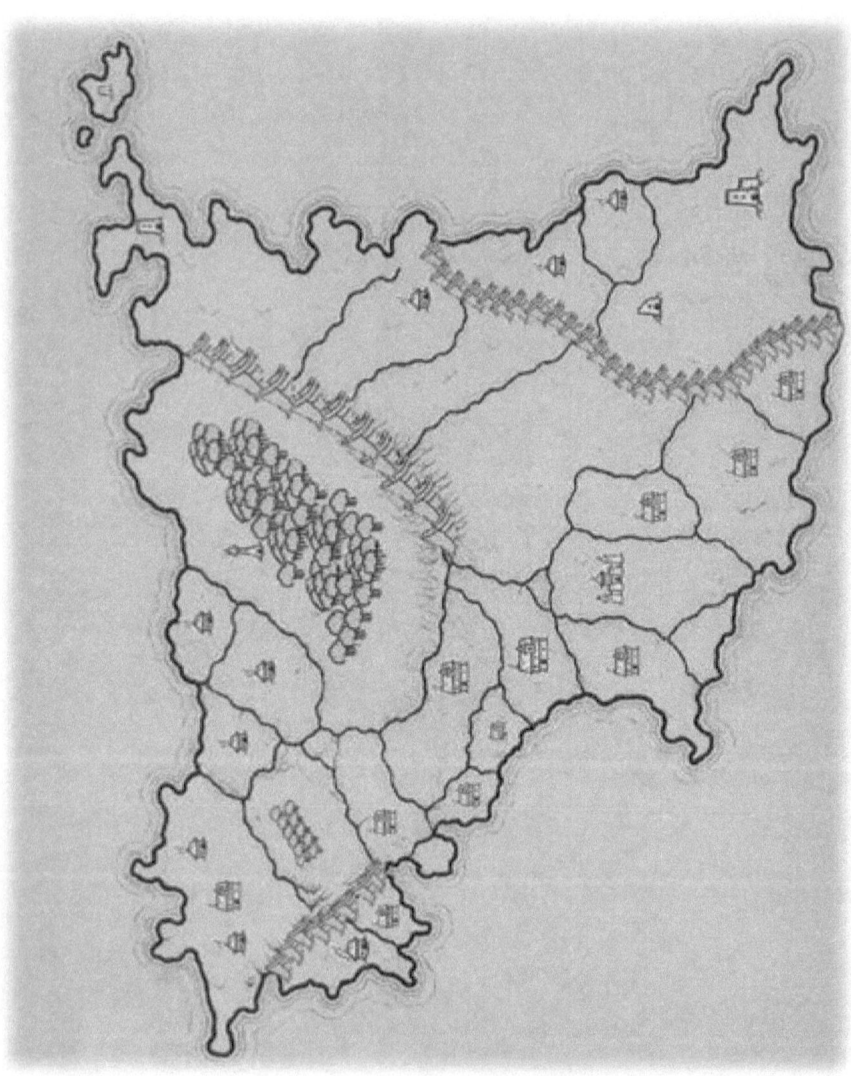

www.ingramcontent.com/pod-product-compliance
Lightning Source LLC
Chambersburg PA
CBHW050021120726
47903CB00006B/1863